BY HIS RULE

CALLAHAN BILLIONAIRES

TRACY LORRAINE

Development Editing by Pinpoint Editing

Content Editing by Rebecca at Fairest Reviews Editing Services

Proofreading by Lisa Staples

Photography - Michelle Lancaster

Model - Doug Mason

The things you regret most in life are the risks you didn't take.

PROLOGUE

Lorelei

"You look lonely." The deep, familiar voice rumbles through me as his shadow swallows me whole.

Sucking in a deep, hopefully calming breath through my nose, I close my eyes and pray for strength.

I love my best friend dearly. She has been hands down the best person who has ever entered my life. But the world she inhabits, the people she is connected with...yeah...not exactly my type.

I come from nothing, and despite working my ass off to try and better my life, I already know that I'll leave this Earth with exactly the same as I entered it. Unlike those currently surrounding me.

Watching Tatum get married was...a headfuck.

She looked beautiful—beyond beautiful. She was a vision wrapped up in the most incredible dress. She was so perfect that no one else in the room would believe that she was suffering from the effects of our drinking session last night.

She wanted to be good, but I'm pretty sure she was lying to herself from the second she thought about those intentions, let alone said them out loud.

She was marrying her brother's best friend. A jerk she's

1

spent her entire life hating. A man her father handed her over to in his will. And if she wants to secure her inheritance, then she has to see it through for a year.

Crazy? Yeah, totally fucking crazy.

But also...

Some might say it's romantic in a way—secretly, I might just be one of them.

They've been enemies their whole lives, both doing anything they can to rile the other up. Now they've been brought together in a way they never expected, and well...who knows what the future will hold?

The sparks are already flying—and not just the angry ones.

They're hot together. Anyone with eyes can see that.

Disappointment niggles inside me, but I don't have time to focus on the fact I'm here as Tatum's only bridesmaid, alone.

Instead, I straighten my spine and attempt to prepare myself for turning toward Kingston's best man, his younger brother Kian.

"Not lonely, just...taking a moment," I say coolly.

Refusing to look at him, I track the closest barman's movements in the hope he can feel my burning stare and supply me with something that will help me get through the next few minutes.

But it never happens—he's too busy with a group of pretentious older men who are drinking top-shelf whiskey as if it's water.

The overt show of wealth makes my skin crawl.

"Well, you look too good to be having a moment alone. Care if I join you?"

But it's too late, he's already sitting on the stool beside me as if there isn't a chance in the world of me saying no.

I guess that's the kind of ego you grow when ninety-nine percent of the female population wants to screw your brains out.

Well, Kian Callahan, welcome to the one percent who

would rather scratch their eyes out with a corkscrew than worship at your stupidly expensive shoes.

Schooling my features, I finally spin on my stool to face him.

"Seems like a pointless question, don't you think?" I ask, dropping my eyes down to where he's sitting.

If I didn't know that his navy suit had been tailored to fit him to perfection, then it wouldn't be hard to figure it out. The way he wears it...well, it's probably the only positive thing I can come up with about him, if I'm being honest.

That and just how fucking good-looking he is.

I bite down on the inside of my cheek.

It's not fair. In fact, it's really fucking unfair that, not only was he born into one of the wealthiest families in the country, enabling him to walk straight into a high-profile, well-paying, and powerful job, but he was also gifted with model-like looks.

How are the rest of us mere mortals meant to compete with the likes of him?

A rush of copper fills my mouth as bitterness floods my veins.

"I'm amazed I'm the first to try and join you," he says smoothly before looking in the direction of the barman and immediately getting his attention. Of course.

It physically pains me not to roll my eyes.

"Macallan, please," Kian orders. "And another—" He glances over at me for confirmation of what I'm drinking.

I refuse to comply or allow him to buy me a drink. Buy— what a joke. Of course this wedding includes an open bar. Other than watching my best friend say her vows, it's the best part of the whole day. Hopefully, if I drink enough, I'll be able to ignore the stench of pretense that permeates the room.

You could leave, a little voice says.

Tate has gone. Kingston literally dragged her away to celebrate their nuptials alone.

Lucky her...

"I'm fine, thank you."

Kian's eyes narrow in irritation before his hand darts out, stealing my glass from the bar before me.

"What are you—"

"Porn star martini," he says to the barman after sniffing my glass. My chin drops. "She'll take another."

"H-how did you..." I stutter like a fool once the barman has retreated.

He smirks, making perfectly symmetrical dimples pop in his cheeks before he winks cockily.

Jesus.

"I'm not just a pretty face, Lorelei," he rasps, his smirk growing.

His voice flows through me, and damn him if my thighs don't involuntarily clench.

It's a natural reaction to a virile man, I try telling myself. It has to be that because there is no way on earth I'm in any way attracted to this arrogant jerk.

"Debatable," I mutter under my breath as I turn my attention back to the bottles lining the bar. They're almost as pretty, and they certainly contain less bullshit.

"I'm sorry, I didn't quite catch that," he says, shifting his stool closer so that the heat of his arm warms mine.

"Yes, you did," I say confidently. "Was there something you wanted other than to interrupt my peace, Kian?"

I don't look over to see his reaction. I don't need to. The reflection of the gold trim that covers the bar does the job perfectly well.

His nostrils flare and he sucks in a sharp breath as his lips part in surprise.

I mentally give myself a high five. I'm not sure it's often anyone gets the upper hand when it comes to any of the Callahan brothers.

"I don't feel like we got off on the right foot," he says, attempting to turn this back around again.

"Is that right?"

4

We've actually met a few times over the years, thanks to our mutual friends, but I don't know him. I've never cared to.

He exudes more than enough of everything I hate to put me off for a lifetime.

I guess it should be expected that he's forgotten we're already acquainted. He was with some fake blonde bimbo the first time we met, and he was as big an asshole that night as he has been every other time I've met him.

"I was merely pointing out that it's tradition that the best man and Maid of Honor hook up at a wedding if they're single."

"Then I guess it's good that I'm not single, isn't it?" I retort as our drinks are placed before us and my feet hit the floor.

"If that's true, then he isn't worthy of you."

Walk away.

Just walk away.

"And why is that?" I ask, unable to follow my own advice.

Spinning on the balls of my feet, I find myself at eye level with him. Many would cower the second his eyes locked on theirs. But while I may not be as powerful or as important as him or anyone else in this room, I refuse to bow down to them.

Money doesn't make you more important. Your job title doesn't make you more or less worthy of anyone's time or attention.

The only thing that matters is the kind of person you are. And the one staring back at me with a mixture of mirth and expectation lighting up his green eyes is a selfish jerk who only cares about his reputation.

"Because a beautiful woman like you should never be attending an event like this alone if you're not single."

I raise a brow but keep my expression neutral.

"It's a huge risk when, instead of missing him..." he explains before throwing his whiskey back and pushing to his feet, moving closer. He towers over me even in my heels, forcing me to raise my chin to keep eye contact. "You could be spending your time getting to know me better."

His alcohol-laced breath rushes over me and his eyes bounce between mine as if I'm meant to be...what? *Impressed* at that pathetic attempt to pick me up?

"Fortunately for him, it's a risk he doesn't need to worry about. Goodnight, Kian. Good luck with your next victim." And with those words hanging in the air between us, I walk away, making sure I put as much sway into my hips as possible.

1

LORELEI

"I'm sorry, Lorelei, but we have reason to believe you've been stealing from the company. We have no choice but to let you go."

My heart stops and my blood turns to ice, my entire body freezing as I stare at my boss in disbelief.

I've felt fear before in my life, but this moment is right up there with the worst.

I'm not a thief.

Not even close.

I've never...

Okay, that's a lie. There have been times in my past where I've made bad decisions. But only because there was no other choice.

My childhood...it wasn't like my best friend's or of any of the people in my life now.

It was hard. Brutal at times.

Times when we didn't have money or food, and never any heating or hot water.

Sometimes things were so desperate there was only one way of getting the things we needed.

But that was then. I left that life behind when I got accepted into my place at college, when I left my hometown and started over.

I haven't worked this damn hard to throw it all away by stealing from this insufferable jerk.

"S-Stealing?" I stutter, unable to believe what I'm hearing.

"Yes. Stealing. From right under our noses."

"I haven't. I wouldn't. I—"

"I'm sure it goes without saying that your employment here has been terminated with immediate effect," he says cooly and calmly. As if this isn't affecting his life in any way.

But then, I guess it's not.

He's hated me from the first day I started here. He's probably silently celebrating that he's finally found what he believes is a concrete reason to get rid of me.

"You can't do this. You don't have any evidence."

His brow lifts as amusement and accomplishment glitter in his dark, calculating eyes.

"I'm willing to hand what I do have over to the authorities if I need to," he warns.

"Or?" I ask, anger beginning to overtake the disbelief.

"Or you can leave and put your time here behind you."

Sounds awfully convenient.

I don't love my job.

In fact, I fucking hate it. But that's not the point.

I need it. I need it and the money I earn more than anyone here could understand.

He leans back in his chair and folds his arms over his chest as if he's already won.

I'd love to fight him on this, but I can't afford it. The smug asshole knows it too.

I can't risk a cent of the money I've got in my bank account, even more so now that I'm unlikely to get any more out of this place.

I've given it my all for two years. Sure, it's far from my dream job. It's not the reason I came to Chicago, but I always hoped it would be a good steppingstone to get where I really want to be.

I close my eyes for a beat and one building, one company, comes to mind.

I was in my junior year in high school when I came across a job advertisement for a well-known hospitality company. I immediately Googled them, and right there and then, I promised myself that I'd do whatever it took to get there.

I was desperate to live in a cool city. To have a fancy job. To commute, to live in a flashy apartment. To spend my evenings out with friends and party as hard as I worked.

The excitement I felt when I received my college acceptance letter was beyond ridiculous. I was giddy in a way I'd never felt before.

It was my first step to the life I'd been dreaming of.

Girls like me who come from families like mine don't get the opportunity to go to college. They don't get to leave their hometown, let alone get a chance to embark on their dream life and career.

I told myself that I was one of the lucky ones. But really, it was nothing but hard work and dogged determination.

Dragging my eyes open, I focus on my boss. My ex-boss.

"You're making a mistake," I warn.

"It's a risk I'm willing to take."

With my head held high, I turn my back on him, desperately trying to ignore my rising emotions.

I need to hang onto the anger. If I'm focused on how best to hurt him, then I'm less likely to crumble into body-trembling sobs.

I've experienced my fair share of them recently, and my asshole of a boss isn't worthy of them.

Nor was the first jerk who caused them, but here we fucking are.

The office is suspiciously empty as I make my way back to my desk with my eyes burning and my nose itching with my need to cry.

Fighting the lump that's growing faster than I can control

9

in my throat, I gather up the few things I care about on my desk and place them in my purse.

I've got two photos of me and Tate. One at graduation and another on a holiday last summer. The sight of my best friend makes my need to cry even more insistent. I grab the plant she bought me for my first day that I've somehow managed to keep alive, and then leave everything else.

This place was never my home. It was just a stopgap until I found something better.

Unfortunately, that something better hasn't made itself known.

It gets even harder to contain my frustration when the warm autumn air hits my face.

Sucking in a deep breath, I look up to the sky and silently beg my eyes to contain the tears.

Wait until you get home.

Woman up. You're stronger than this.

You're better than this.

I take three steps away from the office I never want to look at again when my watch buzzes with a notification.

I almost ignore it. I'm too lost in my own misery to focus on anything someone might have sent me. Assuming it's not just a spam email, of course.

Or worse...*him*.

My heart knots as the face of the man I once believed was the one, fills my mind.

Hopeful now, that he's finally got the message to leave me alone, I shift everything in my arms and dig my phone from the bottom of my purse, praying it's someone with some good news. Hell knows I could use a little positivity in my life right now.

And to think I assumed that finding out my loyal and doting boyfriend was actually living a double life, was as low as things were going to get for me...

How fucking delusional I was.

Hendrix: I failed.

"Fuck," I breathe. So much for some good fucking news.

> Lori: I'm sorry, bud.

I stare at my typed message, my thumb hovering over the send button, wishing I could come up with something a little more eloquent and supportive.

He's worked so damn hard. He deserves more than a fucking fail.

But then, I should know better than most that we don't always get what we deserve.

Shaking my head, I delete the message. He'll read those words as pity, and he doesn't need that right now.

> Lori: I'm so fucking proud of you, bud. You should be proud of yourself too. You worked your ass off. Screw the result. It's a bullshit letter on a piece of paper.

I hit send and the second it shows as delivered, I second-guess it.

Maybe I should have sent the first one.

A scream threatens to erupt as my frustration begins to get the better of me.

> Hendrix: I know. I do. I just thought that this time…

A pained sigh spills from my lips as I grip my cell tighter and continue toward the bus stop.

> Lori: How was the rest of your day?

> Hendrix: Meh. It was fine.

I can't help but chuckle. I can practically hear his unamused grunting. He sounds exactly the same whenever I ask him about school.

> Lori: Do I risk asking about Wilder?

Hendrix and Wilder are my younger half-brothers.

They are the only two good things about my hometown.

Leaving them behind ripped me in two when I embarked on college. But their lives back then were somewhat stable.

Wish I could say the same for now.

If I had my way, I'd move them both across the country to live with me.

But it would be selfish to do so.

They both have lives in California. School. Friends. Our mom...if she can even be called that.

He laughs at my message.

> Hendrix: Last time I saw him, he was molesting a cheerleader.

> Lori: Of course he was.

Whereas Hendrix struggles with school and would prefer to be locked away in his room playing video games, Wilder is the captain of the football team, the boy all the girls want to date, and the kind of student who makes everything look easy. It drives Hendrix to distraction, because no matter how hard he works, he's always at the bottom of the class, fighting to survive and not be held back.

For identical twins, they couldn't be any more different.

> Hendrix: Pretty sure he's already blown through that massive box of condoms you bought him...

I groan loudly as I stand in line at the bus stop.

> Lori: Really, Rix? Really?

The need to pull up my chat with Wilder and chastise him for his behavior burns through me. But it would make me a massive fucking hypocrite, something I try to never, ever be when it comes to my little brothers.

12

I remember all too well what it was like to be seventeen at their high school.

I remember the peer pressure, the need to fit in, to be grown up beyond your years.

Hell, the three of us have more than enough experience of being older than our years, thanks to the shit we were born into.

The boys had it better than me. At least their father hung around and actually attempted to bring them up.

I still have no fucking idea who my sperm donor was beyond the fact he was of a different ethnicity from my mom. My darker skin tone and coarse, curly hair is proof enough.

> Hendrix: You know he loves the game…

> Lori: So long as he doesn't make us an aunty and uncle too soon.

> Lori: What about you? How's it going with Noelle?

I smile to myself as I think about my geeky little brother's best friend. I'm pretty sure he's been in love with her since the first time he saw her, not that he was—is—aware of that, of course.

> Hendrix: Lorelei

My smile grows as I hear his voice in my ear as if he's standing behind me.

> Lori: What? I'm just asking…

> Hendrix: She's great, thanks.

"Oh fuck," I screech when the bus pulls up beside me, hitting a puddle from an earlier rain shower and soaking my feet.

Glancing around, I notice that everyone around me moved out of the firing line.

It's fine. Totally fine. Everything is fucking fine.

Closing down our chat for now, I walk toward the bus doors with my head held high.

Hendrix has made me feel a little better, but no amount of banter with my little brother is going to fix the shitshow that is my life right now.

I find myself a seat and lower my bags on the aisle side, allowing me to sit beside the window and ensure I won't be subjected to an unwanted neighbor.

Ignoring everyone else around me, I stare out of the window, my eyes locked on the building I've spent at least five days a week inside for the past couple of years.

What a fucking waste of my life that was.

The bus jolts forward and I lose myself in the passing buildings with my arms wrapped tightly around my waist as if they'll hold everything together.

Fat chance of that. Everything is crumbling around my feet faster than I can control.

By the time I let myself into my apartment building, every ounce of adrenaline has seeped out of me.

I just about manage to hold it together until I push the key into the lock. Then all hell breaks loose.

The tears that have been burning my eyes since the moment my boss accused me of stealing finally spill free.

By the time I kick the door closed behind me, loud, ugly sobs are erupting from my throat.

Dumping my stuff in the entryway, I all but run toward my bed and throw myself on it as I finally succumb to my emotions.

Just two weeks ago, I thought I had everything together.

I had an amazing boyfriend that I could see a real future with. I had a job that I...endured. But most importantly, I had hope.

Right now, I have nothing.

I can no longer even come home to my friend. Those times

of us pulling out a bottle of tequila and drowning our bad days in margaritas are long over.

That thought only makes me cry harder.

I spent a lot of my former years being lonely. I thought I'd experienced the last of it. But right now, all I feel is alone and hopeless.

2

LORELEI

By the time I emerge from my bedroom, now dressed in a pair of too-big-for-me sweats, a tank and an ugly cardigan that I think might actually be Tate's, the sun is setting outside and casting the living area in a gorgeous orange hue.

I don't appreciate it like I should, and I hate myself for being so up in my head.

I love this apartment. I always have. But it's not the same anymore.

We chose this place together the day after I secured my job. It was our first apartment as independent working girlies.

Tatum and me against the world. Or at least, our little slice of it.

I never imagined a time when one of us would move on.

Sure, I've always been looking for my Mr. Right—it's a compulsion that I can't quite kick; whereas, Tate was always looking for Mr. Right Now.

I guess, looking back, maybe I assumed I'd be the first one to disrupt life as we knew it here.

But that's so far from the truth it's laughable.

Tatum is married. Hell, she's six months pregnant with her brother's best friend's baby. A man she's hated all her life

—well, until she ended up having to say "I do" if she wanted to secure her inheritance from her father.

A sigh falls from my lips as I stare out the window at the city that owns my heart.

I miss having Tate here more than I'd ever confess.

I miss Griz, her kitty, too.

There used to always be someone to talk to. Even if the little furball never actually looked like she cared about the drama in the human world, at least she was a pair of ears.

But while her aura might still permeate the walls, she's no longer here. Neither of them are.

I'm alone.

My fingers grip the windowsill so tight my nails dig into the wood as I attempt to get a grip of myself.

I tried to convince Tate to give up the lease on this place once it became clear that she wouldn't be moving back in after the timer runs out on her arranged marriage, but she wouldn't have any of it.

So as much as I hate taking money from anyone—especially my best friend after everything she's done for me over the past few years—I've had little choice but to stay.

She's still paying her half of the rent despite the fact she hasn't slept a night here since Kingston moved her into his flashy penthouse, and hell knows that I can't afford to take it all on now. Even when I was employed, this place was well beyond my reach.

But what happens now?

A bitter laugh spills free.

I know exactly what will happen.

Tate will take over the rent, and she won't accept anything else.

I love her. I really do. But I don't need or want her money. That isn't—and never has been—the reason why we're friends. Of course, I love her big heart and her need to help. But I hate being anyone's charity case. Even my best friend's.

I earn what I have. I pay my way. For everything.

And, for what it's worth, I don't fucking steal.

"ARGH," I groan loudly before spinning on my heels and marching toward the freezer.

There's only one answer.

Vodka.

Will it help? No.

Will it answer any of my questions right now? No.

Will it stop my boyfriend from being a cheating asshole who deserves to fall into a beehive, or stop my boss from being a jerk who seriously needs to get fucked up the ass with a cactus? Also, a big fat fucking no.

But it will numb the pain.

Oblivion. That's what I need right now.

Total fucking oblivion.

I don't bother with a glass. Why waste the time and effort in decanting it into something else when in these situations, drinking straight from the bottle is perfectly acceptable? At least, in my opinion, it's totally fucking fine.

"Shiiiiit," I hiss when the neat alcohol burns down my throat.

A thought flickers through my head that I should probably eat something before heading down this road, but it doesn't settle. Instead, I allow it to be washed away with my next gulp.

"Alexa," I shout. "I need break-up songs."

It takes a couple of seconds, but Alexa pulls through. Of course she does, she's a fucking woman. "My Happy Ending" by Avril Lavigne erupts from the speaker.

"Yes, Alexa. Louder," I call before taking another swig of vodka.

That song bleeds into another, and then another, and another, until I've no idea how many have passed. What I do know is that the vodka is having an effect, and everything that is currently trying to bring me down feels a million miles away as I belt out my best Whitney Houston.

I think I sound damn good. My neighbors, however, may disagree.

I'm so lost in the music that I don't hear the front door open. I also don't notice anyone walking toward me as I stand with my head tipped back and my eyes closed, channeling my inner diva, so when the music suddenly cuts and only my flat tone fills the apartment, it scares the shit out of me.

"What the—Tate?" I screech, my eyes taking a moment to focus on her standing on the other side of the room with her beautiful baby bump covered in a gorgeous floral dress.

Aw, my bestie is so fucking pretty.

"What's going on?" she demands, effectively stomping on my warm, fuzzy thoughts about her.

"Err..."

"I've been calling you for an hour. We were meant to meet after work."

My heart sinks.

"Fuck. I forgot."

Her eyes narrow in suspicion. I get it. I never forget shit like that.

"I'm sorry. Today...this month has just been—"

"What's happened?" Tate asks again, knowing me well enough to know this is not just cheating-asshole related.

"Men are stupid. That's what's happened."

"I thought Matt had stopped hounding you."

Just hearing his name sends a shooting pain through my heart.

He was so perfect.

So fucking perfect.

Laughter erupts from me, making Tate frown and study me as if I've gone mad.

Maybe I have.

Too fucking good to be true, that's what Matt was.

I should have seen it.

All the red flags and warning signs were there.

How he'd fall off the face of the Earth for days at a time.

How when his "grandmother" died, he wouldn't respond to anything I sent. How he refused to give me his parents' address he was apparently staying at so I could send flowers for his mom.

It was all right there, screaming in my face.

But when we were together...

Fuck. I'm such a moron.

"He has," I confess quietly.

I should be relieved of that fact. I mean, I am relieved. Having him hounding me from dawn to dusk, begging for forgiveness, was only making things worse.

Maybe he was telling the truth about it being over with his fiancée. Maybe they have now finally called time on the relationship and canceled the wedding.

Or maybe he is just a compulsive liar who will tell me whatever I want to hear so that he can continue getting his rocks off.

I let out a sigh that feels like it comes from the pit of my soul.

"So, what's this about?" Tate asks, plucking the half-empty bottle of vodka from my fingers and waving it in front of my face.

Was that full when I started?

I can't remember.

"I got—*hiccup.*" I pause, staring into the compassionate eyes of my best friend.

Changing tactics, I reach for her bump.

"How's my favorite girl?" I ask, gently caressing her belly.

Honestly, we have no idea what the sex is. But I can't imagine my bestie growing anything but a fierce little lady.

Plus, it'll be hilarious watching Kingston get his ass handed to him by both his wife and his daughter on the regular.

"She's fine. Now stop deflecting. Why are you here with Whitney instead of hanging out with me?"

Guilt twists me up inside.

"I'm sorry I forgot."

Taking my hand, Tate tugs me toward the couch and doesn't let go until I fall onto it beside her.

"Talk to me, Lor. What's going on?"

Her eyes bounce between mine, trying to read the truth within them.

Tears come faster than I can control, and before I know what's happening, I'm in her arms.

I sob as if I hadn't already purged the anger and disbelief in my bedroom when I first got back.

But despite the tears and snot I cover her in, Tate doesn't once try to pull away. Instead, she's the unwavering friend she's always been and just holds me. She's my rock. Has been since the moment I walked into our dorm room our freshman year at college.

I was terrified. I'd only ever known our little shithole of a town. Suddenly, I was on my own in the big wide world, and I had no idea what I was doing.

And then there she was. This angel wrapped in a college hoodie and a pair of sneakers more expensive than every pair I'd ever owned put together.

But she didn't care that most of the clothes in my suitcase were barely rags or that my makeup was all grocery store crap, and my shampoo had all the sulfates and silicones despite my desire to embrace my natural curls.

It was all I could afford. Actually, it was more than I could afford, but I was determined to change that.

"I got fired," I blurt, unable to keep it in any longer.

"What? Why?" she barks, anger on my behalf piercing through her voice.

"It doesn't matter. I'm better off out of there, right?"

Her expression softens as I sit up. Unwilling to see it, I drop my face into my hands.

I hated my job.

She's been trying to get me out of there since my second month when I confessed as much.

Honestly, I've no idea how I didn't admit to how much I

21

despised it on day two. But I didn't want Tate to think I was failing before I even gave it a chance. And there was no way I was going home so soon.

Mom had expected me to drop out of college. Hell, there were times she came close to being right. Especially when the twins' dad finally got fed up with her shit and left, leaving them at her mercy. But I refused to be a statistic. Another failed attempt to get out of the down-and-out town I was forced to grow up in.

"What happened, Lori?"

I suck in a shaky breath as I prepare to tell her the truth.

"Clive pulled me into his office and—" I hiccup again as I fight to get the words out.

"And?"

"Heaccusedmeofstealingandfiredmeonthespot," I say so hysterically it comes out as one long word. "Can I get you a drink or anything?" I ask, hopping to my feet and out of her reach as quickly as I can move.

"Wait. He fired you for stealing?" Tate asks, with a deep frown marring her brow.

"So, no drink?" I ask, still hoping to deflect.

"Lorelei," she snaps, getting fed up with my bullshit.

"I didn't steal shit, Tate."

The tone of my voice makes Tate's eyes pop wide open. "I know that," she states firmly. "That is not in question. I want to know why the fuck he would accuse you of that? You're the best member on staff that asshole has had in years."

I shrug, unable to come up with any kind of reasonable answer.

I've no idea why he thinks I was stealing. I haven't so much as taken a fucking pen from that place.

"This is bullshit," she spits, reaching for her purse on the floor and pulling out her cell.

"What are you doing?" I ask in a rush when she begins scrolling.

"This is unfair dismissal, Lori. That asshole isn't going to get away with this. Our legal team will sue him for everything he's—"

"No," I cry, snatching her cell clean out of her hands.

"Lori, we can't let him get away with this."

"I'm not letting you get involved. Nor am I letting Warner Group, or Callahan Enterprises, for that matter, pay for a legal battle on my behalf. I hated that job. I wanted to leave. And now, I don't have to go back."

"You can't leave it at this. What if they report it?"

I swallow as the weight of that possibility sits heavily on my shoulders.

But so what if they do report it? I didn't steal anything, so they don't have a case. It'll be dropped, and I'll be free to get another job.

Right?

I stare at Tate, silently begging her to let this go.

I just want it all to go away.

The cheating boyfriend, the asshole boss. All of it needs to just get out of my life.

I deserve more than this.

3

LORELEI

"I can't," I whine. I sound like a little bitch, and I hate it.

"Of course you can. Maybe this was all meant to be," she says, sounding a hell of a lot more hopeful than I feel right now.

"I can't apply for this, Tate. I just can't."

My heart races as I stare at a job advertisement for the opportunity of my life.

But I can't apply.

My best friend is married to the freaking CEO of the company, and I refuse to let anyone think that I only got the job because of my connections to the boss and his wife. And if that wasn't bad enough, now I'm unemployed. My ex-boss is hardly going to write me a glowing reference after firing me for stealing.

If—and I really mean if—I got the job, it would be a pity job. And I refuse to go anywhere near that.

"Lori, this job was made for you. It's perfect."

"No. It's a disaster waiting to happen. Even if I might have considered it a few weeks ago." Big fat lie. I wouldn't. I couldn't.

My best friend narrows her eyes at me, but I'm not going to budge on this.

"But working for Callahan Enterprises is your dream, Lori. Remember that teenage girl who wanted this?"

"Tate," I warn.

I remember all too well.

The old Callahan building and the images of the glitz and glamor inside were what my teenage dreams were made of.

I wanted it so badly.

Hell, I still do. But I'm not about to tell her that.

The time has passed for me to have a career at Callahan Enterprises. From the moment Tate and I became friends, that dream died. I just didn't know it until I discovered how close her family and the Callahans were. I knew then and there that it wasn't my destiny.

That doesn't mean it doesn't hurt, though.

Callahan Enterprises has since moved to new, even swankier offices. Ones that I gaze at dreamily every time I'm lucky enough to pass by.

"What? King and Kian won't care about what that prick has done to you. They'll—"

"That's the problem, Tate. They'll give me a free pass because I'm your friend. I don't want free passes. I want to work for everything I achieve."

"Lori, you have worked for everything you've achieved. You never should have started your career at that place. You deserve so much more."

Unable to listen to her reasoning anymore, I reach for the bottle of vodka that's taunting me from the coffee table and twist the top off.

"That's not going to help," Tate chastises.

"You're just bitter because you can't have any," I shoot back before lifting the bottle to my lips and swallowing a huge mouthful.

It burns all the way down, making me hungry for more.

"Have you eaten?"

"Jeez, T. When did you become my mother?" I mutter. "No, wait. My mother doesn't care that much."

Tatum sighs. I don't look back at her. I don't need to. I can feel the sympathy oozing out of her.

Silence stretches out for a few minutes. I hate the reprieve just as much as I love it.

"What are you going to do?" she asks softly, finally breaking the silence.

I shrug one shoulder as I swallow another shot of vodka for good measure. "I'll start job searching tomorrow."

"Or you could just send your resume in for this job."

"Tate, you need to stop."

"I'll never stop supporting you and helping you make the right decision."

"Callahan isn't the right decision," I argue as I push to my feet and place the empty bottle back on the coffee table.

The room around me spins as the glinting lights from the city beneath us twinkle in the dark.

"You should go home to your husband," I say, unable to keep the bitterness from my tone.

If I wasn't aware that Tate knows me well enough not to take my attitude to heart, then I'd feel bad about it. But Tate is closer to me than anyone, and she understands that this is just my way of dealing with everything.

"He knows where I am. It'll do him good to be waiting around for me to return home."

Usually, I'd agree and encourage her to be bad and drive him wild. But I don't have it in me tonight.

I don't have anything in me right now. All I want to do is curl up in bed in the dark and pray this was all a bad dream.

"I'm okay, Tate," I say, sounding anything but convincing as I come to a stop beside the front door. "Go and spend the night enjoying your man. One of us might as well."

I look up just in time to see that expression on her face that I hate.

"Everything will work out, Lor," she promises as she moves toward me with her hand on her growing bump.

"Yeah," I say quietly. "I know. It always does, right?" What I really mean is that it does for the likes of Tatum and the people she's usually surrounded by. For people like me, however, it seems that nothing ever works out. We just constantly keep getting knocked down, dragging ourselves back up again, each time a little more broken and beaten than before.

"Will you do something for me?" she asks once she's standing before me, ready to leave.

"Anything," I say before I get a chance to realize my mistake.

She smiles, only confirming my suspicion.

"Apply for this job." My heart thumps against my ribs at the thought of putting myself out there.

What's worse than only getting this position because of my friendship with her?

Applying, not being successful, and then having to face those who didn't think I was good enough.

"Lori, if you don't do it, I'll do it for you," she warns before kissing my cheek and slipping from the apartment, leaving nothing but her ominous threat behind.

———

"Fuck off," I bark as my phone continues ringing from somewhere way too close to my head. "Fuck off. Fuck off. Fuck off."

But it doesn't stop.

Sliding my hand around under the covers, I search for the thing so I can throw it at the wall to make it shut the hell up.

I wince, the brightness of the screen burning through my eyeballs and making my hangover feel a million times worse.

I've woken up in a similar state for the past four mornings.

I start each day with good intentions, but then, just like my life, everything goes to shit.

Job searching has been painful. I've applied for a handful of positions, but none of them really suit me. There's a real fear that I'm going to be applying to Starbucks and

McDonalds in the coming days if the situation doesn't resolve itself. It won't be the first time I've made coffee or flipped burgers; I enjoyed my time doing both. But after working so hard to get here, I really don't want to go back to that.

But beggars can't be choosers and all that.

I need money. Not for me—well, a little for me—but I'm not the only one relying on my pay check.

Wilder and Hendrix are depending on me. It's not like they can trust Mom to keep food in their bellies or a roof over their heads.

When my vision clears, I find an unknown number staring back at me.

Before my brain has fully woken up, my hand moves and I find myself swiping across the screen to answer the call.

I don't know why I do it—maybe so I can shout at whoever thinks it's okay to call me so bloody early, or maybe it's the slightly less hungover part of my brain that knows it could be a job opportunity.

"Hello?" I croak, cringing as I hear my own raspy voice.

If this is about a job, I think it's safe to say I've fucked it up already.

"May I speak with Lorelei Tempest?"

My head spins as I try to place the voice, but I come up short.

"Speaking," I croak again.

"Good morning, Miss Tempest. This is Rebecca Hamilton from Callahan Enterprises. I'm sorry this is so last minute, but I wanted to invite you in for an interview for the position you applied for."

If I thought my head was spinning before, then it's completely out of fucking control now.

"I-I didn't—" I cut myself off as a hazy, drunken memory of my best friend flickers through my head.

"Apply for this job. If you don't do it, I'll do it for you."

Fuck.

Fuck.

I drop my head into my hand.

"Miss Tempest, are you still there?"

"Yes, sorry."

"Fantastic. Is there any chance you could come in this afternoon at three?"

With my heart pounding like a runaway train in my chest, I shoot a look at my alarm clock.

It's already past one.

How is that possible?

"Like I said, we know it's last minute and we apologize for that, but—"

"Yes," I blurt, the volume of my voice shocking me as much as I assume it does her.

"Th-that's great. We were really impressed with your application and CV. We're excited to meet with you."

Oh. My. Fucking. God.

"Do you need me to forward our address, or are you—"

"I know where you are," I interrupt rudely without thinking.

"Brilliant. I'll meet you downstairs and escort you to the interview with Martin, our finance manager."

"Okay," I squeak as something heavy and unpleasant sinks in my stomach.

"Wonderful. See you soon."

Before I get a chance to tell her that I've made a terrible mistake by accepting this, she hangs up, leaving me with nothing but my regrets.

I can't work at Callahan Enterprises. I can't—

"FUCK," I scream, throwing myself back onto my bed. "Tatum Warner-Callahan, this is all your fault," I snap as if she can hear me.

I take a couple of minutes to compose myself before I lift my cell to my ear and repeat those exact words to my best friend.

"You're welcome," she responds happily.

"Tatum, this isn't fucking funny. I told you that I can't work there."

"And yet it seems to me that you didn't turn down the opportunity of an interview."

"You can't say no to the Callahans, Tate. You of all people should know that by now."

She chuckles down the line, letting me know that she's more than aware.

"Just go and have the interview. The role might not be for you. It might be you who turns them down."

Fat fucking chance of that ever happening.

"Does Kingston know about this?"

Silence.

"Tatum," I warn.

"I mentioned it, but he doesn't have any involvement in the recruitment of the finance team. That's Kian's domain."

Oh, Jesus. This is just getting worse and worse.

"And does Kian know?"

"I haven't told him, if that's what you're asking."

A memory of the last time I saw Kingston's younger brother plays out in my mind like a high-definition movie.

He tried hitting on me and I gave him the cold shoulder and told him where to go.

No woman in their right mind tells any of the Callahan brothers where to go.

"But he would be my boss," I reason.

"No, Martin will be your direct boss. You won't have many, if any, dealings with Kian."

I never told Tate about our interactions at her wedding, but she's more than aware of my opinion about the likes of Kian Callahan.

"Martin is lovely. I think you two could work together very well."

"I have to do this, don't I?"

"Do you have any other options right now?" Tatum asks smugly, already knowing that I don't. "Exactly," she adds when I don't respond.

30

"I'm hungover, Tate. I can't go to an interview with alcohol oozing from my pores."

"Go and get yourself a strong coffee, have a hot shower, and pull out that killer dress we bought that day," she demands, making me think of the little black dress I treated myself to for a special occasion.

"That's too much."

"Lorelei," she says seriously. "You have an interview at Callahan Enterprises. That fourteen-year-old girl deserves for you to go in dressed to the nines and be ready to impress. Make her proud, Lor. You've got this."

I suck in a deep breath, trying to find that little girl with stars in her eyes that lives inside me, but she's harder to grasp than ever right now.

"I'll call you later," I say, hanging up before Tate can say anything more. I walk toward my closet and pull the doors open.

Have I got this? Honestly, I have no idea.

But I owe it to that little girl to give it my very best shot.

Consequences be damned.

4

LORELEI

"**L**orelei, this is Martin, our finance manager," Rebecca says as we approach a man, who's probably in his fifties, standing at the entrance to a meeting room.

Attempting to swallow down my apprehension, I hold my head high and reach my hand out to shake his.

"Hello, nice to meet you." Thankfully, my voice is firm and steady. The complete opposite of how I'm feeling.

From the second the Callahan Enterprises building came into view from the Uber that I splurged on, I've been a nervous wreck. To the point that I almost talked myself out of stepping through the entrance.

I'm never going to live it down if I fuck this up.

Kingston already knows, and no doubt Kian will be right behind him.

How am I going to be able to face them if I get rejected from their company?

I already feel small when I'm around them. I can't even imagine how I'd feel after that.

"Thank you so much for coming in at such late notice," Martin says politely as he gestures for me to step into the room first.

"No problem. Thank you for inviting me in."

"Well, I didn't have much choice after seeing your resume."

Heat rushes up my neck as I smile awkwardly at him.

I've no idea what was on my resume. I can only imagine what my best friend thought would be a good idea to fill it with.

"Please, take a seat," he says while Rebecca makes sure I have a glass of water. "We're going to start by talking through the role, if that's okay?"

"Of course."

"Fantastic," he says, shuffling some papers around as Rebecca grabs a tablet and sits to the side of him, ready to take notes.

The second he begins talking, his passion for his role and the company shines through. And it's infectious.

I find myself happily being pulled along for the ride.

Being here, inside this building, with the fancy darkened glass walls, flashy décor and polished furniture, feels right in a way I could before have only imagined.

I've been to Warner Group to meet Tate time and time again, and while those offices are nice, this is on a whole other level.

I love it. Which means it's only going to sting that much more when I discover that this is probably going to be my only visit.

At least I got the chance to find out what it's like. That's something, I guess.

All too soon, Martin focuses his attention on me and begins asking all the usual questions about my previous role and what I believe my strengths and weaknesses to be.

Everything is going well. I think I might have even impressed him with a couple of my answers.

But, as expected, it all comes crashing down around my feet with one sudden knock on the door.

With the windows darkened, it's impossible to see who's on the other side when the strong and confident knock rips through the air, cutting me off mid-sentence.

Both Rebecca and Martin's eyes shoot to the door, openly irritated about the interruption.

But I don't look.

I don't need to.

I already know who it is.

My fingers curl around the edges of the chair I'm sitting in as my already increased heart rate races to dangerous levels.

Please be wrong. Please be wrong, I silently chant.

But as per usual, I'm not that lucky.

The second the door opens, a ripple of anticipation goes through the room that's quickly followed by his expensive scent.

Martin doesn't waver at the sight of his boss standing in the doorway, interrupting the interview he's conducting.

"Kian, how can we help you?" he asks, holding his eyes as the man in question moves farther into the room and lets the door close behind him.

"My apologies for intruding," he says, his deep, rich voice flowing around me like velvet.

Do not react. Do not react.

"Rebecca, you're needed upstairs." Instantly, she hops to her feet, clutching her tablet to her chest. "I'll take over, make sure Martin here makes the right decision about his future assistant."

Before I have a chance to register what he just said, Rebecca is gone and Kian is lowering his suited body into her seat.

He pops open the button on his jacket before getting comfortable.

I can't see because of the table separating us, but I just know that his pants stretch over his thick thighs in a way that should be illegal. It's one of many things I remember from our brief interaction at Tate and King's wedding.

"So, Miss Tempest," he says, commanding my attention without any effort.

Despite knowing better, my gaze immediately lifts to his.

I suck in a sharp gasp the second our eyes connect. My hazel to his green.

Amusement and wicked intent flicker in his, and my stomach knots.

I'm about to pay for that stunt I played at the wedding.

"Can you explain to us why you were able to attend an interview here at such short notice? You are currently employed, correct?"

My eyes narrow.

Fucking asshole.

"No, Mr Callahan. My employment recently came to an end."

"Ah, I see," he muses, relaxing back in his seat and rubbing his chin.

He already knows the truth.

"I haven't been happy there for some time. I always felt underappreciated for what I did."

"Okay, but surely that's not the reason you were fired, was it, Miss Tempest?"

"It's Lorelei," I correct. I hate being called the same name as my mother. It's one of the biggest reminders of where I come from. Of all the reasons I don't fit in here. "And no, that wasn't the reason. There was a misunderstanding, which led to my employment being terminated."

I slam my lips shut, refusing to say any more.

That's not enough for Kian, though.

His eyes hold mine firmly, silently demanding that I continue talking, that I effectively tank my own interview.

Was turning him down really that much of a crime?

I guess it's true what they say; no woman dares to turn down a Callahan.

He smirks. "Please could you elaborate on the details of that...*misunderstanding*?"

I don't say anything. Instead, I keep my lips closed and bite down on the inside of them, forcing myself to remain silent.

"I understand it's uncomfortable, Miss Tempest," he explains, still refusing to use my name as I requested, "but I'm sure you can comprehend that we need to know the details if we're going to consider the possibility of employing you."

Acid swirls in my stomach.

He might already know the truth, but that doesn't make having to say the words out loud any easier.

Our stand-off continues, the atmosphere in the room growing thicker and thicker as Martin continues to look between us.

Knowing that I need to put an end to this charade so I can leave and pretend it never happened, I release my lips and let the truth spill free.

"He accused me of stealing, which is absurd. All I've ever done is work my ass off for him and the company. Was it my perfect job? No. But that didn't matter to me. I pride myself on doing the best I can in any situation. And as for the accusation..." I shake my head, a bitter laugh tumbling free. "He really needs to think again, because that man doesn't have anything worth stealing.

"I earn my money. I work hard for what I have. I expect absolutely nothing to be handed to me on a platter. Everything I have, everything I have achieved, I have fought for. My life. My education. My career. Every. Single. Thing.

"If he doesn't see my value, then fine. I have a better future ahead of me than that place and his petty bullshit."

With my heart slamming wildly against my chest, I push to my feet and focus my attention on Martin. His eyes are wide and his lips are parted in shock from my little tirade. For a second, I think he's going to say something, but then he just swallows, leaving nothing but silence and my previous words hanging in the air between us.

"Thank you so much for inviting me in, and for your time today. It has been an honor to even be considered for this role. I'll see myself out."

I nod at Martin in an attempt to convey just how truthful

those words are, and then I spin on my heels and march toward the door without giving Kian another moment of my time.

Watch me walk away for a second time, you conceited asshole...

And with that, I slip out of the room, ensure the door is firmly closed behind me, and then bolt toward the elevator as if the devil is snapping at my heels.

Stepping inside the fancy mirrored elevator alone doesn't help my unease. I stand right in the center and keep my eyes locked on the descending numbers, praying that it'll move faster. But it doesn't, in fact, I'm pretty sure it's slower than any I've ever experienced before. By the time it hits the ground floor, I'm sweating and my nerves are shot.

And it only gets worse when the doors begin to slide open and a thought hits me upside the head.

What if he's followed me?

What if he's waiting for me?

With my stomach in knots, I keep my head held high as I step out and scan the virtually empty reception.

Two perfectly dressed staff members sit behind a humongous desk in the center of the vast space, and two doormen guard the entrance.

All four of them look up at me the second my shoes click on the shiny tiled floor.

Their attention puts me even more on edge and makes my skin prickle. But there's also relief, because he isn't here.

Silently, I chastise myself for thinking he'd have even considered following me as an option.

Men like Kian Callahan don't chase anyone. Especially women.

Without giving any of them my full attention, or a chance to talk to me, I walk straight out of the building, thanking the doorman who makes the process as easy as possible.

Without stopping, I continue down the block and then around the corner so the Callahan Enterprises building is no longer in sight. And it's not until I step into a deep doorway that I finally release the breath I was holding and sag back against the wall.

"Fuck," I breathe.

I fucking told Tate it was a bad idea.

It's why I never applied.

I just never expected...

As if she knows I've just left, my watch begins vibrating.

Digging my cell from my purse, I debate ignoring her. But it's pointless; she's like a dog with a bone when she wants something.

"How'd it go?" she asks the second the line connects.

"About as disastrous as I predicted. You never should have applied for me, Tate."

"It can't have been that bad," she argues.

I can't help but laugh.

"Kian decided to interrupt," I explain, "and thought it was highly amusing to dive into all the details about why I'm currently unemployed."

"He what?" she shrieks.

"It was going really well before that," I reluctantly confess. "It all felt and sounded..."

"Perfect?" she finishes for me when I trail off.

"Yes," I snap, hating that she's right.

Everything about that place is perfect, from the décor to the people inside. I want to be a part of it all so badly.

But I can't. Now for even more reasons than before.

"I'm going to kick his ass into next year when I see him."

"Just leave it, T."

"No. I won't. You deserve this job, Lor. It was practically made for you, and the timing couldn't be any more perfect."

"Stop, please?" I beg, unable to listen to it anymore.

"What are you doing tonight?"

Going home and crying myself to sleep...

"Might see if Cory is free for a drink. I've ignored his calls all week," I confess with a wince.

"He's got a date," Tate informs me, ruining my plans.

"Come to ours for a drink."

"Tate," I warn.

"Come on. Griz misses you."

"That's a low blow," I mutter.

"What? She does. King's working late, and I'll be lonely."

"You'd better not be pouting right now, Mrs. Callahan."

"Then maybe you should agree and stop me."

I let out a huff. "Fine. But you're ordering Chinese from that place you found, and the alcohol better be strong."

"That's more like it. You can have my share of the alcohol," she offers. "You need me to send a car?"

"No, I'll get the bus."

"Shut up, Lor. Where are you?"

"Around the corner from Callahan. I'll—"

"Lewis is already there. Stay where you are, he'll bring you to me."

"Tate—"

"Stop arguing, Lorelei Tempest," she snaps teasingly. "For once will you just do as you're told?"

"Yes, boss."

"Good. See you soon. Love you, bye."

She must immediately get on the phone to Lewis, her and Kingston's driver, because not two minutes later a sleek black town car appears at the end of the street before slowing to a stop in front of me.

"Good afternoon, Miss Lori," Lewis says with a wide, genuine smile as he climbs from the driver's seat.

"It's okay, I've got it," I say in a rush, pulling the back door open myself.

Having a driver is strange enough; having him open the door for me, is more than I can handle.

"Let's go find the other troublemaker then, shall we?" he teases before taking off.

5

KIAN

"Long day?" I ask Kingston, my older brother, when he falls into the seat on the other side of my desk with a loud sigh as I finish reviewing the spreadsheet in front of me.

"Something like that," he mutters, slumping back and getting comfortable.

"You look exhausted," I point out.

He grunts. "Tatum," he says as if that explains everything.

"Ah, I see. I gotta say, I'm impressed that the honeymoon stage has lasted this long. I had money on her having killed you by now."

"Fuck off. She'd never do that. She needs my dick too much."

"Evidently," I mutter as a weird feeling knots my stomach.

I want to say it's jealousy, but that's fucking crazy.

I don't want what he's found with Tate.

The same woman day in, day out.

No, thank you.

I fucking love my life and the variety of women I have the pleasure of spending time with.

Maybe it's pity. That's a similar kinda feeling, right?

"Sadly, I wasn't awake half the night because I was balls deep in my wife," he mutters disappointedly.

"Oh? Arguing with Grizzy again?" I chuckle, thinking of the hate/hate relationship King has with Tate's cat.

"Fuck off. Me and that annoying little fluff puff are like this now," he says holding a hand up to show me his crossed fingers.

"Of course you are." My cell lights up beside me with a message from my little sister. "So, what's the problem then?" I ask, focusing on my brother for now.

"Tatum's taken to talking in her sleep."

"What?"

He shrugs. "Fuck knows, Bro. I've read all the books and tried to understand everything she's going to experience in the next few months, but not one book or website says anything about women talking in their sleep during pregnancy."

"Right," I mutter, trying not to openly laugh at him. I can't help it; the thought of catching him with his nose in a book that's called something along the lines of *What to Expect When You're Expecting* is just too much to handle.

I always knew that he'd have to have a kid or two. As the eldest of three brothers, it's his responsibility to produce the next lot of Callahan heirs to hand all this down to.

It's one of the few things that makes being the second, and middle, child almost bearable.

I've lived in his shadow all of my fucking life, watched as he had everything handed to him without question. But I've never forgotten about the responsibilities that come hand in hand with all those benefits.

"What?" he snaps.

Rubbing my jaw, I try to picture my big brother as a dad. The only time I've ever seen him hold a baby was when we were kids and Kieran was born. Since then, he's had zero interest in anyone's womb goblin.

"You're gonna be a great dad," I say, turning the conversation more serious.

I don't need to hear that he's been reading up on it all to know that fact.

There isn't one single thing that Kingston Callahan has ever failed at.

Hell, he even succeeded in making Tatum fall in love with him after she was forced to marry him to get her inheritance.

At this point, I find it hard to believe that there is anything out there that my big brother can't conquer, take over, or turn into a success. And that includes managing to keep a newborn baby alive and well.

Of course, he'll have Tatum by his side. Together, they are a force to be reckoned with. In all honesty, I feel a little sorry for my unborn niece or nephew—they have no idea about the kind of parents they're going to have to contend with.

"I've no idea if you're being serious or not," Kingston mutters, narrowing his eyes at me.

"Good. You know how I like to keep you on your toes. Anyway, what are you doing here? I thought you had meetings at Warner Group all day?"

"Last one finished early. Thought I'd better show my face, make sure you're not running this place into the ground in my absence."

I glare at him.

Sure, I might not be the almighty Kingston Callahan; I'm merely his mostly overlooked younger brother, but I was born just as ready for this as he was.

"Things are going swimmingly," I state through gritted teeth. "In fact, I've got the last quarter figures right here."

I spin my monitor around to show him—not that he'll be able to decipher the mass of figures.

Kingston might be a kick-ass CEO, but his skills do not lie within the sheets like mine do. Pun intended.

His eyes scan the figures before he nods confidently and finally spins the conversation to why he's really here.

"How'd the interviews go earlier? Find the one?"

Martin's assistant suddenly handing in her notice with immediate effect, after she discovered both her parents had been in a life-threatening car accident back home, wasn't an ideal situation.

Karla was so much more than his assistant, though. She was his right-hand man. And in turn, she was also mine.

It's only been a couple of weeks without her, but already, we're feeling her loss.

Martin is fantastic at his job, but if left alone for too long he can be a bit chaotic. He needs someone to keep him grounded.

And I need...Well, I haven't had an assistant for quite some time, if I'm being honest.

Since embarking on this job after college, I've been through...a lot of them.

None of them stood up to the job expected of them.

In the end, I gave up trying. All of them made more work for me than necessary, and I discovered life was just easier without one.

Melissa, Kingston's assistant, will help out where necessary, but more often than not, I called on Karla.

"Yeah, they were good," I say simply.

"So? Did someone make the cut?"

Pushing to my feet, I stalk around my desk and toward my drink cabinet.

Without asking, I grab two glasses and pour a generous measure of scotch into them. From the look of Kingston's dark eyes, he needs more than one to get him through the rest of the day.

"Martin has a couple of options," I say as I pass him a glass.

"Lorelei?" he asks, abandoning beating around the bush.

"I'm not hiring her just because she's Tate's best friend," I scoff.

"Did I say you should?" he counters.

No, he hasn't. But the fact he told me that she'd applied and spilled the tea on the reason why she was currently unemployed in the hope of making the process as easy for her as possible, clued me in on his intentions.

I get it, he'd do anything for Tatum. But I refuse to put someone we can't trust in a high-profile position like that; someone who will have access to our figures, our accounts, our everything.

She's been fired for stealing, for fuck's sake.

Tatum might have some kind of magical pussy or whatever it is that turns my hard-assed big brother to mush around her, but that doesn't mean her demands have the same effect on me.

My focus is on the business and our future, and it always will be.

Lorelei might be the best candidate Martin saw today, but if we can't trust her, then it doesn't just put her at the bottom of the list, it makes her fall off it completely.

Our father, our grandfather, and those who came before them, didn't work as hard as they did for us to lose our minds because of a woman and watch it all disappear from beneath us.

Not fucking happening.

"Kian?" Kingston warns when I don't respond quickly enough.

"What?" I snap.

"What did you do?"

I sit forward, studying my brother, trying to figure out when he started being able to read my thoughts without me saying a word.

"I assisted Martin with her interview."

"For fuck's sake, Kian," he groans, lifting his glass to his lips for another drink as if someone has magically refilled it for him. "I promised Tatum that—"

"And there lies the fucking problem, brother," I taunt. "Tate's great. I love her, I do. She's fantastic at her job, and the fact that she can keep you in check is a fucking bonus, but I'm not taking her assurances about her best friend at face value like you are."

"Lorelei isn't a thief, K. Her boss was an asshole."

I smirk, shaking my head.

"Do you have any fucking idea how whipped you sound right now? The Kingston Callahan I remember wouldn't even have considered interviewing someone with a possible theft investigation hanging over their head."

His mouth opens to respond, but he quickly changes his mind.

"I need more scotch for this," he finally mutters. "You done for the day?" he asks before standing from the chair and stalking toward the door.

"Uh..."

"Sorry, I'll rephrase. You are done for the day. Shut down and let's go."

I want to argue. I've got a shit ton of work to do, but I know that when Kingston is in this mood, I've got very little choice but to agree.

There are times you can attempt to say no to him, and this isn't one of them.

"Sure," I mutter, turning my monitor off before grabbing my cell and jacket. I'll message Kenzie back on the way. "Lead the way, boss."

One drink while we discussed business quickly turned into four, maybe five, possibly even six or seven. However many it is, it's safe to say that they hit Kingston hard after his sleepless night.

I can count on one hand how many times I've seen my big brother drunk; he likes to treat his body like a temple, but it seems that tonight is one of them.

"Fucking hell." I laugh as he catches his foot as he

attempts to climb out of the car and flies toward a very unprepared-looking Lewis.

"Whoa," Lewis grunts, just managing to catch Kingston before he takes both of them down.

"Come on, you drunken imbecile," I tease as I wrap my hand around his upper arm and drag him toward the elevator. "Tate is going to rip me a new one for this. It wasn't even my idea," I point out. "Lewis, any chance you could hang around to take me home?" I ask over my shoulder.

"Of course, sir," he agrees with a smile.

The car rises through the building as Kingston attempts to tell me that he's fine and barely even drunk.

It's funny. I just hope that Tate will see it the same way.

"She loves me," he slurs when I say just as much. "She'll be fine."

"Yeah, we'll see." I snort as I throw his front door open and shove him through it.

The second I step inside, a loud, angry voice hits my ears.

"Yeah, well, he's a fucking asshole."

Instantly, my hackles rise.

I know that voice.

I heard it only a few hours ago.

"And he just sat there staring at me as if he owns the fucking world. It was unbelievable."

"What's going on?" Kingston slurs, storming toward the living area faster than his legs should be able to move in his condition. "Oh hey, Lorelei. I didn't expect to see you here."

I cringe hard, and it only gets worse when Tatum announces, "Oh really? So my message letting you know that she was here didn't give you any kind of clue?"

"Fuck my life," I mutter under my breath, a beat before rounding the corner and making my presence known. "Good evening, Tate," I say happily before turning my eyes on Lorelei. She's still wearing the same black dress as she was for her interview, although she's lost her jacket, allowing me to see just how fitted it really is. Her hair is wild, as if she's spent

46

every minute since she left the Callahan building running her fingers through it. Her cheeks are flushed red and her eyes are burning like a wildfire. And on her lap sits my favorite fur ball.

Griz's eyes light up at the sight of me, and she launches herself from Lorelei and straight into my arms.

As I drop my gaze to Griz, Lorelei's stare burns into the side of my head.

She might be as drunk as King is, but that hasn't lessened her anger at all.

She's furious, and the knowledge that I've affected her so much lights something up inside me.

6

LORELEI

Anger continues to simmer just beneath the surface.

It doesn't matter how many times I vent about the mortifying experience that was my interview for Callahan Enterprises, or how many porn star martinis Tatum plies me with, the frustration and disbelief never leave me.

He was such an asshole.

How dare he sit there and say those things to me?

I don't care who I am. Tate's friend or not, no one should be spoken to the way he spoke to me today.

It's infuriating.

But the memory of what happened isn't as infuriating as being forced to look him in the eyes again just a few hours after the event.

"Lorelei," he greets, his stare holding mine firm as the air thickens around us.

Well, if this isn't the perfect fucking way to end my disaster of a day, then I don't know what is.

"Brilliant," I mutter.

"I'm sorry," Tate says, her concerned stare burning the side of my face as I keep my eyes on Kian. If it wasn't already bad enough, he's got my kitty in his arms. "I had no idea he'd be here."

He's lost his gray suit jacket and has his white shirt sleeves rolled up to his elbows, exposing his strong forearms.

Thick veins run up them, covered in what I consider the perfect amount of dark hair and irritatingly tanned skin, considering he spends all his time locked in his fancy office at the top of the Callahan building.

Add the ginger fur ball into that, and...goddamn, he's pretty.

"Drink, Bro?" Kingston asks, swaying as he moves through the kitchen.

"Don't you think you've had enough for a school night?" Tate asks lightly.

"That's the thing about being the boss, baby. No one can say shit."

Kian scoffs.

"You know it's true. Remember that night we—"

"Your wife is right. You should probably stop and call it a night."

"Pfft, you're meant to be the fun one," Kingston sulks, making a detour and placing his hands on Tate instead of a bottle of whiskey.

His hands look massive as they span her growing belly.

"Missed you," he slurs sappily.

"Christ," Kian mutters.

"You could just leave," I point out, turning his attention back to me.

"So could you," he counters. "You are known for walking away when things get too much, after all."

My lips purse and my nails dig into the underside of the stool I'm sitting on.

"You being the thing that's too much."

"Missed you today, baby," King groans from my other side as Tate gasps in a way I'm all too familiar with.

I glance over in time to see him back her up against the counter, lift her onto it, and then step between her thighs.

My chest aches with jealousy, and everything beneath my waist knots with desire.

I want that again.

I thought I'd found it...

A pained sigh spills from my lips before I can catch it.

"Oh god, King," Tate cries as he sucks on the skin beneath her ear.

"So much for you being too exhausted to hold your liquor," Kian mutters, also watching the show with a mixture of curiosity and discomfort in his eyes.

"What can I say?" King mutters, letting us know that he's listening despite being distracted. "My wife is hot as fuck. Stay and watch if you want. We've got nothing to hide."

I shake my head, both loving and hating my best friend right now.

King is hot; I can't deny that. And from what I've heard, his looks aren't where his gifts end, if you know what I mean.

Christ, how long has it been since I got laid...

"Yeah, that's not happening."

"What's wrong? Worried that I'll be better than you?" King teases without so much as looking back at his brother.

Kian chuckles. "Absolutely not. I think we both know who can make a woman scream louder."

"You're a pig," I scoff as my feet hit the floor, ready to do what he just suggested and get the hell out of here.

"Aw, babe. You don't want to test out the theory?"

In utter disbelief, I wobble on my heels and stumble forward, straight into the man in question.

His rich, masculine scent assaults my nose as the soft, luxurious fabric of his shirt slides against my palm.

But there isn't only softness. The abs hiding beneath that shirt...holy shit.

The deep rumble of his laughter fills the air around me as I fight to right myself.

The second he speaks, any thoughts of what his body might be like beneath his clothing are wiped away as I remember what an asshole he really is.

A hot body is one thing, but a shitty personality...nope. Can't do it.

"If you're interested, all you had to do is say. No need to throw yourself at me, Lorelei."

My skin erupts as my name drips from his lips like silk.

"Don't flatter yourself, Callahan. I'm leaving. If you want action, I suggest calling one of your whores. I'm sure you've got more than a few who'd be willing to drop everything for twenty minutes of disappointment."

"Disappointment?" he calls as I storm toward King and Tate's front door, snatching my jacket and purse from the counter as I go.

"Call me tomorrow," I shout, leaving Kian alone with his drunk and horny brother and my pregnant best friend.

"Make sure she gets home," Tate barks, making my legs move faster.

That is absolutely not necessary.

Focusing on my escape, I keep moving, and the second I'm in front of the elevator, I slam my hand down on the button, swallowing down my unease and praying the car is waiting for me.

Only, my reactions aren't quite as smooth as I expect them to be, and I miss the button by a mile.

His laughter rips through the air a beat before his breath rushes down my neck, making my entire body erupt in goosebumps. I close my eyes, trying to fight my reaction to him as a wall of heat burns my back. Reaching out, he efficiently presses the button, calling the elevator, proving that he's not as wasted as the man he delivered home.

"I don't need your help," I snap. "I'm more than capable of looking after myself."

"Sure," he mutters, not believing a word.

"I don't need anything from you."

Thankfully, the doors open the second I finish talking and I rush forward, this time successfully hitting the button for the ground floor and praying the doors will close before he has a chance to join me.

Wishful thinking, but something has to start going my way soon. Right?

I deserve for the tide to change. At least for a short time, surely.

Sadly, long before the doors slide close, I sense him move closer.

"I think we both know that's not true," he says calmly as if none of this is affecting him in any way.

I guess it's not.

I'm...I'm a no one.

A silly woman who thought for some stupid reason that attending that interview this afternoon was a good idea.

I should have stuck to my guns when I told Tate it was a mistake.

I just...I didn't want to believe it.

I wanted the chance.

I wanted the dream.

And it was nice to imagine that it could be a possibility for just a little while.

Gritting my teeth, I ignore him, refusing to give the cocky smirk that I just know is playing on his lips even a second thought.

"Got a bit of a chip on your shoulder, haven't you, Miss Tempest."

I don't want to give him the satisfaction of knowing that he's getting to me, but despite telling myself to remain silent, my mouth runs away with me.

"Don't pretend that you know anything about me," I hiss.

That irritating smug laugh of his fills the enclosed space around us.

"I know plenty. I read your resume."

"That makes one of us," I mutter.

"Admitting to falsifying your application won't look good on top of everything else," he informs me with way too much amusement in his tone.

"I don't give a shit how I look to you."

"Huh," he muses.

His response to my retort gives me pause, and before I know what's happening, I'm turning around to look at him.

I regret it instantly.

He looked perfectly put together when he walked into my interview earlier. His suit was sharp, his hair was perfectly styled. But now, with his jacket gone and his shirt rumpled, his messy hair and his scruffy chin, he looks entirely too delicious, considering what a five-star asshole he really is.

"What is 'huh' supposed to mean?" I snap.

"It's weird. Women usually really care what I think about them."

I narrow my eyes, glaring at him as hard as I can.

"I am not *women*. Whatever you're used to with your easy hookups, I suggest you forget it all when it comes to me. I do not want what they do."

I take a step back and make a show of checking him out.

"I do not have any interest in this," I say, gesturing up and down the length of his body. "And I have even less interest in your bank account or any wild idea about being the special lady who will change your manwhoring ways."

I gag.

"You disgust me, and if I had my way, I'd have nothing more to do with you." The second the words are out of my mouth, I regret them.

Sure, he's an asshole who thinks he's something special, but he doesn't deserve to be on the other end of my issues.

A memory of him sitting before me in that interview earlier pops into my head, and I quickly change my mind.

He deserves every word of my wrath for that stunt alone.

The doors open behind me and I take a step back. If I thought I could do it in my heels, I'd run. But I'm not drunk enough to forget that I'd fall spectacularly on my face, giving him even more reason to mock me.

I force a smile onto my lips. "Thanks for the ride. You've certainly made today...memorable."

I hold his eyes for a second before spinning on my heels and miraculously storming out of the elevator without falling on my ass.

Putting as much sass into my walk as possible, I make a beeline for the doors, more than ready to suck in a breath that isn't laced with his scent.

I march toward the main entrance of Kingston's building and spill out into the cool evening air.

I shiver, regretting that I didn't pull my jacket on sooner, but I can't stop to do so now.

Without so much as a glance at the road, I take off toward a busier street where I can hopefully get lost in a crowd while I figure out my next move.

I need to call a car. I need to go home.

But there's this wildness bubbling under the surface. The need to let go, to break free, to forget all the tethers that hold me down.

Emotion burns the backs of my eyes as I move faster, attempting to escape the demons that continue to haunt me no matter what I do or where I go.

You don't belong in this life, Lorelei.

You're not good enough. You've never been good enough.

You're nothing. You have nothing and you will never have anything.

I'm almost running when a car pulls up beside me. I give it a double take, not expecting anyone to be idling beside me, and I instantly recognize the driver.

"Get in, Miss Lori," Lewis demands from the driver's seat.

I shake my head, unable to speak through the lump in my throat.

I continue moving down the street, and he keeps up with me, not caring about anyone who might be behind him.

"Lorelei," he warns.

Curling my fingers, I let my nails dig into my palms in the hope it'll help me pull my shit together.

Be normal, Lorelei.

It's just a bad day. You've had plenty of them in the past.

This is just another one. Everything will seem better in the morning.

"I'm okay," I squeak. There's no chance he can hear me over the rumbling engine. "I'm meeting someone."

It takes a couple of seconds, but the car disappears from my peripheral vision and I breathe a sigh of relief that he's given up.

The relief is short-lived, though, because instead of hearing Lewis trying to convince me to get into the car, another deep, commanding voice rips through the air.

"Get in the car, Lorelei."

7

KIAN

She stills the second my command hits her, and I watch as her entire body tenses up.

She remains frozen in place as she debates her options.

There's an easy one and then there's a whole heap of others.

Why is it that I already know which one she's going to choose?

Her foot lifts from the sidewalk a beat before she continues forward.

"So predictable," I mutter loudly enough to ensure she hears.

Her shoulders tighten with anger, but she doesn't bite.

"I guess we shouldn't be surprised that you were fired really, when your go-to seems to be walking away from anything good in your life."

I know I've got her before she even spins—there's something in the way she holds herself, readying herself for battle.

"Good? You think you come anywhere close to being something good in my life? The best thing I ever did that night was walk away from you. I've no interest in anything you have to offer, Mr. Callahan, employment—" Her eyes drop down my body. "Or otherwise," she sneers.

"Take your fancy-ass car and go and find some bimbo who'll happily blow smoke up your ass to boost your ego."

"Babe," I taunt, tilting my head to the side like a puppy. "Didn't you know? My ego doesn't need any kind of boosting."

"Ugh," she cries, throwing her hands up in despair. "You're an insufferable jerk."

She stomps forward, throwing every bit of sass she possesses into it. And fuck if the way her hips sway back and forth doesn't hit me straight in the dick.

I bet she'd be fire in bed right now...

I surge forward, fully prepared to keep the promise I made to my sister-in-law in the moments before my drunk brother screwed her brains out.

"What the fuck are you doing?" Lorelei screams as I wrap my hands around her waist and effortlessly lift her from the ground.

Predictably, she begins kicking out. But she's drunk and erratic and misses me every time.

"You're a pain in my ass," I growl, marching her back toward the car she forced me to jump out the back of.

"Put me down," she demands as Lewis watches us with amusement dancing in his eyes.

"Feel free to take over anytime," I bark at him as we approach the open back door.

"But you're doing such a wonderful job. I'd hate to take that away from you."

I snarl at him, making him laugh before attempting to wrangle Lorelei into the car.

I've never done it, but I can only assume that getting her into the car is akin to wrestling with an octopus. Fuck knows how she manages it when she's three sheets to the wind, but every time I try to push her inside, an arm or leg shoots out to stop me.

"Will you just do as you're fucking told for once?"

"Bite me."

As she spits those words, her ass brushes against my crotch, and I suck in a sharp breath.

"Be careful what you ask for," I muse darkly in her ear. "I'm more than happy to bite...anywhere you want."

"Get fucked. I don't want you anywhere near me."

"Then can I suggest you stop rubbing your ass against my dick sometime soon?"

She goes deathly still, her arms falling to her sides, allowing me to finally deposit her in the back of the car.

"We're taking Lorelei home, Lewis," I instruct once we're all safely inside.

Lorelei sits in the corner, as far away from me as she can physically get with her arms crossed under her breasts and a defiant tilt to her chin.

We move back onto the right side of the road in silence while she continues to fume beside me.

"So...do you think Grizzy watches them fuck?"

Silence follows my question.

"The fuck is wrong with you?" Lorelei shouts.

I shrug, fighting to keep the accomplished smile off my face. "Just wondering."

"Jesus," she mutters, keeping her eyes focused out the window.

"If I were a cat, I'd totally watch."

She shakes her head and mutters something I don't quite catch under her breath.

"Oh, come on, you totally would too."

Her top lip peels back in disgust. "It would be like watching your parents fuck. It's wrong. And gross."

"If you say so."

"Have you ever watched your parents at it?"

"Fuck no," I bark.

"Then you understand my point. Griz is Tate's baby. Tate is Griz's mom. Ergo..."

"You know, Martin was impressed with you earlier," I

confess, feeling weirdly compelled to say something nice for a bizarre reason I can't figure out.

"That's good. Maybe he can write me a decent reference, seeing as I'm shit out of other options," she sulks.

"I don't think you'll have an issue finding a new job," I say as my cell buzzes in my pocket.

"I beg to differ," she snaps as I glance at my cell.

A groan rumbles in my throat as I stare at a name I'd happily never see again.

"What's wrong? Your favorite fuck bunny suffering with a case of crabs?"

I roll my eyes. "If only I was so lucky," I mutter.

"Aw, trouble in manwhore paradise?" Lorelei mocks, making Lewis laugh, although he attempts to cover it with a cough.

"Nothing you need to worry about," I say, pushing my cell back into my pocket without opening the message.

"Oh, trust me, I am not worried about anything you do. Haven't I already made that clear?"

"I get mixed messages. Every time you walk away, I can't help but wonder if you're summoning me to follow."

"Rest assured, I am not."

"Just trying to make me jealous with that ass of yours then, huh?"

"I-I'm n-not—" She swallows, cutting herself off, and I mentally give myself a high five for making her lose her train of thought. "Don't look at my ass, Mr. Callahan."

"Hard to look at anything else when you're so intent on running away from me."

Her lips part to bark another cutting retort, but Lewis beats her to it.

"Here you go, Miss Lori. Home sweet home."

Sitting forward, she smiles before sweetly thanking Lewis for delivering her home safely.

In contrast, she doesn't so much as glance in my direction as he opens the door for her and helps her out.

Fire burns through me as I watch her place her delicate hand in his.

Before I've had a chance to think about my actions, I'm shooting toward the door and climbing out behind her.

"I'll be two minutes," I explain to Lewis as I follow Lorelei to the front door of her building.

"You don't have a doorman or any kind of security," I say loudly as she approaches the elevators.

"Well done, Sherlock. Glad to see that private education of yours wasn't wasted."

She hesitates, looking between the staircase and the elevator, but she finally chooses the easy option.

The second the elevator doors open, she darts inside and pushes the button for her floor.

I don't move immediately, letting her think that I'm not going to follow, but then just before the doors close, I jump inside.

"What did I ever do to you?" she asks, glaring up at me as I encroach on her personal space. "Other than turn you down, of course," she adds smugly.

"Promised Tate I'd get you home safe. Just following through."

Her lips twitch with the beginnings of a smile.

"Do you do that a lot?"

"What?"

"Follow through?" This time, she's unable to contain her amusement at her own joke and snorts.

On anyone else, it would be completely unattractive and off-putting.

But on Lorelei...it's weirdly not.

"S-sorry. That was..." She waves her comment off and exits the elevator as it stops on her floor. "I would say thank you for delivering me home, but it wasn't enjoyable, and it was totally unnecessary, so...yeah. Have a nice life and enjoy your crabby booty call."

She angrily pushes the key in the lock and throws the door to her apartment open.

She immediately swings it closed again, proving her need to put an end to our time together, but before it slams in my face, I lift my hand and catch it.

"Lorelei?" I ask, loving the way she pauses the moment I say her name. Just like she did on the sidewalk earlier.

For such a fiercely independent woman, she sure likes following orders.

"What?" she snaps, risking a glance over her shoulder.

I hesitate for a moment, wondering why I thought it was a good idea to stop her retreat.

Curiosity, I guess.

"You were right."

She stands a little taller, shocked by my words.

"Really?"

"Yeah, your ex-boss is an asshole. Getting fired was probably the best thing that could happen to you."

"Could you call my landlord and maybe explain that to him? My credit card company too?"

One side of my mouth kicks up in a smirk. "Everything happens for a reason, Lorelei. As one door closes, another opens. You just have to be ready to embrace the challenges."

"Well, thanks for that nugget of life-changing advice. Now, if you're done, I've got a date with someone who is way more entertaining than you."

Spinning back around, she wraps her fingers around the door handle and attempts to push it closed.

"What?" she snaps.

"I think we both know that your vibrator can't do the things I can do."

"Goodnight, Mr. Callahan." This time when she attempts to close the door on me, I let her.

The second it's closed, she double-locks it as if she's worried about me forcing my way back inside.

With a smile playing on my lips, I back up toward the elevator.

"Until next time, Temptress," I muse.

I descend through the building with the scent of her perfume surrounding me, before rejoining Lewis outside.

"You look pleased with yourself," Lewis muses as I approach.

"Entertaining evening."

"You don't say," he mutters. "She's really something, huh?"

"Yeah," I agree, running the events of the day through my head as I climb into the back of the car.

Pulling my cell from my pocket, I stare at the screen. Any amusement I was feeling withers when I see a whole stream of messages since the first one she sent earlier.

> Sasha: Too much work and no play makes Kian a very stressed boy.

I groan, letting my head fall back against the seat as Lewis drops into the driver's seat.

Another message pops up. It's as if she knows she's got my attention.

> Sasha: I can come to you. I'm already dressed for the occasion.

"Of course you are," I mutter to myself.

"Home, sir?" Lewis asks, oblivious to my irritation.

I consider my options briefly, but really there is only one answer.

"Yes, please."

Putting my cell back to sleep, I close my eyes as we make our way through the city.

There would have been a time not so long ago—hell, maybe even as recently as a week or two ago—when I would have jumped at her offer.

Sasha is...a lot. In every single way. But I've always focused on the fun side. Sadly, though, that's also opened me up to her eager, slightly obsessive side.

I'm no stranger to stage-five clingers. My brothers and I have been dealing with them for years. But Sasha is...fuck. I drag my hand down my face. She's...up there with the worst of them.

I'm sure there were probably signs before I hooked up with her that first time. But they were easy to ignore. She's a model, and she's not just beautiful on camera. She's the kind of woman that every guy would give their left ball for a night with. And, lucky me, that night a few months ago, I was the one she decided to turn her charm on.

It was a great night. The problem came the next morning and the weeks that followed.

While I went into it thinking we were going to have a wild night and then go our separate ways—she's busy with her career, and hell knows I'm run ragged with mine—that hasn't been the case. Almost daily, she's in my messages, trying her hand at another chance.

I'm ashamed to confess to caving a time or two.

What? I'm a red-blooded male with needs. And she's...a fucking supermodel who can fold herself up like a pretzel. Would I even be considered a real man if I turned that down when it was offered up on a plate?

Fucking hell, Lorelei is right. I am an asshole.

As Lewis closes in on my building, the temptation to reply and accept her offer is strong. So strong that I actually open our message thread and have my thumb poised, but something about her profile photo stops me.

Something doesn't feel right.

So instead of losing myself inside a more-than-willing woman, I stalk through my apartment alone, strip down, and step into my shower.

But as I stand there with bubbles sluicing down my body, it isn't the image of a hot blonde supermodel that lingers in my mind. Instead, it's vivid memories of a feisty brunette I can't stop thinking about.

8

LORELEI

I sit on the couch, staring at the same job advertisements that I have for the last week, feeling even more hopeless as the minutes tick by.

"Everything happens for a reason, Lorelei. As one door closes, another opens. You just have to be ready to embrace the challenges."

That jerk's smooth voice rings out in my ears as if he's right in front of me once again. The hairs on my arms rise and a shiver rips down my body.

He has no right to be inside my head, even if it is with annoyingly good advice.

Although, it's not that good, because I don't see any doors opening for me right now. Unfortunately, all of them seem firmly fucking closed.

A waitressing job at a local restaurant stares back at me. It's only a couple of blocks away. I could walk. I might even save a bit of cash on meals if my experience of working in the food industry is anything to go by. It might go a little way toward helping with the significant pay cut.

I'm good with people...sometimes.

I wince as I think about someone complaining about their perfectly good meal.

Do I want to deal with that? No, I really fucking don't. But at this point, I don't have much choice.

My thumb hovers over the "apply now" button, but I don't get a chance to hit it because my cell begins ringing, the name Wilder appearing at the top of the screen.

I frown before glancing at the time.

He should be in class.

Answering the call, I put my cell to my ear.

"What do you need bailing out of this time?" I ask lightly.

Wilder's best fake laugh fills the line, and my stomach knots.

Shit. Something is wrong.

"Wilder? What's going on? Shouldn't you be in class?"

Concern for my little brother floods through my veins, and I find myself on my feet, pacing back and forth through my living room.

I haven't told them that I've lost my job. I don't want them to worry. They've already got more stress in their lives than seniors at high school should have as it is. I don't need them to lose sleep over the fact I'm currently unemployed.

"Yeah, I should. I just...my cleats are fucked, and Coach is gonna rip me a new one if I turn up in sneakers again."

My stomach sinks.

"How is being out of class helping here, exactly?" I ask, mentally trying to figure out how I'm going to get him a pair there in the next...I look at the clock again. Three hours.

"I was trying to get some money together. I've got some friends who owe me, but—"

"Why didn't you just call me?" I ask, although I already know the answer. It's the reason why they both have jobs of their own.

"You know why, Lor. I fucking hate this."

"I know, but sometimes we've just got to swallow our pride and ask for help." The words taste like ash on my tongue.

That's all Tate wanted. It's why she applied for that job. She wanted to help me when I refused to help myself.

"I know," he mutters.

"Send me the link for what you need. I'll sort it," I say, sounding a lot more confident than I feel. He's going to want the best. Hell, he deserves the best. He's one hell of a player.

He sighs heavily.

"I mean the ones you really want, not the second-best pair that will lessen your guilt over this. I want to buy them for you, okay?"

"I'll pick up some more shifts. I'll—"

"No, Wilder. Your focus needs to be football right now. It's your final chance to—"

"Lori, I—"

"I want to see you go all the way this year, Wilder. There might be miles between us, but I'm right behind you. And I'll be there. Your playoff game, the final. I'll be there screaming louder than everyone else."

I don't need to be able to see him to know he's scrubbing his hand down his face and rubbing at the designer stubble on his jaw.

On the outside, he's the stereotypical quarterback and bad boy. But there is so much more to Wilder. He has a sweet and vulnerable side that he doesn't let out very often.

"Okay," he finally says.

"Send me the link. I don't care how expensive they are. I'll order them right now and get the fastest shipping possible. I'll also email Coach and explain."

"No, you don't—"

"Wilder," I warn. "Let me handle this. You need to go back to class."

"But—"

"Do not 'but' me, young man," I chastise, pulling out my best parental voice. "I might want you to kick ass on the field, but I also want you to graduate."

"Fine," he says, as the sound of him moving around echoes down the line.

"I'll let you know when they're arriving."

"Thank you, Lor. You're the best sister in the world, you know that, right?"

I smile, my heart swelling.

"I love you, Wild Child."

He groans, hating that nickname just as much as he did as a kid.

"Love you too. Speak soon," he says before cutting the line to hopefully send me a link and then turn up to class. Late is always better than never.

It takes all of twenty seconds for my cell to ping with a link.

I'm pretty sure it takes longer for the site to open than it did to receive it, making me think Wilder was sitting there staring at the webpage as hopelessly as I was at the job ads.

"What a fucking—" My gasp of shock cuts off my muttering and my eyes widen at the price of what he's just sent through. "How much? Jesus, it really is a good thing I love you."

I find his size and then add them to the basket, all the while wondering how I'm going to swallow this cost.

I have savings, sure. But not enough to keep me afloat without an income for any substantial amount of time.

After putting the cleats and the stupidly expensive next-day delivery onto my credit card, I pull up Wilder's coach's email and send him something that I hope will pacify him. I like Coach Hardin. He's a ballbuster, but he's also fair. Wilder, and all the other boys, respect the hell out of him. They always have. He's the exact male role model that Wilder needs in his life if he stands any chance of keeping his head screwed on and making something of his skills on the field.

Without second-guessing this time, I return to that waitress job and apply.

It'll just be a stopgap while I wait for the perfect position to make itself known.

Something is better than nothing.

Abandoning my cell on the couch, I pull a blanket over me and grab the TV remote. I aimlessly scroll through the rom-com section of Netflix before I find a movie I've never seen before and snuggle deeper into the cushions.

It's a dubbed movie, and it takes all of three minutes for it to irritate me, but I don't turn it off. The guy is cute, and I figure that's good enough to put up with the non-existent lip sync.

As the movie continues, I sink lower and lower, and eventually, my eyes drift close.

I've no idea how long I drift off for, because when I'm startled awake, the sun is still streaming through the windows, the movie is still playing, yet my head is fuzzy, as if I'd fallen into a deep sleep.

I stare at the TV for a beat as my heart races. It takes a second to register that my watch is vibrating with an incoming call.

Rebecca.

Rebecca?

I'm about to ignore the call when reality hits.

Rebecca from Callahan Enterprises.

My stomach sinks. She's calling to thank me for my application but to let me know that I've been unlucky this time.

Honestly, the call is not necessary.

Although, I can't help but think that Kian would probably love to be the one to make it. I can almost hear the amusement in his voice as he explains that I won't be a Callahan Enterprises employee anytime soon, or ever.

I should cut the call and get on with my life. But my curiosity gets the best of me, and instead of shutting it down, I swipe the screen.

"Hello?" I ask, cringing that I once again sound half asleep when speaking to this woman.

At least I'm not hungover this time...

"Hi, Lorelei, it's Rebecca from—"

"Hi Rebecca, how are you?" I ask politely, interrupting her full introduction.

"I'm good, thank you. I'm calling with news that I hope will make your day brighter."

My brows pinch and I sit up on the couch.

"Y-you are?"

"Congratulations, Lorelei. I'm thrilled to tell you that your application has been successful."

"I-I'm sorry. My w-what has what?"

Rebecca chuckles down the line.

"Your application for finance assistant," she explains as if there's a chance I've forgotten about the mortifying experience.

"B-but—"

"I know this is last minute again, but I understand you're available to start immediately?"

"I—" I swallow, giving myself a moment to gather my thoughts.

What the fuck is happening right now?

My interview was up there with some of the worst of all time.

How am I being offered the job?

How fucking awful must the other candidates have been?

"Yes, I'm available."

"Fantastic. I have a few things to go through with you, and I'm going to need you to send me copies of your ID, but as long as everything is in place, how do you feel about starting the day after tomorrow?"

"Th-Thursday? This Thursday?" I stutter.

Honestly, if she had a concern about making me this offer, she really should now. I am not behaving like a Callahan Enterprises employee.

All of them are so confident and self-assured. I'm nothing but a bumbling idiot right now.

"Is that okay? I'm sure we could wait until next week if—"

"No," I blurt as I hop to my feet. "Thursday is perfect."

I try to listen to everything she explains to me after that, but honestly, most of it goes in one ear and out the other.

I've got a job.

No. Not just a job.

A job with my dream company. A massive step toward my ultimate dream.

And I'll be able to buy Wilder a whole closet full of those cleats and Hendrix as many VR headsets and gaming computers as his heart desires.

Okay, that might be pushing it, but the pay increase I'm going to receive here is insane.

It's...

Fuck.

My head is spinning by the time I hang up, and my face aches from how wide my smile is.

"As one door closes, another opens. You just have to be ready to embrace the challenges."

Damn him for being right.

The fucking door just opened, and I am running through it at full speed before someone figures out that Rebecca just called the wrong candidate, and this is all a massive mistake.

I squeal in excitement and practically run through the apartment in the direction of my closet to try and figure out what the hell I'm going to wear on my first day.

9

KIAN

With my eyes locked on the CCTV footage on the screen before me, I sit back in my seat with one leg resting over the other and wait.

And wait...

There are a hundred and one things that need my attention right now, but none of them interest me as much as what's going to happen in the next few minutes.

She'll be early. I know she will. Which means—

"Bingo," I breathe when a familiar figure moves toward the main entrance.

One of our doormen steps forward and pulls the door open for her, and my skin prickles the second she turns her attention on him.

What the fuck is that?

Ignoring the odd reaction, I keep my eyes on her as she moves toward reception to announce her arrival.

Rebecca is meeting her to get her paperwork and security passes sorted.

She comes to a stop at the desk to introduce herself and my eyes drop down her body.

She's wearing a fitted light gray jacket with a matching skirt that fits her hips and ass like it was stitched onto her body.

Leaning forward, I try to get a better view.

On her feet are a pair of purple heels that make my dick twitch as the image of those stilettoes digging into my ass emerges in my mind.

A smirk pulls at my lips as I make my way back up her body and to her long, dark curls that are hanging around her shoulders. The perfect length to wrap around my fist as I—

She turns abruptly, forcing me to take my eyes off her enough to realize that Rebecca is standing before her.

The two women greet each other before Rebecca gestures for Lorelei to follow her.

Only a few minutes later, they disappear into the elevator, heading for Rebecca's office to complete the outstanding paperwork.

I beat them there, already staring at her empty office when they walk in laughing.

My stomach does some weird tightening thing as I take in Lorelei's smile.

Fucking hell, I'm one stupid son of a bitch for this.

But when I want something...

I watch as Rebecca goes through everything before they walk off again, but I follow closely behind.

The team in the security room is ready, and as they hand over her ID card and security pass it's impossible to miss the way her brows pull together in confusion.

I know exactly what our head of security just explained, and I can't help but feel like I just won this round despite her still being unaware of what's about to happen.

My heart kicks up its pace as they turn to leave.

I know their next destination, and I can't fucking wait.

Clenching and unclenching my fists, I watch their journey back down the hallway and then into the elevator.

Switching to a camera a little closer, I stare at the closed elevator doors, watching the number on the small LED screen climbing through the building until it hits the top floor.

My floor.

I can't stop my smile from spreading when she steps out of the car with a confused expression on her face.

Her eyes dart everywhere as she takes it all in. The rest of the building is nice, but the décor up here is on another level.

The floor is covered in white marble tiles, the furniture is dark, rich walnut, and all the accents are gold.

To us, it's normal, but I've seen more than a few visitors taken aback by it all, and it seems that Lorelei is one of them.

She's still looking around ominously as they approach Melissa's desk. The other two up here are empty. Dad's assistant seems to be here even less than he is these days. I've no idea if they're together wherever they are, and to be honest, I'd rather not know.

What our father does is his business. He may not have officially handed everything over, but we're as good as in charge around here now.

If we need him, he's always at the other end of the phone, but that has been happening less and less recently.

As far as King and I are concerned, Callahan Enterprises is ours now.

Ours to run as we see fit. And fuck, we're doing a damn good job, if I do say so myself.

Profits are higher right now than they've ever been. Our staff turnover is almost non-existent. People love being here and working for us. The results of that speak for themselves.

Lorelei stands with her fingers twisting nervously behind her, a habit I would guess she's not aware of, considering she's standing as tall and as confidently as possible.

I give her another five seconds to settle in on the top floor before I push my chair out behind me, smooth down my tie, and straighten my jacket.

Excitement bubbles in my stomach as I pull my door open and march out to reception.

My shoes tap against the expensive floor, but if Lorelei hears or suspects my approach, then she doesn't turn around.

When the hallway opens up into the huge reception area, I slow my pace.

"Good morning, Lorelei," I state confidently, letting my voice fill the space around me.

Her entire body flinches as if I physically struck her.

Did she really think I wouldn't personally welcome her to the organization this morning?

I really thought she was smarter than that.

It's been a week since I delivered her home from Tate and King's apartment.

A week since I've seen her.

Clearly, I haven't been on her mind as much as she's been on mine, if that's her reaction.

After rolling her shoulders back, she spins toward me.

Her eyes find mine instantly and she holds my gaze firm, daring me to be the one to step down.

I almost outwardly laugh at the thought alone.

You're going to need to try harder than that, Lorelei. We're in my territory now.

A wicked smirk plays on her lips. One that I'd love to make better use of.

"Mr. Callahan. What a surprise," she says, refusing to cower under my heated stare.

"Really?" I ask. "I would have thought you'd have expected to see me today, seeing as I'm your new boss."

My pulse continues to race as an army of butterflies threatens to erupt from my stomach.

"Hmm," she says letting her eyes drop from mine in favor of my body. She's doing it on purpose, trying to put me on edge, but she's going to learn very soon that it takes more than one suggestive glance to knock me off kilter. "I'm sorry to disappoint you, sir," she says, putting a little more emphasis than necessary into the final word. "But I believe that you're actually my boss's boss. Hopefully, that means that our paths won't cross all that often."

Both Melissa and Rebecca's eyes widen in surprise.

"Right, well," I say, moving closer. "That security pass in your hand...did anyone explain what it gives you access to?"

She swallows nervously. She knows the answer. I made it very clear that I wanted her to know the second it was handed over.

"Th-the whole building," she stutters, a little of her initial confidence beginning to wane.

"Correct," I confirm, coming to a stop right in front of her.

Melissa and Rebecca are watching our exchange with more than a little interest, but I don't so much as glance in their direction. My entire focus is on the woman before me.

"But here's the thing, Miss Tempest," I say, lowering my voice a few octaves. "No other finance assistant has ever been granted permission to step foot on the top floor of this building, at least not without a very specific invitation."

A frown mars her face, and her chest begins to move faster as her pulse rate increases.

"I have no interest in having access up here, Mr. Callahan."

"Well, that's a real shame, Miss Tempest, because without access to this floor, you're going to fail at your new role before you've even started."

"But the finance floor is—"

"Follow me, please," I demand before abruptly turning around and marching toward my office. "Back to work, please, ladies," I shoot over my shoulder.

She hesitates behind me, but Lorelei obviously makes the right choice, because a couple of seconds later, the tapping of her sexy purple heels sound against the tiled floor.

The hair on the back of my neck stands on end as accomplishment floods my veins.

Oh, this is going to be so much fun.

I hold my office door open and watch her closely as she walks inside before closing and locking it behind her.

She studies my space with intrigue, but she doesn't react until I pick up the small remote on my desk and darken the glass wall that would allow anyone passing to see inside.

A sharp gasp fills the room, and I swear it sucks all the air from the vast space.

"What is going on here, Kian?" she demands, walking toward the floor-to-ceiling windows that showcase the city outside.

I chuckle at her confusion. I can't help it; riling her up is just too much fun.

"Why are you finding this so fucking funny?" she snaps, finally losing her patience. "Is all of this one big joke? Was the job offer bullshit? Are you just doing this to get revenge because I turned you down? I've got to say, if that's true then—"

"There is a job, Lorelei," I say, interrupting her rant.

"Then why am I up here and not down with Martin?" Her hands land on her hips as she glares nothing but pure hatred at me.

"Another candidate was chosen to be Martin's assistant," I explain as I undo my jacket and lower my ass to my chair. "Someone a little more suited to the role."

"What the hell is that supposed to mean?"

"It means that it went to someone with a little more experience with the kind of tasks that role demands."

"And what? I wasn't good enough?" she spits.

I stare at her while she fumes. I'm pretty sure if I wait long enough, steam is going to begin billowing from her ears.

"Something like that," I muse.

Her eyes widen and her mouth opens and closes like a fish as she fights to come up with a suitable retort.

"You are unbelievable. I need this job, Kian. And to think, I actually believed that something good was happening in my life. What a fucking idiot I am," she storms toward the door, ready to flee.

"You weren't given the job as Martin's assistant because you're too good for it, Lorelei. That role is beneath you."

She pauses with her hand on the door handle as my confession lingers between us.

"We didn't need a reference from your previous employer. We already know what you are capable of and where your skills lie."

Her shoulders rise and fall with every deep breath she sucks in.

"What are you saying, exactly?" she asks, her voice weak and vulnerable.

I push my chair back and stand before stalking closer to her.

"I'm saying that I have a better offer for you."

I don't stop until I'm close enough to her that there is no chance she can't feel my warmth against her back.

"You're not going to be Martin's assistant, Lorelei." I swear she trembles before me as she waits for the words she fears that are about to fall from my lips. "You're going to be mine."

10

LORELEI

Oh, fuck no.

He has got to me fucking with me.

I suck in a deep, steeling breath, hoping it gives me enough strength to deal with this delusional asshole.

I had no issue being Martin's assistant. It's a job I'd do willingly and happily.

Is it my dream job?

No.

If I'm being honest with myself, I want to be the manager. I want to be the one with the role that requires an assistant.

But being in this building, learning how things work, is a huge step in the right direction. It brings me within touching distance of my dream job.

Just being here...it means everything.

That over-excited fourteen-year-old girl who lives inside me is doing endless cartwheels and screaming at the top of her lungs right now.

"You made it. You did it," she cries proudly.

But no matter how loud she is, Kian's words still hang ominously in the air between us.

They're almost as oppressive as his immovable form behind me.

The heat of his body sears through my clothes, making my skin prickle with awareness.

I take another breath before I hold my head high and turn around, facing him head-on.

I smile sweetly before saying, "I'm sorry, I think I just misheard you, Mr. Callahan."

His lips twitch before pulling into what has to be the best panty-melting grin that has ever existed.

"Okay," he says, mirth dancing in his dark green eyes. "Let me say it again. You're not Martin's assistant. You're mine."

Mine.

That word hits me like a baseball bat.

"I am not, nor will I ever be yours, Mr. Callahan."

The green staring back at me darkens even further before his eyes narrow slightly.

"That's a real shame, Miss Tempest, because from what I hear, you don't have any other choice."

His grin is wicked, and hell if it doesn't do things it shouldn't between my thighs.

I've heard plenty of stories about this man's antics—many of which have come directly from his annoyingly full lips.

He knows his power over women, and he uses it to his advantage.

Well, Mr. Callahan, you've met your match here because there is no way I'm falling for any of that.

A pretty face and a hot body will only get you so far with me. Both of those assets are easily forgotten when the personality lingering behind them is as arrogant and pig-headed as Kian's seems to be.

There was a fleeting fear that maybe I'd got him all wrong. That the man I met before was an act. But standing here now, staring him dead in the eyes, I know that's not true.

This man is every inch of the person I first believed him to be.

But, unfortunately, as much as I might see him for who is he, he can also see me. And he's got me.

I can't walk out of this building unemployed. Neither my bank account nor my pride will allow it.

Is agreeing to this farce the stupidest thing I've ever done?

Quite possibly.

Am I going to turn it down?

Fuck no.

"Mr. Callahan, with all due respect, I think assisting you will require an increase in the benefits I've been promised for this role."

Something akin to pride flashes in his dark eyes before he finally takes a step back, leaving me with enough space to draw in a breath that isn't laced with his scent.

"One thing you need to learn about me, Miss Tempest, is that I'm always one step ahead," he says, his tone oozing arrogance.

He stalks around his desk before pulling out a black folder with "Callahan Enterprises" in raised gold foil shining in the corner and sliding it toward me.

"I suspect you'll be more than happy with the benefit that comes with working closely with me."

"I'm not sure that's actually possible," I mutter under my breath, although loud enough for him to hear every word before swiping the folder from the desk and flipping it open.

I scan the page, shamelessly looking for the most important piece of information to me right now.

And when I find it, my eyes practically pop out of my head.

"Holy shit," I breathe. My knees give out and I crash very inelegantly into the chair behind me. "That's—"

"Agreeable?" Kian asks smugly.

"Um..." It's fucking crazy. There is no way on earth that I deserve a salary like that for following him around like a puppy and doing his bidding. Not unless— "What exactly do you expect me to do for that figure?" I ask suspiciously.

I swear to God if he's expecting "benefits", then he's about to find this entire folder shoved so far up his ass that he'll never be able to retrieve it.

"You'll find your roles and responsibilities listed on the next page," he says without bothering to look at me.

Instead, he presses a button on the phone console sitting on his desk before demanding that someone bring us both a coffee. He rattles off both our orders as if we've been working together for years, not the last thirty-five seconds.

"How did you know?" I ask once he's hung up.

"I always do my research, Lorelei," he says, holding my eyes across his massive walnut desk.

A wave of nerves rushes through me as I think about all the things he could discover about me. About my family.

Internally, I cringe. Girls like me don't belong in fancy offices like these. I've felt out of place since the day I left my hometown. Not that I've let anyone know that.

Holding my head high, I keep my mask firmly in place.

If he didn't like what he found, then I wouldn't be sitting here right now. My past holds many, many reasons as to why I shouldn't have a job like this, but he's allowing it nonetheless.

"Of course you do. Heaven forbid the great Kian Callahan isn't fully in control of everything at all times."

He glares at me—and probably questions his life choices and decisions.

This is on him, though. I could have been downstairs right now, being welcomed into the finance team. But no, here I am, sitting in his fancy office, discovering what this all-powerful man requires from his assistant.

His jaw ticks with annoyance, but he refrains from responding. Instead, he turns to his computer and allows me to continue reading the list of requirements he has of me.

Most of them are to be expected. Managing his schedule. Monitoring email, mail, phone calls, and other company logistics. Providing administrative support. Attending and minuting meetings. Planning events both on and off-site. And then there are a whole host of finance-related tasks that I'm not sure a standard assistant would ever be expected to do, but the sight of them warms something inside me. Maybe he doesn't just want me to be his little bitch. Maybe there is more to this than I first thought.

"What's this?" I ask before reading a line about travel.

He glances up, studying me for a beat before he responds.

"When I need to travel, you'll make the arrangements and then travel with me."

"W-with you?" I squark.

His smirk grows. "Yes," he confirms simply before turning back to his screen.

"O-okay."

He waits a moment, allowing me to get to the bottom of the page before sitting back in his seat, his lips parting to say something, when a knock sounds on his office door.

Kian reaches for something under his desk before calling for whoever it is to enter.

The lady Rebecca introduced me to, after we exited the elevator, steps inside the room with a tray in her hands.

"Thank you, Melissa."

Melissa, I say to myself, making a mental note. If she works up here, then something tells me that I'm going to need her support in the coming weeks and months.

"Thank you so much," I say when she places a mug before me.

"You're welcome," she replies softly before looking up at Kian. "Be nice, remember. And maybe try to keep this one a little longer than the last," she teases.

"Thank you, Melissa. That will be all."

I wait until the door clicks closed behind her before asking the obvious question.

"How long did your previous assistant last?"

Honestly, I'm not sure I want the answer, but I can't not know now that it's been brought up.

Lifting my mug to my lips, I blow across the top of the surface before taking a sip.

It's hot. Too hot. But something tells me it's less painful than what I'm going to experience working for Kian.

"Six hours," he states, making me almost choke on my coffee.

"Six hours?" I balk. "What the hell did you do to make her leave after six hours?"

He shrugs one shoulder. "She didn't have what it took. I can be..." He trails off, and I can't help but wonder if he's expecting me to fill the blanks.

I could. Easily. But it will probably end with me having an even shorter stint as Kian's assistant than my predecessor.

"A lot," he finally says.

"Oh, really? Can't say I've noticed."

He quirks a brow at me as he sips his coffee.

"Is there anything else on that list that you'd like to discuss?"

I scan the page again, trying to find something untoward that I can pull him up on. But the truth is, it's a really good job description.

"There are a lot of financial tasks on here. Are they usually things you expect your assistant to do?"

He shakes his head once before lowering his mug.

"I've never had anyone working this closely with me before who has an understanding of what I do."

"And you think that will make this partnership more successful?"

"Possibly." He studies me as he swallows thickly, his Adam's apple bobbing as he thinks. "I don't trust easily, Lorelei. It's one of the many reasons why I've never found an assistant I've connected with. But, since KC and I took over from our father, I'm finding my workload growing with tasks I'm not willing to pass down for many reasons."

"But you trust me with them?"

"Hmm," he mumbles.

"So, I did only get this job because of Tate," I say with a frown.

"Yes and no. I don't usually go around hiring friends of friends. I just..." My brows lift, impatiently waiting for him to continue. "I don't know," he muses, scrubbing the perfectly trimmed stubble on his chin. "I'm interested to see how this will work out."

"Because I turned you down," I reason.

He smiles.

"Not many women do that," he says, leaning forward to press a button on his phone again.

A deep male voice greets him not a second later. "Please could you bring Miss Tempest's computer and cell phone up. She'll meet you at her desk."

"Yes, sir."

Kian cuts the call and focuses on me once again.

My temperature increases as our eye contact continues.

"Simon will meet you at your desk and get you logged into the network and go through everything you need to know.

"You will already find emails in your inbox with your first tasks for the morning, then we have meetings all afternoon. I've sent you notes from some of the previous ones. Make sure you're prepared."

"Y-yes."

"Yes?" he asks, quirking a brow.

"Yes...s-sir," I guess, my stomach knotting.

It's not the first time I've called him that, but something feels very different right now.

He studies me for three more seconds before dismissing me in favor of his monitor.

"I'll be unavailable for the next two hours. Any questions, Melissa will be able to assist you."

"O-okay. Sure. Yes."

His lips twitch with amusement, but he's too focused on whatever he's reading to respond, and a couple of seconds later, I let myself out of his office.

It's not until I'm standing on the other side of the door and able to suck in a deep breath that reality begins to dawn on me.

11

LORELEI

"I'm not sure if I should be offering you a seat or the trash can to vomit in," Melissa says as I shuffle back down the silent hallway toward her desk, which is perfectly positioned to intercept any visitors risking a visit to the top floor of this building.

I hold her eyes for a beat before a manic laugh tumbles from somewhere within me.

"Oh sweetie, how about you come and test out your new desk?" she asks, before wrapping her arm around my shoulder and guiding me forward.

The desk is as big and as ridiculous as hers. The second I step behind it, I feel like a tiny bug that's about to be squashed beneath someone's—namely Kian's—shoe.

My ass hits the soft cushion of the chair and I take a moment to suck in a few deep breaths of air.

"This is crazy," I whisper. I'm not sure if I'm talking to myself or Melissa, but she takes it upon herself to answer nonetheless.

"The Callahan brothers are a law unto themselves," she muses as if this is something that's going to be news to me.

"I'm Tatum Warner's best friend," I blurt.

Melissa taps the back of my hand and smiles

sympathetically at me. "I know, sweetie. I know who you are. Tatum always talks very highly of you."

"At least someone does." I blow out a long, pained breath as I try to figure out the big question. "How did I end up here?"

Melissa chuckles. "What Kian wants, Kian gets. The sooner you learn that about your new boss, the easier this will probably all be for you."

"Easier?" I blurt. "Nothing about this is going to be easy. I can't stand the man. He's an egotistical, self-assured—shit," I hiss as instant regret hits me.

He's her boss, too. He's everyone's freaking boss.

Dropping my head into my hands, I allow myself another moment of wallowing in the unbelievable situation I've found myself in before pulling on my big girl panties and sitting up tall.

"I'm sorry, that was unprofessional of me. I'm sure Kian is a fantastic CFO and—"

"It's okay. You're allowed to have a moment over this. Would you like another coffee?"

"Or a shot or five of vodka," I mutter under my breath.

"Probably not the best first impression," Melissa jokes.

"Coffee would be great," I say while mentally kicking myself for being such a moron.

I sit there in my new chair at my new shiny, massive desk and just look.

I'm pretty sure it's possible to see my reflection on every surface up here, they're all so polished.

Every single inch of the décor screams unbelievable wealth, something that makes me very uncomfortable.

I grew up in the slums surrounded by dirt, violence, and disregard. This is like nothing I've ever experienced before while being the exact thing I've always dreamed of.

A life with a high-flying career, a position in a fancy high-rise building, polished floors, and suited staff. They've got a freaking doorman and actual security, for fuck's sake. This place is the shit. Far more than I am.

My stomach knots as I once again feel about a foot tall and nowhere near grown up enough, or prepared enough, to embark on this kind of life.

"So, what do you need to know before the IT guys get here?" Melissa asks, perching herself on the edge of my desk and sipping her coffee.

"Um…" I hesitate, not knowing where to even start. "Has Kian been looking for an assistant for a while?"

The second the question is out of my mouth, I regret it, but it's too late now.

"Nope. He hasn't been actively looking since he ran the last one out of here crying."

"If that's meant to make me feel better about this, I've got to say, it doesn't."

"Sorry." She chuckles. "If you want me to sit here and tell you that I was expecting someone to be occupying this desk anytime soon, then I'd be lying. I honestly didn't think he'd ever have an assistant again. He's too…"

"Stubborn?"

"Yeah, that works."

"Okay so…how about telling me all the things I shouldn't do instead of what I should. I'm pretty sure I've already pissed him off enough for one day," I say with a sweet smile.

I'm lying, of course. I'm pretty sure that the favorite part of my new job from here on out will be finding any way I can to drive my new boss to the brink of insanity.

I may or may not have gotten this job because of Tatum and my—albeit loose—connection to the Callahan family, but something tells me that's also going to make it harder for him to fire me.

My smile grows.

"Oh, now that look is dangerous," Melissa says with what I suspect is a wicked glint of her own in her eyes.

"You know what, Melissa," I say, my grin still firmly in place, "I think I'm going to enjoy my time here."

She nods as something—an understanding—passes between us. It gives me a little confidence boost, knowing that I have at least one person on this floor who has my back.

The sound of the elevator arriving stops any further conversation, and in the next breath, a nerdy-looking guy with thick-rimmed glasses and curly hair strides toward me with a laptop, tablet, and cell phone in his hands.

Melissa makes herself scarce, returning to her desk and whatever task she was doing before I interrupted her with my little freakout.

"Okay, Lorelei, is it?" the guy says, lowering everything to my desk. "I'm Paul, and I'll get you set up and ready to start work as soon as possible."

"Great," I say nervously as he slides me a piece of paper with my email and login details on it. "I can't wait."

He glances at me as if he's able to read between the lines.

I force a smile onto my face and do my best to listen to every word he says about the server, the printers, the email, and everything else I might need to know about the three devices he leaves me with.

"Oh, thank god." I sigh when my third call to my best friend is finally answered.

"What's going on? I was in a meeting."

"Oh my god, Tate," I cry, thankful that the ladies' bathroom is empty. Honestly, why anyone thinks that Melissa and I need a bathroom with six stalls just for the two of us is a little insane, but right now, I'm grateful for the pacing space.

The past few hours have been nothing but a whirlwind. I've no idea which way is up, and something tells me that it's only going to get worse as the day progresses.

My two-hour relief from Kian is coming to an end, and I

can only imagine what is going to happen when he summons me to his office for whatever the rest of my day holds.

"What? What's happened?"

I freeze, staring at myself in the spotlessly clean wall of mirrors that sits behind what I can only assume are hand-carved basins.

"You mean, you don't know?"

"No," she says in a rush. "I have no idea."

"Fuck, Tate. I told you this was stupid."

"Do you need me to come over there?" she offers.

"What? No," I cry. "Do not do that."

I can only imagine how that'll look to Kian.

Day one and I've already called in backup in the form of his sister-in-law to deal with his irritating ass.

"Okay, so..."

"I'm not Martin's assistant, Tate."

"O-okay, but—"

"I'm Kian's," I interrupt, unable to keep it in any longer.

"Y-you're...what?"

"Exactly. That's why I'm freaking the hell out. Do you know what happened to his last assistant, Tate? She left crying after six hours. And those before her? God only knows, but something tells me that crying is the best of it."

"Um..."

"Tate, you're meant to be telling me that I'm overreacting. That he's not that bad. That it won't be—"

"It'll be fine," she says in a weirdly high-pitched voice that sounds nothing like her usual one.

"Tate," I complain.

"What? It will be."

"And how do you know that?" I demand.

"Because none of his previous assistants were you. There is no way Kian Callahan will send my best friend running from her new job in tears. Not a chance in hell."

I can't lie, her confidence in me does light a fire under my ass, and I stand a little taller.

"If anything, I'd say that he'll be the one crying."

A smile spreads across my lips. "Hey, what are you trying to say?" I tease.

"That he has never had an assistant like you before, and that he has no idea what's about to hit him."

A laugh breaks free.

"See? The Lorelei Tempest I know would never cower down to a man like Kian. She isn't intimidated by money, or power, or good looks."

"You're right," I whisper, more to myself than her.

"She'd stand tall on the other side of his desk and tell him how it is. She'd call bullshit on his stupid, irrational demands, and make him do better. She wouldn't bow to his nonsense."

"Is that how it is with you and King?" I tease.

"Oh, hell no. We both know that I'm the boss and that he's the one running around completing my errands."

"I think you're going to have to share your wisdom. I need to know how to tame a Callahan."

Tatum laughs, and I picture her in the new swanky office at Warner Group as she throws her head back in amusement.

"Oh, Lori," she muses once she's finished laughing at my expense. "You are in so much trouble right now. But it could also be the best thing that's ever happened to you."

"Struggling to see that right now," I confess.

"Yeah, he's going to be a hard ass to work for, but Lori..." She pauses for effect. "You made it. You are exactly where you've always dreamed of being."

My new work cell begins buzzing with the alarm I set so that I wouldn't get lost in my conversation with Tate and end up back at my desk late.

Something tells me that when Kian said he'd be unavailable for two hours, he meant it to the second.

And while I might want to drive him crazy, being late on day one is not the way to do it.

"Tate, I gotta go."

"Oooh, duty calls," she teases.

"We'll talk later, yeah?"

"We should go out. Celebrate."

There's a part of me that wants to agree, but there is also another that is already exhausted and just wants to go home to sleep.

It's not even lunchtime yet.

How the hell am I going to endure endless days of this?

Of him.

"Maybe. Let's see how the rest of the day goes."

I hang up after quickly saying goodbye before setting about and attempting to get myself ready to face my boss again.

With my curls tamed and my lips freshly stained in a bright fiery red, I stride out of the bathroom with my head held high and my purple heels tapping loudly against the tiled floor.

Remember who you are, Lorelei.

You laugh in the faces of men like Kian Callahan.

12

KIAN

Like a creeper, I stare at the closed ladies' bathroom door, waiting for my moment.

The previous two hours have passed slower than any I've ever known.

I wasn't lying, I had back-to-back meetings that would have been too much for her to keep up with on her first morning.

She might have been trying to put on a brave face earlier, but I could see the turmoil bubbling behind her eyes.

I'd thrown her for a loop by having Rebecca escort her up here and announce that she was to be my assistant and not Martin's.

Fuck Martin.

She's way too good to be hanging out on his floor.

Something unfamiliar stirs in my stomach as I think about her following him around, about the way I know the younger men down on the finance floor would watch her in turn.

Not fucking happening.

Glancing at the clock, I note that there are only five minutes left of the two hours of freedom I gave her.

Smoothing my tie down, I turn my monitor off and push to stand. Pocketing my cell, I throw my jacket over my arm and march from my office, aware that she's still hiding in the bathroom.

She's been in there for so long that there can't be any other explanation. A smirk pulls at my lips as I think about her in there, psyching herself up for facing me again.

Melissa looks up from her desk as I approach with her usual soft smile playing on her lips.

"How is she getting on?" I ask before she gets a chance to say anything.

Melissa nods, her smile widening.

I trust her judgment. Always have. She's steered both King and me in the right direction more than a few times over the years.

"Yeah, she's great. Different," she adds.

"What makes you say that?" I ask, thinking of those who've come before her.

My assistants have come in all shapes and sizes over the years in the hope of finding one that fits.

Young, old, male, female, experienced, fresh out of college.

None of them worked out.

I don't know what it is about Lorelei that makes me think that she might be the one, but Melissa is right—there is something different about her.

"She's...feisty. Something tells me that she's not going to take the kind of shit the others have."

I cock my head to the side. "What are you trying to say, Melissa?"

"Oh, don't give me that innocent puppy-dog look, Kian Callahan. It will never work with me."

I smile innocently.

"Just give her a chance, yeah?"

"I have. I got her here."

"Yeah, about that..."

The sound of a door opening down the hallway cuts off Melissa's question. I'm grateful because other than spinning a line about seeing potential in Lorelei, I don't really have a reason for stealing her from Martin.

It was a hot-headed, rash decision that I'm not sure I could fully explain to anyone. Thankfully, having an office on this floor of the building means that I don't have to explain anything.

Well, that's not entirely true. King likes to grill my ass for anything I do that he doesn't agree with or understand. And I'm pretty sure he's going to have something to say about this when he finds out.

Honestly, I'm amazed he hasn't turned up here yet to confirm that what he's heard is true.

There is no way that Lorelei didn't immediately alert Tate the second she left my office earlier.

Goosebumps erupt across my body as heels clicking against the polished tiles beneath our feet echo around us.

Slipping away from Melissa's desk, I stand beside Lorelei's.

Her new laptop and a few messy sheets of paper are strewn across it haphazardly.

My eyes lock on the only item of hers that sits on top of the papers.

At first, I think it's an innocent pen. But then as her footsteps get closer, I focus on the writing down the side.

I watch porn at work.

Well then...

The second she turns the corner and finds me standing here, her steps falter and a loud gasp fills the air.

"Mr. Callahan," she whispers.

"You're late," I state, knowing full well that it's bullshit.

There's a second of silence while she decides how to react. Then her eyes narrow and a fire erupts within me, because I know which route she's going.

Her chin lifts and she holds my eyes firmly.

"I think you'll find that I still have a full two minutes before you require my services."

"Two minutes before we need to leave."

"Leave?" she balks.

"Yes. We have a meeting to attend. You are accompanying me. But before we go..." Leaning forward, I pluck the pen from her desk, holding it up for her to see. If she's shocked by what's on it, or my actions, then she doesn't show it. "What is this?" I demand.

Her lips twitch with amusement. "Oh, that." She laughs. "I stole it," she says simply, plucking it from my fingers before she reaches for her purse hanging over the back of her chair. "From your desk. Now, are we leaving or what?"

I stand there with my chin dropped as she sashays toward the elevator, ready to head out.

Melissa's quiet laughter behind me fills the air and my temperature soars.

"Maybe I was wrong. Maybe you shouldn't be giving her any chances. She's got you pegged from day one."

She's still chuckling behind me as I march toward where Lorelei is waiting.

As I get to her, the elevator doors open and she steps inside with her head held high.

Unable to do anything else, I follow her, allowing the doors to close and cage us in.

The sweet scent of her perfume permeates the air, ensuring that my heart continues to race.

"That pen isn't mine," I blurt like a moron.

What I should do is ignore the whole thing.

Clearly, it was a joke. One at my expense. But a joke nonetheless.

"Is that right?" she muses, refusing to look me in the eyes despite the fact I'm glaring into hers. "What is the meeting we're attending first? I would like a little heads up before walking in."

"We're meeting with our lawyer about a future investment. I'm going to need you to take notes."

"Okay," she agrees with a smug smile playing on her lips.

The sight of it irritates me instantly.

She knows she got to me with that pen stunt, and I fucking hate it.

"There weren't any minutes about an investment. Anything else I need to know?" she asks as we begin to descend through the building.

"No."

The second we hit the ground floor and the doors part, I stride out, leaving her to rush to keep up.

"Are we late or something?" she calls after I've greeted the doorman and come to a stop beside my car as Jamie, my driver, pulls the back door open.

"Afternoon, sir," he greets as I climb in.

Jamie has been my driver for about a year, but no matter how many times I tell him to call me Kian, he refuses. A part of me loves it. Another part...not so much.

"Good afternoon, ma'am. I'm Jamie, Mr. Callahan's driver," he says politely behind me.

"Hi Jamie," Lorelei says softly. "Please, call me Lori. I'm Mr Callahan's new assistant."

"How wonderful to meet you. I'm sure you'll love working for Callahan Enterprises."

"Oh, Mr. Callahan will make sure of that," she all but sneers as she joins me in the back of the car a beat before Jamie closes us in.

Forced to suck in yet another breath laced with her scent, I turn to look out the window as she gets comfortable beside me.

With an efficiency I'm used to from Jamie, he swiftly pulls into the passing traffic in the direction of our lawyer's office.

Ignoring my assistant, I pull my cell from my pocket and open a message I know is waiting for me.

> Makenzie: I'm bored.

I shake my head, picturing my kid sister staring out of the window instead of paying attention at school.

Kian: You should be in class.

Makenzie: I am. It's history. I'm over it.

Kian: If you listen, you might actually learn something.

Makenzie: You're meant to be the fun one. Come and get me, let's go and do something crazy.

Kian: I'm at work.

Makenzie: As yes, the big important CFO of Callahan Enterprises. Don't tell me, you're in a boring meeting too.

Kian: Nope. I'm too busy trying to make my new assistant cry.

Makenzie: I never want you to be my boss. You're mean.

Kian: Pay attention, Makenzie. I'll test you later.

Makenzie: You don't even know the topic.

Kian: Maybe not but you can bet that I'll find out before you get home.

Lorelei might not be looking at me, or paying me any kind of attention, but I know she's just as hyper aware of me as I am her. The skin down the right-hand side of my body is burning red hot despite the fact there's more than a handful of inches between us.

"So," she says, finally breaking the silence between us. "There really is nothing that I need to know about this meeting that will help me assist you?"

I don't say anything. Instead, I continue to keep my eyes trained outside of the car as I take slow, calm breaths.

If this is going to work, I'm going to need to let her in.

I'm going to need to trust her.

But...do I even want this to work? Or did I just want to fuck with her head?

"We're meeting Kingston, our father, and our lawyer to discuss a possible investment. We're still in the beginning stages of the process. No decisions have been made. We're just information gathering to see if this would be a good move for Callahan Enterprises to make."

"What is it?"

"There is a chain of British hotels that are weeks away from bankruptcy. King is interested because—"

"Of Tate," she finishes for me.

"Because it could be a good investment," I correct. "Business deals are made with the head, Lorelei, not the heart."

"You mean you have one?"

My teeth grind at her quick comeback.

"We're talking about Kingston here if I'm not mistaken. Not me."

"Right," she muses as her rapt attention burns the side of my face.

I want to turn farther away from her, stop her from seeing more than I want her to, but I hold firm and keep my head high.

Let her look all she wants—my mask is better than her inquisitiveness.

"We don't have a lot of assets in the British market. It's somewhere we've talked about branching out to in the future, so this is just a part of that. If the numbers don't add up, it won't happen," I explain simply.

The truth is, Lorelei is right. From what I've already seen, the numbers are a fucking mess and there is a very good reason why this chain is going under.

Of course, bad management and structure have a massive part to play in that, but it will be a huge challenge and need a sizeable investment to turn it around.

But it isn't the potential profit that is appealing to Kingston.

It's the fact his wife loves being in England. And if this works out, then...

Before I know what I'm doing, my hand has lifted from my lap and I'm dragging my palm down my face.

It's always been me and King. Or should I say, King and me?

I've followed him everywhere. Sometimes by choice, I guess, but mostly because it's been expected of me. The only real difference between us growing up was our majors at college.

King did business, I did finance. But then, while we might have somewhat "chosen" our directions, I think we both knew deep down that we'd been groomed into the decisions we made. Our father knew what our lives were going to look like long before we were born, and unlike Kieran, we just...went along with it.

I never really questioned it. It felt right.

But now, watching Kieran living out his dream every weekend, I can't help but wonder if there was ever anything else out there for me.

Or was I always destined to end up here, always living in the shadow of my big brother while watching my little one live the life that no one ever thought he'd achieve?

A heavy sigh threatens, but I keep it locked away.

The car slows to a stop and only a second later, Jamie has the door open and I'm climbing out.

Should I wait and allow Lorelei to go first? Probably.

Do I? Hell no.

Her heated glare burns into my back as I smooth my jacket down and stride toward the front doors.

With a nod at the doorman, I march inside and toward the lift.

I don't need to look back to know she's following; I can feel her.

Nothing is said as we move toward the floor we want, and

the second we step out, I find both my big brother and father waiting for us.

"You're late," Dad barks.

I raise a brow at him, unamused that he dares to reprimand me when he barely bothers to turn up to work week after week.

I've already lost King's attention, which has been on Lorelei since the second she appeared behind me, although he doesn't look shocked by her appearance, confirming what I already knew. But Dad takes a little longer to clock her, and when he does, his entire face lights up.

"And who do we have here?" he asks, letting his eyes run up and down the length of her.

Disgust swirls in my stomach and my fists clench at my sides.

Dad might be married—again—right now, but I'm pretty sure he'll always be a womanizer who is always looking for an upgrade. I could tell him right here that Lorelei isn't that.

"Lorelei, I heard a rumor you might be here. What a surprise," Kingston says with an amused smirk. "Dad, you remember Tatum's best friend from the wedding, right?"

13

LORELEI

Micheal Callahan's attention makes my skin prickle in the worst possible way, and without realizing what I'm doing, I take a step back, using Kian as my human shield.

The second I notice, I hate myself for it.

So what, he's a stupidly powerful and wealthy womanizer. I can hold my own.

A shiver rips down my spine at just the thought of being the sole focus of his attention.

I know all about him and his antics. Tatum has told me about the way he lives his life, hopping from one young bride to another.

I must admit that hearing more about his relationship with King's mom recently did tug at my romantic heart. But still, just because he had his ripped out and stomped on by the woman he loved, doesn't mean he was innocent in any way, or that he should be trading women like fucking Pokémon cards.

"Yes," Micheal says. "I remember Tatum's Maid of Honor. How could I forget?'

My stomach rolls at the thought of him watching me that day.

Gross.

"I do find myself wondering why she looks like she's about to walk into this meeting with us, though."

"Dad," Kian warns, and I can't help but wonder if it's because he doesn't want to explain himself and his decisions, or if he wants me out of the limelight.

Honestly, right now, if it takes Micheal's eyes from me, I'd happily go with either.

I thought Kian was everything I hated about this world. But his father...shudder.

"Just curious, Son. It's not like you to turn up with an assistant who doesn't look like they want to throw themselves in front of a bus just to escape you."

Okay, so maybe there is something more to the senior Callahan than just his disgusting ways with women.

Straightening my spine, I hold Micheal's eyes firm.

"I have no plans on getting up close and personal with a bus anytime soon, sir. Although, this is only my first day, so..."

Micheal and Kingston laugh.

"Most don't make it to the end of their first day, so things are looking promising for you right now."

I'm about to respond when Micheal turns his attention to Kian and completely changes the subject, as if I'm not standing here.

"Have you had a chance to read through that email I sent you?"

"Briefly," Kian admits. "I'll give it some more attention tonight and let you know my thoughts."

As I study father and son, a shadow falls over me, forcing me to look away.

"How is it really going?" Kingston asks quietly. "And you can be honest."

"It's...unexpected."

"Tatum said. You want me to kick his ass for you?" Kingston offers, making me smile.

"Nope. If anyone is going to be kicking his ass, it's me."

Kingston chuckles. "This could be the best decision that idiot has ever made."

102

"I'm pretty sure he's already regretting it," I confess.

"Exactly. It's fucking perfect. It's about time he had someone call him out on his bullshit."

"Isn't that your job?" I muse.

"Fucker doesn't listen to me. You though...something tells me that you're going to have magical powers."

My lips part to ask what he means when a door opens and an older man with salt and pepper hair and deep frown lines across his forehead steps into the room, immediately apologizing for his lateness.

Kingston takes off toward the room the man emerged from, and I step forward to follow.

"Are you sure about this, Kian?" Micheal says behind me. It's a whisper, but not one that's designed not to be overheard.

My teeth grind as I wait for Kian's reply.

"Are you questioning my decisions?" he growls quietly.

"You're like me, Son. Your head is easily turned by a pretty face and a hot body."

Asshole.

"Be very careful mixing business with pleasure. There is a reason why we keep those kinds of activities outside the office."

"I'm more than capable of controlling myself," Kian snaps before marching forward. "Shall we?" he asks before resting his hand on the small of my back and ushering me forward.

"Just don't let me have to say the words, Kian," Micheal warns as we all file into the room.

I glance at Kian as he pulls a chair out and gestures for me to take it.

"What was that all about?" I whisper.

"Nothing," he snaps. "Are you sitting or what?"

Shaking my head, I accept the chair and pull my iPad and Apple pen out, ready to take notes.

Kian lowers himself beside me, and I've no idea if it's me being hyper-aware of everything right now, or if he does actually sit a little too close to be professional.

The heat of his arm only an inch from mine means that I have to fight to keep my focus on what's being said and not lose myself in his warmth, his scent.

Keep your head, Lorelei.

The meeting is short. No more than thirty minutes later, Micheal is thanking the lawyer and seeing himself out of the room.

The second the door closes behind him, the atmosphere in the room instantly dissipates.

"He's not happy with this," Kian points out once the lawyer has also said his goodbyes.

"I don't really give a shit," Kingston says simply.

"He kinda has a point though, don't you think?"

The two brothers glare at each other in a silent battle of wills.

"It's a good investment," Kingston finally states.

"It's a money pit and a huge risk," Kian counters.

"With huge potential if it works."

"If," Kian points out.

"We don't fail, Kian. I thought you knew that."

Kian opens and closes his mouth, but he quickly realizes that he doesn't have a comeback to that.

"Just look at The Retreat," Kingston says, mentioning his health and wellbeing project up in Kohler, Wisconsin.

Tate has told me all about it and shown me everything she and her team have come up with for its launch.

It looks incredible, and just like this, it was a passion project of Kingston's that Micheal didn't believe in.

It's going to be a huge success; I just know it is.

"That's different," Kian argues.

"How? The place was a money pit," he says, trying to mimic the way Kian said the words a moment ago. "But it's going to be huge. This could be too. We'll be stamping our brand over every corner of the UK. It's what we've always talked about."

Kingston's excitement about this project shines through, but even I can see Kian's concerns over the figures.

"Bro." Kian sighs, dragging his hand across his jaw.

"I know. I fucking know, okay? I can see the numbers just as well as you can. But this is going to work, I can fucking feel it."

The two brothers continue their silent argument before Kingston rips his eyes away and turns them on me.

I want to shrink under his intense stare, but I don't. I hold my head high and pray that he's not about to drag me into his argument.

Apparently, I didn't pray hard enough.

"Lorelei, you've just listened to everything. What do you think?"

"Err...I'm not sure my opinion is important here."

Kingston glances at Kian briefly before coming back to me.

"Of course it is. Tatum trusts you. Kian clearly does, too. So, if you had to make the call on this, what way would you go?"

My heart races and my palms begin to sweat.

This wasn't what I signed up for.

"Umm..."

"You don't have to answer that," Kian mutters, clearly pissed off as he pushes his chair back and stands.

"I just want her thoughts. Nothing wrong with that, little brother."

Kian tenses, his fingers curling into fists beside me.

"I do love your vision for it," I tell King honestly hoping it stops them bickering. "But I also agree with Kian. The figures I've seen today are bad."

Kingston sighs heavily, falling back into his seat and looking up at the ceiling.

"Are you done? We have other meetings to attend," Kian snaps.

"Sure," he agrees.

Kian immediately marches through the door, not bothering to wait for me to catch up.

"Christ," I mutter as I rush to put my iPad and pencil into my purse.

"You've got your work cut out for you with him, I hope you know that, Lorelei."

"I'm learning fast," I say quickly before racing to the door.

"He's not used to having someone else take the weight, but he needs it. Recently, he's been..."

I pause with my fingers wrapped around the door handle, unable to take another step until I've heard the end of Kingston's statement.

"I don't know," he mutters, forcing me to look back at him. "Stressed, I guess. He's not a bad person. He's just..."

"An infuriating jerk who makes rash decisions and has a hot head?"

Kingston throws his head back, his laughter bouncing off the walls around us.

"You two are either going to be a match made in heaven or you're going to kill each other by the end of the year."

"He'd better watch his step then because I won't be the one losing that battle."

Kingston shakes his head, amusement still dancing in his eyes. "If you need anything, call me, yeah?"

"I can handle your little brother, Kingston. You just focus on looking after Tate and my future goddaughter," I tease before finally pulling the door open and going in search of my boss.

I have to navigate my way to the exit alone, but it doesn't take me long to discover where Kian is hiding, because as I emerge from the elevator, I find Jamie standing beside the car with the door open, waiting for me.

"Thank you," I say sweetly as I step inside to find a brooding billionaire in his fancy suit.

"Where have you been?" he snaps.

"I'm your assistant, not your slave, Kian," I counter.

He turns his eyes on me, and I swear I feel his wrath all the way down to my toes.

"I was talking to your brother. Problem?"

"We have another meeting to get to."

"Then maybe you should have said that before storming out and expecting me to follow you like a little puppy. And to think, I fucking agreed with you," I add quietly.

"Agreeing with me would have been telling my brother that it's a stupid idea."

"You mean lie, then?"

He sucks in a deep breath as he straightens and stares out the windshield.

"We're meeting with our accountant to review the past quarter," he tells me, all back to business.

"Fantastic. Looking forward to it." The sarcasm is heavy in my voice, and if the way his jaw ticks tells me anything, it's that he didn't miss it.

Silence falls and the air turns heavy and oppressive.

Long, painful minutes pass, allowing me to lose myself in my own head and attempt to forget who I'm sitting beside.

Our next meeting isn't nearly as short as the last, and despite there being cup after cup of coffee, no one delivers any food.

I scribble down notes about the previous quarter's performance like they're going out of fashion, but two hours in and my concentration is shot.

I couldn't eat this morning, I was too nervous, and now, I swear I'm bordering on passing out.

Thankfully, the men sitting around the table before me haven't stopped talking, ensuring my growling stomach has gone unnoticed. Or at least, I hope it has.

By the time the meeting is drawing to a close, my hands are trembling with my need for food.

"Thank you, gentlemen," Kian says, his voice firm and

unwavering. "I'll get back to you by the end of day tomorrow with those outstanding queries. Lorelei?" he questions, watching as I make quick work of putting everything away.

This time, he waits for me, and once I'm on my feet, he gestures for me to leave first.

Just like our arrival here, he doesn't say a single word to me as we descend through the building and climb into the waiting car.

"Where to, sir?" Jamie asks once he's joined us.

"Callahan building, please," Kian says, making me breathe a sigh of relief.

Sitting back, I attempt to rest, but I'm just as on edge as I have been all day. And the exhaustion and hunger are making it all that much worse.

The afternoon traffic is horrendous, and with only the rumble of the car and Kian's thumbs tapping against his cell screen as he replies to emails, there is nothing to hide my grumbling stomach.

"Sorry," I mutter, my cheeks burning up as it gets louder.

Kian doesn't so much as look over, let alone acknowledge that he's dragged me around the city without feeding me.

The car continues to crawl forward at a snail's pace. I pick at my fingers, staring out at all the food places we could be stopping at.

Something tells me that Kian isn't a fried chicken kind of man.

I know what Kingston is like for healthy eating. I bet Kian is equally as irritating.

"Jamie, can you pull up a little down here, please?" Kian asks suddenly, his deep, commanding voice startling me.

"Of course, sir."

Jamie pulls over, and Kian immediately slides out.

"Do you need me to—"

"Stay there," he barks, making my brows lift.

His attitude makes me want to do the opposite and follow

him just to be a brat. But I don't. Instead, I remain in my seat with my arms folded across my chest and a pout on my lips.

I'd even take one of Kingston's superfood smoothies right now.

Fuck. I must be desperate.

"Where is he going?" I ask Jamie when he gets back into the car, having not been fast enough to open the door for his boss.

"I have no idea," he says, giving me the impression that this is a regular occurrence. "With Mr. Callahan, it could be anything."

"Wonderful."

I swear to God, if he's just abandoned me on the side of the road for a quick hookup then I'll—

My thought dries up as he climbs back into the car as fast as he left. The scent of something mouthwatering follows him and not a second later, a bag lands on my lap.

"What's—"

"Eat, Lorelei. I can't bear listening to your stomach any longer. In the future, you'll eat a full, nutritious breakfast. I can't guarantee you a regular lunch break, so you need to be prepared for anything."

My mouth opens and closes, both in shock at his actions and in disbelief at his demands rendering me mute.

When I don't move fast enough, he turns his mesmerizing green eyes on me.

"I said eat."

"What if I don't like it?" I ask, unable to stop myself.

"You will. Now eat."

14

LORELEI

Kian was right. Damn him.

The sandwich he bought me was one of my favorites. Did he know, or was it just a damn good guess? I've no fucking idea, but all afternoon I've been grateful for his moment of thoughtfulness, even if it was accompanied by a side of demands.

Our afternoon has been busy and full of meetings, just like he promised. One of which was with Martin and his new assistant, Charlie.

She was lovely, and I've no doubt she will be great at her job. I wasn't sure if I was jealous that she was down there embarking on the job I was meant to have, or happy that I managed to score myself something better...

Is it better?

On paper, I'm sure the role of Chief Financial Officer Assistant trumps that of Finance Manager Assistant. But the reality...

I bet she didn't have a sandwich dumped in her lap and was told to eat.

But equally, I bet she hasn't spent the day trying to push her boss's buttons just to see how long it takes to make him blow, purely for her own amusement.

I smirk. Maybe my first day hasn't been all bad. Even if I was meant to go home an hour ago.

I'm lost in the numbers filling the spreadsheet before me when the ding of the elevator floats around the room. I don't look up. I've no reason to. Melissa is positioned to greet anyone who dares come up here. I, however, have been strategically hidden behind a big plant.

I've no idea if he's actually done that on purpose, or if it's just a happy accident on Kian's part that I can't see what's happening in my own workplace, but whatever. I guess it stops me from getting distracted.

"Oh my gosh, look at you," Melissa gushes, giving me a tiny hint about who might have just invited herself up to the top floor of the building.

I haven't seen her husband again; I can only assume he spent the rest of his day at the Warner Group office, trying to strengthen his argument for why that chain of hotels is right for them.

"She's growing nicely," my best friend says. I can picture her clearly rubbing her rounded belly with a wide smile on her face. "How's my girl done today?"

"Your girl is hiding behind the plant," I call out at the same time as a deep voice growls, "Managed more than six hours."

"I warned you, dear brother-in-law, my girl will stand up against all your bullshit and throw it straight back."

Pride is evident in Tatum's voice, and it makes a wide smile spread across my face.

"I don't know what I was thinking," he muses, his form moving on the other side of the plant, making my stomach erupt with a million wild butterflies.

Tate laughs. "That you're jealous of the way I boss your big brother around and you want in on the action."

"Oh yeah, it was definitely something like that," Kian mutters before he finally appears, approaching my desk, looking as suave and put together as he was first thing this morning.

Asshole.

I feel like a hot mess after running around the city all day and trying to focus harder than I'm sure I ever have in my life to ensure my notes stand up to Kian's exacting standards. And don't even get me started on this spreadsheet I'm attempting to make and populate.

I like to think I'm pretty skilled where spreadsheets are concerned, but this is pushing my limits. And I do not want to get caught Googling formulae by Kian.

I've got a list in my notes for all the things I need to look up tonight to make this work before showing him tomorrow.

My stomach knots just thinking about it.

Will anything I do ever be good enough for him?

Something tells me no.

He makes a show of looking at his stupidly expensive watch before glancing at my screen.

"Careful, Lorelei. I might get used to having you at my beck and call all hours."

"I wouldn't," I mutter, making Tate laugh.

My confidence quickly wanes when he stalks behind me and studies my spreadsheet over my shoulder.

"How are you getting on?" he asks, his warm breath rushing across my exposed neck.

My hair had been down and wild most of the day, but I couldn't cope this afternoon and it's been pinned up out of the way, something that I'm now regretting.

"I-I...yeah. Good. Should be done in the morning."

I gasp when he reaches around me and steals my mouse, moving my cursor and clicking on a couple of cells.

"Hmm," he hums.

"Is it wrong?" I ask, hating feeling like I might have disappointed him.

I shouldn't care. I'm learning here. But still...the need to please him, to prove that I can do this job takes over.

"No, not wrong exactly."

Abandoning my mouse, he begins tapping on my

keyboard, changing formulae and making numbers shift and change before my eyes.

My spreadsheet.

Emotion burns the backs of my eyes as I watch hours of work vanish before my eyes.

Well, not vanish. But…it's not the same anymore, and I've no idea what he's done.

"See?" he says, pointing at a column. "Now it's pulling data from each sheet and populating the result here instead of up there."

Unable to speak through the lump in my throat, I nod.

"Easy, right?"

"Uh-huh."

"Great. We'll review it once you've finished tomorrow at eleven. You can then move on to the next stage."

I nod, and thankfully, he steps back, allowing me to suck in deep lungfuls of air.

"Great. Can't wait."

"In the meantime," Tate announces as if nothing just happened—I guess it didn't, in her life. She didn't watch her past few hours' work evaporate with just a few taps of a keyboard.

He probably thinks he just helped me.

Maybe he has.

But…

Reaching out, I slam the lid of my laptop down harder than necessary.

"We are going out to celebrate my bestie's new job. Something tells me that her boss will have been an asshole and she deserves a drink."

"No idea what you're talking about," Kian mutters before picking something up from Melissa's desk and disappearing out of sight, but not before calling, "See you in the morning, Lorelei. Our first meeting is at eight o'clock. Do not be late."

I sink lower in my seat, all the air rushing from my lungs, my adrenaline and energy going with it.

"Been that good, huh? King said you looked a little stressed."

"It's been fine." It's not really a lie. As far as jobs go, it's probably been up there with some of my best. It's a hell of a lot better than my last place, that's for sure. And yes, Kian has had his moments, but so far, he's got nothing on the one who came before him.

I shudder. If I never have to see that asshole again, it'll be too soon.

When Tate frowns, not believing a word I've said, I follow up with, "Just a lot to learn in a few hours."

"Nothing like easing you in gently, then?"

"I don't think Kian knows the meaning of the word gentle. He did buy me lunch, though."

A wide smile lights up Tate's face. "See, he likes you."

I briefly think back to our interactions over that sandwich. "Oh yeah, we're like that, me and the boss," I say, holding my crossed fingers between us.

"Give him time. He takes a while to warm up."

"That's bullshit, and we both know it." Kingston is the one who takes a while to get used to. Kian is everyone's friend. Mainly because he's so fucking big headed he thinks everyone wants to be.

"Whatever. Grab your stuff. We're going out for dinner and drinks."

I wince. "I can't, T. I've got—"

"To celebrate your epic new job with your best friends." Her final word makes me look up. "Cory is downstairs, chatting up the doormen."

"He is not," I gasp.

"He's trying. But they're as straight as they come—just ask their wives."

I laugh, picturing him down there pulling out his best moves.

"We should probably go and rescue them."

After saying goodbye to Melissa, who's also finishing up

for the day, we step into the lift and hit the button for the ground floor.

The second the doors close, Tatum squeals, "I can't believe you're up here. It's so freaking cool."

"Tate," I warn.

"What? You can't still think this is a bad idea."

"Bit late, even if I do still think that."

"First days are always hard. But give it a few weeks and you'll figure out that I was right."

"You're insufferable."

"And you deserve this. You worked your ass off for nothing in that last place. Here, you'll get paid what you deserve, along with a whole host of benefits along the way."

"Benefits," I balk.

"Yeah," she says with a calculated smirk. "Someone told you that you have free access to the gym on level two, right?"

"The gym. Oh yeah. That's a massive benefit right there."

"You should use it. Rumor has it that Kian does a couple of times a week."

"Why would I—"

"First thing in the morning, then he showers in his office bathroom."

"Why are you telling me this?"

"Why not? I think it's important information to have about your boss."

I don't get a chance to respond because the doors open and Tatum spills out into the foyer in search of Cory. I want to say I follow hot on her heels, but that would be a lie. My head is lost in visions of Kian, hot and sweaty in a gym.

I wonder if he uses the sauna...

"Lori," Cory calls, ensuring all sets of eyes leaving the building for the day turn on us. "How is Callahan Enterprises's newest and best employee?"

Heat burns my cheeks and down my neck.

"Shut the hell up," I hiss before he wraps me in his strong arms and kisses my cheek.

"It's been too long, girl. I've missed your sexy ass."

"I'm sorry. Things have been—"

"Girl, don't. I know all about you kicking that cheating fuck to the curb. Good for you. My girl deserves so much better than that. You deserve this," he says, holding his arms out from his sides and spinning around. "It's fancy as fuck."

"It's sure something," I mutter, still unsure how I feel about it all.

"It looks so fucking good on you," he praises with the widest smile I think I've ever seen playing on his lips. "Now, let's go celebrate." He threads his arm through mine and marches me toward where Tate is laughing with the doormen. "You're paying, by the way. I have it on good authority that you've had an epic pay rise."

Laughter tumbles from me, and I finally feel some of the stress from my first day beginning to leave me.

My shoulders relax, and my smile loosens, becoming more genuine and less forced.

I think of the figure on that job description Kian handed me earlier and shake my head.

Something is going to have to give soon because this is all too good to be true.

Even Kian and his stupid demands and irritating remarks can't bring me down from this high.

"Hell yeah," I say as we collect Tate and emerge into the autumn evening sun. "Where to?"

"Where do you think?" Tate laughs before Lewis opens the door and gestures for us to climb inside.

"I have the best friends in the freaking world," Cory announces as Tate pops a bottle of champagne that she had waiting for us inside the car. "Now, I have a question," he says, sounding a little more serious.

"Shoot," Tate says as she begins filling our flutes full of bubbles.

"What are the chances that I can turn Kieran so that I can have a brother too?"

Tatum barks out a laugh. "Sorry, but I don't think that's going to be happening anytime soon. That man is about as addicted to pussy as they come."

"Worse than Kian?" I blurt, regretting the words the second they spill from my lips.

"Pretty sure they're in competition," Tate explains.

It's nothing I haven't heard before. But now that Kian is my boss, it's not something I need to be thinking about, let alone talking about.

"Oh, because Kingston was any different before he got stuck with you," Cory teases.

"Nice. I think I'll take this back then," Tate says, trying to steal the champagne back.

"I don't think so," Cory argues before downing the entire glass. "What's the problem? You tamed that beast. Someone out there will do the same to the others, and until that happens, I'm going to continue thinking that one is secretly gay and longing for a man like me."

"Dude, you're not even gay," I tease.

"I will be whatever I'm needed to be for the right person."

"Whore." Tate laughs.

"Just the way you like me," he says, blowing her a kiss.

15

KIAN

"Any plans for the night?" Melissa asks me once Lorelei and Tate have left.

I glance at Lorelei's desk, irritated when I find that she's left sheets of paper messily on the top.

"I've got a date," I say, deciding not the tell her about the history lesson I'm going to force my little sister through first. At least I don't need to worry about Tilly, Makenzie's little sister. She'll have listened to every word at school today.

Walking around the plant, I study her desk. My eyes land on the pen from earlier and my fingers twitch to take it. Or at least hide it.

"Oh, anyone I might know?" She asks me this every time I tell her I'm meeting a woman. I'm pretty sure she's hoping I'll name-drop some celebrity or something. But I'm not really one for discussing my sexploits at the office. Over a glass or two of whiskey with my brothers, maybe, but that's where I draw the line.

I chuckle, walking away from Lorelei's desk, leaving it in the mess I found it. "I doubt it."

"Well, have a wonderful night. Don't do anything I wouldn't do," she calls as I walk toward the elevator.

My cell burns a hole in my pocket as I descend through

the building, and by the time I climb into the back of my car, I can't ignore it any longer.

I open up my emails and hit compose.

From: Kian Callahan
To: Lorelei Tempest
Subject: *Housekeeping*

Dear Miss Tempest,

I hope your first day was enlightening.
Please may I request that in future you leave your desk clear before leaving at night?
We have an image to uphold, and a desk holding that kind of pen does not scream professionalism.
Also please ensure you never involve yourself in those kinds of activities in the office.
I look forward to what tomorrow brings...

Regards,
Kian Callahan
Chief Financial Officer
Callahan Enterprises

"Good day in the office, sir?" Jamie asks as we make our way through the city.

It takes me a second to answer—I'm too busy remembering my day and the highlights that Lorelei's presence brought.

"Yeah," I finally say, a smile firmly playing on my lips as I do so.

"Your new assistant was something."

I still the second his words hit my ears and look up, finding his eyes in the rearview mirror.

"What was that?" I demand, my voice a little deeper than it was before.

"O-oh, I didn't—shit," he hisses under his breath. "I didn't mean it like that. She looked professional and like she could..." He trails off, piquing my interest.

Jamie doesn't usually give me his opinion about much. Maybe the weather or the state of the traffic. But never about a woman, or even a staff member.

"She could what?" I ask.

"Be a good addition to the team, sir," he says after clearing his throat.

My shoulders shake with a laugh. "You mean she can handle me?"

"Um...handle isn't the word I'd use."

"Oh really?"

"I'm sorry, sir. I shouldn't have said anything."

I glance down at my cell, disappointed that she hasn't already replied with some snide comment about my demands and expectations.

Sitting forward, I hold Jamie's eyes in the mirror as he's forced to stop at an intersection.

"Appreciate her from afar all you like. But you will not be getting any closer than that. Do you hear me?"

He swallows nervously before a car behind beeps, alerting him to the fact he can now go.

"Shit," he hisses again.

Happy that I've made my point clear, I sit back and open my emails again.

Without a reply from Lorelei, I'm forced to go through the others sitting in my inbox. They're nowhere near as exciting.

I've almost read and replied to all the ones worthy of my time when Jamie pulls up out the front of my apartment building.

"There you go, sir."

"Thank you. Have a good night. Try to stay out of trouble."

"You got it, sir."

"It's Kian," I say for the millionth time.

I've no idea who his parents are, but they instilled some serious fucking manners in this kid.

He smiles at me, silently letting me know that it'll never happen.

With a nod, I take off toward the entrance of my building, greeting the doorman as he lets me inside.

"Good evening, Kian. Good day?" Maurice is in his sixties, and I'm pretty sure he's been guarding the door of this building for the better part of his life.

He's been married since he was twenty-one, has four kids, eight grandkids, and a great-grandkid on the way. He is hands down the nicest man I've ever met. His wife is equally as lovely. He's a hardcore Chicago Chiefs supporter and loses his mind every time he has the pleasure of opening the door for my little brother.

A few years ago, we organized for him to have a season ticket. Since we did, he's attended every single home game, proudly wearing his Callahan shirt.

"Yes, thank you, Maurice. It's been great. How about you?"

"Can't complain, young man. Can't complain. What are your plans tonight then? Anything I should be jealous of?"

I smile at him.

"I've got a date."

"Another one?" he balks. "How many are you going to turn down before you find the one?"

"Maurice." I laugh. "I'm not looking for the one, you know that."

He shakes his head. "You've got it all wrong, kid. Women are great, sure. But *the* woman. Sheesh." He smiles, obviously thinking about his wife. "You'll know about it. And when you do, you do not let her go for anything. You got that?"

"I'll see what I can do. You on all night?"

"You know it."

"I'll see you later then. Gotta go clean up." I wink and he groans, shaking his head at my antics.

Secretly, he loves it. He's living vicariously through me; I know he is.

The second the elevator doors open and I spill out into my private entrance, I begin undressing.

By the time I'm in my bedroom, only my boxers remain, and after tugging on a pair of shorts and a t-shirt, I make my way to my home gym, press play on my favorite playlist, and hit the treadmill.

Putting the speed up as fast as I can cope with, my feet pound against the belt and my heart begins to race.

I try to empty my mind and focus on the movements of my body, of the beat of the music thumping through the room, but I can't get there.

Instead, my head is full of the day's events.

No. Not just the day's events.

It's full of one person who was a part of them.

Long curly hair. Purple stilettoes. Gray pencil skirt and a mouth that never ceases to amaze me.

Fuck.

I squeeze my eyes closed as I push myself to the max and try to remember who I'm meeting tonight.

Fuck if I can remember her name or anything about her.

We met at an event the other week, and seeing as she didn't annoy the shit out of me from the get-go, I agreed to go out with her. Something that I'm now second-guessing. And I never fucking do that.

Slamming my palm down on the stop button, I jump off and bend over, resting my hands on my knees.

What the fuck is wrong with me?

I've got a date with a hot woman. A night that will no doubt end in pleasure, and all I can think about is walking into work tomorrow and seeing if Lorelei beats me in so she can tidy her desk.

She won't. She's too fucking stubborn to do that. But I still can't help wondering. Waiting.

"Fuck's sake."

Killing the music, I march out of my gym in favor of the shower.

"Get your head in the fucking game, Kian."

The temptation to blow the date off entirely is almost too much. But knowing that I'll hate myself for being such a pussy tomorrow, I dress and head out.

I don't feel any of the usual excitement I do when I know I've got a woman's sole attention for the night. And as I drop into my Maserati to head to the restaurant, all I want to do is turn around and lock myself in my apartment.

The fact that my date has managed to book a last-minute table at the Barrel and Grill should impress me. There is a chance that she used my name to secure it, of course. But seeing as I can't remember who she is, she might not have needed to.

"Kian," Rob, the owner greets me the second I step through the door. "What a pleasant surprise," he says, holding his hand out to me.

"How's it going, man?"

"Great. Booked out for months right now."

"That's awesome. You deserve it."

"Is it just you? I'm not sure I'll be able to squeeze many more in tonight," he says with a wince.

"Actually, I'm meeting someone."

"Ah," he says, a wicked grip pulling at his lips. "What's the lucky lady's name?"

"Err..."

"Fucking hell, K," he says, throwing his head back, laughing.

"I've got a lot going on," I explain.

"Sure. Sure. Let's see..." He taps on his iPad; I assume scrolling through tonight's bookings for two in an attempt to save this date for me before it's even begun.

"Ah ha," he announces, looking up at me with a smug-as-fuck smile on his lips. "Does Claudine Bernard ring any bells?"

Honestly? No, not really.

"Yeah, that's it," I say confidently. If I'm wrong, this evening could be about to go from bad to worse, but there's a niggle in the back of my mind that I'm right.

"Great. Right this way then, sir. I'll grab you a drink. Something tells me that you're going to need it."

"Thanks," I mutter, lowering my ass to the seat. "Rob?" I ask before he takes off.

"Yes."

"Any idea who she is?"

He smirks again, shaking his head in amusement. "You're something else. I'd pull up Google if I were you, or this date could be heading south fast."

Fuck my life.

The second he turns his back, I pull my cell out and tap her name into the search bar.

My eyes widen as a photograph of her pops up.

Yep, that's why I agreed to this date. Fuck. She's stunning.

Long, sleek red hair, mesmerizing light blue eyes, pouty full lips, and if my memory does serve me correctly, a body to die for.

So why is it that as I stare at her photo, I don't feel even one ounce of excitement about spending the night with her?

I should. I really fucking should. But...I don't.

Am I broken?

Opening up her Instagram, I quickly discover that while I might not have had a clue who she is, it seems a lot of other people do.

Along with hundreds of thousands of followers, I find endless photographs of her posing in an array of beautiful places.

Travel influencer. Of course.

Explains why she might have made a beeline for me.

With a sigh, I close down the app and push it back into my

pocket, although not before I check my email for a reply from Lorelei. Nothing.

My whiskey arrives and I take a sip as I wait.

It's no surprise she's late. Apparently, it's fashionable or some shit. Maybe it's meant to build anticipation. But honestly, right now all it's doing is pissing me off.

This woman only came on to me because of my job. The only reason she's interested is because she wants a step up in hers.

Why else would a travel influencer want to be out on a date with me?

Well, I mean...there are a few other reasons, but still...

I'm about to give up and blow her off when a shadow falls over me.

Glancing to my right, my eyes roll up a fitted dress before I find the exact same face that was staring back at me from my cell only a moment ago.

Fuck. Those images didn't even have filters.

"Good evening, Kian," she says in her sultry French accent that takes me back a few weeks to the event I met her at.

"Claudine, good to see you again," I say, forcing some lightness into my voice hoping she won't notice that I've no interest in being here right now.

It doesn't matter how hot she looks, or how every other man in this place is looking over, wishing that he was me right now.

Like a moron, I hold my hand out to greet her. She takes it with a teasing smile playing on her lips before leaning in close and pressing a kiss to both of my cheeks.

"I've been so looking forward to seeing you again, Kian." She takes a seat, leaving me little choice but to do the same as Rob comes over with a bottle of champagne for her and a fresh whiskey for me.

"No more," I tell him, placing my hand over the glass. "I'm driving."

Claudine frowns, but she quickly recovers as she holds her glass out. "To a wonderful evening."

My stomach knots as I clink my almost-empty glass to hers.

Something tells me that this is going to be anything but wonderful.

16

LORELEI

"**O**f course, you're going to have to travel with him. I thought that would be kind of obvious," Tatum says as he sips on her virgin margarita.

We've had the best night catching up. It feels like it's been a long time since we've all managed to spend some quality time together. But as is usually the case, Cory got a message a few minutes ago, offering him a night of mindless fun, and he bailed, leaving us to finish up our Mexican feast alone.

"I thought I was going to be working for the finance manager, T. I doubt he goes very far."

"Nope. But Kian does. They've got hotels and resorts around the world. You could end up anywhere."

Something flutters in my stomach as I think about the kinds of luxury resorts I know the Callahans own.

White sand, clear blue sea, sun, sun, and more sun.

They offer the kind of vacations that a girl like me can only dream of.

Kian's personality aside, this job sure does have its benefits.

"This is crazy," I breathe, lifting my drink to my lips and taking a big sip. I might have had one real cocktail when we first arrived, but I switched after that. I need to keep a clear head for tomorrow. Kian will be able to see if I turn up unfocused, and he'll never let me forget it.

"Yeah, but awesome. It's so much better than the job you applied for."

"That I applied for?" I ask, lifting a brow.

"Semantics. It was the right thing to do. I felt it in my waters."

"No, that was a baby kicking your bladder," I tease.

"Well, whatever it was, it was one of the best things I've ever done."

"Hmm...we'll see."

"It's going to work out. Now all you need is a man," she says wiggling her eyebrow.

"I do not need a man, T. No freaking way. They're too much trouble."

"I'm not talking for keeps, I'm talking for fun. You need to let your hair down. Get under another to get over the asshole."

"I'm okay."

"Oh, come on. You know some of your old fuck buddies would be down. Ryder," she says holding up one finger. "Harry. Jake."

I cringe. "You make me sound like a whore."

"Hell, no. Just a woman who knows what she wants and enjoys herself while getting it."

"Thanks for the suggestion, but I think I'm good."

Tatum shakes her head. "You'd feel better for it."

With my best friend's words ringing in my ears, I let myself into my apartment alone a little over an hour later with a smile on my face.

I needed those few hours with my people.

But as fun as that was, there is a spreadsheet taunting me from my laptop.

Setting myself up on the kitchen island, I lift the lid I

slammed down in irritation earlier and prepare to figure out what the hell he did.

What I really want to do is ctrl+alt+z to just get rid of it all. But...the asshole knows what he's doing and that formula he put in did exactly what I was failing to make happen.

Once I understand his thought process and have written it all down, I finally do what I was burning to do the second he took control of my computer and delete it all.

It's a small victory in the grand scheme of things, but still, watching his formulae disappear gives me great satisfaction.

"Right, you can do this, Lorelei. You are going to walk in there tomorrow morning and blow his socks off with this spreadsheet."

I work long after the sun has set, and I get through more cups of coffee than anyone should ever drink this late at night in order to complete it. But finally, I think I get it working as I want it to, and I sit back with a smile playing on my lips.

"Eat your heart out, Kian Callahan," I mutter, double-checking that I've hit save before switching to my emails.

Honestly, I'm not expecting to find any. No one knows I exist yet, and I cleared down everything Kian had forwarded to me earlier in the afternoon. Surely, he hasn't—

"Motherfucker. Couldn't even give me a night without you, could you?"

I stare at the subject of the email with my mouth open.

Housekeeping?

Tell me he's not expecting me to clean.

I knew all the roles listed were too good to be true.

Hesitantly, I open the email, and what I find has my chin hitting the floor.

"What the...it's my desk," I shriek. And it's hidden behind a freaking plant, for fuck's sake.

Fuelled by anger, caffeine, and exhaustion, I hit the reply button harder than necessary and try to summon up an epic reply.

From: Lorelei Tempest
To: Kian Callahan
Subject: *Housekeeping*

Dear Kian,

My first day was indeed enlightening, although I'm not sure that's the exact word I'd have used to describe it.
I apologize if my choice of pen has offended you—that was not my intention. I will ensure all my personal items are more discreet in the future.
And, as for your final point, I can assure you, I am in no mood to be watching such entertainment when I am in your company.

Respectfully,
Lorelei Tempest
Assistant to Kian Callahan, CFO
Callahan Enterprises

My hand trembles as I hit send. It might say everything I want to say, but it's entirely too polite.

But then, I guess it will be more fun to tell him to shove his professionalism and stuck-up attitude up his ass in person. I wouldn't get the full effect over email.

I'm still muttering curses as I get ready for bed. I wash the day's makeup from my face before piling my hair on top of my head and wrapping it in my favorite silk scarf, and then I crawl into bed with my cell in hand.

Anger continues to simmer just beneath the surface as I open the photo Tatum sent earlier of the three of us with wide, happy smiles.

She's glowing; it makes me so happy to see. She deserves it more than anyone else I know.

I scroll through my socials, making a point of checking

both Wilder's and Hendrix's to find out what they've been up to.

I'm yet to tell them about my job. I didn't want to jinx it. I want to know that it's going to stick before I give them any hope for the future.

The truth is, the pay rise that has come with this job will help them so much more than it will me.

I only need enough money to pay my way here. Every other penny I have goes to them.

They're expensive. Both of them have expensive hobbies that our mother has no interest in helping with. Hell, most days she doesn't have any interest in getting out of bed and making sure they have food, let alone anything else.

She has no idea what their dreams are for the future. She doesn't know that Wilder is good enough to have a real shot at the NFL. She has no idea that Hendrix doesn't just play computer games but builds them, too. She has no idea that both of them plan on going to college as far away from her— and as close to me—as they can get next year. She also has no idea that they have savings accounts open in their names with money that will hopefully help with their dreams. To be fair, they don't know about that either. But they will soon.

No one helped me, and it was so fucking hard that I almost gave up time and time again. I'm glad I didn't. I'm so fucking proud of the fact I stuck at it, even on my darkest days. It would kill me if I knew they both had to go through all of that alone.

I want to help them. I want to see them both succeed. I want to see them embark on the lives they crave, not be stuck in that shithole, drowning as their dreams vanish before their eyes.

I can't help but smile as I flick through the photos Wilder has posted. On the outside, it looks like he's living the kind of high school life that everyone dreams of. He's got friends, girls, looks, and his team. Even though I know the truth about his life, the look of it makes that little loner girl inside me jealous.

I just wish it was all true. I wish the smile he gives everyone was his real one. They might not be aware of it. Hell, the only other person who knows the truth in that school is Hendrix, because he wears the exact same mask.

Hendrix's life is quieter. His circle of friends is tighter, and he prefers to live his life out of the spotlight, but he still posts things. I'm pretty sure he only does it to stop me worrying, and as much as I hate that he feels the need to, I fucking love it too.

"Aww," I breathe when I find a photo of him and Noelle after school on the beach.

If they don't end up together and have all the babies, I'm going to be heartbroken. She is the sweetest, and together they're so perfect.

It terrifies me that another guy is going to see how incredible she is before Hendrix does, and she's going to be stolen from under his clueless nose.

With my brain fully awake from the caffeine, I continue scrolling, losing myself in snippets of other people's lives that they like to show the world.

But eventually, my need to know if Kian has responded to my email gets the better of me. Although, my curiosity isn't enough to get my ass out of bed and go in search of my new work cell. So instead, I load up my new email account on my mail app and wait for it to load.

When my inbox shows nothing new unread, I jump back to Instagram, and before I can stop myself, I'm typing his name into the search bar.

His account doesn't hold much of any excitement. In fact, it's downright fucking boring.

For someone who lives a life as exciting as his, you'd really think he'd show it off.

I shake my head, trying to force out the idea that I should bring it up tomorrow. He's something of a celebrity in Chicago. He really should have a better account than this.

Bored of his almost non-existent feed, I turn to tagged photographs of him.

"Aha." *See, you do have a life.*

However, I soon discover what that life involves.

Women.

A lot of freaking women.

Almost every single photo of him with a model-worthy woman on his arm. I shouldn't be surprised—the first few times I met him, he was doing the exact same thing.

Without thinking, I tap on the most recent image of him with a gorgeous redhead. Then my eyes drop to the date and time.

"Holy shit," I gasp. That was posted two minutes ago.

Right this second, he is on a date with this woman, and I'm sitting here like a loser waiting for him to email me back.

Christ. Could I be any more pathetic?

I immediately close Instagram before I start digging any deeper into his date. Hell, for all I know, she could be his girlfriend.

The less I know about my boss's extracurricular activities, the better.

I snuggle down into bed and just get myself into the perfect position when my watch buzzes.

"Fuck's sake," I mutter, flipping over to grab my cell and put it on do not disturb. But my good intentions are squashed when I find a message from someone I'd hoped had left my life.

I stare at it for a beat, debating deleting it without even opening it. I silently beg myself to do just that, but when my thumb moves, it isn't to rid my cheating ex from my life again but instead to see what he's decided to say after a blissful week without him.

> Matt: I'm sorry, I know I said I'd let you go but…I miss you, baby.

My hand trembles and emotion burns the backs of my eyes as I stare at his words.

I don't want to miss him.

He lied to me. He played me. He hurt me.

But...

"Fuck," I breathe.

Closing my eyes, I let my head sink back into the pillow as I fight against falling apart again because of a jerk who doesn't deserve it.

I just think I've got it together when my cell buzzes again.

Fuck.

He's seen that I've read it and he's going to try and lure me back in.

Hesitantly, I crack an eye open and look at the screen.

But to my surprise, there isn't another message alert.

There's an email.

From a man who is currently on a date...

From: Kian Callahan
To: Lorelei Tempest
Subject: *Housekeeping*

Dear Miss Tempest,

Thank you for your swift and clear reply.
I am glad to read that you're too fully focused on your job to be thinking about other pleasurable ways you could be spending your time.
Your dedication from the outset is commendable.

Regards,
Kian Callahan
Chief Financial Officer
Callahan Enterprises

17

KIAN

I didn't get much sleep last night between waiting for Lorelei to reply to my email and reviewing the documents Dad sent over a few days ago. He's waiting for my opinion. Fuck knows why—he doesn't usually listen to a word I have to say. King, though...

I shake my head, trying to lose the bitterness that thought drags up.

Lorelei didn't reply. I can't say that I was surprised. It was late. But there was a little bit of me that hoped she'd still be awake and willing to spar with me. Hell knows I needed it after the night I'd had.

Claudine was beautiful, smart, funny, and apparently, everything I wasn't interested in last night.

No matter how hard I tried, I just couldn't ignite any excitement for the woman sitting on the other side of the table.

I told myself that it was because I was waiting to discover the real reason for our date. I just knew that at some point she'd try for an invitation to one of our exclusive five-star resorts. But the request never came.

Although the expectation for me to take her home and continue our night was as clear as day on her face after I paid the bill and escorted her outside.

Don't get me wrong, I've turned down more than a few women in my time. I'm not that much of a whore that I'll take anything that's on offer. But I can say that last night was the first time I've turned down a woman who ticked every single one of my boxes.

Kieran would have kicked my ass into the middle of next year if he knew.

But I couldn't do it.

Sure, taking her home would have been fun, and pleasurable. But I'd have felt like an asshole afterward.

Fuck knows why I care all of a sudden. Being an asshole has never stopped me before.

I let out a sigh, letting my head fall back as the call I was on ends, plunging me into silence.

It goes without saying that I've been an asshole.

I was here early. Earlier than anyone else on this floor. I wanted to be here when she arrived. I wanted to see her face when she found me waiting at her messy desk.

What did I just say about not caring about being an asshole? Apparently, that only extends as far as Claudine, because all bets are off when it comes to my new assistant.

And just because I can, I sit forward and press the button on my phone that will connect me with her.

"Hello," she answers as if she has no idea who's going to be on the other end. I've done this exact thing more times than I can count today.

Every time I've wanted something, I've pressed that little button that will connect me to the person who can't say no.

I mean, she can, but seeing as she's only on day two of her employment, she hasn't dared yet. There's a really fucked-up part of me that's looking forward to the moment she does.

"Get us both a coffee, and then I need you in my office."

I hear the words the second they leave my lips, and a hit of desire shoots through my veins.

While my head might not have been in last night, my body

was more than ready, and don't I fucking know it this morning.

I woke up tenting the sheets like a fucking teenager, but thoughts of my date were far, far from my mind.

Instead, as I'd wrapped my hand around myself in the hope of finding some relief, it was a head full of dark curls that emerged in my mind.

It was wrong. So fucking wrong.

But also...

I stare down at my desk, trying to picture how she'd look bent over and—

"What did your last slave die of?" Lorelei snaps down the line.

"She didn't. She ran off crying and never returned. Feel free to follow suit if you don't think you can cut it."

She mutters something under her breath that makes me smirk. I might not be able to make the words out, but I get the gist.

"I'll see you in ten," I say, hanging up before she has a chance to respond.

Spinning my chair around, I stare out at the city beyond, watching the ant-sized people on the sidewalk below going about their days.

It's already four o'clock, and the sun is beginning its descent. It's been a beautiful sunny autumn day, and something tells me that the evening will be just as nice.

My cell buzzes on the desk behind me and I spin back around to see who it is.

> Makenzie: Will you come to our next cheer comp? It's in Seattle.

She follows up that message with all the details.

> Kian: Can I let you know closer to the time?

Makenzie: Sure, but Mom needs to buy tickets.

"Shit," I hiss, guilt flooding through my veins as a knock sounds out from my door exactly nine minutes and fifty seconds later.

"Your coffee, sir," she mocks as she moves across the room and lowers the mug to my desk.

She's already spent a few hours in here today going over her spreadsheet and discussing the next set of data that needed to be inputted. It's a job I'd usually have done myself so that I could get a better picture of the company as a whole, but it's not the most exciting job in the world, and I wanted to test her.

The spreadsheet she's built...I have almost an exact replica sitting in my documents that I made years ago. I wasn't going to tell her that, though.

Honestly, I expected her to struggle. Just because someone has a finance and business degree, it doesn't mean they have the skills they actually need to succeed. But I might admit that I've been impressed with her.

Sure, my intel told me that she did a good job at her previous place, that her dismissal was nothing more than a clash of personalities and a company that is on the decline. But still, it's nice to see for myself that my decision to make her mine was the right one.

"Thank you," I say after long, silent minutes.

"Did you need me for anything, or can I return to my desk?"

"I said that I needed you, didn't I?"

I might not be looking at her, but I can see enough of her reflection to know that she stands a little taller as she prepares to go into battle.

Fuck if my dick doesn't jerk at the thought.

Finally, I push my foot against the floor and spin around. The second her eyes land on me, they widen, her lips parting in surprise.

I get it. I don't look like I did earlier. I'm no longer dressed for meetings. It's Friday afternoon, and I'm dressed for the occasion with my tie hanging loosely around my half-unbuttoned shirt and my sleeves rolled up to my elbows.

"I hope you didn't have any plans tonight, Lorelei," I say with a smirk as I comb my fingers through my now messy hair.

"Um..."

"Good," I state before she comes up with an answer. "Kingston is still adamant that this hotel chain in the UK is for us. I want to put up an argument based on all of this," I say, pushing a whole stack of papers in her direction. "That he's wrong."

Lorelei swallows nervously as she looks between me and the paperwork.

"What's wrong? I thought you agreed with me," I say, cocking my head.

"I-I did. I mean, I do." She has more to say, the words are practically dancing on the tip of her tongue, but she refuses to let them free.

"Go on," I encourage. "You're not usually one to keep your opinions to yourself."

Her eyes narrow, and my smirk grows.

"Fine. Do you really think Kingston cares about the financial implications of this potential deal? Like you said before, he's not going into this with his head. It's fuelled by his heart. No amount of paperwork or business plan is going to deter him."

I nod, completely agreeing with her.

"You're right," I say, pushing to my feet and walking around my desk, closing the space between us. "But I wouldn't be doing my job if I didn't present this to him like I would any other acquisition we've gone into. And anyway, I didn't have any other plans for my evening. Did you?"

I can tell from the expression on her face that she did, and it leaves me wondering what it was.

She saw Tate and Cory last night. And I know for a fact

that Kingston is taking Tate out for a date tonight, so she's otherwise engaged.

I also know that she's single, unlike the night of the wedding. The jerk who didn't attend with her proved his true colors the other week when it became apparent that he was living a double life and had a fiancée.

So, if she does have plans tonight, then—

"Nothing I can't cancel," she says through gritted teeth. Irritation comes off her in waves, but I don't let it affect me.

"Fantastic," I say, stepping up behind her, letting the sweet scent of her perfume flood my senses. "Shall we get started?"

"The sooner we start, the sooner we can leave."

"Hmm, my thoughts exactly," I lie.

"This is a fucking disaster," Lorelei announces from where she's sitting on the floor at my coffee table, surrounded by the chain's previous accounts. We have the past five years to go through. I might only have scratched the surface of them, but I already know that it's not pretty reading.

"Did they really think they could turn this around?" she asks.

"I guess so. I don't think anyone sets out to go under."

She stills and looks up, glaring at me.

"What? You asked."

"It was rhetorical," she hisses before sitting back in her haunches and grabbing her cell.

A deep frown mars her forehead before she begins tapping the screen frantically.

"Everything okay?" I ask, still curious as fuck about what her canceled evening plans entailed.

"Great," she lies before letting out a heavy breath.

"Your date not impressed that you had to cancel?" I hedge.

"I didn't have a date. I'm not dating right now." Her cell lights up again, distracting her. "Not that it's any of your business," she adds absently as she starts typing again.

"Just trying to get to know you better."

"Okay, so for reference, only one of us has a different member of the opposite sex warming their bed every night of the week."

My brows lift at the bitterness that accompanies that statement.

"I don't sleep with a different woman every night," I say before thinking better of getting into this with her.

"Okay, cool. Whatever you say."

This time when she looks at her cell, she sees something she likes and a wide, genuine smile appears on her face.

My breath catches at the sight of it.

"For someone who isn't dating, you sure look happy about those messages you're getting."

She pauses typing and lowers her cell. "I'm sorry, you must not have heard me when I said it was none of your business." Holding my eyes firm, she climbs to her feet and straightens her skirt. "I don't need to be here right now. My working hours ended hours ago. Excuse me," she says before marching across the room and slipping out of the door.

Sitting back, I can't fight the grin that spreads across my face.

"Take your time," I mutter, knowing that she'll be back. Her shoes are on the floor next to my desk, after all.

18

LORELEI

"Insufferable asshole," I mutter as I march from his office with my cell in my hand.

The coolness of the tiles beneath my feet works its way up my body and I shiver.

I can't even leave...

Ignoring the jerk I just left behind, I pull up my contacts and hit call on Wilder's number.

It only rings once before his deep voice fills the line.

He was waiting for me. He always is before a game.

"Hey, are you ready?" I ask.

"It's a big night. They were our worst loss last season."

"That was last season. You're a better team than you were then."

"So are they," he says nervously.

"Then the win you're about to take will only be sweeter."

"Lor," he warns.

He secretly loves my positivity before his games. It's the reason he has this little pregame ritual.

"How are those cleats?" I ask.

"Oh my god, they are the best." So they should be, for what they cost. "Thank you so much."

"They're gonna get you this win. I just know it."

142

He blows out a long, nervous breath that makes butterflies erupt in my own stomach.

It doesn't matter how many games he plays, how many touchdowns he scores, or how many wins he gets under his belt, I am always a nervous wreck for him.

As much as I hate being so far away from them, on game nights, I can't help but think it's probably for the best. I have never been more stressed than sitting in those stands, watching Wilder get taken down from every which way while the timer counts down, ready to decide their fate.

"There are scouts, Lor," he says quietly. "They—"

"Wilder," I snap, trying to drag him from his panic. "You are the best football player I've ever seen." No need to mention that I never watched a single game until he started playing. "Forget about everything but the game. Focus on the ball, on your plays. Even if this one doesn't go the way you hope, your skills and talent will still shine through."

"I want this so bad," he confesses.

"I know you do. And you're going to get it."

"Fuck," he huffs.

"I believe in you, Wild Child. Rix does too. He's in the stands waiting for you to come out."

"I know. I know."

My free hand curls into a fist. I wish there was more I could do to reassure him.

"You'll be watching, yeah?"

Guilt twists up my stomach.

I want to. I watch every single game.

Glancing up, I gaze down the hallway that will lead me back toward Kian.

"I've got to work late, but I'll have it on my phone," I say, unable to lie to him. "I'll be right there with you, okay?"

"Yeah," he says quietly.

"You've got this, Wilder. You're going to kill it."

He falls silent, and my nerves quadruple for him.

There's noise down the line and he sighs. "I need to go."

"I love you. I can't wait to see you."

"I love you too, Lor. Come visit us soon, yeah? I want to see you in the stands again."

My heart constricts.

"I'll be there, I promise. Message me later, yeah?"

"Might be too busy partying," he says with a laugh.

Shaking my head, I can't fight the smile that spreads across my face.

"Bye, Lor. Love you," he says again before hanging up on me.

"Love you too," I add as I lower my cell from my ear.

I'm still smiling when I turn back toward Kian's office.

But it falls the second I find him standing there, watching me closely.

"Who was that?" he asks.

"What the hell has that got to do with you?" I hiss, all the happy feels vanishing.

His eyes narrow as he studies me. There's a silent warning there, which I choose to ignore.

"Excuse me, we've got work to do, and I for one don't plan on spending my entire Friday night with my boss."

I take off in his direction, refusing to cower to his demands or the look in his eyes.

"I thought you were single."

"And I thought you were my boss, not my father."

He's standing right in front of the door, refusing to allow me entry, but I'm not the kind of woman who'll be stopped by a man with more muscle in one arm than I possess in my entire body.

"Excuse me," I say again, attempting to squeeze between his massive body and the doorframe.

My arm burns red hot the second my bare skin brushes against the soft cotton of his shirt. But that reaction is nothing compared to when I press the length of my body against his side to squeeze past him.

Closing my eyes, I ignore the sparks that shoot around my body.

144

I've almost done it. I'm almost past him and back into the room when he suddenly turns and wraps his hand around my upper arm.

Twisting me around, he backs me up against the door, his hard eyes boring into mine.

"Who were you talking to?" he asks darkly.

A smile curls at my lips as I remember the final words I said to Wilder.

I shake my head, unable to believe what my brain is conjuring up right now.

"Are you...are you jealous, sir?" I ask, tilting my head to the side, silently mocking him.

His jaw tightens, a vein I haven't seen before popping up at his temple.

"I want to know who's important enough to stop you mid-task."

"It's Friday night, Kian. I shouldn't even be here right now."

"You agreed to stay and work."

"Yeah," I say, a bitter laugh following the word. "But I'm wondering why I bothered. It's a bullshit task we're doing right now."

"No," he growls, making my skin erupt with goosebumps.

"It is. You just want to prove Kingston wrong. But it's pointless. He's going to do whatever the hell he wants. He doesn't care what you say about the figures."

His eyes darken, letting me know that I've just hit on something.

"He will make the right business decision," he argues, although it's weak. He knows I'm right. He's just desperately trying to cling to some authority when it comes to his brother.

"Whatever you say. Can you let go of me now?"

His grip loosens a little, but he doesn't release me. Instead, his other hand comes up to rest on the door beside my head, effectively caging me in.

I lift my chin, refusing to show any kind of weakness.

"I'm going to ask you one more time." I roll my eyes and his expression hardens. I'm pretty sure he's seconds from losing his shit. And I am here for it.

I smirk, already hearing his question in my ears.

"Who were you talking to?"

"You're an insufferable asshole, you know that?" I say, ripping myself from his grip and quickly ducking under his arm, marching deeper into the room to resume the task at hand.

"Lorelei," he rasps.

Fuck. The sound of it does all kinds of things it shouldn't between my legs.

"What, Kian?" I snap, my patience giving out.

I look up and my eyes instantly lock onto his dark, angry ones as he stands before me with his arms crossed over his chest.

Oh, he's pissed. He's really fucking pissed.

And damn, if it doesn't look hot on him.

Heat surges through my veins as I sit on my knees staring up at him.

An image I really don't need of me crawling toward him suddenly pops into my head, and I fight to banish it.

Not fucking appropriate, Lorelei.

With an irritated huff, I decide to just give in. If I want to watch even a second of Wilder's game, then I'm going to have to come clean anyway.

"My little brother," I state. "Happy now?"

He blinks. Once. Twice. Three times.

O-oh, he was not expecting that.

How cute.

"Careful, Kian. You look awfully close to losing control right now."

I smile up at him innocently.

"Just get back to work, Lorelei," he hisses before turning on his heels and marching from the room.

"Well then," I mutter to myself once the door has closed behind him.

Waking my cell up, I find the app that will allow me to watch a live stream of Wilder's game that's due to start any minute, and I prop it up so I can see as I return to the endless sheets of paper, showcasing what has to be the most depressing set of company accounts that I've ever seen.

Kian is gone longer than I was expecting, and I can't help but feel smug about riling him up so much that he had to go and have a serious word with himself.

Good. Fucker deserves to give himself a dressing down for his overbearing behavior.

The game starts and I quickly forget about the paperwork, instead focusing on the tiny players running around my screen.

It's almost impossible to identify any of Wilder's teammates, but I can spot my little brother from a mile away, and from the second the whistle blew, he's been on it.

"Yes," I hiss when he makes a pass that earns them the first touchdown of the game. "You can do this. Make those scouts proud, baby."

I startle when a throat clearing on the other side of the room rips through the air.

"Shit," I mutter before glancing nervously at my cell.

Kian takes a step forward, and the unmistakable scent of takeout fills the room. My stomach almost immediately rumbles.

"What are you doing?" I ask as he clears off the coffee table before me and places the bag on it.

"I ordered us dinner," he says simply, as if the event that sent him running from his office never happened. "What are you watching?"

I climb to my feet, taking my cell with me.

"Umm...hey?" I complain when he snatches my cell to look for himself.

"At least it's not porn," he deadpans, making my cheeks blaze, before tapping on my screen.

"What the hell are you—" My words trail off as the huge flat screen on the opposite wall lights up and Wilder's game appears before me.

The players are no longer unrecognizable little ants on the screen. Now they all have limbs, and I can even make out the names and numbers on their jerseys.

"Which one is your brother?" Kian asks.

"Seriously?" I balk, blindly dropping onto the couch beside him as my eyes track Wilder across the screen.

"Protective much?" Kian mutters as he begins unloading the bagful of food.

"Don't start. You have no idea what our—"

"I'm sorry."

I rear back. "Y-you're—"

"Sorry," he repeats.

"Right. Okay," I mutter, unsure what to do with that apology.

"Eat," he demands, sounding much more like himself.

Unable to deny the lure of good Chinese, I select a container and grab..."Chopsticks, really?"

Kian shrugs one shoulder.

"If you're going to do something, Lorelei, then you should do it properly," he states.

"I agree, and to eat properly, I need a knife and fork."

"Sorry, we're going authentic tonight," he explains as if this isn't the only time we're going to be eating dinner together.

I don't remember that being in the job description.

"Brilliant," I mutter, attempting to wrangle the two sticks into submission as a cheer goes up around the room.

I look up and immediately jump to my feet, screaming at the TV as Wilder makes a touchdown.

"What?" I ask once I've calmed down and find Kian staring up at me with an unreadable expression on his face.

"Don't worry, I caught the chow mein before it hit the floor," he says, lifting the container to show me.

"Oh shit, that was on my lap."

He grins. "Maybe I'll just eat it all myself."

"Oh hell no. I'm starving. I'll figure these bad boys out even if it kills me," I say, retaking my seat and attempting to copy his hold on the sticks.

He smirks at me before expertly collecting up rice and pushing it past his lips without dropping a single grain.

"How?" I ask in disbelief. I can't even pick up a vegetable.

"We spent a few weeks in China when were kids and—"

"Of course you did," I mutter, unable to contain my eye roll.

"Here, let me show you," he offers, scooting closer and wrapping his arm around me.

19

KIAN

Lorelei's sweet scent floods my senses as her hair tickles the side of my face.

Fuck. This was a bad idea.

But as my hand slides against hers, I realize that it's too late.

If I back away now, she's going to know.

Fuck my life.

"Hold them a little more like...this," I say, my breath racing over her exposed throat.

She sits frozen. I'm not even sure she's breathing as I adjust her chopsticks so she'll stand a chance of picking up some food.

"Now, if you..." I take control of her movement and lower her hand to the container sitting in her lap. "That's it. Got it?"

She nods. The movement is so slight that I wouldn't see it if I weren't so close.

"Now, lift it and—" I swallow thickly as we push the food into her mouth and her full lips close around the chopsticks.

"That wasn't so hard," she says before glancing back at me over her shoulder.

"N-no, not hard at all," I mutter before shifting to my side of the couch and turning my attention back to the sweet and sour pork I should be eating.

No more words are said as the game continues playing on the TV, the air so thick around us it's hard to draw in a breath let alone eat.

Thanks to her little celebration earlier, I've figured out that her little brother must be number thirteen, Kemp.

He's good. Really good.

"Does your brother want to go pro?" I ask when I'm confident I can speak without my voice sounding all desperate and pathetic.

"Yeah," Lorelei muses, keeping her eyes on the screen, watching as her brother calls a play. "That's his plan, anyway. He's got scouts watching this game. He's nervous as fuck."

"He isn't showing it."

"Knew he wouldn't. He was born to do this."

I nod, watching the play he called turn into a seamless touchdown.

A wave of nostalgia hits me from watching every single high school game Kieran played back in the day.

"He's important to you," I state. It's not a question—it doesn't need to be. Love and pride ooze from her.

"He's my little brother. Of course." She glances at me briefly, and for the first time, I realize that her guard is down.

If it's possible, she's even more breathtaking.

"Annoying little shits, aren't they?" I joke.

She laughs, and it's light and genuine in a way that makes my chest contract.

"Yeah," she agrees before we both fall silent again as we watch his team obliterate the opposition.

"He should be really proud of that performance," I say, breaking our stalemate once the final whistle blows and his team piles themselves on top of him in celebration.

"He's meant to call me, but—"

"He'll forget in favor of celebrating?" I guess.

"Yeah. He's a little wild. Works hard and parties harder."

I smirk. I know it well. "Nothing wrong with that."

"I don't want to be an auntie yet," she says under her breath.

"I think you'll be okay. He looks like he has his head screwed on. He just commanded that entire game and barely broke a sweat. He's not gonna risk screwing up his future."

Abandoning her food container on the coffee table, she turns to look at me.

Her lips part, but for a few seconds, no words spill free. She studies me in a way she hasn't before, and I can't help but wonder if she's seeing something different, just like I am with her.

"I hope you're right," she says before she begins tidying up. "We should probably carry on or we'll still be here doing this in the morning."

I watch her as she places all the containers into the bag. "I'm going to the bathroom. I'll get rid of all this on the way."

Wordlessly, I watch her go.

The second the door closes behind her, I push to my feet and stalk to the windows.

It's dark out now, and all the buildings are lit up around us.

There are people in their apartments going about their evenings. I stand there and watch as some prepare dinner in their kitchens and others get ready for nights out.

It's something I've spent too much time doing since moving into this office.

I find it fascinating, watching others live their lives, completely unaware that they've got a spectator.

I scan the windows, searching for people, and I quickly come to a stop when I find a couple dancing in the middle of their living room.

I might be too far away to see any detail, but it's more than obvious that they're laughing.

I'm so lost in their moment that I don't hear Lorelei step back into the room, and it's not until she speaks, startling me, that I realize she's standing beside me.

"And here you were worried about me watching porn at work."

"W-what are you—"

She jerks her chin to the left and I scan the windows again.

"Oh shit." I laugh when I find something I hadn't before.

A couple going at it against the window.

"No wonder you have those fancy darkening windows on this office. What exactly do you do in here?"

"Unfortunately, not that," I mutter before ripping my eyes away from the show.

"I find that hard to believe."

"What is that meant to mean?" I snap as she returns to the paperwork neatly piled up on the coffee table.

"You have a reputation, Kian. I'm sure that's not news to you."

"Maybe so, but that doesn't mean I'm fucking in my office on the regular."

"I didn't say anything about regularity," she says with a smirk.

"Put all that down, I'm taking you home," I say, making a rash decision.

She freezes instantly and looks up at me. "But I thought you wanted this done."

"I do. But it's Friday, it's late, and...you should call your brother and congratulate him before he gets too drunk."

"Wow, that's very...thoughtful of you."

I laugh. "I have my moments. Now, get your stuff together before I change my mind."

Without wasting a second, Lorelei begins tidying up and then rushes from the room. After shutting down my computer and grabbing my jacket, I follow to ensure she doesn't bolt from the building the second she's out of my sight.

"I'll give you a lift h-home," I stutter when I find her with her ass up in the air, pulling her purse out from beneath the desk.

"That's not necessary, but I appreciate the offer. The bus is due in five min—"

"No," I bark, a little more aggressively than I was expecting. "I'll take you home."

Placing her purse and new laptop bag over her shoulder, she turns to stare at me.

She wants to argue—I can practically hear the words falling from her lips. But she can't.

She knows as well as I do that she doesn't want to get the bus.

Not when I've got a perfectly good car sitting in the underground parking lot.

"Thank you," she finally whispers through gritted teeth.

Silently, we step into the elevator, and no sooner have we started moving than Lorelei lifts her cell to read a message.

"Your brother?" I ask.

"Yeah," she says as another of those genuine smiles appears on her lips.

"Are they local?" I ask, needing to find out more about her. I didn't recognize the high schools, but that doesn't mean they're not close.

When I told her that I'd done my research, I wasn't lying. But I kept it focused on her life here, and admittedly, I got most of the intel from her best friend one night when I had dinner with her and King.

"No," she replies curtly.

"Do you have any other siblings?"

"What is this?" she snaps. "Twenty questions?"

"Just trying to get to know you better," I confess.

"You know everything you need to know."

Her cell buzzes again, but this time when she lifts it up, a smile doesn't form. Instead, she frowns.

"Everything okay?" I ask before thinking.

She turns to look at me as the elevator descends the last few floors.

"Fucking brilliant," she hisses before stepping from the enclosed space the second the doors open.

"O-okay," I mutter. "My car is this way." I point out as she takes off randomly through the empty parking lot.

With a huff of irritation, she spins on her heels and begins following me.

"Why am I not surprised?" she says as all the lights on my Maserati illuminate when I unlock it.

"Not a fan?" I ask with a smirk.

"Of over-the-top shows of wealth and pretense? No, not really."

I want to point out that she probably still has time to catch her bus, but I keep my lips sealed.

Stopping at the passenger side of the car, I pull the door open and wait.

"It's okay, I won't tell anyone you got in and actually enjoyed your ride."

She raises a brow. "I can guarantee you that I won't."

"We'll see," I say, closing her in the second her ass hits the seat.

Damn, she looks good sitting there.

"That doesn't impress me," she sneers when I bring the engine to life. Admittedly, I do rev it a little more than I usually would, but only because I know it's going to cause a reaction. Something I'm becoming more and more addicted to achieving with Lorelei.

"No?" I ask, glancing over at her with a shit-eating grin on my face. "What about this?"

I slam my foot on the gas and the car races forward, throwing us both back into our seats. Lorelei squeals, her grip on the leather so tight her knuckles turn white.

"If I thought I was going to be risking my life getting in here with you, then I definitely would have got the bus."

"Nah, the bus is boring. Life is about living."

"Oh my god," she whimpers as I race through the empty parking lot like it's my own personal race track. "Where the hell did you learn to drive like this?" she demands.

My lips part, but she beats me to it.

"Wait, don't tell me. You had race car training as a kid. Same year you vacationed in China, I bet."

I chuckle. "Yes, actually. Although it wasn't the same year as China. A couple later."

"Of course. Can you please—fuck," she gasps as I bring the car to an abrupt stop before pulling out onto the street.

"Everything okay over there?" I tease.

"Great. Just great. If you could slow down a little, that would be—shiiit, Kian," she screams when I take off again.

"Getting your heart rate up is good for the soul," I tell her as I ease the car around the corner.

"I can think of better ways of making that happen," she cries.

Sadly, we hit congestion and I'm forced to slow down.

"Thank fuck for that," she mutters, finally releasing her grip on the seat.

"Didn't have you down as the kind of woman who shies away from a little adrenaline."

"There's adrenaline and then there's fearing for your life. Two very different things."

"If you say so."

"Do you remember where I live?"

"Please, give me some credit, Lorelei."

"Fine," she hisses before her cell goes off again.

She groans at whatever she finds waiting for her.

"You sure everything is okay?"

"Brilliant."

"He's not drunk already, is he?" I tease.

"No, it's not my brother, it's—" She slams her lips closed.

"It's..." I prompt.

"None of your business. Here is great," she says the second we pull onto her street.

"Absolutely not. I'm not leaving you on a street corner on a Friday night."

"You're also not walking me to my door. You can forget it."

"We'll see," I tease.

"Yeah, we will."

20

LORELEI

"**W**hat are you doing?" I snap when Kian kills the engine and reaches to open his door as if he's going to walk me inside. Exactly what I just told him not to do.

"Lorelei," he warns, sending tingles shooting around my body.

"I don't need you to pretend you care, Kian. I have let myself into my building alone at night more times than I can count. I didn't need a babysitter then, and I still don't need one now."

"What if I told you that I'd sleep better tonight if I knew you were safely tucked inside your apartment."

"Then I'd tell you that I don't care how you sleep and stand my ground."

"You're a real pain in the ass, you know that, Miss Tempest?"

"Takes one to know one," I shoot back as my cell buzzes with yet another message from Matt.

Any thoughts about the message he sent last night being a one-off because he was feeling bad about what happened between us vanish. It was a stupid hope. I already know he doesn't care about my feelings or anyone else's.

All I want to do is get inside, talk to Wilder, have a shower, and crawl into bed. Is that too much to ask?

"Touché. So shall we?" he asks, pushing his door open.

"Watch me into the building. I'll message you once I'm safe inside my apartment. How's that?"

He shakes his head. I get it. The feeling of irritation is most definitely mutual.

"I'll see you on Monday," I say before we end up arguing about this any longer and push the door open, pressing my foot to the sidewalk.

"Thank you for tonight."

"Sure," I mutter before slamming the door closed and taking off toward the entrance to my building.

Despite my need to turn around and make sure he leaves once I'm inside, I don't. I keep my sights set on the elevator and keep moving.

He's my boss, not my father. I don't need anyone to take care of me.

No one else has, so why should someone start now?

I take care of me, that's how it's been for as long as I can remember, and it's the way it'll stay.

Sure, I might always have one eye out for Mr. Right, but that doesn't mean I want to end up as a little wife who relies on her husband. I will never be the kind of girlfriend or wife who asks her man's permission for anything. I want someone who will give me space to breathe and make my own decisions and mistakes, while always being there waiting for me to return with his arms and heart open.

Am I asking too much of the male half of the population? Yes, I very much could be. But I refuse to compromise for the sake of being in a relationship.

The elevator delivers me to my floor, and in only seconds I have my front door open, ready to lock myself inside and put the day behind me.

My cell buzzes again, and I groan.

"I swear to God if you're messaging me already—" My

words are cut off when it continues vibrating, and I jump into action.

"Oh my god, Wilder," I cry the second the line connects. "You were incredible."

Kicking the door closed behind me, I dump my things in the entryway and walk toward the kitchen as he talks me through the entire game as if I weren't watching it. Every word he says makes my heart sing. I love hearing his excitement, his pride.

I barely get a word in as he explains about meeting the scouts at the end of the game and discussing what his future plans might be.

College football has always been a pipe dream—one that I've encouraged as much as I can, but Wilder isn't stupid. He knows that the chances of actually making it from where we come from are slim. He knows how much college costs, and he knows that even with a scholarship, it's going to be hard—especially with Hendrix wanting to go as well.

I don't think they understand, though. I'd sell my soul to the devil if I had to, to get them there.

"Shit, Lor, I need to go. We're having a party on the beach and then heading to Jackson's house. His parents are away and...you probably don't need to know that."

"No." I laugh. "Just please—"

"Be good. I know, Lor. I know."

"Good. I love you, Wild Child. Send your brother my love if you happen to see him."

"At a football party? Not really his scene."

I can't help but laugh. "I'm sure he'll want to congratulate you," I say, knowing full well that Rix usually shows his face just to support Wilder. Despite their differences, they are tight as hell. It makes me jealous as fuck. I was so alone when I was their age. I would have given anything to have a bond with someone even close to what they have.

"Love you, sis. Speak soon, yeah?"

"Have a good night."

Placing my cell on the kitchen counter, I grab a bottle of water from the refrigerator and take off toward my bathroom to wash the day away.

My jacket has already been abandoned in the kitchen, and I unbutton my blouse as I walk, letting it fall to the floor to pick up later.

I step over the threshold with my hands on the zipper of my skirt when someone knocks on the front door.

I pause and tip my head back, asking anyone who will listen to give me strength.

Watch me into the building. I'll message you once I'm safe inside my apartment. How's that?

"Fuuuuck," I groan as I spin around and try to summon the strength to face him again.

"This is so un-fucking-necessary," I mutter as I unlock the door and pull it open.

But the man I find staring back at me isn't my infuriating boss.

It's worse.

"What do you want?" I snap, my fingers gripping the door so tight with my need to close it on him that they start to cramp.

"I miss you, baby," Matt says, his voice raspy with emotion, his eyes full of regret and pain.

But it's not enough.

"I'm not interested. Goodby—"

He presses his palm against the door as I attempt to slam it in his face.

"I'm sorry, Lori. I fucked up. I should have told you. But it's over. I swear to God, it's over with her. It was, I just...we had obligations we couldn't—"

"I'm not listening to this. You're a liar. I don't believe a word that comes out of your mouth."

"I swear to you, it's over. You're the one I want."

We might have only been together for a short amount of

time in the grand scheme of things, but he feels so familiar, standing there.

Memories of our time together are still so vivid, the feelings he evoked within me still just within touching distance, although clouded with pain and anger.

I remember how easily he made me laugh. How electric his touch was. How he made me feel beautiful and sexy. He made me feel like I was the only woman in the world. What a fucking joke that was.

"I don't care. We're done."

I try to close the door again, but he steps closer, putting his foot in the jam.

"Matt," I warn, my heart pounding at a mile a minute as my head spins.

I don't want him back. I refuse to spend my life with a man who is capable of lying to me like that. It wasn't a little white lie to make himself look better, to impress me early in our relationship. This was huge.

"Please, Lori. Just let me explain properly."

My breath catches as he reaches out like he's going to touch me, but before he makes contact, another voice booms down the hallway.

"Get your fucking hands off her."

All the air in my lungs comes out in a rush as Matt immediately takes a step back and turns to the man who is glaring pure death at him.

"Who the fuck are you?" Matt demands.

"The man who's not going to let you get away with that bullshit you're spewing. Lorelei asked you to leave, and yet you're still fucking standing there. Why?" Kian spits.

Not once has he looked up at me, his attention purely focused on Matt.

Oh my god.

What the fuck is he doing? He should have driven away in his fancy-ass car by now and be safely locked inside his pretentious penthouse. He should not be here.

Matt shakes his head. "This has got nothing to do with you."

"Oh, but you're wrong," Kian counters.

I cringe, dreading what's about to come out of his mouth next. But despite needing to put an end to this car crash, I can't force any words past my lips.

"I refuse to let anyone talk to my girl like you are now."

The fuck?

If I weren't so shocked myself then I might be able to appreciate the look of pure disbelief on Matt's face.

Kian makes the most of Matt's inability to do anything and slips past him into my apartment.

"Your presence is not welcome here. Goodnight," Kian states before swinging the door closed.

I stand there frozen in place as the events of the previous few minutes repeat over and over in my head.

The only thing I can hear is the blood rushing past my ears as I stand there with my chest heaving and my head spinning.

"Lorelei?" Kian says after long seconds of silence. His intrigued stare burns into the top of my head, but I can't drag my eyes from the floor to look at him.

I've no idea if I'm relieved that he's here or pissed off beyond belief. Everything is just too...confusing.

He moves closer, his perfect shiny shoes appearing in my line of sight before he whispers, "Are you okay?" The second his warm breath rushes over my bare chest, my nipples pebble and I become very aware of the fact that I'm standing here in only a silk cami with an unpadded bra beneath.

Forcing down my shock, I stand tall and lift my eyes to his.

"That was completely unnecessary. You need to leave."

He smirks, his gaze dropping to my chest for a beat before returning to my eyes.

"Really?" he rasps.

"Yes. Really. Or do we need to go back to our previous conversation about me not needing a babysitter?"

"Who was that jerk?" he asks, changing tactics.

"No one you need to know about. I'm tired, Kian. I want to go to bed."

"I'm not leaving unless he's gone."

I sigh, very quickly losing patience. "I only opened the door because I thought it was you."

His annoyingly pretty smile emerges upon hearing my confession.

"To shout at you for ignoring me," I add. "Trust me, I won't be making the same mistake twice in one night."

"You're lying. If that were me on the other side of the door, you'd have invited me in...for coffee."

My chin drops.

"No, I wouldn't. But if you didn't turn up and ruin...that," I say, throwing my arm out toward the door, "then I might be getting my brains screwed out right now. It would certainly improve my day." The grin I give him is pure malice.

"You're lying. You didn't want him anywhere near you," he counters, stepping forward again, his body now dangerously close to mine.

"Don't pretend you know anything about me or what I want," I snap.

"I'm not pretending. I can read you, Lorelei. I know exactly what you want right now."

Just like Matt, Kian reaches out—only no one stops him.

My entire body burns up the second his knuckles brush my cheek before tucking a lock of curly hair behind my ear.

"No," I snap, my own arm shooting out to bat his away. "You do not get to do this."

"Do what?" he asks innocently.

Shaking my head, I pull my front door open once more.

"Leave, please. We're done here."

"Lorelei, come on. What if he returns?"

"Then I will deal with it how I see fit. This is my life, Kian. You are my boss. That is it."

I glare at him until he gets the message and finally steps back outside.

"See you Monday," I mutter before swinging the door closed and twisting the deadlock into place.

With my head held high, I return to my previous plans. I'm fully undressed by the time I get into the bathroom, and after popping my shower cap on my head to save my curls, I step into the shower, finally washing off the day and everything I want to forget from my body.

21

LORELEI

I lie on a sun lounger, sipping on fresh orange juice as my best friend flushes from head to toe at whatever her husband is saying to her on the other end of the phone.

My nose wrinkles as I study her. She's wearing a red bikini that makes her pregnant body look incredible. It's really no wonder her husband is clearly whispering all kinds of freaky things in her ear right now.

"Is that a promise?" she purrs back.

The jealousy rushing around my veins only increases.

After giggling like a schoolgirl, she finally hangs up.

"What?" she asks when I groan loudly.

"I need to get laid," I complain, making her laugh. I might have meant what I said the other night about not wanting a hook-up but I still have needs.

"It hasn't been that long. I'm sure you've had longer dry spells," she points out, quirking a brow.

"Oh, that's rich, T. I remember all too well you complaining if more than a week had passed since you saw some action."

Her smile turns wicked. "Don't have that problem anymore.'

"So I just heard."

Her eyes widen. "You heard that?"

"Well, no. But I got the gist. And I already know your husband is as freaky as you are. Oh, wipe that satisfied smile from your face, Tatum Callahan," I tease.

"So, go and get laid. It's not like you don't have options," she says, taking me right back to our conversation Thursday night.

"I know, I just..."

"Do not tell me that you're still yearning for Matt."

"Oh hell no. I am not going there again. We're done. Over. Finished."

Sensing that I've got more to say on the subject, Tatum turns in my direction and studies me closely.

"What happened?" she asks, a deep frown appearing, twisting up her beautiful face.

"What? How...How do you know something happened?"

"I can read you, Lor. I noticed something was off with you from the second you climbed into the car earlier. I was just hoping that you'd spit it out before I had to drag it out of you."

I blow out a long breath.

"He turned up at the apartment last night."

"What?" Tate gasps. "What did he say?"

"Tried apologizing again. Told me that he missed me."

"Ugh, what a fucking asshole. I hope you slammed the door in his assholey face."

I bite down on my tongue to stop any more of last night's events from erupting.

Once I'm confident I'm not going to say more than I'd like, I force out a simple, "Yep. Deadlocked it too. Hopefully, that'll be the end of it."

"You really believe that?" Tate asks with a raised brow.

"No, not really," I mutter under my breath.

"Stick to your guns, Lor. Do not let that lying prick back into your life. You are worth so much more than him."

"I know." And I do know. No matter how hard he tries, I'm not going backward.

Look to the future, always.

Leave mistakes in the past, where they belong.

The hardness of her glare increases.

"I mean it. We're finished. He is nothing to me."

Pain slices through my chest as I say the words. I mean them, I do, but it still hurts. For a while there, I really thought he was the one I'd been looking for.

"You'll find him, Lor," Tate says, reaching out to squeeze my hand in support.

"I know," I whisper, although I feel more doubtful than I think I ever have.

Maybe he isn't out there.

"I do agree with one thing, though. You need to get laid, and you just need the right opportunity to fall in your lap."

Ignoring the suspicious look in her eyes I mutter, "We'll see. What time are our next treatments?"

"Massages in thirty minutes."

"Perfect," I sigh, stretching myself out on my lounger.

One benefit of my best friend being married to Kingston Callahan? Easy access to one of the best spas in the city.

"I needed that," Tate sighs happily as we emerge from the spa a few hours later, and I can't help but agree.

I have fresh nails, a newly waxed...well, everything, my muscles are loose, my face is glowing, and my troubles are far away. Okay, that last one might be wishful thinking.

"Cocktails, then we can go," she instructs before hooking her arm through mine and dragging me toward the bar. "One porn star martini," she says, ordering my favorite without bothering to ask. "And a virgin mojito, please."

We find ourselves at a seat by the window and continue our previous conversation, although it's cut short a few minutes later.

"Lorelei?" a deep voice asks a beat before a shadow falls over me.

Looking over my shoulder, I have to do a double take.

"Holy shit, Ryder," I say, hopping to my feet so I can hug him.

But the second his familiar scent hits my nose, so does reality.

The moment he releases me, I turn toward my best friend and narrow my eyes.

She smiles innocently at me. But I know. I know exactly what she's done.

"Tate, it's good to see you," Ryder says.

"You too. Long time, no see."

"What are you doing here?" I ask as he drags a chair over.

"I've just come from meeting a client," he explains, although it doesn't actually answer my question.

"Excuse me, I'm just going to the bathroom. Babies and bladders don't mix," Tate says, just in case Ryder didn't notice her belly.

"Oh, shit. I heard you were expecting. Congratulations."

"Thank you," she says before walking away.

"So, how have you been? I was actually thinking about messaging you the other week."

So, he's single again then.

"Yeah, I'm good. Just started a new job so things are a little crazy."

"It's congratulations all around then. So where are you working now?"

Tate and I met Ryder at college. We all hit it off easily. He was easygoing, fun-loving, everything we were.

The two of us have had some very, very good times together. And sitting here looking at him now, I know why. He's hot. A total player who's never going to settle down—a little like someone else who shall not be named—but he's... easy. He doesn't take life too seriously, and despite the fact he's hot as hell, he doesn't flaunt it. He just...loves life. And quite honestly, Tatum might just be onto something, because this is a little bit of what I need right about now.

"I'm working at Callahan Enterprises," I say honestly, knowing that Ryder isn't going to judge like many will.

Instead, he just grins. "That's awesome. That's what you always wanted, right?"

"Yeah," I muse, impressed that he remembers. Hell knows most men wouldn't.

"Shit," he curses as he glances at his watch. "I've gotta head out. But I'll message you, yeah? We should hang out. It's been too long."

A genuine smile pulls at the corners of my lips.

"Yeah," I muse. "We should."

Familiar tingles spread through my body as I think about the kind of hanging out that Ryder and I usually do. The kinky kind that never fails to scratch an itch.

"Sweet. Speak soon, yeah?"

After pressing a quick, chaste kiss to my cheek, he's gone almost as fast as he arrived, leaving me with nothing but the image of his hard ass in his tight suit pants as a parting gift.

"Where's Ryder gone?" Tatum asks when she finally returns from the bathroom.

"Oh, you've finished hiding?" I tease.

"What? I needed to pee."

"Did you?" I snark, raising a brow in question.

"I did. So...how was he? Been a while, huh?"

"You are so fucking transparent."

She stares at me, her lips twitching with amusement.

She can't lie for shit. Especially not to me. I know her too well.

"Fine. Fine. He popped up on my Facebook feed and...well...I thought he might be of some use to you."

"You think he's going to fuck all my problems away, like they don't exist."

"Fucking hell, if he's that magical, I might have a go myself," she teases.

"Oh yeah, like you'd ever stray from King's magic dick," I deadpan.

She gets this far-off dreamy look in her eye.

"Please, stop thinking about his dick. We're in public."

She laughs before her expression turns serious.

"I swear, Lor, since I've been pregnant, it's actually got better."

"Fucking hell."

"I mean it. Sex before was amazing. But now, the extra hormones or something...Fuck. It's beyond incredible. I really do recommend it."

"Umm...hard pass for me, but thanks for the advice."

I might be interested in finding my Mr. Right, but kids... that's a whole other issue for me. A therapist might say it has something to do with my own childhood, and do you know what? They'd probably be right.

"Oh, you say that now. One day, everything will change."

"We'll see," I mutter, lifting my drink to my lips as Tatum checks her cell.

"Mr. Perfect Dick want to know where his baby mamma is?"

"Yep," she agrees happily. "I should probably take you home so I can go enjoy him. It's been a few hours."

"Whore," I cough.

"Loud and proud, baby. Loud and proud."

It's Saturday night and I'm...staring at a spreadsheet.

Is this really what my life has become?

I should put work and Kian freaking Callahan behind me for the weekend. It's bad enough that he took my Friday night.

But I can't. And anyway, it's not like I've got anything better to do.

My head is spinning with numbers and formulae when my watch buzzes.

I glance down and immediately burst out laughing.

> Ryde my dick: It was good to see you today.

Reaching for my cell, I open our conversation, noting just how long has passed since his stupid contact name has popped up on my screen.

I remember the morning he did it. I was hungover as hell, and every inch of my body hurt. Most of it courtesy of him and the lack of sleep we'd had the night before.

I'd never had sex like it. It was wild, and I couldn't help but gaze at him in wonder that next morning. The things the man could do with my body.

Shit. It had happened to me, and yet I still struggled to understand it.

Before he left that next morning, he found my cell on the floor in the middle of my small dorm room and put his number into it.

I had no idea what he'd called himself until later that day when he messaged me to let me know how much fun he'd had.

Ryde my dick.

What a fucking idiot.

But just like a few moments ago, that name has made me laugh every time it's popped up on my screen over the years. And despite how it might sound, they haven't always been booty call messages. We have hung out with clothes on as well. Once or twice...

I stare at the screen, trying to come up with a reply that sets the right tone.

Despite Tate's meddling, do I really want to fall back into old habits with Ryder?

Of course, my body screams yes. Yes, we fucking do.

But my head...that's a little more reluctant.

> Lori: It was good to see you too.

I hit send before I ask a question that could be misconstrued.

Ryde my dick: Any good plans for the evening?

Well, there goes my good intentions.

Lori: Quiet night in. Been a long week.

Ryde my dick: That's boring. I'm heading out with the boys later. You should join.

I can't lie, there is a part of me that wants to. I want to put on one of my dresses, do my hair and makeup, and dance the night away.

But also...

Lori: Maybe another time. I hope you have a good night. Don't do anything I wouldn't do...

Ryde my dick: That sounds like a challenge.

Lori: Maybe it is. You can tell me all about it tomorrow.

Ryde my dick: Maybe I'll be too busy wishing I was spending the night with you. You know, for old times' sake.

Lori: Who says I'm single?

Ryde my dick: Tatum.

"Of fucking course she did."

Lori: She's meddling. Ignore her.

Ryde my dick: I quite like her meddling, if I'm being honest.

Lori: Of course you do. You always were looking for trouble.

Ryde my dick: Takes one to know one.

Ryde my dick: So, what are you really doing tonight that's more important than meeting me?

Lori: Netflix and spreadsheets.

Ryde my dick: Wow, I'm really getting blown off for the good stuff here...

And just like that, I find myself sucked back in by arguably the best ride of my life.

I mean, what's the harm? My only other option right now is my ex, and there is no fucking way I'm going back there.

22

LORELEI

It's late by the time I roll out of bed the next morning.

My intentions of having a quiet evening followed by an early night were shattered the second Ryder popped up.

He might have gone out, evidenced by some of the selfies he sent me during the evening, but he didn't forget about me.

I'm not sure if he was keeping me on the back burner in case he didn't have other options or what, but he'd thoroughly reeled me in, and I couldn't switch off despite knowing better.

As it turned out, he didn't hook-up, and he went home alone. Well...not entirely alone. I was happily burning up his messages by that point.

I stretch as I walk into my bathroom, feeling pretty sated despite spending the night in bed by myself.

Tate was right; Ryder is what I need in my life for a little stress relief right now.

Feeling inspired and full of life, instead of starting the coffee machine and curling myself up on the couch to laze Sunday away, I pull on a sports bra, a pair of leggings, and throw my hair up into a messy bun.

I haven't been running properly since Matt and I started getting serious. Any spare time I had, I was spending with him. And my exercise was courtesy of him as well.

The pain of the breakup threatens, but I stretch my neck out and force it down.

Being sad over that lying piece of shit is a waste of time.

Instead, I need to be focusing on myself. That is a much healthier way of dealing with everything.

With my cell strapped to my upper arm and my earbuds firmly in place, I close the front door behind me and take off.

It's a beautiful fall day outside, and I feel better about my life every time my foot hits the sidewalk.

Considering how little I've exercised in the past few months, I find my stride easily, and I soon discover that I've run farther than I anticipated.

When I find a coffee shop with a free seat outside, I order myself an iced latte and a panini and continue with my self-care day.

It's perfect.

Tate was right. I just needed a bloody good orgasm to fix me right up. Sure, she was expecting it to be delivered by a man and not my favorite toy, but whatever.

The endorphins are running rampant through my system nonetheless.

It's mid-afternoon when I finally walk back into my building.

My skin is covered in a sheen of sweat, my hair is... probably better off not being thought about, and I'm pretty sure that when I strip off my clothes I'll discover that my waning summer tan has had a boost.

I'm more than ready for a shower and to kick back and relax before another working week begins.

A trickle of unease works its way through my body as I think about facing Kian again after what happened Friday night, but I quickly lock it away to worry about tomorrow. I'm not allowing him to ruin any more of my weekend.

My legs are burning from the run up the stairs of my building, but I'm too busy fiddling with my earbuds and cell to pay any attention to what's happening in my hallway. Something I soon discover is a mistake.

"Good afternoon, Lorelei."

The second the deep voice hits my ears, I freeze.

No.

No.

He is not standing outside my apartment on a Sunday freaking afternoon.

Dragging my eyes up, I find that I'm wrong, because he is standing there beside my front door like he owns the place.

"What are you doing?" I snap, trying to hold my head high and stand my ground despite the fact I'm a disgusting, sweaty mess.

"Waiting for you. What does it look like?"

"It looks like you're standing somewhere you don't belong."

A smirk kicks up one side of his mouth, and it makes one of his dimples pop.

A sigh falls from my lips, and I tell myself it's out of frustration, not how damn good-looking he is.

He tsks before letting his eyes drop down my body. I might be dressed, but the way his pupils dilate, I may as well be standing here naked.

"What do you want, Kian?" I snap, frustrated that he's ruining my day.

Everything was going so well.

"We're going out," he states as if it's the most obvious thing in the world.

Popping a hip, I rest my hand on my waist. "I'm sorry. We're what?"

"Going out. You're probably going to want to shower first though, right?"

My mouth opens and closes to say something, but no words emerge.

What the fuck is this asshole playing at?

"Come on, open up. We don't have all day. Got places to be."

I continue to stare at him in disbelief.

"Where is your key, Lorelei?" he snaps, his patience quickly disappearing.

My eyes drop to the fake plant that sits in a pot beside the front door, and he follows my gaze.

"You're fucking kidding me. That's where you keep your key? Are you asking to be robbed and attacked in the middle of the night?"

My brows jump. "N-no, that's not—"

"Never. And I mean fucking never, leave your key here again. Do you hear me?"

"I hear the words, Kian. But I am not listening to them. Who the hell do you think you are to tell me what to do with my own goddam key?"

He holds my eyes for a few seconds, the hardness of his expression letting me know exactly what he thinks of my statement before he spins around and plucks the key from beneath the pot.

My eyes catch on the "Callahan" that's branded across his back, giving me little choice but to appreciate what he's wearing.

The suit I'm used to is nowhere to be seen. Instead, he's wearing a Chicago Chiefs jersey and a pair of what I can only assume are stupidly expensive jeans and sneakers.

I hate to admit it, but the casual look really suits him.

Without another word, he opens my front door, and after pressing his big palm against the small of my back, he physically pushes me inside, immediately closing us in.

"I have no idea what is going on here, but I have plans this afternoon, and they don't involve you."

"Cute," Kian muses. "You have thirty minutes to get showered and dressed. Do not make us late."

He takes a step forward, stupidly assuming that I'm going to follow his orders.

"You do not get to force your way in here and then start barking orders like I'm a dog, Kian Callahan."

"Oh, and you need to wear this," he says thrusting a carrier bag at me before disappearing into my living area.

"What the actual fuck, Callahan?" I seethe.

"Just do as you're told, Temptress," he rasps back.

Fire burns through me and I storm after him.

"What did you just call me?"

He spins around and holds my eyes as if I'm the crazy one here.

"Tempest. Your name, Lorelei." He says the words with so much confidence that I question my own hearing.

Shaking my head, I drop my eyes to the bag in my hands.

Reaching inside, I pull out the fabric hiding inside and hold it up.

"What the—"

"We watched your brother's game. Now we're going to do the same for mine."

I stare down at the Chicago Chiefs jersey in my hands with my head spinning out of control.

"Y-you're taking me to watch a football game?" I ask in complete bafflement.

"Yes, Lorelei. I'm taking you to watch a football game."

"You know I don't actually like football, right?"

He shrugs. "Doesn't matter. We're there to support Kieran."

I'm speechless. Utterly fucking speechless.

"The game starts at four thirty, and I'd quite like to be there before then," he says, making a show of glancing at his watch.

"Y-you're—"

"Taking you to watch a football game. Yes, Lorelei. Is there another way you need me to explain it to you?"

"B-but why?"

"Because I am, okay? Now stop questioning me and go and get ready."

Unable to come up with any kind of argument to get

myself out of this—not that I think any would be good enough —I spin on my heels and march toward my bedroom, clutching the jersey in my hands with a death grip.

It's not until I kick my bedroom door behind me that I suck in some much-needed air.

Kian Callahan is standing in my living room, waiting to take me to a football game. What fucking universe is this?

And more importantly, why am I even considering going?

He's right. He did watch Wilder's game with me. I owe Kieran, right?

Before I can talk myself in circles, I strip out of my running clothes, pull my shower cap on—because I do not have time to deal with that—and step into the shower.

"This is a really bad idea, Lorelei," I tell myself as I stand in front of my floor-length mirror, staring at the name plastered across my back.

Of course Kian couldn't bring me just any Chicago Chiefs jersey. Oh no, he had to bring me one with "Callahan" splashed across it.

Sure, as my boss, he may have some kind of ownership of me right now, but this is taking it to a whole new level.

I. Am. Wearing. His. Name.

This was not in my job description.

But that doesn't stop me from double-checking my hair and makeup in the mirror, slipping my feet into a pair of sneakers, and heading out to discover what he's done to entertain himself.

I guess I shouldn't really be surprised when I find him sitting at my kitchen island with my laptop open and a spreadsheet filling the screen before him.

"What the hell are you—"

"Some of your formulae were wrong," he states simply.

"You don't even know what I was trying to do."

"Yes, I do. I was the one who asked you to do this. I know how it needs to work."

Red-hot anger shoots through my veins.

"Then maybe you should just do it yourself."

He stares at me with a slight frown between his brows, as if he isn't understanding my issue here.

"Then why have an assistant?"

"Well, isn't that the question? Please, can you stop interfering with my work? If I need your help, I will ask."

"No, you won't," he says confidently.

He's right. I probably wouldn't. Google is my friend. He is not.

Closing my laptop, he gets to his feet and steps toward me.

"Shall we go?" he asks, and then as if suddenly realizing that I'm actually standing here, he takes a moment to let his eyes drop down my body. "Shit," he breathes.

"Why am I agreeing to this?" I ask, trying to ignore the way my blood heats under his perusal.

"Because I'm your boss, and you have to say yes to me."

"Wow, you really are delusional," I mutter, holding my ground as he steps right into my personal space.

Alarm bells go off, and my head screams for me to step back.

My body, though...the warmth from his calls to me, draws me in. If I were to move just a couple of inches, then...

"You look beautiful, by the way. Chiefs' colors suit you."

I stare up at him, unable to come up with any kind of intelligible response to his comment.

"We need to leave. Do you have everything?" he asks as his large hand gently wraps around my upper arm, spinning me in the direction of the front door.

"M-my purse," I stutter like a fool. Anyone would think that I've never been touched by a man.

His hand moves to the small of my back, and he sucks in a sharp breath. Glancing back over my shoulder, I find him staring at his surname branded across my shoulder blades, and my heart jumps into my throat.

His hand presses against my back, encouraging me forward. My feet move of their own accord. No sooner do I have my purse over my shoulder than I'm guided out of my apartment and into the elevator.

The air is thick with his cologne and sexual tension as his eyes remain on me. And not just on my face. He is way too blatantly looking at my body, and I've no idea what to do with it.

"W-who are the Chiefs playing?" I ask, my voice shaky and weak.

I hate it.

No man should have the power to make me second-guess myself.

But there is something about Kian that totally disarms me.

He is the perfect specimen of everything I hate in a man. He should not affect me in any way, other than to disgust me and turn me off. But I'm learning that I have a very different reaction when I'm in this man's company and the object of his attention.

Fucking hell. I'm just like all the others.

Do not fall for it, Lorelei. He's just trying to make a point. And right now, he is winning.

Straightening my spine, I repeat my little pep talk over and over as we descend through the building, and I pretend to listen as he talks football.

23

KIAN

"What the fuck was that?" Lorelei screams, making my smile grow wider.

For someone who claims not to like football, she's sure invested.

Her face, when we arrived and I directed her to a box, was priceless. Anyone else would have been beyond excited to have such incredible seats for this game. But, oh no, not Lorelei Tempest. She was pissed not to be in the stands with everyone else.

She is like no other woman I have ever spent time with. It's as amusing as it is confusing.

I wasn't trying to impress her—at least, I don't think I was. But it's becoming more and more obvious that my usual way of impressing women—anyone really—is having zero effect on my new assistant.

And let's not even get started on why we're here in the first place. I was meant to be coming with Dad, but when he called this morning to cancel, there was only one other person I could imagine watching this game with. Fuck knows why. She drives me crazy.

But watching her little brother on Friday night was...fun. So, I figured that she owed me a game.

It made sense until I said the words out loud and to her face. Then I just felt like a bit of a moron.

I have plenty of other associates who would love to watch the game from up here. But I didn't want a single one of them here with me.

I wanted her. And that is fucking terrifying.

"Who the fuck is that?" she barks, pointing down at the field as I finish my beer and abandon the glass.

Following the direction of her finger, I watch as a Seattle Saints player gets to his feet, leaving a trail of Chiefs' carnage behind him.

I glance at his number. Eighty-eight.

"Kane Legend."

Lorelei nods as if she's aware of his name.

He just took out almost all our defense in one play.

"He's good. The Saints are really fucking good. Have you been watching their quarterback?"

She scans the field, trying to find him. "Dunn?"

"The one in blue, yeah."

"Wait, there's—"

"Luca Dunn is the Saints' quarterback. Leon Dunn is one of our wide receivers. They're twins."

"Huh. You know a lot about football," she points out.

"I grew up listening to Kieran talk about it every chance he got. It becomes second nature after a while."

"You follow him and the Chiefs closely."

"Of course. He's my little brother. No different from you and yours."

"Something we have in common," she says absently.

The game continues with our offense lining up to make a play, leaving Luca, Kane, and the rest of the Saints' offense on the sideline.

Leon and our other receiver Braxton Whitlock take their positions, ready for the snap.

"Come on," Lorelei screams in encouragement as Whitlock makes the catch before passing it off to Weston

Rogers, our running back, who scores a touchdown, making the entire stadium erupt. "Yesssss."

I watch her with amusement as the Chiefs celebrate their touchdown, my eyes searching out my little brother for a moment before turning back to her.

"You might need to reconsider not being a football fan," I point out.

"I get sucked into the excitement. I can't help it."

The smile on her face and the twinkle in her eye when she turns to look my way do things to me. Things I'm unable to acknowledge, let alone even try to explain to myself.

The only thing I know is that I made the right decision to bring her here this afternoon. And I already can't wait to do it again.

It's dark by the time we leave the stadium. If I were here with Dad, I've no doubt that we'd head toward the Chiefs' locker room to congratulate Kieran on an epic win. But I shut the idea down the second it pops up. There's no fucking way I'm sharing Lorelei with a bunch of sweaty guys who are running on nothing but pure adrenaline right now. I know all too well what they're all like after a win, and that isn't something I want her anywhere near.

Instead, I lead her toward my car with my hand pressed against the small of her back.

"That was fun," she confesses once we're in the car.

"Better than high school games?" I ask since she confessed to never going to an NFL game before.

She thinks for a moment. "Different. Bigger obviously, louder. But there's something nice about those smaller high school games with boys who have everything to play for."

As much as I love the buzz of watching the pros, I can't help but agree.

The car falls silent as Lorelei pulls her cell out and replies to some messages as I drive.

We haven't discussed what to do after the game. It's Sunday night. We both have a long week ahead of us, but still, I can't quite convince myself to take her home. Not yet.

"Who are you talking to?" I ask after she bursts out laughing.

I assume it's Tate. Lorelei is probably giving her best friend the lowdown on her day. Internally, I groan, because I know it will end with a phone call from my big brother demanding to know why I chose to take my assistant to Kieran's game.

"Just an old friend," she says absently, more focused on the new message that's popped up than talking to me.

"It's not him, is it?"

"Him?" she asks, finally turning her eyes on me.

"The asshole who was trying to force himself on you the other night."

"He did not—" She cuts herself off and finally lowers her cell, turning her full attention on me. I feel the heat of her glare all the way to the tips of my toes. "You had no right to get involved on Friday night."

"He was harassing you. I had every right to protect you," I counter, my grip on the wheel tightening as I remember the way he leered at her, unable to read her reaction to him.

"I don't need protecting, Kian. Not from Matt, and certainly not by you."

"If you say so."

She sucks in a sharp breath, ready to continue coming at me with reasons, but then she looks around and takes in our surroundings. "Where are you going?" she asks firmly.

"For dinner."

"For dinner?" she echoes. "Why the hell are we going for dinner?"

"Well, there are a number of reasons. First and most pressing is because I'm hungry," I mock. "Second, and only very closely second, is because I just love being on the wrong end of your temper, and I'm not ready to say goodbye to it yet.'

"You're not funny," she snarks, crossing her arms beneath her chest and lifting her chin.

"And you're not going to win. Not against me, Temptress."

"I knew it," she shrieks at a pitch that I'm sure only dogs should hear. "You called me that earlier."

"And?" I ask, refusing to be embarrassed by the fact she is a fucking temptress. Her last name fits her to a tee.

"Do not call me that. It's Lori. Anything else is unnecessary."

"I'll call you whatever I want to call you," I say as I take the next left, our destination appearing up ahead.

"As long as the same goes for me."

I smirk. "As long as it's sir, boss, or maybe even daddy, I'm pretty sure I can get on board with it."

"Pig," she scoffs.

"That wasn't on the list, Temptress."

"Kian," she warns, only dialing up my amusement over this.

"Dinner, then I'll take you home. Deal?" I ask as I pull the car to a stop.

"What is this place?" she asks before committing.

"This is where you get the best buffalo chicken wings in the state."

Lorelei's eyes widen in interest. "Oh?"

"So do we have a deal?"

She makes a show of pretending to think about it.

"Okay, fine. But let me make this clear—I'm only doing it because of the wings."

"Sure you are."

Without waiting for me to even kill the engine, she pushes the car door open and climbs out.

"Fucking pain in my ass," I mutter as I follow her out.

By the time I catch up to her, she's already asking for a table for two.

The server opens his mouth ready to speak, but then he looks up at me.

"Kian, long time no see."

I might be standing behind Lorelei and unable to see her face, but I know she rolls her eyes hard enough to hurt as I'm greeted personally.

"Good evening, Ash. Table for two?"

"You got it, sir."

He takes off, leaving us to follow.

"See," I say, dropping my head so I can speak directly into Lorelei's ear. "He's happy to call me sir."

"He'd probably happily drop to his knees and worship at your feet as well. Another thing I am not going to do."

"We'll see," I rasp before she lowers into her chair.

"Can I get you some drinks?" Ash asks.

"Two sodas, please," I say before Lorelei has a chance, mostly just to piss her off.

There is something very endearing about the way her nose wrinkles and her lips purse when she's irritated.

I'm not sure if it's a reaction she only has to me, or everyone who riles her up, but I kinda hope it's the former.

"Seriously."

"Trust me, Temptress. I won't steer you wrong here."

"Not the point. I don't need or want a man who will order for me, or think he knows better than I do."

I smirk.

"Don't say it," she warns, her eyes narrowing.

"Well, have you been here before? Are you an expert?"

"Sodas," Ash announces, stopping Lorelei from snapping back. "Are you ready to order?"

"We are." I rattle off our order while Lorelei threatens to end me with a look alone.

"You're unbelievable," she mutters, pulling her cell from her purse and staring down at it.

"And you're ignoring me again."

"I know it might be a hard pill to swallow, but there are other people in the world who are more interesting than you."

I move faster than she can compute and pluck her cell from her hands.

I glance at the screen and find exactly what I was expecting, a message thread with Tate.

"Kian," she cries, leaning over the table to snatch it back, but I'm faster and tuck it into my pants pocket before she gets anywhere close.

"You're insufferable," she huffs.

"Takes one to know one," I counter.

"Mature," she mutters.

"Tell me something, Temptress. Something not everyone knows."

Dropping her eyes to the table, she falls silent as I reach for my soda and wait.

"There's nothing to tell. I'm a small-town girl who wanted the bright lights of the big city," she says, but there's something in her tone that doesn't sit quite right with me.

"Where'd you grow up?"

"California."

"Parents?"

"Single mom," she explains reluctantly.

"I bet she's something."

A bitter laugh erupts from Lorelei, making me frown. "Yeah, you could say that."

"You don't get along?" I guess, reading between the lines.

"You could say that. What about you?" she asks, turning the tables on me.

"Yeah, things are about as good as they can be when families get separated. Dad...Dad likes replacing the woman in his life almost as often as he changes his underwear."

"Your stepmom at the wedding?"

"Gone. Think he's had two others since then."

"Wow, okay." She says, her eyes widening with surprise. I get it. Dad is nothing but a serial womanizer. It's his coping mechanism from how things ended with Mom.

"Mom's happily married. Has been since leaving Dad. She's happy. Our half-sisters are...hard work," I confess. "That's siblings, right?"

"Yeah," she muses. "Mine are awesome, though," she says with a soft smile playing on her lips as two huge platters of wings appear before us, putting an end to our serious conversation.

The plate has barely touched down when I dive for my first wing.

The heat and spices hit my tongue, and I groan in appreciation.

Lorelei, though, doesn't move an inch. Instead, she just stares at me with her lips parted and her eyes getting darker by the second.

"Eat, Lorelei," I demand, aware that it'll annoy her.

Her eyes narrow, but unable to deny herself, she finally reaches out for a wing. The second she begins eating it, I discover what the issue is.

I've only ever eaten wings with the guys before. I've never taken a girl out for them, and I'm starting to wonder why, because the way Lorelei is working that wing right now...fuck.

24

LORELEI

I can't lie, watching Kian Callahan devour more buffalo chicken wings than should be humanly possible is addictive.

In this moment, he's no longer the wealthy CFO of Callahan Enterprises. He isn't the pretentious jerk who thinks the world owes him something because of his surname. He also isn't my demanding, overpowering boss. He's just...a young man enjoying some hot wings after watching a football game.

All the pretense has fallen away. Suddenly, we're just... us.

Two people on a...date? Enjoying good food and each other's company. Okay, so that might be pushing it a little bit. More like tolerating each other.

Who the hell am I kidding? This afternoon has been great. Kian has been...pretty great too.

Shit.

Am I actually starting to like my boss?

He drops some bones to the plate in front of him, and I take a moment to study him in this bizarre environment.

This isn't the kind of restaurant I ever pictured him eating in. It isn't fancy. I can't imagine it's won any prestigious awards—they totally should, though, because these wings are insane. Hell, it's even got a napkin dispenser on the table. And yet, Kian looks more at home here than I've ever seen him.

"Kieran killed it this evening," the server who greeted Kian personally when we first arrived says while delivering our drink refills.

"Yeah," Kian says, a proud smile appearing on his messy face.

I laugh; I can't help it. He looks like a little kid who went at the chocolate sauce too hard.

Instantly, I reach for my cell, needing to capture the unbelievable moment on camera. But then I remember. The asshole stole it.

Shaking his head, he pulls a couple of napkins free and wipes his mouth.

"They're going to have an epic season, I can just feel it."

"We can only hope. Kieran is desperate to make the playoffs."

After a little more football talk, the server finally leaves us alone again.

"You need to stop looking at me like that," he says, reaching for another wing.

"Like what?"

"Like you'd rather eat me than the wings."

My chin drops in the hope of looking shocked at his words.

"Seriously?" I hiss.

He smirks and shakes his head.

"I'd make it worth your while; it's not only a chicken wing I know my way around, you know."

"Once again, not interested, thank you."

"Are you going to try to tell me you have a better offer on the table?"

I think about the messages I was exchanging with Ryder last night. All it would have taken was for me to invite him to my place, and he'd have been there and between my thighs in a heartbeat.

At the thought, an image appears in my head—only the face between my legs doesn't belong to my old friend.

Dangerous territory, Lorelei. Very fucking dangerous.

"Yeah, actually, I do," I state firmly.

"Your ex isn't a better offer," he counters.

"Couldn't agree more. He was good, though," I muse, loving the way it makes Kian's jaw tick with annoyance.

"Lorelei," he warns.

I shrug before focusing my attention back on the wings.

"**A**re you going to listen to me today and drive away the second I step out of the car?" I ask as we sit outside my building.

The sunny fall evening has given way to a torrential downpour that I'm happily avoiding for a few more seconds by arguing with Kian.

"Absolutely not. I would be a very bad boss if I didn't see you to your door."

"It's raining," I point out.

"Is it? I hadn't noticed," he deadpans.

"Asshole."

"Nope. Sir, boss, or daddy, remember?"

Deciding that I'm better off battling with the rain than him, I push the door open.

"Thank you for today—it was tolerable. See you in the morning."

I swing the door closed before he has a chance to respond and then sprint toward my building.

The main doors are locked, and it takes me longer than it ever has before to locate my keys at the bottom of my purse.

In seconds, I'm soaked through, my jersey sticking to my body as the chill of the rainwater makes me shiver.

"At last," I cry as I pull them free and let myself in.

Shivering, I race toward the elevator for once, not second-guessing my actions and more than ready to peel my wet clothes from my body.

The doors close and I reach for the back pocket of my jeans for my cell but...

"Fuuuck," I groan.

That asshole didn't give it back.

I'm too busy debating whether to march back out there and have it out with him or say fuck it and just wait until tomorrow morning.

Thoughts of missing messages from Wilder or Hendrix finally force me into action, and I hit the button to open the doors.

Praying that he's still going to be there, I race out of the small space but come to a very abrupt stop when I crash into a hard body blocking my exit.

"What the—" A sharp gasp cuts off my question. "Kian?"

His hands wrap around my upper arms and I'm forced into the elevator until my back presses against the wall.

I'm so shocked, I don't realize that he's hit the button to my floor until we begin moving.

My heart races and my chest heaves as I stare up into his dark green eyes.

He continues to hold me with one hand on my arm. It's innocent, but my entire arm burns red hot.

"What are you doing?" My voice barely comes out as a whisper, and I mentally kick myself for letting him get to me.

His eyes bounce between mine before dropping to my lips.

Everything beneath my waist clenches, my stomach somersaulting.

He swallows, his Adam's apple bobbing before his full lips part.

"You forgot your cell," he explains roughly.

"A-and you couldn't have just given it back?"

The elevator dings, announcing our arrival, before the doors open.

Cool, fresh air rushes in, and I suck in a deep breath before Kian finally releases me, allowing me to duck around him and step into the hallway.

I don't stop until I'm at my door, my key in the lock, ready to escape inside.

"Can I have my cell, please?" I ask, holding my hand out for it.

He studies me closely before his eyes shift to my outstretched hand.

"Or you could invite me in?" He looks at me through his lashes and damn him, he looks so fucking cute.

His hair is wet from the storm and rain droplets are running down his face, disappearing into his weekend stubble. I don't need to let my eyes drop to know his shirt is as wet and as clingy as mine. I really do not need to see how it sticks to his muscles.

I. Do. Not. Need. To. See. That.

It takes every ounce of self-control I possess to listen to myself and do the right thing.

"I don't think that's a good idea, do you?"

He steps closer. His body and scent completely overwhelm me.

It could be a really good idea...

"Only one way to find out, I guess," he rasps, no longer even trying to hide the fact his attention keeps getting stolen by my lips.

Kiss me.

No. No, don't fucking kiss me.

He's your boss.

He's an asshole.

But he's so hot.

"Cell phone please, Kian," I demand again, determined to think with my head and not my pussy.

Movement catches my eye, and my attention drops as he pushes his hand into his pants pocket, making the fabric tighten across his crotch—and successfully showing off the reason he's able to be such a cocky motherfucker.

Oh, sweet mother of Jesus.

Every muscle in my body tightens.

I don't doubt what he said earlier is true about his skills. Hell, there are enough women out there who've happily shared their stories about their night of pleasure with him to prove it. Not that I've looked them up or read any, of course.

But that doesn't change the fact that he's my boss, and that this is a really, really bad idea.

"Temptress." His deep voice vibrates through me, making it even harder to do the right thing.

"Cell phone."

I breathe a sigh of relief when he places it in my hand.

"See you in the morning, Boss," I say before forcing myself to take a step back and swing the door closed.

But I don't walk away. I can't.

Instead, I reach up on my toes and look through the peephole.

My heart is still racing, my body screaming that I just made the wrong decision as he lifts his hand and combs his fingers through his wet locks. His eyelids lower and his lips part.

He looks tortured. It occurs to me that I should probably be enjoying watching him struggling to pull himself together. And all because of me. But I'm not.

Instead, I feel...confused. Conflicted. Guilty, even.

As proud as I am that I've made him lose control like that, I'm also a little ashamed.

Did I lead him on tonight? Was that reaction my fault?

My breath catches when he steps closer as if he's going to knock. As if he knows I'm here watching him. But then he changes his mind.

It takes him long minutes, but eventually, with one final long look at my front door, he disappears.

My chest constricts as he walks away with his head

bowed. He doesn't even take the elevator; he opts for the stairs instead.

"Fuck," I breathe, my head spinning with the events of the day.

I never in a million years would have predicted that he'd turn up here and take me out. It's happened and still, I'm struggling to get my head around it all.

Stepping back from the door, the coldness makes itself known once again, and after abandoning my purse and toeing off my shoes, I make my way through to my bedroom.

I abandon my cell on the bed until I've showered and dealt with my hair. After grabbing a bottle of water, I slip between my sheets and finally check my notifications.

I start with the messages from Wilder and Hendrix, smiling to myself as I read their words. They're just checking in, but it means everything to me that they've taken a few minutes of their day to do so.

Tatum's comes next, and I follow orders and fill her in on the rest of my night with Kian— although I keep those final moments to myself. I don't understand them, so how the hell am I meant to explain what happened over texts?

And finally, I open the message from Ryder.

I ignored the one he sent earlier today. It didn't feel right messaging him while hanging out with Kian.

> Ryde my dick: Have you had a good day?

I tap the side of my cell as I contemplate my answer.

Have I had a good day?

Honest answer... yes. I've had a really good day.

I hate that I have. That I enjoyed spending time with Kian. Sure, he's still demanding and overbearing, and everything I hate. But I'm beginning to see glimpses of another side to him.

Take him away from Callahan Enterprises and he's actually a half-decent person. It is not what I wanted to discover about my boss.

Keeping the wall up between us, that he seems determined to knock down, would be so much easier if he kept the mask in place and continued to show me that he's a cold, uncaring asshole.

> Lori: Yeah, I have. You?

> Ryde my dick: Had a quiet one. Mostly just waiting for you to reply and bring me some excitement.

> Lori: Oh yeah? What kind of excitement did you have in mind?

It's wrong. I shouldn't engage. Not when my head is full of the man I've just turned down and slammed the door on. But also...it's the perfect distraction from the man who needs to get out of my thoughts.

Nothing good can come from him getting up in my head and featuring in my dirty thoughts.

Nothing good at all.

25

LORELEI

I f I didn't have very, very vivid memories of Sunday, then I'd be questioning if it really happened.

I turned up at work on Monday morning and it was business as usual.

Kian had reverted back to the hard businessman I've always known him to be.

I want to say that I'm disappointed that the softer side of him seems to have vanished almost as quickly as it appeared, but honestly, I'm not.

It's much easier to hate him and keep a level head when he is barking orders at me and dragging me here, there and everywhere for meetings that really should have been fucking emails.

I barely saw him all day yesterday. He was in meetings all day that didn't require my presence. So instead of having to tend to his needs and demands, I was able to spend the day at my desk getting through some of the tasks he'd given me and the hordes of emails he'd forwarded to me to deal with.

It also gave me time to get to know Melissa better. She helped me with everything I couldn't do, and we had lunch together. It was nice to have someone to talk to who wasn't Kian. Not that we did a lot of talking. He mostly either issued demands or completely ignored my existence.

It should be fine, but there's a part of me that has been mourning the loss of the man I spent Sunday with.

It's stupid. I really need to get over myself, because it's more than apparent that he has.

I've just lowered my ass to my seat and placed my coffee on my desk Thursday morning when the phone rings.

I suck in a deep breath when I see that it's Kian as I prepare to deal with his first demand of the day.

"Good morning, Boss," I purr, loving the way his own breath hitches down the line. Something tells me that he won't think I heard it, but I did. Loud and clear.

He might act like Sunday didn't happen, but he remembers just as clearly as I do. I know he does.

"My office, Lorelei." I lower the phone from my ear, not bothering to even respond to his rude demand. "And bring coffee."

"Would love to," I snap once I've hung up.

"Kian's here today then?" Melissa laughs.

"And in a fantastic mood, it seems," I say as I gather my things up.

When Melissa went out yesterday, we did a little shopping as well as grabbing lunch, and I found the most perfect office supplies.

I couldn't help myself. And as I clutch my new notebook to my chest, I giggle like a naughty schoolgirl.

Kian is going to love it.

With both our cups of coffee in hand, I attempt to smoothly let myself into his office, seeing as the jerk has shut the door despite demanding my presence while carrying loads of shit.

"Good morning, Miss Tempest."

Oh good, we're on surname basis this morning.

"Sir," I sneer.

I keep my eyes focused on where I'm going instead of looking directly at him.

He's not the only one who can be an asshole.

After placing our coffees on his desk, I take a seat and then lower both my notebook and pen in front of me.

"We need to go through my calendar for the rest of the month. I have some travel plans that need—" He abruptly stops talking, and I fight to keep the smirk off my face. "What the fuck is that?" he barks.

"What is what, sir?" I ask sweetly, finally looking up at him.

He's wearing a navy blue shirt with a silver tie. His hair is styled, and the scruff on his chin has been trimmed to perfection. He looks the total opposite of what he did with his messy hair, scruffy beard and football jersey on Sunday.

I miss that version of him.

"That?" he barks, his eyes dropping to my notebook.

"Oh, it's new. Do you like it?" I ask, holding it up to face him to ensure he can read it.

His eyes narrow.

"I'm not sure a notebook with 'things I don't give a fuck about' written across the front is entirely appropriate."

"Do you not? Well, that's a shame," I mutter, placing my notebook back down and flipping it open. "Now, please continue. You wanted to discuss your schedule."

I grab my pen, making sure the writing down the barrel is facing him too.

It says, "This meeting is shit," and I know he's really going to appreciate it.

Sucking in a deep, steeling breath, he opens up his calendar and begins talking me through it.

Hours pass as he makes plans and I scribble notes to make sure I don't forget any of it.

I have a whole list of meetings, both in person and virtual, that I need to organize along with a whole host of things.

As we close in on lunch, my stomach begins to growl—and none too quietly, either.

One particular growl is so loud it makes Kian look away from his computer screen with a scowl on his face.

Despite wanting to apologize, my lips remain closed.

He doesn't deserve an apology when he's the one stopping me from eating.

"I have a gala on tomorrow night," he explains. "My suit will be delivered here this afternoon. If you could get it to Jamie when it does, I'd appreciate it."

"Would you rather me pick it up from the dry cleaners and then deliver it home for you? Perhaps I could help dress you in it as well?" The second I say those last few words, I regret them. The man from Sunday night would definitely take me up on the offer, and that is not the version of Kian Callahan I am facing right now.

"That won't be necessary," he says tersely.

I breathe out a sigh of relief. I might be annoyed that I've got to intercept his dry cleaning, but it's nowhere near as bad as finding myself in the middle of his fancy penthouse. I'm already more involved in his life than I want to be.

"That leads us to travel plans. Next week, I'd like to—"

A knock on the door cuts his words off.

He looks at me as if I know who it is. But when I say nothing, he finally concedes.

"Come in," he commands.

Honestly, I'm expecting it to be Kingston, or maybe even Micheal, so when the door opens to reveal what is probably the most stunning woman I've ever laid eyes on, I can't help but give her a double take.

As shockingly beautiful as she is, and as well as her obviously designer clothes fit her, it's the picnic basket hanging from her fingers that really catches my attention.

"We're in a meeting, Sasha," Kian says sharply.

"I can see that, sweetie. But it's lunchtime and—"

Pushing to my feet, I close my notebook, more than grateful for the interruption and the reason to escape.

The woman—Sasha—steps farther into the room as I retreat toward the door.

Almost instantly, I notice just how tall she is.

Christ.

Any self-confidence I might possess withers and dies, seeping from my feet and into the floor as I step up to her.

What the hell was Kian thinking Sunday night when he has this woman at his beck and call? And she comes with food. I bet there is caviar and champagne in that basket.

He took me for wings, for fuck's sake.

With a discreet shake of my head, I duck out of the office.

"I'm going out for lunch. We can continue this after," I mutter.

I take off, my heels clicking against the tiled floor as I leave Kian to his supermodel lunch date.

Something unpleasant swirls in my stomach, and as I approach Mellissa's desk, she also looks less than impressed.

"Everything okay?" I ask hesitantly.

"She just...she..." Melissa huffs in irritation. "Just because she's young and pretty, it doesn't mean the world owes her anything."

Okaaay.

"I'm going to grab some lunch. Would you like me to get you anything?" I ask, forcing a smile on my face in the hope of looking unaffected by Sasha and her picnic basket. I bet she doesn't even have plastic plates and cups. I bet it's fine China and crystal in there.

"Cake would be fantastic. I'm having one of those days."

You and me both.

"Did you want to come with? We could—"

"I can't, I'm due in a meeting momentarily. But thank you for the offer."

With a smile, I grab my purse from beneath my desk and head out, more than ready to put some space between me and the romantic picnic happening in Kian's office.

I've almost managed to escape the building when a familiar voice calls my name.

Spinning around, I find Tate talking to a security guard.

"Hey, what are you doing here?" I ask.

"Coming to take my bestie for lunch. Why else would I be here, silly?" she says with a wide smile. "So, what do you fancy?"

"Umm..."

"You're right. That sandwich place a couple of blocks down. That's exactly what I'm craving."

With a laugh, I say, "Sounds good, T."

Linking her arm with mine, she leads me from the building.

I shouldn't need a distraction from Kian and his supermodel, but fuck, I really do.

"H e's busy," Melissa informs me once I've returned from lunch and delivered her a mouthwatering piece of chocolate cake.

"Still?" I balk.

My lunch with Tate might have run over a little—enough that I'd no doubt receive a dressing down about my punctuality if Kian were to notice, but it seems that he's still otherwise engaged.

Images of what the two of them could be doing behind those darkened floor-to-ceiling windows make a shudder rip through me.

Melissa smiles sadly at me, and I cringe.

He's just my boss; why should I care what he's doing right now?

"Great. At least that will give me a chance to catch up."

Pulling my office chair out, I drop down into it a little heavier than intended and reach for my notebook, staring at the cover.

Things I don't give a fuck about...

My boss screwing a supermodel over his desk.

That is something I really don't give a fuck about.

I lose myself booking in all the meetings he's requested,

along with a host of things that were added to my endless to-do list while we were talking.

Hours pass, but neither he nor his model emerge, and as the end of the day approaches, I find myself glancing down the hallway more and more frequently.

I've had no emails or messages, no phone calls demanding anything.

Nothing but radio silence.

I should love the peace. But...I kinda hate it.

Deciding against going down there to say goodbye, I tidy up and shut my computer down almost ten minutes after the time I should leave for the day. If he's expecting me to hang around while he has an afternoon-long fuck fest with Sasha, then he's got another thing coming.

Melissa has already left to run an errand for King, so without looking back, I step into the elevator, more than ready to put the day behind me.

With plans for my evening spinning around my head, I ignore everyone else who steps into the car with me. Seeing as I came from the top floor, I end up squashed at the back, something which I'm sure never happens to Kian. I'm the last to leave—everyone else has already rushed out of the building, ready to enjoy what's left of the sunshine.

The sight of Kian's car sitting out front makes my stomach tighten, and it only gets worse when Jamie notices me and pushes the door open as if he's going to come over.

Not wanting to get into an argument with him, I put my head down and hurry down the sidewalk, hoping to blend in with the crowd.

"Excuse me," I say, when someone steps right in front of me.

I attempt to dart around him without bothering to look up and realize my mistake the second his voice hits my ears.

"Lorelei, I miss you. Please."

Oh, for the love of fuck.

Finally, I lift my head and look Matt dead in the eyes.

"That's a real shame. Maybe you should have thought about that before lying to me. I have somewhere I need to be. Excuse me."

I try once again to get around him, but he isn't having any of it. His hand darts out and he grips my upper arm tightly enough to hurt. It's nothing like the way Kian held me Sunday night. He wasn't gentle, but he also wasn't vicious and angry like Matt seems to be right now.

He's got a fire burning behind his eyes, and it's not the good kind.

"I see you managed to make your dream come true," he sneers. "But then I guess it's easy now that Tate has married in."

"I'm not listening to this," I hiss, trying to free myself from his grip. "We're done, Matt. I am not interested in anything that comes out of your lying mouth."

"I just want you to reply," he says, sounding hopeless all of a sudden. But I don't get a chance to focus on the sudden shift in his emotions because his hand loosens on my arm a second before he stumbles back, crashing into the building. A dark shadow looms over him as he clutches his face. A face that Kian Callahan's fist just plowed into.

26

KIAN

"Yes," I snap the second I accept Jamie's call.

"It's Lorelei, sir. She's—"

"Where?" I bark, not needing to hear any more. If he thinks it's important enough to call me—which he never does—then I don't need an explanation. I just need to get there.

"Outside. Turn right."

"Coming."

Without another word to our head of security that I was having a discussion with, I turn and race from the room which is, thankfully, on the ground floor of Callahan Enterprises.

I'm halfway through reception when I see her.

When I see him.

Anger burns through me, and it only gets worse when I see his hand on her.

Shoving more than a couple of our employees out of the way, I race the short distance down the sidewalk with fury like I haven't felt in a long fucking time, bubbling just under the surface.

I see red when she tries to get out of his hold but is unable to.

Asshole has no fucking right to lay a finger on her.

My fist is curled and my muscles are pulled tight, ready for the hit I know is coming long before I reach them.

He doesn't see me approaching—he's too focused on trying to make her listen to him—so my punch comes as a massive shock.

Thankfully, he releases her arm before he crashes into the window behind him.

"Fuck," he barks, covering half of his face with his hand like a fucking pussy.

"Get up," I demand as I loom over him.

My breathing is erratic, and my fist fucking hurts, but it won't stop me from doing it again.

Motherfucker deserves it for what he's done to her.

Yeah, after their exchange on Friday night, I made sure to get all the details from King.

The jerk is fucking scum.

"Dude, what the fuck?" he seethes.

"The fuck? The fuck is that you're man-handling a woman who doesn't want anything to fucking do with you. If you're man enough to lay a hand on her, then you're man enough to stand up to me."

"Leave it," Lorelei snaps, but I'm not having any of it.

There's movement and noise behind me, the thought of this whole thing being filmed and put online should stop me.

But it doesn't.

Instead, I step forward, ready to drag the asshole to his feet if he doesn't get on them willingly.

"Get. The. Fuck. Up."

"Kian, please. Just leave it. He isn't worth it."

"You can fucking say that again."

Thankfully, the jerk pushes to his feet and holds my stare.

I'm about to throw another punch when I'm suddenly hauled backward.

"Get the fuck out of here," a deep voice barks from behind me. I've no idea if he's talking to me or the crowd that's predictably gathered.

"I don't need your fucking help," I seethe, trying to shake both sets of hands off me.

"You're throwing punches out the front of the office, little brother. I think you very much need our help right now."

Jamie ushers Matt away, and the fucker runs like the little pussy that he really is while King continues to get rid of our audience.

"Kieran, take Lorelei to the car and see she gets home safely."

I spin around just in time to watch my little brother throw his arm around Lorelei.

The anger, that had barely lessened, surges forward once again.

"No," I bark, reaching out to throw his arm from around her. "Don't you fucking touch her."

Silence rings out so loud between the four of us it's deafening.

"I'm taking her home."

"No, you're not. You and I need to talk."

"Talk?" I balk. "I've got nothing to talk to you about right now."

"How about the media shitstorm that's going to come from videos of you going viral punching an innocent man outside our offices?" Kingston sneers.

He's pissed. I acted before thinking about the consequences. But so fucking what? If it were Tate in Lorelei's position just now, he'd have done the exact same thing.

"You'll figure it out," I mutter as I grab Lorelei's hand, tugging her away from Kieran.

To my surprise, she doesn't let go as we close in on the car.

I clutch her hand tight, wondering what might have happened if Jamie hadn't been here.

Would he have hurt her worse?

"Get in," I bark, the red haze beginning to dissipate, allowing reality to trickle in.

"I don't think so," Lorelei spits, finally attempting to tug her hand from mine.

As if her touch burns, I drop her hand. But I'm not letting her get away. I will see her safely to her door, even if it kills me.

"Kian?" King demands from behind me.

"Get in the fucking car, Lorelei. I won't ask you again."

She looks between me and my brothers, who are standing behind me.

She wants to argue, I can see the fire burning deep in her eyes, but for a reason I may never know, instead of continuing to battle with me, she nods once and then concedes and steps into the car.

"Good girl," I muse, following her inside.

"Don't," she warns. "Just...don't."

I follow her orders as Jamie closes the door, blocking us off from outside, plunging us into silence and our own little world.

My hand throbs from where I hit that motherfucker, but I don't let it be known. Something tells me that Lorelei would delight in knowing I was in pain.

The engine comes to life, and the moment I can, I lean forward and put the privacy screen up.

Sitting back, I turn to look at Lorelei. Her back is ramrod straight. She's got her purse and laptop bag on her lap, her arms clutching them as if they're a lifeline.

Her brows are pinched together, leaving a deep crease between them that I desperately want to reach out and smooth away. Her lips are thin, and I can't help but wonder if she's biting down on them to stop herself from saying anything.

"What did he want?" I ask after long, agonizing minutes.

It takes her a moment to register that I've said anything, but I know the second she does because her expression hardens even more.

"That is none of your business. What were you even thinking?" she demands without bothering to turn to look at me.

"He was touching you," I seethe quietly, my fists

tightening on my lap, sending a shooting pain up my right arm.

It might hurt now, but fuck did it feel good.

I can't remember the last time I hit someone that wasn't one of my brothers. That fucker deserved it, though.

She shakes her head, unable to accept my words.

"I'm your assistant, Kian. Not your problem."

"That's bullshit and you know it," I snap. "It doesn't matter if you're my assistant or the part-time cleaner, I will not have any of my staff treated like that."

A humorless laugh falls from her lips.

"What?" I ask, confused.

"Nothing. It's nothing. I'm..."

"You're what?" I ask when she trails off.

"Nothing. Literally nothing."

My brows pinch.

A heavy sigh passes her lips and her shoulders lower as if she's got the weight of the world on them.

Before I manage to find a response, she finally turns to look at me.

The sight of tears glistening in her eyes ensures that any words I might have had shrivel up and die.

I hate it. I hate that someone like him has the power to do this to her.

Asshole deserves so much more for the pain he's caused her.

"Just..." The car stops and my heart lurches, knowing without looking that Jamie has just pulled to a stop outside her building. She's going to get out and walk away, and there is fuck all I can do about it. "Just forget it. He's not worth risking an assault charge."

"He's not, no, but—" Before I get a chance to say any more, Jamie has opened her door and she's climbing out.

"I'll see you tomorrow, Kian. Have a good night," she shoots over her shoulder.

I'm out before Jamie has a chance to close the door, chasing her toward her building.

"Lorelei, wait."

She spins around on her heels and glares at me with a look that would make a lesser man's balls shrivel up into their body.

"No. You do not get to pretend to be the better man here. Not when you have spent all afternoon with Model Barbie bent over your desk instead of doing any work."

Model Barbie?

Shock renders me useless long enough for her to flee inside.

I take a step forward to follow, but before I can take another, Jamie's hesitant voice carries through the air.

"Sir. M-maybe you should give her some space?"

All the air rushes from my lungs, and I hang my head.

He's right. I know he is.

But...but fuck.

I really want to follow her. I want to make sure she's okay.

I want to make sure she doesn't fucking call him.

"Yeah. Yeah," I say, pulling myself back together and returning to the car.

Lorelei's a big girl. She can take care of herself.

I shouldn't be surprised to find two men waiting for me when I step into my apartment a little over thirty minutes later. But I am.

"Fuck's sake," I mutter as I throw my suit jacket onto the kitchen counter and toe my shoes off, leaving them abandoned in the middle of the room.

"Lovely to see you too, big brother," Kieran mocks.

"Is that really a good idea?" Kingston barks like the overbearing asshole he is when I reach into the cupboard and pull out a bottle of Macallan.

"It's been a long day," I say absently as I reach for a glass and pour myself a measure.

I don't bother offering either of them a drink, and they don't request one either.

Instead, they continue to silently stare at me.

Waiting.

They're waiting for an explanation.

Well...they're going to be waiting a long time because I don't even know where to start.

I swallow my whiskey in three big mouthfuls before slamming my glass down on the counter hard enough for it to shatter. Thankfully, it doesn't, and I take off through my apartment announcing, "I need a shower."

Something tells me that my absence won't be enough to get rid of them, but at least I can put off the two-man firing squad a little longer.

Just as expected, when I return to the kitchen, the two smug assholes are in the exact same place; only this time, they've got food from my favorite restaurant.

"Hungry?" King asks with a smirk.

"Fuck off," I grunt as I lower my ass to one of the stools and pull the lids from the containers.

The scent of rosemary and garlic chicken floods my senses and my mouth waters.

Okay, maybe they aren't so bad...

"So...first, you bring her to my game, and then you're fighting random men in the street for her. Your new assistant must really be something, huh?" Kieran starts, not bothering to beat around the bush.

"Do we have to?" I mutter around a mouthful of dauphinoise potato. This food is too good to be ruined by them and their curiosity.

"If I've got to deal with the press because you can't keep a cool head, then yes, we're doing this."

With a sigh, I reluctantly tell them about watching her brother's game on Friday night and then making her return the favor.

But my explanation doesn't pacify them. If anything, it makes them more curious.

"Have you fucked her?" Kieran asks.

I swear, King leans in closer to give himself a better chance of hearing the answer.

Not fucking necessary.

"No. I have not fucked her. Nor am I planning to."

"Liar," King coughs like a child, making me roll my eyes.

He might be the oldest, and arguably the most sensible out of the three of us, but every now and then he proves that there's still an element of that little boy lingering inside him.

"I am not," I protest, although I'm barely able to believe my own words, so I'm not surprised when they stare at me in disbelief.

"She's just...she's having issues with her ex. She's been the best assistant I've had so far, and I wanted to help."

"By making a spectacle of yourself and the company? Didn't want to wait until the world wasn't watching?"

"Saw an opportunity," I mutter before shoveling a huge piece of chicken into my mouth to give me an excuse to keep quiet for a few more minutes.

"You're a fucking idiot," King happily points out. "But you did the right thing. That prick needed to be taught a lesson."

27

LORELEI

Unknown: My hand hurts.

I've been staring at the same message for the last five minutes, trying to get my head around it.

It's obvious who it is. I don't need to double-check the number that I haven't bothered to store in my personal cell.

Did I think he'd reach out after the way we left things earlier? Yeah, I guess I did.

Did I expect him to send something like that, and to my personal cell, no less? No, I really didn't.

What the hell am I meant to send back?

I've typed out a few responses, all of which I've second-guessed and deleted almost immediately.

Thankfully, I haven't heard anything from Matt. However, I can't help but think that that might be worse.

He could be at the station right now, reporting Kian for assault.

I cringe at the thought.

CFO of Callahan Enterprises arrested for the assault of his assistant's ex-boyfriend...

That is not the kind of headline news I really want to wake up to.

In the moment, I was horrified at what I was witnessing, but now, a few hours after the event, I can't help feeling a little smug.

Potential criminal record or not, Matt is currently nursing one hell of a swollen face, and when he wakes up in the morning, I have every hope that he'll have an ugly bruise that matches his ugly morals.

Unable to come up with something more eloquent, I tap out one single word and finally hit send.

Lori: Good.

It shows as read immediately and my heart lurches, but he doesn't begin typing.

Taking a moment to save his contact, I wait patiently for what he might respond with.

I wait for so long that my cell goes to sleep, and when it goes off again, it startles me.

Lifting it in a rush, I don't bother reading it before opening the notification.

My eyes almost bug out of my head when I find a dick pic staring back at me.

Admittedly, it's a very nice dick pic and can only come from a man who sends them often and knows all his best angles.

I don't need to look up at the name of the person who sent me this, I know the appendage well enough, and I'm so fucking relieved that it doesn't belong to my boss.

Or am I...

I'm still staring at it, wondering how Kian's might look in comparison, when my cell buzzes again.

Boss: He deserved it. I just hope it hurts worse than my hand.

> Lori: Baby. Anyone would think you hadn't thrown a punch before.

I smirk, trying to imagine his childhood and education compared to mine. Pretty sure half of his middle school didn't burn down because some assholes decided that setting off fireworks in multiple classrooms at once was a good idea, or that the police had to attend at least once a week to pull students off each other when the teachers failed to deal with the brawling.

Even the best students learned how to protect themselves very quickly in that place. It's one reason why I don't really need to worry about Wilder and Hendrix. What they might lack in motherly love and support, they make up for in street wisdom.

That school might not teach the standard lessons, but every student definitely leaves with some kind of education.

I know from Tate that all three Callahan brothers went to the same boarding school and spent their spare time clay pigeon shooting and learning to play sports like polo and golf.

It's two different worlds, and every time I think about it, I feel like I belong here less and less.

> Boss: I grew up with an older and younger brother. Trust me, I know how to fight. I was always the one in trouble for it, too.

> Lori: Is that meant to make me feel sorry for you?

> Boss: Not at all. I can punch harder than both of them combined; your sympathy should be with them.

> Lori: I once broke a girl's nose.

The second I hit send, I regret it.

> Boss: Mud wrestling can be brutal. How did your bikinis fare?

Laughter bursts out of me.

> Lori: There was no mud involved. Ironically, she kissed my boyfriend at the time. She had it coming.

> Boss: You have questionable taste in men, Temptress.

Seeing his nickname for me typed out on my screen has butterflies erupting in my stomach.

One word should not cause such a visceral reaction. But it does.

> Lori: Thank you for pointing out the obvious, Sherlock.

> Boss: Things can only get better, right?

I think of the dick pic sitting in my messages. That's looking pretty good right now.

The temptation to blow Kian off in favor of Ryder is strong. He would know exactly how to make me forget about the drama of the day.

And why shouldn't I? It's not like Kian didn't spend the afternoon getting his rocks off.

I deserve a little stress relief too, don't I?

But just as I'm figuring out how to wish him a good night, he sends another message.

> Boss: My brothers were waiting to rip me a new one when I got home.

> Lori: Did that hurt more or less than your hand?

> Boss: You concerned about my ass, Temptress?

> Lori: Naturally. I have no interest in going out tomorrow to buy you a special pillow for your delicate behind.

> Boss: I think you're safe.

> Lori: So what did they say?

> Boss: King is pissed about the publicity that will come from this. Kieran is just amused. Wants to know what's so special about my new assistant that I'd risk broken bones AND take her to his game.

> Lori: We're all wondering the same...

> Boss: Are you digging for compliments, Miss Tempest?

My cheeks heat because, yeah, I guess I am a little.

Seeing that woman standing in the doorway to his office earlier was a knock to my confidence, I can admit that to myself.

I can also admit that the man she was there to see shouldn't be the one to build it back up again, but here we are.

Acid floods my stomach the second I think about her. Fuck, she really was beautiful, and totally Kian's type.

I don't know why I care, but I do.

> Lori: No, just wondering why you've yet to send me running out of the building crying.

> Boss: Because you don't take any of my shit.

I smirk, the jealousy ebbing away.

She might have it all in the looks department, but does she have anything else about her?

Could she stand up against the mighty Kian Callahan and not end up crying?

Something tells me no, and I'm more than happy to run with that thought.

> Lori: I'm glad you've noticed, Sir *smirky emoji*

> Boss: Trust me, it's impossible not to.

I sigh, lowering my cell to my stomach. I don't know why him appreciating my strength means so much to me, but it does.

When I don't reply, he obviously gets bored of being ignored and sends another.

> Boss: What are you doing?

> Lori: Practicing my mud wrestling. Championships are coming up…

> Boss: Give me the date and time. I'm there.

My light laughter fills the room as my blood heats.

Biting down on my bottom lip, I imagine the insanity that would be a mud wrestling championship, or more so, what having his eyes on my bikini-clad body might feel like.

Fire.

Red-hot, burning fire.

> Lori: I'm reigning champ, don't you know?

> Boss: Can't say it surprises me. Your opponents don't stand a chance.

> Lori: What are you doing?

I'm expecting something equally stupid to come back, so I'm more than surprised at his response.

> Boss: Lying in bed, wishing I'd thrown a few more punches into that prick's face.

I can't help but agree. Only…he hasn't finished, because he continues typing.

> Boss: Wishing you'd let me follow you up to your apartment.

"Oh, Jesus."

There was a very good reason why I didn't want him to follow me earlier, and the heat that's coursing through my veins is exactly it.

> Lori: You're more than capable of icing your own fist. And anyway, I don't have any peas in my freezer.

> Boss: I was more worried about you than my hand.

My chest tightens and my heart rate increases.

> Lori: No need. As you so helpfully pointed out, I have a habit of picking the men who hurt me. Just another day, just another asshole.

Fuck. The truth hurts more than I was expecting.

> Boss: That's not the point.

> Boss: Are you okay?

Tears burn the backs of my eyes and make my nose itch.

I don't want his sympathy or his concern.

I don't...

> Lori: Yes.

That one-word response taunts me, and I quickly find myself following it up with another message.

> Lori: Thank you.

I manage to stop myself from telling him that no one has

ever stood up for me like he did today. That is definitely an overshare that doesn't need to happen.

> Boss: You're welcome. Maybe let me vet the next one before you fall head over heels, yeah?

> Lori: That won't be necessary. I won't be falling for anyone anytime soon.

> Lori: Good night, sir. See you in the morning.

I tell myself to turn my cell off and put him out of my mind, but before I can convince myself to do it, he replies.

> Boss: That's good. It'll give my hand time to recover. Good luck with your training. If you need any advice, make sure you bring photos. I'll willingly check over your form.

> Lori: See you in the morning, Boss.

A fter that last message, I was good and put my cell on airplane mode. I want to say that I rolled over and went straight to sleep, but that would be a lie. With Kian's actions and messages, and Ryder's dick pic circling around in my head, it was well into the early hours of the morning by the time I drifted off. When my alarm started up this morning, my eyes refused to open, and my body ached with exhaustion.

At least it's Friday.

And if I thought things were already bad, the second I step out of the elevator on the top floor of Callahan Enterprises with a large iced latte in hand, I find none other than Kian Callahan perched on the edge of my desk with his hands folded across his chest.

I'm late. I know I am. The line in the coffee shop was

beyond a joke. Apparently, I'm not the only one in the city who needs a pick-me-up this morning.

He looks between my drink and my eyes with an expectant expression on his face.

"Where's mine?" he demands.

I smirk. He's so predictable.

"Well," I start as I walk around him and behind my desk without reacting to his presence.

Melissa isn't in yet, which is almost a shame, because she will miss this.

"I figured you might want something, but I wasn't sure what you might fancy this morning. And then as I was standing there, I had a lightbulb moment." His brows pinch, but I keep my expression blank as I wrap my fingers around the cool bottle in my tote.

My lips twitch with amusement as I pull out a bottle of superfood juice that looks about as disgusting as the homemade one Kingston forces Tate to drink.

Kian stares at it, his eyes darkening with frustration.

"Where is my coffee, Lorelei?"

"So, I got you this. It's really good for you." I lift it up to read the label, but it's ripped from my hand before I get a chance.

"I punched that asshole for you, and this is the thanks I get?" he scoffs, slamming the bottle down on my desk.

"Sorry, I wasn't aware I needed to repay you for that little stunt. As you're a free man here, I'm assuming he didn't press charges."

Kian's jaw ticks with irritation.

"Cancel all my meetings today," he demands as he pushes from my desk and starts to walk away. "My office, two minutes. Do not be late again."

28

KIAN

Exactly two minutes later, Lorelei walks into my office with her notebook tucked under her arm and two— yes, two—coffees in her hands.

My eyes narrow.

"Cappuccino with a double shot, extra hot. Just the way you like it, sir."

She places it in front of me with a smirk playing on her lips.

"All of your meetings have been canceled. They'll need to reschedule, so if you could let me have—"

"Sit."

"I-I'm sorry, it may have escaped your notice, but I'm not a dog. Nor do I appreciate being spoken to like one."

I shake my head as I reach for my coffee and take a sip, watching with amusement as she lowers herself into the chair on the other side of the desk like I instructed her to, despite her little tirade.

"Noted."

"What is happening today?" she asks curiously.

"Something has come up."

"Right. Do you require me to do anything for whatever situation has arisen?"

"Yes, actually, I do."

She grabs her notebook from the corner of the desk and places it before me, giving me enough time to read the front.

Internally, I laugh, but I don't let her see that.

Instead, my lips press into a thin line and my eyes narrow dangerously.

My pointless notes from meetings...that could have been an email...

She's trying to rile me up, but I will not rise to it.

And today's pen...

This job is shit.

Wonderful.

Finally, she flips the book open on a fresh page and is poised ready to scribble down notes...that could have been an email.

I take another sip of my coffee.

"Ten AM: Appointment with a personal shopper."

She scribbles it down, but not before she glances up at me suspiciously.

She may have joked about collecting my dry cleaning and delivering it home for me the other day, but contrary to popular belief, I don't actually want my assistant doing personal tasks for me. Lorelei is here to assist me at work, not with my personal life.

"One PM: Lunch reservations. Three PM: Hair and makeu—"

"M-makeup?" she stutters, confusion written all over her face.

"Yes," I agree, swallowing the rest of my coffee and pushing to stand. "Are you ready?"

"Ready?" she balks.

"Yes. I hate being late, and the traffic across town to your first appointment will be horrendous."

"My appointment?"

"Yes," I say for the third time. "You didn't think it was all for me, did you?"

With a smirk playing on my lips, I pull my jacket on and

pocket my cell. I may have gotten her to cancel all my plans, but that doesn't mean the end of my work for the day.

Her mouth opens and closes like a fish, but she fails to find any words.

"I have the charity gala tonight," I explain. "And you're my date."

The statement lands exactly as I predicted it would.

Hard.

She jumps to her feet, her eyes wide with shock.

"Your...your date. No, Kian. That is absolutely not—"

"It is. Your name is already on the guest list. We just need to get you ready."

"B-but—" She cuts herself off as she looks up to the ceiling as if it might give her some divine intervention. "What about Sasha?"

When her gaze comes back to mine, the fire burning in the depths of her eyes makes my breath catch.

It only confirms that I'm making the right decision.

"What about Sasha?"

"Isn't she your date to this thing? Or one of the other women you spend time with?"

"No," I state simply. "Get your things together, we're going to be late. Jamie is waiting."

Striding toward the door, I pull it open and wait for her to walk through it.

She's reluctant, but after a silent stand-off, she finally concedes.

"Good girl," I say quietly behind her.

It's so quiet that there's a chance she won't hear, but the second her shoulders bunch and her steps falter, I know she has.

She likes it too.

I had a suspicion she would.

The reception area is still empty. Melissa is in a meeting with Kingston, allowing me to do this without being under her watchful eye.

"Ready?" I ask when she emerges with her purse hanging over her shoulder.

"Not in the slightest, but I'm not sure I have a choice."

"You're learning fast."

Pressing my hand to the small of her back, I gently push her forward and into the elevator once the doors have opened.

"For the record, I want you to know that I'm against this."

"Why? What could possibly be so bad about spending the night with me?"

"Plenty of things," she mutters under her breath.

"You get to get all dressed up, eat incredible food, and enjoy outstanding company."

"Debatable."

"Don't even try to convince me that you didn't have fun on Sunday."

"Donning a Chiefs' jersey and going to a football game is very different from attending some fancy gala. What's it even for, anyway?"

I smile, knowing that this is the exact moment I change her mind about the whole thing.

"How much do you know about Kieran's career outside of on the field?"

"Uh...I know that like you, he gets pictured with the world's most beautiful women on a weekly basis, and that more than a handful of them have sold stories about their... activities together."

"So not a lot, then," I muse making her roll her eyes.

"He runs a foundation that helps kids from underprivileged backgrounds get the education and training they need to stand a chance at playing professional football."

Her chin drops.

"And tonight, there is a silent auction to help secure funding for scholarships for students around the country."

"Right..."

"Changing your mind about attending now?"

She sucks in a sharp breath.

"What makes you say that?"

She's been very closed about her family, but it doesn't take a genius to work out why.

"Your little brother...does he plan on attending a college with a successful football team next year?"

Her lips purse in frustration.

"He plans on it, yes."

"And does he have the funding in place to make that happen?"

"He has scouts attending his games, as you well know. He's hoping to secure something soon."

"And should he not get a scholarship? Is your family able to support him?"

The second the question rolls off my tongue, every muscle in her body pulls tight.

"That is none of your business."

There is it again. That sore spot she doesn't like me poking.

"I'll take that as a no. And in case you're wondering, I've already put your brother's name on Kieran's radar. He's impressed."

"No," she snaps. "My brother has nothing to do with you. His future, his career has nothing to do with you."

I study her for a moment, loving the way her cheeks glow and her body trembles with pent-up frustration.

"No, he doesn't. But he also deserves the best chance at getting the life he wants, no?"

We hit the ground floor and the doors open, allowing us to walk out before she gets a chance to respond.

A couple of people try to stop me as we exit the building, but I put them all off in favor of getting Lorelei into the car and en route to finding her a dress for tonight.

The atmosphere is tense as we drive across the city, and despite my words from the elevator still floating around us, Lorelei doesn't make a comment.

In fact, she doesn't say a word. Instead, she pulls her laptop out and continues working on a spreadsheet.

I watch her, impressed with her skills until she makes a predictable and common error.

"That won't work."

She freezes, her fingers hovering over the keyboard.

"Then I'll learn that myself when I test it and find a way to fix it."

"Or you could let me tell you the correct way."

"I prefer to learn for myself. I don't need anything to be spoon-fed to me," she snaps.

"Fair enough."

Unwilling to pull my cell out and continue trawling through my emails, I watch her experiment with different formulae.

The desire to blurt out the answer she's looking for is strong, but this time, I refrain. I think I've probably already put enough on her this morning.

She's still got her head in her laptop when we pull up at our destination.

"As much as I appreciate your work ethic, we have other places to be right now."

She barely looks up as I climb from the car, and it's not until she joins me on the sidewalk that reality hits her.

"We're on Oak Street," she says, her eyes wide as she looks up and down the rows of designer shops.

"Uh...yeah. Where did you think we were going?"

She swallows thickly before taking a step back toward the car.

"I-I don't belong here."

I study her as she tries to retreat to the car.

Those pink cheeks and the fire in her from earlier have gone. In their place is nothing but trepidation.

"What are you talking about? Of course you do."

Glancing at my watch, I find that we have five minutes until her appointment.

Reaching out, I take her hand in mine. "Come on, they're expecting you."

I hold her with enough force that she can't slip free, giving her little choice but to follow me.

We pass several boutiques before we get to the one Melissa suggested—not that she was really aware of what I was looking for, of course. I knew asking Tate for advice wouldn't work. She'd go straight to Lorelei and tell her what I was doing. Honestly, I wasn't sure that Melissa wouldn't do the exact same thing, but she was my only other option.

I certainly couldn't call up Sasha and ask her advice.

A shudder rips down my spine at the thought alone.

"Here we go," I say, coming to a stop beside a fully glass-fronted store.

The security guard inside sees us coming and opens the door to invite us in.

Aside from two members of staff, we're the only ones here.

Perfect.

"Good morning, Mr. Callahan," one of them gushes as she strides over with a smile on her face. "Lorelei," she says, turning to the woman currently hiding behind me. Her hand trembles slightly in mine.

It's bizarre. She is so strong in so many ways, and yet, at the flip of a coin, everything can change.

I've seen it twice in two days now, and I can't say I like it very much.

No. I fucking hate it.

"My name is Magda. I'll be assisting you today."

Tugging Lorelei around in front of me, I allow Magda to get a good look at her.

"Okay, I think I've already got some fantastic ideas for you. Sir, if you'd like to take a seat," Magda says, gesturing to the back of the store. "Lorelei and I will get started. My colleague will get you both drinks, and if there is anything we can do during your time with us, please, don't hesitate to ask."

Lorelei remains frozen on the spot, not that Magda seems

to have noticed. She's too busy mentally dressing her in luxury gowns that will make her sing tonight.

Reaching out, I grip her upper arm and duck my mouth to her ear.

"Trust her. She knows what she's doing." She trembles again, although something tells me that it's more of a shudder this time.

"I don't," Lorelei hisses back. "This...this isn't the kind of place I shop."

"Today it is. Consider this a work event. I require you to represent Callahan Enterprises in the way we see fit. You're just doing your job, Lorelei."

29

LORELEI

"Okay," Magda says with a wide smile on her face as she rubs her hands together.

She eyes me like I'm her new favorite toy and I'm about to be subjected to a whole new kind of playtime.

My stomach knots and my hands tremble.

It's not just her overexcitement that makes me feel more anxious than I ever want to experience, but this whole place.

My heart races as I drag my eyes from the perfectly styled woman before me and gaze around the store.

Everything about it screams perfection, from its designer labels to its almost mirrored floor, which reflects the strategically placed lighting and artistic mannequins.

I do not belong here.

I find Kian relaxing back on one of the huge couches with one ankle resting on the other knee, but while I might have expected him to have his nose back in his cell, his sole focus is me.

It doesn't help in any way.

"I know exactly what we need to try," Magda gushes excitedly, but I'm barely paying any attention.

Kian's lips curl up in what I assume is meant to be a supportive kind of smile, but it does very little to calm me. The only thing it manages to achieve is to put me more on edge.

Not only do I feel like a fish out of water, but my boss, that man I always try to stand strong against, has a front-row seat to it.

Hold your head up high, Lorelei.

This is your job.

"Great," I lie, turning back to Magda just in time to see her pull a stunning royal blue gown from the rack before us.

It's the kind of thing that Tatum would wear and look a million dollars in.

Me, however...

I trail around behind her, trying to look enthusiastic as she adds another four gowns to the rail. She's pulling it along with as much ease as I'm sure she does her designer suitcase on the morning of a vacation.

"Let's go and see if we have a winner, shall we?" she asks excitedly as she leads me to the dressing room.

I lost Kian's attention a while ago. I felt it the moment he looked down. A weird coolness washed over my body, a coolness I've tried really hard not to think about too much. But as I move toward the dressing room at the back of the store, I can't help but look over my shoulder.

The second I do, my eyes collide with his and a shot of adrenaline shoots through my veins.

I might not have any interest in being his date to anything, but he knew exactly what he was doing with this: taking me to a charity event that supports underprivileged young footballers. This is my kryptonite.

I may not be able to put much money into the pot, but I will support this cause in every way I can. Even if it's only with my presence and sharing it on my pitiful social media platform.

I can't say no. And that means I have to stand beside the mighty Kian Callahan and look the part.

Something flutters down low...he's going to wear a tux.

Oh, help me, God.

"Nope. Nope. Nope," Magda says when I pull back the curtain on the black dress she selected. "It's beautiful, but no. Get back in there."

She pulls the curtain closed with a flourish, leaving me once again standing in the middle of the biggest dressing room I've ever seen.

My own reflection stares back at me from all three walls, and I hesitantly look at myself.

She's right, the dress is beautiful, but it's not the one. I don't expect to feel comfortable in any item of clothing from a shop as exclusive as this one. I feel like I'm wearing a costume, not a luxury dress that costs more than a car, I'm sure.

Obviously, there are no price tags on anything. I don't want to imagine how many figures would be staring back at me if there were tags.

My stomach lurches at the thought of how much money Kian might be throwing away just to have me attend this event with him.

He certainly wouldn't have to if he invited Sasha or any of the numerous wealthy socialites he usually spends time with.

Blowing out a long, slow breath, I will myself to put them out of my mind.

You are worthy of this, Lorelei.

You are as worthy as all those other women.

Turning to the final option, I let my eyes roam down the stunning royal blue dress before reaching for it.

Here goes nothing.

The gown's weight shocks me when I remove it from the hanger, but it feels like silk as I step into it and pull it up my body.

My skin erupts with goosebumps as I adjust the single strap over my shoulder and reach for the side zipper.

I haven't looked up, but I don't need to. I already know this is the one.

Was this how Tate felt when she tried her wedding dress on?

Shaking that thought from my head, I finally look up.

"Oh my god."

My stomach knots so tightly, it hurts as my heart begins to race.

This dress...it...

Fuck.

Was it made for me?

My chest heaves as I stand there staring at myself in disbelief.

The smooth lines of my body, the way it cinches in my waist, smooths over my hips and pushes my tits into the perfect place is mind-blowing.

"How are you doing in there?" Magda asks, impatiently waiting outside for me to reveal myself.

I'm pretty sure she thought she hid her disappointment when the other three dresses didn't have the desired effect, but I could read her every thought.

This one is going to change everything, though.

My hand trembles slightly as I reach for the heavy curtain cutting me off, and I suck in a deep breath as I prepare for her reaction.

But it turns out that it doesn't matter how deep that breath was; I could never have been prepared for the ridiculous screech she lets out the second her eyes land on me.

"Yes, yes, yes. That is the one," she announces excitedly, her eyes a little glassy with pride and awe.

Having been disturbed by Magda's over-the-top reaction, footsteps race our way before a large shadow appears at the entrance to the dressing rooms.

"What's—oh fuck," Kian gasps the second his eyes find me.

Heat unfurls inside me as he slowly takes me in from head to toe.

But it's got nothing on the moment his eyes find mine. They're nothing but deep pools of desire, and damn if they don't suck me right in.

"She's going to show you up in that dress, Mr. Callahan," Magda tells him.

His smirk ensures his bottom lip is released by his teeth.

"As it should be. Please can you ensure Lorelei has everything she is going to need for that dress? Your colleague already has my credit card details."

With one last smoldering look, he turns on his heels and walks away.

"I-I already have shoes and a purse," I stutter like an idiot.

Kian shakes his head.

"Everything, Magda," he instructs before walking away.

With a beaming smile, Magda announces, "I know exactly what you need to complete this outfit," and then rushes behind Kian.

"Are you really accompanying me to this appointment?" I ask as Kian slides out of the car behind me, in front of what is arguably the most famous salon in the city.

Women wait months to get an appointment here. God only knows how he managed to get one at the last minute.

"Yes. Something tells me that you'd run away if I left you alone right now," he says confidently, standing to his full height beside me on the sidewalk.

With his hand on the small of my back, he guides me toward the entrance with his words ringing in my ears.

Would I have tried running if he sent me to do all this on my own?

Yes. One hundred percent, I would have run.

I may not have totally defied him. I possibly would have bought a new dress, although my limit would have been a trip to Macy's, not the boutique he took me to. But I definitely wouldn't have been standing in the reception of this salon with the most groomed woman I've ever seen in real life staring back at me.

She's beautiful, sure. Wide eyes and nice high cheekbones, but she's trying too hard. I bet she would look even better without the filler, fake lashes, and makeup. But that's just my opinion. I'm not exactly an expert.

I'm half decent at doing my own makeup, and I've figured out a decent routine for my curly hair over the years that I often get compliments, but that's about my limit. Everything about me is natural, and I intend to keep it that way.

Mom loves all this stuff. But then, she has spent her entire life trying to be someone she's not. Whereas all I want to be is nothing like the woman who birthed me.

"Mr. Callahan," the woman gushes, staring at him with blatant come-fuck-me eyes.

Does every woman in his city know this man standing beside me?

Yes. Yes, they do.

"It's so wonderful to see you. It's been too long," she continues, resting her forearms against the desk and pushing her modest chest up to give him a show.

But to her disappointment—and my delight, not that I'd admit that to anyone—his eyes don't so much as flicker to her chest.

His reaction to her is nothing like the one he had to me in that dress earlier.

"Lorelei has a hair and makeup appointment," he states, completely unaffected by this woman's attempt at flirting with him.

"Oh, yes," she breathes before finally ripping her eyes from him and glancing at me.

Both her eyebrows shoot up.

I barely contain the need to roll my eyes the second she looks at the computer.

She taps away before announcing, "Yes, we have you in one of the private rooms upstairs. I'll take you right up if you want to follow me."

Reluctantly, I follow her, and I'm hardly surprised when the tapping of Kian's shoes against the tiles beneath us rings out behind me.

She takes us to an elevator at the back of the salon and escorts us upstairs.

The whole way, she attempts to engage Kian in conversation while completely ignoring my presence.

"If you need anything during your stay with us, please don't hesitate to reach out," she says before none too discreetly slipping Kian a business card. Something tells me that it doesn't hold the number for the salon...

Thankfully, my stylist is much more excited to see me, although that doesn't mean that he doesn't check out Kian the second he steps into the room.

"Lorelei," he sings, rushing over to take my hands and kiss both of my cheeks. "I'm Richie, and I'm going to work my magic on your hair today." Releasing my hands, he reaches for my locks. "Beautiful curls. And in such good condition as well."

I stand there while he inspects me before ushering me over toward his station. After wrapping a gown around me, I take a seat, allowing him to continue with...well, whatever he's doing, and move my hair this way and that while muttering to himself.

My eyes catch Kian's in the mirror, and I can barely hold in my laugh at his expression.

Everyone might know him here, but it's more than obvious that he hasn't attended an appointment with anyone else. That thought does things to my insides that it really shouldn't.

I'm no more important than any other woman he's attended an event with. I'm just...more of a flight risk.

I smirk, loving that he has no idea how to handle a woman who isn't falling at his feet.

There's a knock on the door, and a woman enters with a tray in her hand and two glasses of champagne.

"No, thank you. I'll take a black coffee if you have it," Kian says, having made himself comfortable on a couch in the corner. "Lorelei can have both of those." His eyes lock on mine again. "I think she's going to need it."

30

KIAN

I stand in front of the full-length mirror in my dressing room and adjust myself for the millionth time since putting my dinner suit on.

I've been rocking a semi since the moment I raced into the dressing room at the boutique, thinking that something was wrong.

Something was very fucking wrong.

Lorelei in that dress.

Fuck.

I bite down on my curled fist at the image of her standing before me in that fitted royal blue gown.

My cock gets harder again.

I've jerked off three times since getting back here, but I'm still fucking hard. And I still can't get her out of my head.

I thought that blowing off Sasha and taking Lorelei as my date tonight was genius.

I mean, it is fucking genius, because as much as Lorelei annoys the shit out of me with her defiance and need to rile me up in any way that she can, Sasha—all the others—are worse.

All they do is try to impress me. Try to make themselves perfect in the hope that I might want them for more than a night.

None of them have yet to do either of those things.

Sure, they're fun for an evening. They've given me what I needed. But there has never been anything more to it.

But with Lorelei...despite everything, I'm quickly learning that I enjoy spending time with her.

She's different. Her attitude toward me is refreshing. And trying to figure her out, to peel back a few of the steely layers she has wrapped around her, is fucking addictive.

I'm pretty sure she believes that she's closed off and giving nothing away. But she's wrong. Every single day, I learn more about my new assistant, and every single day, I need more.

"Fuck it," I mutter, attempting to hide my semi for the final time.

Marching out of my dressing room, I swipe my cell and wallet from the end of the bed and head toward the exit.

We may have only parted ways an hour ago after the longest hair and makeup appointment in history, but I'm already yearning to see her all dressed up.

"Good evening, sir," Jamie says from his position beside the limo idling outside my apartment block.

Do I think Lorelei will hate such a show of wealth when we roll up to collect her?

Absolutely, yes.

A smirk curls on my lips as I slide into the back of the limo.

I can't fucking wait to see her face.

I sit back and watch the city pass me by as my anticipation increases for the night ahead.

If I didn't know better, I might even say I was excited.

My knock rings out in the silence of Lorelei's hallway.

I shake my head, unsurprised that she's making me wait.

Anything to infuriate me.

I knock again, picturing her standing on the other side of the door with a mischievous glint in her eyes.

Pain in the ass.

I knock for a third time, the joke becoming less and less funny.

"Open the door, Lorelei. I know you're there."

It takes a few seconds, but finally, the sound of movement inside the apartment hits my ears before the lock releases and the door opens.

A rush of her sweet perfume assaults my nose a beat before she appears before me.

Fuck.

If I thought I had a semi earlier...

"Jesus, Lorelei," I mutter, my hand coming up to my mouth just in case I'm drooling.

I'd seen the final hair and makeup, and I'd seen the dress, but my imagination couldn't put it together as well as this.

"You look..."

"Wow, have I really made Kian Callahan lose his words?" she teases as she slips out of her apartment and locks up.

I take a step back, giving her some space, but it's about all I'm capable of.

"Are we going to this thing or just hanging out in my hallway? I've got to be honest, you overpaid for all this," she says, gesturing to herself, "if you planned on spending the night here."

"We're going," I say gruffly, already hating the idea of sharing her with anyone else tonight.

With my hand on the small of her back, I guide her toward the elevator, willing my body to get a grip of itself.

I should not be this affected by a woman. Especially a woman I made my assistant and a huge part of my life.

The second the elevator doors close, the air turns thick.

"You look beautiful," I say honestly, my voice rougher than usual.

Lorelei stands tall beside me, not giving me even a clue how she feels about that compliment before she responds with, "You don't scrub up too badly either."

One side of my mouth twitches with a smile.

"I didn't think you had a thing for billionaires in designer suits."

"Don't read too much into my compliment, sir. I was merely being polite."

Oh, ouch.

"Good to know. I was being entirely sincere. Every other man at the event tonight is going to wish they were me when I walk in with you."

"Maybe tonight won't be a total bust, then. I guess there could be worse outcomes than hooking up with a hot, wealthy guy."

Something bitter and poisonous shoots through my veins and my lips part to respond, but the doors open and Lorelei glides out. I swear, she could be floating for how smoothly she walks.

My eyes automatically drop to her ass that's perfectly wrapped in the royal blue fabric.

Is she wearing panties under there?

"You flash bastard," she announces long before she gets to the exit.

Jamie notices us coming and rushes to open the doors.

"Good evening, Miss Lorelei," he says, his eyes almost bugging out of his head and his cheeks blazing bright red at the sight of her. "You look incredible."

"Thank you, Jamie. I really appreciate it."

She shoots me a look over her shoulder, her eyes dancing with mischief and her smile downright filthy.

Christ. Tonight is going to be hard. Pun very much intended.

With Jamie's attention fully on Lorelei, I adjust myself once more and trail behind her.

"Well, this is fancy," she muses as I join her in the back of the limo.

"I thought your dress deserved it."

"My dress?" she deadpans as I reach for the bottle of champagne chilling on the other side of the limo.

"Yes. I knew the person wearing it would hate it."

"And you would be right."

"Tonight, we do things my way."

I frown when she throws her head back laughing.

Not the reaction I was expecting.

"What?" I ask when her giggles continue.

She sobers as I pass her a glass of champagne.

She takes a sip, making me wait.

"When do we have a day when we do things any other way?"

"I listen to you," I argue.

"Do you?"

"Yes."

"Okay, so you might listen, but that doesn't mean you agree or go with my suggestions."

"I'm your boss."

"Ah, yes, and that means you're always right. I keep forgetting that."

I watch as she takes another sip, her red-stained lips pressing against the glass and then her throat rippling as she swallows.

I wonder if the skin there is as sweet as I imagine...

As she reaches into her purse and looks at a message on her cell, my eyes drop to the split that's cut almost to her thigh, exposing her muscular, tanned leg.

My mouth waters—I can't help myself.

"Are you going to behave tonight?" I ask. There's a part of me hoping that she'll say no and that she'll be naughty with me, but there's another part that keeps reminding me that I'm her boss. That she's my sister-in-law's best friend. That she hates me and everything I stand for.

My head might know all those things, but my body—my dick—doesn't give a single fuck.

"Oh my god," Lorelei gasps, dragging me from my salacious thoughts. "Tell me that we don't have to get out here?"

I glance up to see what she's talking about and find a huge crowd, paparazzi, and a red carpet.

"I didn't buy you that dress for nothing."

Swallowing what's left of my champagne, I take her glass from her hand and sit forward.

"Ready?" I ask as Jamie pulls to a stop in front of the red carpet in preparation to let us out.

"No. You can get out here and soak all that up. Jamie can take me around the back or something."

I chuckle. "Absolutely not. You're walking in on my arm whether you like it or not."

She harrumphs, keeping her eyes on the crowd.

"You're not nervous, are you, Temptress?"

"Pfft, never. I just...I'm no one. They don't want photographs of me."

Jamie opens the door, and the excitement from outside immediately fills the limo.

Sure, we might be no one compared to the celebrities Kieran manages to get to these kinds of events, but still, I have every confidence that our photos will grace plenty of news outlets come sunrise.

"I strongly disagree." Without another word, I move toward the open doors.

Cameras immediately begin flashing before I hear my name murmured in the crowd.

Leaning back into the limo, I hold my hand out for my plus one. I didn't want to mention it, but the only reason people are interested in my arrival is to know who I've brought with me.

I've been connected to numerous high-profile women in the past, so they're probably expecting someone they know. Someone like Sasha.

Well, they're about to get a shock.

Tingles shoot up my arm the second she slides her small hand into mine, and it only gets worse as she emerges from the car.

No one here knows her name, but that doesn't mean she's any less than any other woman who's walked in her shoes. If anything, she's more, and that thought is fucking terrifying.

"Kian, who is your date?"

"Turn this way."

"Kian?"

"What's her name?"

The second Lorelei is standing, I wrap my arm around her waist and pin her to my side as the volume and excitement around us increase, along with the incessant camera flashes.

"This is insane," she whisper-shouts.

Ducking my head low, I brush my lips against her ear, letting everyone make what they want of the intimate move as we continue toward the entrance.

"Welcome to my world, Temptress."

She shudders against me, and my hand tightens on her waist.

We make our way down the red carpet, turning each way for photos before someone else arrives behind us and steals our attention.

"Oh my god," Lorelei gasps the second we're inside the venue for tonight's event. "That was insane."

"Ow," I complain when she suddenly slaps my arm. "What was that for?"

"Why the hell didn't you warn me?"

"I wasn't aware I had to," I say honestly. She may not have grown up in his life, but she's been friends with Tate for long enough to know she attends these kinds of events.

"Unbelievable."

Another couple steps into the building—the woman immediately locks eyes with me, and I nod politely. She's an actress, one that Lorelei would recognize if she stopped glaring at me for even a second.

They move away without a word as a loud cheer erupts from the crowd outside.

"Ah, sounds like my little brother might have arrived," I say. But when I look at Lorelei she's got her nose stuck in her cell again.

Finally, she puts it back into her purse so she can go and see what's going on.

I follow her lead, watching as Kieran works the crowd like a pro.

Lorelei balks "Has he brought two dates?"

"Quite possibly. He's—"

"A Callahan," she interrupts.

"Hey," I argue.

"What? It's true and you know it."

I shake my head, unable to argue as Kieran gets closer, his dates close behind him.

I don't recognize either of them, but that doesn't mean they're not famous in their own right. Kieran has an image to uphold, and he always chooses his dates wisely. Just like I do... or did...until tonight.

He bursts through the doors with more energy than any adult should possess.

"The king is in the house."

"Oh, Kingston is here?" Lorelei asks without missing a beat and looking around as if he's about to emerge from somewhere.

My brother's eyes land on my date and then widen to the point I'm sure they're going to pop.

"Lorelei Tempest, what a surprise," he says before pulling her in for a hug as if they're best friends and spinning her around.

"Put my date down, asshole," I complain.

Kieran stops, his eyes finding mine.

"Calm down, K. I'm not going to steal your date. I know how important she is to you."

"Shall we go and get a drink?" I suggest, once again wrapping my arm around Lorelei's waist and attempting to steer her away from my shit-stirring brother.

"Yes," she says happily. "But only if Kieran and his dates join us. I'd love to hear more about how important I am."

"I think Kieran will probably be needed elsewhere. This is his event, after all."

"Nah, they can all wait for me." Throwing an arm around each of his dates, he leads the way toward the bar.

"Sorry about him," I whisper to Lorelei.

She smirks, her eyes twinkling.

Oh yeah, I made a massive fucking mistake putting those two together, and something tells me that I'm never going to hear the end of it.

31

LORELEI

"**B**ottoms up, baby," Kieran calls before lifting his tequila shot and downing it in one quick swallow.

The two ladies on either side of him watch him closely as they sip their champagne.

No sooner did we join them at the bar after we first arrived than Kieran was whisked away to deal with some official business, much to his disgruntlement. He wanted to party, that much was obvious.

With the season in full swing, I can't imagine he manages to find much time to kick back, but it seems that he's happily forgetting the pressure that's on his shoulders right now and making the most of his rare Friday night off. I'm sure it'll be back to business tomorrow.

Kian shakes his head as he sips on his whiskey while I mirror Kieran and down my shot.

My cell buzzes again, but this time I ignore it.

"What?" I ask when I catch Kian studying me closely.

I might be willing to support this cause, but I still have to spend my night with all these people. I deserve a drink or, I don't know, five, maybe.

Add the shot to the champagne that's already bubbling through my veins, and I'm probably a little too tipsy already, but I figure we have a full sit-down meal shortly.

It'll be fine. Everything will be fine.

"So, Lori, what did my big brother here do to convince you to be his date tonight?"

"I asked," Kian grunts, making Kieran throw his head back and laugh.

His dates simultaneously follow suit, tittering along with him as if it'll help their chances of securing something serious with him by laughing at whatever he finds funny.

I don't mean to be judgy, but when I overheard them talking about their "jobs" earlier and one of them was expressing how annoying it was that Daddy refused to fund a six-month trip around Europe, I was done.

"Come off it. I saw how pissed she was at you yesterday. There is no way in hell she'd have just agreed."

"Then maybe you don't know enough about the situation as you think you do."

Kieran is about to respond when I add, "He's talking shit. He blackmailed me into coming."

Kieran's face lights up like a kid who's just been told it's Christmas day.

"I knew it," he says punching the air, a smug grin spreading across his lips.

"Asshole," Kian mutters before grasping my elbow lightly and turning me away from his brother and his harem. "Let's go and check out the silent auction before dinner is served."

With a smile at Kieran, I allow Kian to guide me to the room where all the auction items are kept.

I can predict what I'll find inside. Luxury breaks in the most exclusive resorts worldwide, courtesy of Callahan Enterprises, of course. Stays on billionaires' yachts. Luxury boxes for Chicago Chiefs games throughout the season. There are tickets for hockey games, baseball, and basketball. There are track days in cars I've never heard of, flying lessons, and a whole host of other things that get the wealthiest excited enough to pull out their fat checkbooks and make some unbelievable offers.

"How much?" I gawp, looking at the most recent price someone has written down for the exact box Kian and I watched the game from on Sunday. "Did it cost you this much to take me?"

He smirks at me but shakes his head, refusing to answer before scribbling something on another lot.

I don't bother looking at what he's bidding on. It's only going to make my head explode, I'm sure.

Walking off, I take in everything else that is on offer, discreetly watching as men and women alike place eyewatering bids. As someone who's had to fight for every single cent she's ever had, it's mind-boggling to watch people throw it around like it's nothing.

I'm staring at a photo of a mega yacht when Kian steps up behind me. I don't need to look around to know it's him. The tingles and the way my body heats tell me everything I need.

His large hand lands on my waist, and I curse myself when I flinch. I don't want him to know I'm affected by his presence, but I feel it's a fight that I'm losing.

He moves closer still, the heat of his body spreading down my back, making every single inch of my skin prickle with awareness.

His breath rushes over my exposed neck, and I noticeably shudder.

Squeezing my eyes closed, I silently pray that he won't have felt it. But I know he has.

"Have you finished?"

A bitter laugh erupts.

"Have I finished?" I balk.

Does he really think I was about to offer up the next ten years of my salary to spend seven days in the Mediterranean on this mega yacht?

"Let's go and find our seats." His hand once again slips into mine, sending a rush of warmth up my arm.

Instantly, a calmness washes through me.

"The menu for tonight looks incredible," he says after nodding at someone I don't recognize.

"I wouldn't know. I haven't seen the invite," I mutter.

He chuckles beside me before leading me into a huge ballroom.

"Wow," I breathe, attempting to take it all in.

They might be raising money for underprivileged kids, but they haven't held back with the glitz and glamor.

"Wouldn't the money that's been spent on all this have been better off going to the cause?" I ask quietly as Kian studies the table plan and finds our seats.

"In theory, yes. But things aren't always that black and white."

I want to ask more, but I keep my mouth shut, fearing it will only irritate me more.

I need to remember that all those insane figures I just read on the auction lots are going to this charity. It'll help many young athletes with their dreams of playing professional sports that, for whatever reason, they can't achieve on their own. That is what tonight is about...so why we need four-foot floral decorations on our tables and gold cutlery. I've no idea.

Kian holds my chair out for me, being the gentleman that I catch glimpses of every now and then, before slipping his jacket off and sitting beside me.

"Would it be naive of me to ask what you think?" he murmurs.

I've been to events before. But I have never experienced something on this scale.

"Yes."

I squirm in my seat. I'm further out of my depth than I ever have been in my life.

I thought the boutique and the salon were bad, but this... this is next level.

Kian's hand brushes across my back before his thumb caresses my bare shoulder.

"If it makes you feel any better, you're the most beautiful woman here."

My insides tighten at the honesty in his tone.

"Is that supposed to make me feel better?" I hiss, trying to hold onto my irritation and not allow myself to be swept along with his smooth words.

"It isn't meant to do anything. I'm just telling you the truth. Everyone is enthralled by you."

"Kian," I warn.

"They all want to know who you are."

I tense, panic shooting through me.

Why didn't I think about this?

I bet there are people out there right now doing a deep dive on Google to find out who Kian Callahan's date for this event is. They will want to know what family I belong to, if I'm worthy of a man of his stature.

A bitter laugh dances on the tip of my tongue, but I swallow it.

I already know what conclusion they're going to come to.

I'm not worthy. Nowhere even close.

"I don't want that. I'm no one."

The need to escape my own thoughts becomes too much and I reach for my purse, grabbing my cell again and hating that my nose itches with emotion. I almost groan when I find more of the same messages waiting for me.

Lock it down, Lorelei.

You're working.

Be professional.

But that's all shot to shit when Kian reaches out and tucks two fingers beneath my chin, giving me little choice but to turn to look at him.

His concerned dark green eyes lock on mine, searching for a few seconds as if he'll find the answers he wants within them.

"You're someone, Lorelei. Trust me, you're very much someone."

My lips part in shock, and his eyes drop to them.

My heart does a little somersault, and my temperature soars.

He wants to kiss you.

Here.

In front of all these people.

He wouldn't, though.

Would he?

"You two look lonely," a familiar deep voice sings before the chair beside me is pulled out, allowing a large body to drop into it.

Kian's fingers instantly drop, leaving me cold and bereft of his touch.

"How are you enjoying your first KC Foundation event, Lori?" Kieran asks with excitement glittering in his eyes.

I may have witnessed him do a shot or two earlier, but that look isn't from alcohol. It's from knowing he's doing something good. It's pride.

"It's...a lot."

He smirks. "So it should be. I planned it."

"Christ," Kian mutters.

Kieran leans closer. "Want to know a secret, Lori?"

"No, she doesn't," Kian hisses.

"Calm down, Bro. I'm not gonna tell her that I was potty trained before you. Late starter in life, this one," Kieran adds.

"Fuck's sake. Don't listen to a word he says about me."

"Don't worry, K. Lori is a smart girl. She knows the truth when she hears it. Anyway, I digress. Do you know the best way to fleece the wealthy out of their money?"

"Steal it?" I deadpan.

"Nah, way too much hard work, babe."

Kian sucks in a sharp breath through his teeth, but as much as I might want to see his expression right now, I don't take my attention from Kieran.

"Stroke their egos. Make them feel special. Treat them. And in return," he says, sitting back and holding his arm out to gesture to the room, "you can create magic."

"Arrogant fuck."

I can't help but snort at Kian's comment.

"Takes one to know one," Kieran quips, shooting his big brother a look before returning his gaze to me. "You want anything out of my big brother here, I just gave you the keys to the castle, babe."

"I don't want anything from Kian."

A deep laugh rumbles deep in Kieran's chest.

"Babe, from how close the two of you were sitting when we came over, I'd beg to differ. And anyway, every woman on the planet wants something from the three of us. With King now off the market, it's allowed me and K here to do God's work."

"Fuck my life. Is it too late to change tables?" Kian barks.

"You wouldn't want to be anywhere else, and you know it. By the end of the night, Lori is going to know everything."

And to my surprise, Kieran does a very good job on following through with that promise.

Despite having two dates to entertain him, tonight's MVP spends almost all his time talking to me and winding Kian up to the point I'm pretty sure steam started coming out of his ears.

It was during a particularly amusing story about Kian's first crush that he'd finally had enough, shoved his chair back, and stormed away.

"You're evil," I tell Kieran honestly.

"Pfft, asshole is more than used to it. Funny, though, he's never cared this much before. I wonder why that is."

As Kian promised, dinner was incredible. And with a Callahan brother sitting on either side of me, I was saved from making small talk with Kieran's dates or the others sitting at our table.

Kian's still gone when the compere steps up on stage and asks for everyone's attention.

Silence falls around the room before he finds Kieran in the crowd and invites him up to the stage to a thunderous round of applause.

I'm so lost watching the man of the moment move through the crowd, shaking hands with men and kissing women's cheeks as he goes, that I don't notice Kian return.

"That's sure to help his ego," he mutters, reaching for his drink and draining the glass.

"He's doing a good thing. Let him have it."

I feel Kian's side-eye burn down my face, but I don't turn to look. Like the rest of the room, I'm too enthralled with his little brother.

32

KIAN

I'm immensely proud of Kieran. Firstly, for standing up to our father and refusing to bend to his wishes. Kieran had a dream, a dream that he knew he could make a reality. He didn't care that our father had his life already planned out. He knew what he wanted, and he's worked his ass off every single day to get it.

He's kind, caring, smart, determined, hard-working, and a kickass football player. He's also the best little brother anyone could ask for, despite him being a bit of an asshole at times.

But none of that stops a little bitterness trickling through my veins as the entire room—Lorelei included—focuses every bit of their attention on him as he makes his speech introducing the foundation and the good it does.

Kingston is the boss. He's the oldest who's been handed everything.

Kieran is the headstrong one who carved out his own life and gives people a reason to talk about him other than the surname he was born with.

And then there is me.

The middle child.

My stomach knots. I hate that I feel like this.

I've had a good life. No, a great fucking life.

I've never wanted for anything. I had the best education

money could buy. I've had the vacations, the experiences. Lived in lavish homes and driven fancy cars.

But despite all that, I can't help feeling like I'm always overlooked.

I have never been anyone's priority.

I'm just the one in the middle who's expected to do as he's told and toe the line.

Ripping my eyes away from the enigmatic man on stage, I turn to Lorelei.

She looks tense, and I don't think it's just because of the event, but also because of whatever she keeps looking at on her cell. I have a very good idea who's putting that expression on her face and continuing to convince her that she's not good enough.

I should have punched that motherfucker harder.

What I said to her earlier is true.

She is hands down the most beautiful woman here tonight.

And it's not just because of how she looks. It's what I know she hides inside underneath the chip on her shoulder and the sassy attitude.

She isn't from this life, I get that. And I also understand the reason she views rich people the way she does. Hell, half the time she's right. We are a bunch of arrogant assholes.

But there's so much more to some of us than that. Or, at least, I really fucking hope there is.

With her fully distracted, I study her closely.

Her curly hair is pinned up away from her neck with pins encrusted with blue diamonds. Not that she knows that, of course. Just the pins in her hair tonight cost more than most cars. She'd lose her shit if she knew that our lunch date between her appointments earlier was to allow me time to get them delivered to the salon.

But it was worth it. And if I fuck all this up in the weeks and months to come, then she can pawn them and take the cash.

My chest tightens at the thought of her discarding them—me—so easily. But I know she could.

This is just a job for her.

Sure, she might flinch when I touch her and give me those "come fuck me" eyes every now and then, but I know she's not feeling the pull toward me that I am to her.

It's because she doesn't want you...

Shaking my head, I force my eyes away from her. It's unlikely, but she could become bored of Kieran and turn back to me.

Who am I kidding? As far as everyone around me is concerned, there is only one Callahan in attendance tonight. And it's not the one sitting at this table.

I scan the room, taking in table after table, mentally working out how much money Kieran has raised from ticket sales alone, when my eyes lock on someone I was hoping not to see tonight.

And she's looking right fucking at me.

Fuck.

Sasha smirks.

Dread seeps through me.

When I refused to add her name as my plus one tonight, I knew she wouldn't let it go.

Before Lorelei started, Sasha may have been the one to be sitting beside me tonight. She would be the easy choice. I know what I'm getting with her. Taking someone new to an event like this is a risk.

Bringing Lorelei was also a huge risk, if the red flags waving above Sasha's head right now are anything to go by. But while Lorelei might not feel like she belongs here, I'm confident that she can hold her own.

Her attitude, her awe to all of this is addicting. The way her eyes widened when we walked into this room earlier, full of amazement, was enthralling.

I love giving her these experiences. Taking her places and

letting her see things she never thought she would. It's like seeing a flower bloom for the first time.

Sasha is the first to look away. There was no way in hell it was going to be me. I'm not allowing her to think she's won anything.

A round of applause erupts again, signaling that Kieran's speech has come to an end. I look up as he hands the mic back, and the compere invites everyone to visit the auction lots in the room to the right before retiring for drinks and dancing in the room to the left.

No one moves as Kieran weaves his way back through the tables. Almost every person he passes stops him to say something or shake hands.

Pride for my little brother continues to grow, thankfully squashing my own bitterness down enough that I can ignore it.

"Good, huh?" he says, modest as ever before shocking the fuck out of me and pulling Lorelei in for a celebratory hug.

The fuck?

"Who knew you could deliver a speech with as much ease as you do a touchdown," Lorelei praises, making something poisonous fill my stomach.

The second he releases her, I wrap my arm around her waist and pull her into my side. Where she fucking belongs.

He brought two dates. He has more than enough women for one night. He doesn't need to take mine as well.

Mine.

That word hits me upside the head so hard the room spins around me.

When I come back to myself, I find Kieran grinning at me like an idiot.

"What?" I snap.

"Oh, nothing, Bro," he teases, looking between me and the woman tucked into my side. "Thought you'd want to congratulate me, that's all."

"I thought we were stroking other people's egos tonight."

His smirk grows. "Oh, I don't know. You certainly need something stroking."

My grip on Lorelei tightens as the true meaning of his words slams into me at full force.

"We're out. Congrats on another successful night."

"Wait, you can't go. I want to dance with your girl."

I pause, fire flooding through my veins.

"Lorelei isn't my girl," I hiss. "She is my assistant."

Before he can say another word, I lead her forward and toward the doors that will allow us to exit.

Lorelei moves silently through the crowds of people lingering around, probably waiting for a chance to speak to tonight's star.

We move through the bar, thankfully everyone giving us a wide birth and allowing us to make a beeline for the main entrance.

I need to call Jamie to bring the car around, but I also have no intention of stopping. From the comments Lorelei has made about tonight, something tells me that she won't object to making an early departure.

The doors appear before us and I pick up speed, but I'm not fast enough.

"Leaving so soon, Mr. Callahan?"

Fuck.

Lorelei stops dead. I've no idea if she recognized Sasha's voice or if she can hear the venom in her tone just as easily as I can.

Before I can push her forward and pretend I didn't hear anything, Lorelei spins around.

"Sasha, how lovely to see you. Kian didn't tell me that you'd be here tonight."

With a sigh, I also turn around. Just in time to see Sasha sneer at Lorelei.

"Could say the same about you."

"Me?" Lorelei says, pointing at herself, a sickly-sweet smile playing on her lips. "I'm only here because—"

"She's my girlfriend," I finish before Lorelei gets a chance to finish her sentence.

Lorelei's body freezes in my hold, but she doesn't immediately refute my comment.

Sasha rears back as if I just slapped her, although somehow, she manages to keep the fake smile on her equally fake lips.

"I see. Well, congratulations," she forces out before turning her attention to me. "I didn't think you were one to fuck your subordinates, Kian."

Lorelei trembles and I squeeze her waist, silently begging her to keep a lid on it.

"We can't always predict these things," I explain tersely.

"Apparently not, seeing as I was meant to be here with you tonight."

"I'm sure you found a wonderful man to put up with you for the event. He's probably looking for you as we speak. Might want to run along."

Sasha's face turns beet red, and I just about manage to catch my laugh before it erupts.

"We should go, we have plans. Come on, babe. The car is waiting."

Ready to make her escape, Lorelei bids Sasha a forced goodbye before spinning around and marching toward the doors.

"Lorelei," I warn darkly as she pushes through them. Thankfully, the crowd and paparazzi from earlier have disappeared, leaving only the valet drivers behind.

"What?" she hisses, spinning on the balls of her feet and glaring me dead in the eyes. "Don't you want her to witness the fallout from that? Am I meant to be the perfect, doting girlfriend now? What. The. Fuck, Kian?"

Tipping my head to the sky, I stare up at the dark, star-filled sky and pray for some strength.

Did I plan to say that? No, I really fucking didn't.

Am I regretting it? Also no.

If it gets Sasha and the numerous others like her off my back for a bit, then, no, I don't fucking regret it.

But then, I look down again and find Lorelei's murderous expression that promises me a whole world of pain, and I begin to second-guess myself.

"It's a smart idea. I'm surprised I didn't think of it sooner," I explain as I dig my hand into my pocket for my cell to message Jamie.

"A smart idea? Fuck, Kian. How was telling your...your fuck buddy that I'm your girlfriend a good idea?"

I continue typing and hit send before acknowledging her question.

Looking up, I hold her angry eyes for a beat. Dropping my cell into my pocket, I take a step closer to her.

Lorelei immediately backs up, but she doesn't get very far, because the railings are still out from earlier.

"Think about it, Temptress. This is a win-win for both of us."

"How is this any kind of win for me?" I open my mouth to respond, but she beats me to it. "I swear to God, if you try spouting some shit about increasing my social status by being photographed with you, then I will hurt you."

Reaching out, I tug her purse from beneath her arm and flip it open.

"What are you doing?" she screeches as I pull out her cell, wake it up, and stare down at the screen.

I find exactly what I was expecting.

Spinning it around, I hold it up for her to see, not that she needs to. She already knows what's waiting for her.

"That is why, Lorelei. *He* is why."

33

LORELEI

I swallow thickly as I stare at numerous notifications of messages from Matt staring back at me.

When I didn't hear anything from him last night or all day, I thought that maybe he'd gotten the message and was finally going to back off.

Apparently, that was wishful thinking.

"You want him to leave you alone?" Kian asks, his voice deadly serious. "Then let me help you."

I shake my head, unable to process all of this.

I barely hear the sound of the car pulling up, and it's not until Kian reaches for my hand that I realize what's happening.

He leads me toward the limo with his hand resting on the small of my back, and after greeting Jamie, who's holding the door open for us, he follows me inside.

The second the door closes behind us, I swear all the air goes with it.

Kian presses the button to raise the privacy screen, and it only compounds the issue.

When he drops into the seat beside me, I swear he's closer than he was on the way here.

His heat burns down the length of my body, and suddenly, my dress feels too small. Suffocating.

"I'm tired," he says after a few seconds, although his voice doesn't convey the feeling he expresses. He sounds fully awake and alert. "Sasha, Claudine...they all want something from me. Something that I don't have to offer them."

He glances at me when I don't respond, but I stay silent and allow him to continue.

"This arrangement will be mutually beneficial for both of us. It'll get Matt off your back, and it'll give me a break."

Picking at my nails, I consider his words now that the shock and initial anger have ebbed away.

"You really want to be my fake boyfriend?"

"Sure, why not?" he asks as if this isn't a big deal.

"But I'm your assistant."

"Bosses and assistants hooking up is pretty common."

"As common as making them cry?" I quip.

"I haven't fucked any of my assistants before, if that's what you're asking."

"And that won't be changing anytime soon. I said fake boyfriend, Kian. F.A.K.E." I'm not sure which one of us I spell it out for.

We're in dangerous territory right now. Territory that I know I need to back away from as fast as I can.

But Kian Callahan is like a flame. I just can't help but touch. Metaphorically, of course.

There will be no touching.

I don't need to look over to know his signature smirk is fully in place.

"Whatever you say, Temptress."

"I won't do anything for your image. I'm not the daughter of some wealthy businessman, or the daughter of a mogul or philanthropist, or an up-and-coming influencer or celeb—

"Good. Fuck all of those."

I sit up straighter and finally look over at him.

The engine rumbles beneath us as Jamie makes his way across the city toward my apartment.

"You're actually serious, aren't you?" I ask in amazement.

"That asshole is harassing you, Lorelei. Do you really think he's going to get bored and just give up?"

I want to say that he will, but I've been saying that for weeks now. Even a black eye hasn't deterred him.

"He won't. But let him think that you've moved on and he might just figure out that it's really over."

"And you really think you being in a 'fake' relationship will force your harem of loyal followers to back off? I'm not sure you're really giving these women's tenacity and determination enough credit."

"There are plenty of other men they can turn their attention to."

"Wow." I laugh, making Kian's eyes widen in surprise. "How much did it hurt to just admit that you're not all that special?"

"Careful, Temptress, I can redact this offer at any time."

I think for a moment. "Seems to me like you're the keenest party here, seeing as you've already announced it."

"I'm not allowing you to be subjected to Sasha's shit."

"How noble of you."

He narrows his eyes in warning as his patience begins to visibly drain.

"Okay, so say I agree to this inane plan; how would it look exactly?"

Kian relaxes back in the seat as if I just agreed. He combs his fingers through his hair as he thinks for a moment.

"It would look exactly like it does now. Only..."

"Only what?" I ask when he trails off. "I'm not sleeping with you. You can forget that."

"I was going to say that you actually have to look like you like me. But—" He shifts even closer and wraps his arm around my shoulders. "If you want to turn this to the more intimate parts of our arrangement, then I'm more than happy to discuss details."

A shudder rips through me when his fingers gently brush the skin just beneath my hairline.

"Kian," I warn.

"What? If we're fake dating each other, there's nothing wrong with us benefiting from it."

"You laid the benefits out a moment ago. Discourage Matt and send your fan club after other eligible bachelors."

"Aw, you think I'm eligible."

"You're insufferable."

"And you're hot. Sue me."

The car slows and I look out, hopeful that I'll find my apartment.

Nope, just a set of lights.

"What are your plans this weekend?"

"Well...I did consider popping to Paris. It's been a while. Or maybe Rome. But it might just be a little too much for a weekend, so I think I'll probably just hang out at home. Maybe have lunch with Tate. Get takeout. Wash my hair."

"Think I prefer the first options."

"Ah, yes, but then you're a billionaire who can charter a jet and go wherever you want in the world at the drop of a hat. Us mere mortals need to book commercial flights and spend hours in an airport."

He smirks. "Having money sure has its benefits." I roll my eyes hard enough to hurt. "Can I take you out?"

"Sorry, I'm busy."

"But we're dating," he sulks, sticking his bottom lip out like a petulant child.

"No, you have floated an idea about us faking it. An idea I have yet to agree to."

"But you're going to," he states arrogantly.

"Am I?" I quiz.

"Of course you are. You know I'm right. And anyway, dating me would be fucking awesome."

"Correct me if I'm wrong, but you've never had a girlfriend before, have you?"

"Lorelei Tempest, did you Google me?" he asks, quirking a brow.

"I think it's only sensible to know as much about my boss as possible."

"And I'm sure whatever shit has been written about me in the media was very enlightening."

"Like you wouldn't believe. All those scorned women you've left in your wake really had a lot to say."

"Lies. All of them."

"Good to know. So...previous girlfriends?"

"You're right. I've never dated anyone seriously. Ever. I'll be good at it, though." He leans closer, allowing his breath to race down my neck. "I know exactly how to treat a woman."

Oh my god.

Without instruction from my brain, my head turns to look at him.

My breath catches and my surroundings vanish as his eyes drop to my lips again.

Do it, I want to scream when he finds my eyes again.

Suddenly, the door is pulled open and we both jump back. One glance out of the window tells me that I'm home now.

I should probably be glad, but honestly, I'm mostly disappointed that our time is over.

"Right, well. Thank you for this enlightening evening. I'll see you on Monday."

I climb out of the limo with Jamie's help and then walk into my building without looking back.

Leave. Please leave.

I'm not sure I could be held responsible for my actions if he were to do anything else.

Hell, the guy just offered to make one of my biggest problems go away.

Sure, he's going to benefit from it too. But still. People—men—don't offer to do things like that for me.

The elevator doors open the second I press the button and I slip inside.

In seconds, I'm closed into the small car, and it jolts around me as it climbs through the building.

A few years ago, I never would have stepped into something so small and enclosed.

It was a fear that was born from my less-than-memorable childhood, and something I never want to think about again. It's also something that I'll forever be grateful to Tate for helping me with.

Pushing thoughts of my former years behind me, I focus on the present and Kian's proposal.

It's crazy, sure. But it also makes a lot of sense.

I have one big problem with it, though.

Who the hell in their right mind will believe that Kian Callahan has lowered his standards enough to choose me?

I'm lost in my own insecurities when the elevator jolts to a stop.

Shit.

My eyes shoot to the little screen to find that I'm one floor below where I need to be.

Jamming my finger against the button for my floor, I pray that it'll kickstart it into moving.

I might be mostly okay with enclosed spaces these days, but getting stuck in an elevator is a very different situation.

I keep pressing the button over and over, but nothing happens.

"Come on, please," I beg, my pulse beginning to race.

I jam my finger against the emergency call button. But nothing happens.

No alarm rings. No voice crackles down the line with supportive words about getting help.

Regretting my decision to run away from Kian the way I did, I weigh my options.

Normally, I'd call Tate. But she's at a different event with King tonight.

Flipping open my purse, I pull my cell out.

I'm immediately assaulted with even more message notifications from Matt.

"This arrangement will be mutually beneficial for both of us. It'll get Matt off your back..."

"Jesus." As if Kian wasn't messing with my head enough already.

The lights above me flicker, and my heart jumps into my throat.

I can't be stuck in here in the dark. I just can't.

Swallowing thickly, I unlock my cell and open my contacts.

I do have other people I could call in an emergency, but it's Kian's contact I find myself staring at.

My thumb hovers over the call button.

Even if he has left, he'll be the closest person.

Suddenly, I'm plunged into darkness.

I stumble back, colliding with the wall as the space around me instantly begins closing in.

My cell ensures it's not completely dark, but one look at the battery and I know it's not going to help me for very long.

Before time runs out, I hit call.

"You've reached Kian Callahan. Please leave a message, and I'll get back to you as soon as I can."

"Motherfucker," I hiss, watching in horror as my cell dies in my hands. "FUUUUCK," I sob, wrapping my arms around myself protectively.

Sliding down the wall, I tuck my legs against my chest and rest my head on my knees. Instantly, I'm six again, and the shouts and screams I remember all too well echo around me.

Ice fills my veins, making my entire body tremble.

I was useless then, and I'm useless now. Unless someone in this building realizes the elevator is out and calls for help, I'm fucked.

I'm going to be here all night.

A loud sob bubbles up my throat as the sound of Mom's screams haunts me just like they used to every night back then.

Screams. Slaps. Sobs. Punches. Grunts. Moans. Threats.

Without realizing it, tears are streaming down my cheeks as I relive everything I've worked so hard to forget.

What is Kian thinking? I'm not the woman he wants to be faking anything with.

I'm just a broken little girl who is the product of her shitty upbringing.

I can't stand beside a man like him.

I don't belong in the world he inhabits.

I'm no one.

Just a broken little girl trying to outrun her nightmares.

34

KIAN

"Shit," I hiss as the building's emergency lighting flickers to life around me.

The front doors burst open before Jamie's voice fills the foyer. "Is she in the elevator?"

"Yeah, it stopped on level five."

"She needs six."

"Yeah," I call, already running toward the stairwell.

Jamie's heavy footfalls follow me as I take the stairs two at a time.

My chest is heaving by the time I hit the fifth floor and fly through the doors that will lead me to the elevator.

It's darker up here than it was downstairs, but I don't let that stop me.

"Lorelei," I bellow the second I get to the closed elevator doors.

There's silence for a beat that allows a little hope to slip in.

Maybe she got out on this floor for some reason. For all I know, she has a friend on this floor.

But despite trying to convince myself, I don't believe a word of it.

She's in there, I know she is.

"Lorelei."

"Kian?" a quiet voice says.

"Yeah, babe. Are you okay?"

Nothing.

"The power's gone out," I explain. "We're gonna get you out, okay?"

Silence.

"Have you called for help?" It's a stupid question, I know, but I ask it anyway.

When she doesn't respond again, I begin to think she's ignoring me, but then I hear her.

"It's dead. No one is answering."

"Shit." Spinning around, I face Jamie. "We need to get her out."

"Leave it to me," he says before confidently striding back down the hallway and disappearing into the stairwell.

The fuck?

"Jamie has gone to get help," I tell her, hoping like hell it's true. "Can you call me so we can talk properly?"

"My cell is dead," she calls back. There's a waver in her voice that makes my heart fracture.

She's not okay.

"Have you been thinking about my offer?" I ask in the hope of distracting her from the situation.

I'm sure I hear a laugh, but I can't be sure.

"Just think about the benefits."

"Not interested in the benefits, Kian. I thought I'd made that clear."

"I'm not talking about sex, Temptress."

"Then what can you possibly offer me?"

"You said you wanted to go to Paris or Rome this weekend. Which would you prefer? I'll book the company jet."

"You're an idiot."

"Maybe so. But I can be your idiot."

As I say those final few words, Jamie rushes into the hallway.

He briefly looks at me questioningly before turning his attention to the elevator.

"Oh shit," I gasp when I find a crowbar in his hands. "Why are you driving around with that?"

"You never know when it might be useful," he mutters before jamming it between the elevator doors and attempting to wrench them open.

"Is that really going to work?" I ask skeptically.

"Do you have any other suggestion?" he snarks, sounding very un-Jamie-like.

"Uh..." I guess not.

"Then, do you want to help?"

Jeez, who knew my driver was so snappy in a crisis?

"Shit," he barks when we finally manage to get the doors to part enough to see that the car isn't fully on the fifth floor.

"Lorelei," I breathe, peeking through the gap to see her darkened form huddled into the back corner. "We're right here."

"I-I'm—I'm a little claustrophobic."

"We'll have you out in a few minutes."

Her quiet sobs fill the air. I hate it.

"I can't climb up there," she says, staring up at me with wide, terrified eyes.

"Trust us, yeah?" I urge, although honestly, I've no idea how we will make it happen.

Jamie continues to do whatever he's doing that involves a lot of grunting and groaning, and only a few minutes later, the crippled doors finally give.

Dropping to my knees, I reach down into the car for her.

"I'll pull you out," I say, trying to reach her.

"Y-you can't."

"I can, Lorelei. You just have to trust me. Come on," I say encouragingly.

Slowly, she pushes from the back corner and moves closer.

A second later, she lifts her arms for help.

"Get up," Jamie demands.

"W-what?" I ask, ripping my eyes from Lorelei to glare up at him.

"Get up," he repeats. "I'll lift her up to you."

Too baffled to argue, I get up and stand aside, allowing him to drop to his front.

"Take your shoes off. You're going to need to help me by climbing up."

"I can't climb," she whispers.

"You can."

She quickly kicks her shoes off and stretches up.

"Ready?" he asks.

Lorelei doesn't say a word, but she also doesn't back away as Jamie leans into the space as much as he can and lifts her from the floor.

"That's it," he grunts. "Walk up."

The second I can reach her, I grab her arms and pull her higher.

"Hey, babe," I say, giving her my best smile hoping it'll distract her.

A loud rip fills the air, and her watery eyes shoot to mine.

"My dress."

"Fuck your dress," I grunt. "I only care about you."

I hear the words as if someone else says them, but as much as I want to, I can't regret them.

The second her legs are free, I sweep her up into my body and take off.

"My keys are in my purse," she cries when we're almost at the stairs.

"Jamie will get it."

Fuck knows how, but something tells me that he will.

Tucking her face into my shoulder, she allows me to carry her up the stairs.

I hold her tighter than probably necessary, but the sound of her crying and alone in that elevator continues to haunt me.

"What if he doesn't get my key?" she asks quietly once we're at her front door.

"Then I'll take you to my place."

The thought of having her in my space does weird things to me. But as much as I might want to see how she looks in my penthouse, she needs her own place right now.

Her breath catches at the prospect, and I'm unsure if it's with fear or excitement.

I don't get a chance to find out though, because the sound of Jamie's footsteps pounding up the stairs gets closer before he appears with Lorelei's purse and shoes in his hands.

"Keys?" Jamie says, holding up her purse.

"They're inside," I confirm before Lorelei has a chance to say anything.

Jamie hesitates, not wanting to dive into a woman's purse.

"Just get them," I grunt, fed up with standing in the hallway.

"Yeah, okay," he mutters before finally flipping it open and pulling them out.

It takes him two goes to find the correct key, and not a second later, I march through Lorelei's apartment.

Not bothering with the living area, I immediately turn toward her bedroom.

"No," she argues, wriggling in my arms the moment she realizes where I'm heading.

"Stop fighting, Temptress," I mutter as I kick the door open and march into her room.

The lights around us flicker to life, and suddenly, we're once again flooded with light, allowing me to see her room.

The place is a state. There's makeup, clothes, shoes, and all kinds of products everywhere. It's also possibly the girliest room I've ever stepped in. It is not what I was expecting at all.

"It's pink," I state, unable to stop the words from spilling free.

When she fights again, I finally release her, placing her on her feet at the end of her bed.

"You can leave now," she says, her head bowed so I can't see her face.

"Lorelei," I warn, tucking two fingers under her chin and giving her little choice but to look up at me.

"Stop trying to hide from me," I whisper, taking in her red, swollen eyes and tear-stained cheeks. "You've got nothing to be ashamed of."

Moving both hands, I brush my thumbs under her eyes, wiping away some of the darkness and lingering wetness.

"I fell apart," she confesses brokenly.

"So? That doesn't make you weak. Having a fear doesn't make you inadequate."

I study her closely, trying to gauge her reaction, to see if my words register at all.

"You need to leave," she says, taking a step back and severing our connection.

"No," I state. "Not until I know you're okay."

It's the wrong thing to say. Her shoulders tense and a fierce expression appears on her face.

"I'm fine. I've never needed anyone to look after me before, and I don't need you now."

Her words hurt. If it weren't for me—okay, if it weren't for Jamie—then she'd still be trapped inside that elevator. I think it's clear to both of us that she needed me tonight. Needed us.

"Are you sure about that, Temptress?"

The air turns thick around us. So thick that it becomes hard to suck in the breath I need.

She stares up at me with her big, watery eyes. Fear lingers within them, but there's more than just that alone: anticipation, desire, and hope glitter within them.

She trembles in my hold, her tongue sneaking out to lick across her bottom lip.

Unable to do anything but lower my head, I bring our mouths closer as the magnetic pull I feel toward her becomes stronger than ever.

I still when my lips are a hair's breadth from hers, giving her a very brief chance to react, to back away. But she doesn't.

Instead, she holds my eyes steady, silently daring me to do it.

Fuck.

My lips brush hers in the softest, sweetest kiss I think I've ever experienced, my hold on her face tightening in the hope of stopping her from running, should that be an option right now.

Three of the longest seconds I've ever experienced slowly pass as I wait for her to react, and just as her lips move, accepting the kiss, a voice rings through the air.

"I've made you a hot chocolate. I thought that might—oh, fuck," Jamie gasps when he walks into her bedroom and finds us locked in a kiss that is nowhere near finished. Hell, it's barely even started. "Sorry. I'm sorry. I'll just—"

He runs out of the room, this time ensuring that the door is closed almost as quickly as Lorelei jumps away from me.

"You should go," Lorelei says, turning her back on me and wrapping her arms around her waist.

"No, I already said—"

"Leave, Kian. I don't want you here. I don't..." Her words trail off as she marches into her en suite and slams the door behind her.

"Lorelei," I call, rushing over, refusing to accept that she's better off alone right now.

It doesn't escape my attention that if this were any other woman, I'd have left a long time ago without giving her a second thought.

But this isn't any other woman. This is Lorelei.

"Goodnight, Kian," she calls brokenly.

"Shit," I hiss, combing my fingers through my hair, trying to figure out what to do for the best. "Fuck it."

Marching through her bedroom, I rip the door open before slamming it behind me so she knows I've left, only to come face-to-face with my driver.

"I'm sorry, sir. I didn't think—"

"Forget it," I say, waving him off. "I've got a job for you."

"Anything," he says keenly, just like I knew he would.

35

LORELEI

My fingers curl around the edge of the basin as nothing but pure exhaustion seeps through my veins.

Tonight has been...

Tonight has been too much.

The gala alone was too much to process, let alone adding Kian's proposal and getting trapped in the elevator. The last thing I needed was that kiss.

Fuck. That kiss.

My head drops lower as heat rushes through my veins.

If we weren't interrupted...

I want to say that I'd have ended it and backed away. But I'd only be lying to myself.

I wasn't about to put an end to anything; I was balancing right on the edge of doing a very, very bad thing.

"Get it together, Lorelei."

Finally, I lift my head and face the truth.

It is not pretty.

My hair is a mess, and my makeup is ruined. It's smeared around my puffy eyes and streaked down my cheeks.

Why he wanted to kiss me is beyond me. I'm not sure I've looked more like a hot mess in my life.

Lifting my hand to my mouth, I press my fingertips against my lips as softly as his lips did.

My stomach flutters as I recall that very brief moment.

I kissed Kian Callahan.

No, I didn't just kiss Kian Callahan. I kissed my boss.

The man who proposed only hours ago that we should start up a fake relationship to get rid of my stage-five clinger ex.

Christ, this is a mess.

And it only gets worse when I look down at my dress.

My beautiful, ridiculously expensive dress with a massive, ugly rip up the front.

Dropping my hand to the ruined fabric, I fight the lump that crawls up my throat.

Needing to get out of the dress and wash every inch of tonight from my body, I drag the zipper down and let the heavy fabric pool on the floor around my feet.

I push my thong from my hips and leave that on top of the pile as I move toward the shower. After placing my shower cap on my messy updo, I step under the hot water.

I wish I could say that the lingering fear of being stuck in that elevator swirls down the drain, but it's not the case. While I was in Kian's arms, it was easy to push it aside.

But now I'm alone again...

At least the lights have come back on.

Grabbing my sponge, I load it up with as much of my favorite shower gel as it'll take, and then I scrub every single inch of my skin until I'm red and sore. If I wash hard enough, it'll erase my past, my memories and nightmares from my body, right?

Sadly, just like all the other times in my life I've begged for relief, it never comes, and as the water runs cold and I finally step out of the shower, the feelings still linger.

I do the best I can to remember the mess on my face, but I'm losing the fight with my exhaustion, and before I've done a proper job, I'm stumbling into my bedroom to find some pajamas.

The hot chocolate Jamie so thoughtfully made for me sits on my dresser, and seeing as it's in a thermal cup, I grab it before I crawl into bed.

It's no longer hot, but it's not cold either.

I drink it absently, letting the sweetness soothe me in the way that only chocolate can before I sink between the sheets and will sleep to come.

Everything will feel easier in the morning. I'll be able to process my thoughts better in the bright light of day.

My eyes are sore when I open them the next morning, reminding me with agonizing clarity that I cried on Kian's shoulder after freaking the fuck out in that elevator.

I should have been stronger.

Maybe if he hadn't ripped the ground from beneath me with that stupid proposal to be his fake girlfriend, then I might have managed to work my way through it without falling back into old habits.

With a groan of irritation that he's taking up headspace before I've even rolled out of bed, I throw my legs over the edge and pad through to my bathroom to freshen up. What I really need is coffee, but that's going to have to wait.

I throw a zip-up hoodie around my body and finally emerge from my bedroom. The second I step into the hallway, I suck in a deep breath that I pray isn't going to contain the scent of him like I'm sure I can still smell in my bedroom. But I quickly discover it isn't the case.

He may have only been here for a few minutes, but it seems his presence in my life is determined to remain at the forefront of my mind.

Maybe you do get what you pay for when it comes to cologne...

I frown as I step into my living area. The curtains are shut.

I didn't come in here last night, and I know I didn't close them before Kian picked me up for the gala. I hardly ever close them. Not since Tate left. Having them open and being able to see other people living their lives inside their own apartments on the other side of the road makes me feel a little less lonely.

On edge, my next steps come slower, but the second I turn toward the couch, I understand exactly why the room is in darkness despite the fact the sun is up.

"What the fuck are you doing?" I shriek, finding a man stretched out, fast asleep on my couch.

A decent person would probably leave them to sleep. But fuck that.

Why is he still here?

I told him to leave.

I thought he had left. I heard the front door close behind his irritating ass.

"Shit," Kian croaks, lifting his hands to rub his eyes.

"Yeah, fucking shit," I mutter, marching toward the windows and throwing the curtains open, flooding the room with light.

The rain pounding against the windows makes my heart sink, but I don't have time to mourn the loss of the morning run I was yearning for.

"Fucking hell, woman," he grunts.

By the time I spin around, he's pushed himself up so he's sitting, letting the blanket—my blanket—that he was using to cover him slip down to his waist, revealing his naked torso.

Fuck my life.

As much as I fight to keep my eyes on his face, I fail badly.

And holy cow am I glad I do because my boss is fine.

I already knew he was cut. It's obvious even when he's clothed. But Christ, my imagination failed me with this one.

He clears his throat, forcing my eyes back up to his before throwing the blanket off and pushing to his feet.

An alarm instantly begins ringing in my head.

He is wearing gray joggers.

Gray joggers.

Lifting my eyes to the ceiling for a beat, I pray for strength.

He is not playing fair here.

Sculpted chest. Defined abs. That perfect fucking V that sinks to...

Oh my god, he's hard.

"You should be in your own apartment right now," I say firmly, spinning on the balls of my feet and striding toward the kitchen.

I already needed coffee. Now, I need it possibly more than I ever have in my life.

"I needed to know that you were okay."

I suck in a sharp breath at the concern I hear in his voice.

"Why?" I burst, spinning back around to glare at him

Damn it. It's easier to be annoyed when I can't see his hot body and pretty face.

Ugh. He is the most infuriating man on the planet.

"Why do you care? You don't about anyone else."

"Everyone else isn't you."

His words hit me like a punch to the gut.

Our eye contact holds as the air crackles between us.

"Excuse me, I need the bathroom," he says before turning his back on me—his stupidly muscular back—and disappearing into the hallway.

"Oh my god," I breathe, dropping my face into my hands.

"I'll take mine black and strong."

"And in a takeout cup," I mutter.

When he returns, I'm sitting at the island with a mug in my hands, my eyes locked on the liquid gold inside.

He moves around me, I assume scanning the counter for his coffee, but he will soon be disappointed.

"Where's mine?"

"At the coffee shop you'll stop at on your way home. Get dressed, Kian. It's time to leave."

He stops beside me and crosses his thick arms over his chest.

That V and the marginally smaller bulge in his sweats call to me, but I manage to resist.

"Are you usually this rude to your guests?" he asks.

"My guests are usually invited to stay," I counter.

He moves, walking around behind me, making my entire body tingle with the need to turn and watch him.

Only a few seconds later, I discover that I don't need to move a muscle, because he appears before me and sets about making his own coffee.

"I thought you knew, Temptress. I'm not the kind of man who waits for an invitation."

The coffee machine starts up and he spins around, resting his ass against my counter, his heated stare burning the top of my head, demanding that I look up and meet his eyes.

I hold still for a few more moments, not wanting him to think that he can order me around in my own home like he does the office, but eventually, my need to look into his eyes gets the better of me.

A smirk tugs at the corners of his lips in accomplishment, and I internally groan.

"Did you still fancy a trip to Paris?"

"You're annoying."

"And you're grumpy in the mornings," he counters.

I glower at him but say nothing as he picks up his steaming coffee and pulls out the stool beside me.

He clears his throat, and the air instantly shifts around us. Sure, it's still buzzing with desire, but there's something more serious there too.

"I'm worried about you," he says quietly. "Did you want to talk about last night?" he offers like he does genuinely care.

"Which part, exactly?" I ask, taking a sip of my coffee in the hope it drowns out some of my sass and bitterness.

"Well, any part, I guess."

"The part where you accidentally asked me to be your fake girlfriend?"

"That was no accident," he says firmly, squashing any doubt I'd woken up with about the whole situation. "The elevator?" he hedges. "Did you want to—"

"No," I snap. "I don't want to talk about it."

"Okay. Then how about the ki—"

"Don't," I bark, jumping to my feet and backing away from him.

"Lorelei," he warns.

"There is nothing to talk about. Thank you for sticking around long enough to rescue me last night, I really appreciate it. But there is nothing more that needs to be said about the matter."

"Nothing?" he asks, his brow quirking in amusement.

"Nothing. Now, if you could get dressed and leave...I've got things to do."

"Things?" he enquires.

"I want to go for a run, and I...I'm not justifying myself to you. Please, just go."

Spinning on the stool, he looks toward the window and then back to me.

"A run? In that weather?"

"It's just rain. It won't kill me."

His smirk returns.

"I've got a better idea. Go and get dressed for your run."

"Oh no. I'm not."

He steps closer, eradicating the space between us.

"Whose hoodie is this, Lorelei?" he asks, running his finger down the zipper. His fingertip hovers just above my breast as he does, and damn if my nipple doesn't pucker with the promise of his touch.

"No one's," I breathe, hating how desperate I sound.

"It's his, isn't it?"

I clench my teeth, not wanting to go down this road.

But before I can force a lie past my lips, he grabs the fabric roughly in his hand and drags the zipper down. I don't register what's happening, and he's ripped the hoodie from my body and thrown it to the floor before my brain catches up.

"He's gone, Lorelei. It's over. Get him out of your life in every single way."

His green eyes blaze with fire as he silently dares me to defy him.

"Okay," I whisper. Honestly, I wasn't keeping it for sentimental reasons. It's soft and...yeah, okay. When he first left, it smelled like him, too, and I liked it.

But now...now things are very different.

"Go and get ready for your run. Then we're going to see if we can leave those demons of yours in our dust."

He spins me around and gently pushes me toward the door.

I glance back over my shoulder just in time to see him pull his cell from his pocket and focus on the screen.

Grabbing my purse from the hallway from the night before, I take out my own cell and put it on charge as I do as I'm told.

By the time I'm dressed, it's powered up and showing me a whole host of notifications. But it's the top one that really catches my attention.

A whole-staff email from none other than Kian Callahan.

Subject: URGENT - GYM CLOSED FOR MAINTENANCE

"Motherfucker."

His knock on my bedroom door makes me jump a mile, and I drop my cell on the bed.

"Ready?" he asks before poking his head inside and letting

his eyes drop down my body. I might be wearing leggings and a sports bra, but they're skin-tight and leave very little to the imagination.

My blood boils, my core clenching with excitement.

No. I'm most definitely not ready.

36

KIAN

Lorelei and I walk into the gym side by side.

There was a moment when I thought she was going to point-blank refuse. But then she glanced at the rain lashing the windows and I knew I had her.

She needs the escape that running gives her, but she didn't want to get soaked.

"I can't believe you did this," she murmurs as we step inside the deserted gym.

"I can do what I want," I say arrogantly.

"Not sure your dad or King would agree."

I scoff. "Fuck them. I hold just as much power as they do."

I've no idea what she hears in my voice, but from the way she looks up at me, I fear it's far too much.

"So, where do you want to start?" I ask, hopefully diverting the conversation.

"Treadmill. I've never really used any of this equipment before."

"You've never used a gym before?" I ask.

She shrugs. "Wasn't ever really an option," she says, dropping the bag she brought with her and taking off toward the machine.

I'm frozen in place as I watch her ass sway in her leggings.

Effortlessly, she steps up onto the machine and studies the buttons before her.

I smirk and wait.

"Need some help, Temptress?" I ask, taking off after her.

I'm still wearing the gray sweats I slept in. How could I even consider changing when she looked at me the way she did? Shame I had to pull on a t-shirt, really. There was something more than a little addicting about the way she studied my body. It reminded me that last night was real. The almost innocent kiss we shared was actually real.

"I'm fine," she huffs indignantly, her shoulders tightening.

"You know, it is okay to ask for help every now and then," I say, stepping up beside her.

With the treadmill beneath her, it brings us to eye level.

"Do you have to look so smug?" she complains.

"I'm not smug."

"My ass, yo—"

"Looks amazing," I interrupt.

Her cheeks blaze at my compliment. But it's true. It really fucking does.

"On button is here," I say, waking up the screen. "Then all the controls are here. Did you want to set a time limit or speed or—"

"I've got it from here. You...go and do your thing."

"What if my thing is watching you run?"

"I don't believe you got those muscles from watching others work out, Callahan."

"You've noticed my muscles, Temptress?"

"You're an idiot, and you're distracting me. Go away."

"Sure, but only because the view is better from a distance."

Pulling my cell from my pocket, I find my workout playlist, and after syncing it to the speakers, I take a seat on the weight bench.

Lorelei's eyes follow me in the mirror, and with a smirk, I reach my arm behind my head and pull my shirt off.

She shakes her head, a tight smile playing on her lips, but she doesn't take her eyes off me as I shift into position. And even after lying down and losing sight of her, I know she continues watching.

With most of my focus on my workout, I go through my usual routine, trying the best I can to ignore my partner.

But no matter how loud the music is, I still hear her heavy breathing as she continues to run.

I move away from the weights to the bar and begin counting my pull-ups.

"How many have you done?"

Lorelei's voice startles me, and I drop to the ground.

"Twelve, before I was interrupted," I mutter as I reach for a towel to wipe my head and chest.

"Still impressive. I've never had any upper body strength."

"Surely you can do one," I taunt. I let my eyes roam around her body. "You look in pretty good shape to me."

"I'm glad you think so. But there's no chance I could even pull myself up an inch."

"Bet you can."

She raises a brow.

"And what do I get when you lose?" Placing her hand on her waist, she pops a hip.

"I'll take you home after this, and you don't have to see me again until Monday morning."

A smile spreads across her lips before a laugh spills free. "Oh, it's going to be so peaceful."

"And if I win..." I pause for effect, even though she doesn't think she stands a chance at losing. "Then you have to come out for dinner with me tonight, and everything is my choice."

"Normal day for you then," she mocks.

I shrug.

"So, what do you say?"

She laughs again. "I'm excited to see you lose for once in your life."

"Let's see, shall we?" I say, gesturing for her to step in front of me beneath the bar.

"You've got it, sir."

She rolls her shoulders and shakes her arm out as if she's actually going to give this her best shot.

Then she looks up and realizes her mistake.

"Wait, I can't even—" She shrieks when I wrap my hands around her waist and lift her up.

"Got it?" I ask before letting go.

"Yep."

Releasing my hands, I take a small step back.

"Go on, then. Let's see what you've got."

Her entire body locks up and her arms tremble as she attempts to pull herself up.

To give her credit, it really does look like she tries. It's pointless, though. She doesn't move an inch.

"See? I can't do it."

"Hmm...Try again."

"Nope." Before she gives up, I jump from the ground, grab the bar beside where her small hands are holding it, and wrap my legs around her waist.

"What the fuck are you doing?" she screeches, wriggling against me as if she thinks she can escape.

"Proving that you can do this," I say. My lips brush her ear as I speak, and she visibly shudders as my breath rushes over her heated skin.

"I think I just proved well enough that I can't."

"We'll see. Now, engage your core. We're going to lift."

"Oh no, no, no, no," she chants, finally figuring out my plan. "This is not what I agreed to."

"Funny, because I don't remember there being conditions."

"You dared me to do it alone."

"No, I didn't. I dared you to do it. There was no mention of support. Three, two, one."

I lift, and with my legs around her waist, she has no chance but to come with me, completing her first pull-up.

"Fuck's sake," she mutters when her chin meets the bar.

We hold it for a count of three before lowering down.

"See? Wasn't so hard, was it?"

"With you doing all the work? No, it was pretty easy," she confesses as I unwrap my legs and drop to the floor again.

She follows suit, and the second her feet touch down, I spin her around and back her up against the post.

"Kian," she breathes as I pin her against the cool metal with the length of my body.

Lowering my head, I rest my brow against hers.

"I can't stop thinking about it," I confess.

My eyes stay locked on hers as my chest heaves. My heart thunders, and my breathing is erratic.

She sucks in a sharp breath, letting me know that it's not far from her mind either.

"Well..." She swallows. "You need to."

Her eyes bounce between mine as we remain frozen in this position, each of us waiting for the other to react.

"I'm your assistant, Kian. Y-your...your fake girlfriend."

My lips twitch.

"You're agreeing?"

She lets out a long breath, letting it rush over my face and down my chest. Just that is enough to ensure my cock is hard as steel against her stomach. There's about as much chance of her not feeling it as her missing my morning wood when I stood from her couch earlier this morning.

She shrugs one shoulder. "Your reasons were very convincing. But—"

I cut her words off with my lips.

But this time, I don't hesitate or give her a chance to back away this time.

The second her lips move against mine, my tongue joins, and only a heartbeat later, so does hers.

It's what should have happened last night, only, we were interrupted.

But that's unlikely to happen here. We're alone.

All alone with an entire gym to make the most of...

I lose myself in her kiss. My hands roam over her body, or at least the parts I can reach.

But all too soon, she presses against my chest.

"Kian," she says into our kiss.

Unable to deny her wishes, I pull back.

"I agreed to the fake relationship. Not to this."

Taking a large step back, I comb my fingers through my sweat-damp hair, dragging it back until it hurts, my eyes tracing the lines of Lorelei's body.

When I get back up to her face, I find that she's just as mesmerized by my body as I am hers. Although, her attention is focused on just one part of me. The part that's tenting my sweats.

"Temptress?" My voice is deep and raspy—not that she needed any more evidence about how I'm feeling right now.

"It's time to go, Kian," she says, sounding much more stable than me.

"Right. Yeah. Sure." Once she's walked around me, I sink my hand into my sweats to rearrange myself, but not before I squeeze my length, eliciting a groan to spill from my lips.

"I don't think dinner is a good idea," she says.

When I spin around, I find her standing at the door with her bag in hand.

"But I won. You owe me."

Snatching my t-shirt from the floor where I abandoned it, I stalk closer to her.

"But—"

"No, buts, Temptress. Me and you. Dinner."

"Lunch now?" she asks, hoping for an easy way out.

"Absolutely not. A deal is a deal. You owe me dinner, and I'm collecting my winnings tonight."

Reaching above her, I push the door open and give her little choice but to walk through it.

"Nothing fancy," she concedes. "Not after last night."

"It's my choice. We'll go wherever I see fit."

She falls silent and I step up beside her, leading her to the stairs—not the elevator—that will take us to the garage for my car that Jamie dropped off at her apartment last night, along with a bagful of clothes.

The journey back to her apartment is quiet. I'm unsure if it's because she's regretting taking that bet. She really should have known better if she thought she stood a chance at winning.

She was right. I don't lose.

Ever.

I pull the car to a stop outside her apartment and kill the engine.

"I guess I'll see you later then," she says, unclicking her seat belt and hooking her fingers over the door handle, ready to escape.

"You don't have to sound so excited about it."

"Hmm," she mumbles.

"We're going to have fun. You know we will."

"Kian, I—"

Reaching out, I press my fingers to her lips.

"We'll talk later," I promise her.

She sighs as I feel the weight of it right down to my toes.

"This is fake," she says the second my fingers slip away. "Don't get carried away."

"I know," I say confidently, but I can't help wondering just how much of a lie it is.

That kiss earlier felt anything but fake, and nothing at all like a lie.

"Message me when you're safe in your apartment," I instruct.

"I'm taking the stairs. You don't need to worry."

"I still will. Message me, yeah?"

"Fine. See you later."

She pushes the door open and climbs out before disappearing into her building without looking back—just like she did last night.

Only now, I don't follow. Instead, I sit there and wait for my cell to buzz.

I know she'll follow orders. She won't risk me coming up.

She's too scared.

Scared what letting me in will mean.

Unfortunately for her, I have every intention of worming my way in as deep as possible so we can find out.

37

LORELEI

Boss: I'm going to have to cancel tonight.
Raincheck?

M y heart thumps against my ribs as I stare down at his message.

I shouldn't be disappointed. I should be relieved to get out of a date that I shouldn't want.

But fuck...I am.

Without bothering to reply, I throw my cell onto the couch and stomp toward the kitchen.

Grabbing myself a glass, I yank the fridge door open and pull out a bottle of wine.

I treated myself to my favorite when I started at Callahan Enterprises, but I haven't had a chance to celebrate with it yet.

Celebrate...

"Pah, what a joke," I mutter as I pour myself a generous measure before taking a sip. "Mmm."

As I put the bottle back, I study the contents of the fridge. If I really wanted to, I could pull something together for dinner. It wouldn't be very exciting, though.

I can't help but wonder where Kian would have taken me

tonight. One thing is clear—the food would have been outstanding.

My stomach growls unhappily as I walk back toward the couch with my wine.

Picking up my cell, I close down my messages and open my takeout app. I mindlessly scroll through every offering. Every type of cuisine and fast food passes before me, but despite being hungry, none of it steals my interest.

Damn it, I wanted to be waited on tonight and treated like a princess. It's not very often it happens. But it's been too long since someone even tried.

Matt...

All our dates were like a dream.

He was a dream...until he turned into a nightmare.

There are more unread messages sitting in my inbox from him, and my stomach knots. How long is he going to be satisfied by sending messages that go unanswered? At some point, he's going to up the ante again. Maybe once his black eye has faded.

Tonight's date and maybe a photo or two would have helped get rid of him. Or at least I can hope that it would have. But spending Saturday night in my apartment with only a glass of wine for company isn't going to convince anyone that I've moved on with my life.

I'm still scrolling when my cell begins buzzing with an incoming call.

My heart lurches at the thought of it being him, but the second my eyes land on the person calling, I relax.

"Hey," I say the second the video call has connected and my best friend's face fills the screen. "How was last night?"

She rolls her eyes. "Exhausting. I swear every single person wanted to personally congratulate us."

"Aw, that's sweet," I say, fully aware of how much Tate would have hated all the attention. I know because I'd feel exactly the same. The only difference is she's been brought up in these elite circles and wouldn't have stared back at them with her best resting bitch face fully in place. I, however, am less skilled at hiding my true feelings.

"Uh huh," she mutters. "King killed his speech, though, so that was good."

"Were you expecting him to do anything but?"

"No, but seeing him nervous was funny as hell."

"King gets nervous, who'd have thought it?" I tease.

"I know, right? He'd kill me if he knew I told you."

"Your secret's safe with me. Maybe."

"So..." she starts, her eyes twinkling with excitement. "How was your night?"

"Fine," I mutter, reluctantly.

"Oh, come on, Lori. You looked fucking stunning, by the way."

"You saw me?"

"Haven't you been on Instagram?"

A weird mix of dread and excitement war inside me.

Maybe we didn't need a date tonight to publicly announce our fake relationship.

"Clearly not," I mutter as I open the app. "Oh shit," I gasp when I find more notifications than I think I've ever had before.

"Told you so. Everyone and their wife wants to know who the beautiful woman is smiling up at Kian Callahan like he's personally handed her the moon."

My stomach twists uncomfortably.

"I am not looking at him like that. I'm glaring at him in pure irritation."

"Bullshit," she coughs. "Admit it. He looks good."

"When don't any of the Callahan brothers look good?" I mutter, wondering how it's possible that even on their worst days they look like they've just walked off a runway.

Kian in a tux, though...almost as good as those gray sweats from this morning.

Heat blooms in my lower belly as I think about what they were hiding—or not hiding, as the case may have been. And how it felt pressed against my stomach as we made out in the gym.

Bad move, Lorelei. Bad fucking move.

"What's that face for?" Tate asks. We've been each other's ride or die for so long now that one look can tell a thousand words.

"N-nothing."

"Lorelei Anne Tempest," she says, turning on her future stern mother voice as she full names me. "Do you have something you need to tell me?"

I let out a heavy sigh and sink lower on the couch.

"I got trapped in the elevator last night," I confess as horror washes over my best friend's face.

"Holy shit. Are you okay? Why didn't you call? We could have—"

"Tate," I snap, interrupting her. "I wasn't going to interrupt your night. Plus, you were miles away. And anyway, my cell died and—"

"Do not tell me you spent all night in there."

"No. Kian had only just dropped me off and he—"

"Oh my god, he rescued you?" she asks, her voice getting all light and whimsical.

It's weird hearing it because I've always been the more romantic out of the two of us, but it's clear that King has had an impact on my bestie.

"Him and Jamie, yeah. I was freaking out and—"

"He was there in your moment of need."

"Hmm. Something like that."

"You thanked him, right?"

An image of us standing in my bedroom, our lips pressed together as we each questioned our next moves, comes back to me.

"He stayed the night to make sure I was okay."

"He what?" Tate shrieks at a decibel that only dogs should be able to hear.

"On the couch, Tate. He slept on the couch."

She frowns. "What was wrong with my bed?" she asks, offended that he chose the couch over the unused memory foam mattress in her old room.

"I don't know, T. I didn't ask. I was too busy freaking out over the fact he spent the night in our apartment and I didn't know."

"Your apartment," she corrects like she always does. "And how didn't you know?"

I explain how he shut me inside my room—ignoring the part about Jamie interrupting us—and how I thought he'd left as I'd demanded.

"Aw, he likes you," she sings.

"No, he was concerned I'd freak out and never return to be tormented by him at work."

"Oh yeah, that's the reason he slept on the couch. Sure." She rolls her eyes to ensure I know she's joking—as if the tone of her voice wasn't enough. "Then what happened?" she asks eagerly, needing more details.

"He closed the entire gym so the two of you could work out alone?" she cries.

"It's not a big deal."

"You're wrong. It's a huge fucking deal. You know why he did that, don't you?"

"So no one could see how awful I look all sweaty and red in the face?"

Tate laughs. "For a smart girl, you're really freaking delusional, Lor."

My lips purse and my eyes narrow as I glare at my best friend.

Why did I tell her all this? I should have known her opinion wouldn't be helpful.

"He didn't want anyone else to see you. Full stop. He wants you, Lor, and he doesn't want any other man in that office to lay eyes on you.

My stupid romantic heart flutters wildly. "That's ridiculous," I state, trying to ignore my true feelings about her explanation. "He just knew I'd outrun him and make him look weak."

"Kian Callahan might be a lot of things, but weak isn't one of them."

I huff, because what else can I say? She's right. Obviously.

"Soooo...I feel like there's more."

"Fuck's sake, Tate," I mutter, reaching for my wine and taking a massive gulp.

"I know when you're hiding things. You get shifty and weird. You fucked him, didn't you?"

I almost spray my screen with wine. "No," I cry, after thankfully managing to swallow it. "Christ, Tate. I'm not a whore."

"Never said you were. Rumor has it, though, that Kian is a freak between the sheets, and I know you could use a little bit of that in your life right now."

"Dude, you need to stop meddling. First Ryder and now Kian." I shake my head.

"You can thank me anytime," she says with a wide smile.

"I'll give you Ryder. He's...easy, in more ways than one. But I'm not fucking my boss." I'm actively trying not to let that happen.

But that kiss earlier...

Fuck. That was hot as hell. I can only imagine how good things could have been if I hadn't pushed him away.

"So, what are you hiding? And don't try to tell me that it's nothing."

"Ugh, you're a pain in my ass, Tatum Grace Warner-Callahan."

She glares at me, silently demanding the information I'm holding back.

"Fine. Kian suggested we fake date so that he can lose his stage-five clingers for a bit and I have a reason for Matt to leave me the fuck alone." I say it in such a rush that I'm not sure any of it was intelligible. But it's out.

Silence follows my confession, so I can only assume she heard me loud and clear and is trying to process.

"Okay," Tate says, holding her hand up to the screen. "Let me get this straight." I roll my eyes and take another sip of wine. "Kian Callahan—the Kian Callahan, CFO of Callahan Enterprises— who has never dated anyone for more than a few hours, has asked you, my best friend, his assistant, to be his first girlfriend."

"Fake, Tate. Fake girlfriend."

"Oh my god, we're going to be sisters-in-law."

"Okay, now you've lost it. I shouldn't have said anything," I mutter, regretting this whole conversation.

"No, no, you absolutely should have. This is fucking epic, Lor."

"It's fake, Tate. There is nothing worthy of anything even close to epic. It's a means to an end to give us both a breather from the exhausting dating world."

"So you're seriously telling me that if the opportunity presented itself, you wouldn't screw his nerdy numbers brain out?"

I swallow thickly, praying that this is one instance where she can't read every single one of my thoughts.

"Knew it. I fucking knew it." She laughs, a wide smile splitting her face.

"I'm not screwing his brain out. We're just..."

"Faking it. I bet there wouldn't be any faking with him, though. I'm just saying."

"You're almost as insufferable as he is," I complain.

"So, what's the plan? Fake dates? Making excuses to be photographed together?"

The more she talks, the more I realize that this whole plan is insane.

Just look at the last twenty-four hours. I've kissed him twice.

Twice.

I've felt his body pressed up against mine, and I've spent

longer than acceptable imagining just what it could be like if there weren't a couple of layers of clothes between us.

His canceling tonight was the best thing that could have happened.

"I'm going to tell him no," I state firmly.

Decision made. This is a very, very bad idea.

The worst.

"And you think he'll accept that?"

"He's already canceled our first date."

"Ooooh, that explains your hair," she says, making a point of glancing at my freshly styled curls.

My insides twist up painfully. I went to so much effort, and look where I've been left.

Alone on my couch with a glass of wine.

"It needed washing after the gym. There is nothing more to it."

"Why has he canceled?"

"Didn't say. But it's for the best. I'm his assistant. He's my boss. That is all there needs to be between us."

38

KIAN

I could be sitting opposite Lorelei in a restaurant right now, trying to figure out the best way to score myself an invite into her apartment so that our night doesn't have to end at the entrance to her building like our afternoon did.

But no. Instead, I'm sitting in a hospital with one of my little sisters while the other has her ankle x-rayed. Mom is with Kenzie, and I was called in to keep Tilly entertained.

I don't mind. I love my irritating little sisters almost as much as I do my knuckle-headed brothers. But there are other things I could be doing right now than watching videos of the girls' cheer competition this afternoon that ended up with us here.

Kenzie is the flier, and well, let's just say that she didn't fly all too well when their stunt went wrong and she ended up crashing to the floor.

"We'd have won," Tilly complains for the fifth time. She's a year younger than Kenzie, but you wouldn't know it. They're exactly the same height and look almost identical. They get confused for twins on a daily basis. "All she had to do was hold that pose and we'd have smashed it."

"Next time, Tills," I say, hoping to pacify her.

"You should have come," she complains.

"Something came up. I'll be there for the next one," I promise.

"You said that about this one," she says sadly.

Guilt sits heavy in my stomach, and I hate myself for not putting them first.

I tell myself that Lorelei needed me after the elevator debacle the night before, but I'm pretty sure I'm lying to myself. Sure, she needed us to help get her out, but after that, she was more than capable of looking after herself.

"I know. I'm sorry."

"Mom said you used to go to all Kieran's games as a kid. I know cheer isn't the same, but—"

"I'll be there," I say, meaning every word of it.

Pulling my cell from my pocket, I open up my calendar.

"Give me the dates and locations. I'll make sure everything else is canceled. No matter where it is, I'll be there."

Her eyes light up with excitement before she begins rattling off dates and venues.

"I'll make sure my assistant knows that these trump everything else." Wrapping my arm around her shoulders, I pull her closer and press a kiss to the top of her head.

"Love you, Tilly-bob."

"Love you too. She's going to be okay, isn't she?"

"Of course she will."

"But if she's broken it then she won't be able to cheer."

"It'll heal, and then she'll be as good as new. And just think, in the time she's out, you can get even better," I say with a wink.

She smiles up at me with wide, dark eyes, and my heart tumbles.

These two little rugrats stole my heart from the moment they were born.

Our family might be a little disjointed, but when it counts, we all pull together. Even King, when he really has to.

I get it. His relationship with Mom is strained because he remembers more than Kieran and me. I'm pretty sure he'll always hold her infidelity against her. Me, though... sure, her cheating on Dad was wrong. But we don't know what their lives were like back then. Dad loved her, that's more than obvious, but love isn't always enough. We all know that.

She's happy with Neil. Probably happier than she would have been if she stayed with Dad. And Dad? He's...enjoying himself.

I figure that I either believe everything happened for a reason, or I'll end up all bitter and twisted about it like King.

I don't need that in my life. Nor do our sisters.

Our parents' decisions and mistakes are their own. At this point, the only person's actions who can influence my life are mine. Okay, and possibly a certain curly-haired woman I can't get out of my head.

When I glance over at Tilly, I find that she's distracted watching some other video on YouTube, and I take the opportunity to open my message thread with Lorelei.

She's read my message, but she hasn't responded.

I want to say I'm surprised, but I'm not.

She didn't want to go on this date tonight. She's probably feeling pretty smug about the fact that she got her way despite my slightly unethical win earlier.

I hate the thought of her sitting at home alone, thinking about the fun we could have been having.

Wanting to make it up to her, I find the phone number of one of my favorite restaurants and hit call.

"I've got to take this," I say, waving my cell in front of Tilly, not that she's paying any attention.

I make quick work of ordering each of my favorite dishes on the menu, along with a bottle of wine, before giving the guy on the phone Lorelei's address.

He promises me that it'll be delivered within the hour before I return to my seat and find myself dragged into some teenage YouTube drama.

Not the way I was expecting to spend my Saturday night.

"I 'm going to head out," I say, pushing from the chair I was sitting in next to Kenzie's bed.

Her x-ray showed that her break was worse than they were expecting, and she ended up in surgery having it pinned. Something that neither her nor her sister are happy with. It's going to put her out of action for months.

Neil, their dad, arrived an hour ago after being pulled from his golf weekend, and I can't help but feel like we're crowding Kenzie, who's still dozy from the anesthesia.

"Thank you for coming," a weak voice says from the bed.

"Anytime," I promise before glancing up at Tilly and smiling at her. "If you need anything, I'm only a phone call away."

"I'll walk you out," Mom says, her eyes dark with exhaustion.

"It's okay. I can manage. Rest," I say sternly.

But in true Mom style, she ignores me and quickly follows me out of the room.

"Mom," I warn.

"Thank you for coming to help me out."

I dropped everything the second she told me what was happening.

"That's what big brothers do," I say, but the second I look over and see dark shadows in her eyes, I know it was a mistake.

Like everyone else in the world, it doesn't escape me that she'd probably prefer to call King in a crisis. But unfortunately, she's stuck with me. We both know that as much as Kieran would love to drop everything and run to the girls' aid, he's always got something on. I get it. I do. But I also can't help but feel like she ends up stuck with me when she'd prefer one of the other two.

"I hope you didn't have to cancel anything important tonight."

"Nah, you know how it is," I say, playing it off.

"Oh no, how many hearts did I break tonight?"

"Mom," I faux-gasp. "It's only ever one at a time."

She pats me on the shoulder patronizingly. "Whatever you say, darling."

I roll my eyes but give up arguing.

"Well, whoever she is. I hope she understands that your little sisters needed you."

"I'm sure she will."

My cell burns a hole in my pocket as I think about Lorelei. She should have been delivered her dinner by now. I was hoping to have heard from her, or maybe the restaurant to tell me that she refused delivery.

"Go and enjoy the rest of your night," Mom says after giving me a kiss on the cheek. "Don't do anything I wouldn't do."

Shaking my head, I make my way to my car, and the second I'm inside, I pull my cell from my pocket.

Nothing.

The urge to call her burns through me, but I resist.

I don't want to be that man.

I've made my move. Now I need to wait to see what hers will be.

Despite my body wanting to head across town to Lorelei's place, I let my head lead and drive home. Although, once I get there, I don't let myself up to the penthouse. Instead, I wander down the street to the bar.

I need a drink, and for some reason, I don't want to be alone quite yet.

The security guard sees me coming and lifts the rope so that I don't have to slow my stride.

"Evening, Kian. How lovely to see you."

"You too, Brian," I say before continuing.

The place is busy. Almost every table is full, and there are more customers than usual lining the bar.

I instantly regret my decision. Maybe hiding in my apartment would have been the best option.

"Mr. Callahan," the barman smiles when he spots me. "To what do we owe this pleasure?"

"Missed you," I tease as I hop onto a barstool.

"Well, I'm honored. You usually have much more beautiful company on a Saturday night than me."

"Don't I fucking know it."

He smirks. "Usual?"

"You got it."

Spinning away from me, he grabs their finest bottle of scotch and pours me a more-than-generous measure.

"I hope that does what you need it to, man," he says as he places the glass before me.

I'm about to ask what he means, but he's already gone, serving others.

With a sigh, I pick up my glass and swirl the amber liquid around.

Maybe all the answers do lie at the bottom.

I quickly check my cell again in case I missed her message, but when I find nothing but work emails and other shit I don't care about right now, I lift my glass to my lips and swallow every drop.

Tucked at the end of the bar, I'm awarded some kind of privacy, allowing me to watch the comings and goings around me.

I watch the couples on dates and the friends having a long overdue catch-up. Thankfully, everyone leaves me alone to get lost in my own little world. I'm about to call it a night after my third scotch, but just as my feet hit the floor, the worst noise possible hits my ears.

"Kian Callahan. Well, I never."

Fuck.

My body acts of its own accord, and I spin around to face a woman I haven't seen for years.

We had a couple of nights together when we were younger, before she landed a job in Hollywood and disappeared to live the dream on the Golden Coast.

"Tia," I say, sounding much happier than I feel.

Women like her are the exact reason I proposed that fake relationship deal to Lorelei yesterday.

Tia's eyes glitter with excitement and ulterior motives as she moves closer, ready to kiss both of my cheeks.

"Honey, it has been way too long," she purrs, her hand gliding up my arm. We might have once been close, but we're hardly long-lost lovers.

I take a step back, but she follows.

"Can I buy you a drink?" she offers, noticing that my glass is empty. "We've got a lot of years to catch up on."

"I was just leaving."

"Aw, come on. Just one—for old time's sake."

39

LORELEI

"**M**otherfucker," I bark, my grip on my cell tightening to the point I fear the screen is going to crack.

The photo staring back at me does prove one thing, though...I did the right thing last night.

After talking to Tate, I'll admit, I did feel a little guilty for not even replying to Kian.

He didn't say why he had to cancel—for all I knew, he could have fallen ill and his message was a cry for help.

I wasn't all that concerned, though, because I managed to convince myself not to reply.

Then, when the food arrived...I really did want to message him.

But that was what he wanted, right?

Messaging him would have been playing right into his hands.

Kian is a player. He knows how to manipulate women into doing exactly what he wants them to do.

Well...I am not one of those women.

I will not fall for the fancy night out in the designer gown —nor will I fall for the pity dinner after he bailed on our date that I didn't even want.

I totally ate every mouthful of it, though.

How could I not? The second I discovered it wasn't him or Matt standing on the other side of the door and I opened it to the waft of garlic, cheese and a whole host of other flavors, there was only one thing I was doing with the contents of the tray. Devouring them.

I'd only snacked since getting back from the gym, knowing that he'd take me somewhere incredible; I was starving despite my inability to decide on my own dinner.

As I ate it, I couldn't help but try and figure out what pulled him away from me. He was more than keen for the date earlier in the day. I figured that it had to have been something important.

Well, now I have my answer.

Tia fucking Halliwell.

That's who was so important that he had to cancel on our fake date.

Much like Sasha, she's everything I'm not. Blonde, blue eyes, sculpted cheekbones that I'm convinced are fake, as are her tits. She's tall, and slim, and would grace any runway with ease and sophistication. She's also a household name since her success on a Netflix series recently.

A bitter laugh spills from my lips as I continue to stare at them.

Each photograph of the two of them together is worse. He's watching her closely with a smile playing on his lips. It's not the sneer he gave Sasha on Saturday night, either; it's different, and it cuts me right to the core.

"Fucking asshole."

It shouldn't hurt, because I shouldn't care.

I agreed to fake dating.

Fake.

Nothing about it, especially feelings, was ever going to be real.

I guess it just goes to prove that the decision I made while talking to Tate last night was the right one.

Being anything more than Kian's assistant is a mistake.

With fire burning through my veins, I grab my laptop from the coffee table and open my emails.

To: *Kian Callahan*
From: *Lorelei Tempest*
Subject: *Mistakes...*

Dear Mr. Callahan,

After careful thought and consideration, I am turning down the proposal you made on Friday night.
I believe that any other outcome would be unprofessional and unethical.
Good luck with your future conquests. I'm sure you're more than equipped to deal with them.

Regards,
Lorelei Tempest
Assistant—and only an assistant—to Kian Callahan, CFO of Callahan Enterprises

I slam the top of my laptop down hard enough to break the screen.

Another reason why I just did the right thing.

Fuck Kian Callahan.

Fuck him and his pretty little actress and the perfect little babies they're going to have.

Stuffing my AirPods into my ears, I shove my feet into my sneakers and take off running in the hope I can leave all this behind and never think about it again.

> Ryde my dick: Hey, beautiful. Missed me?

S omething flutters in my belly at the sight of Ryder's message.

He's been away in Europe on a business trip. The time difference has made it hard to continue the sexting we'd embarked on earlier in the week. It was probably for the best while I had my momentary lapse in judgment where Kian was concerned.

But now, that is over, and I can jump back into the thrill of flirting with Ryder, knowing that I'm not putting my heart at risk.

I put off coming home for as long as I could earlier. I knew that I'd have a reply to my email, and I wasn't ready to deal with his demanding ass.

But to my surprise, when I eventually stumbled back into my apartment on jelly legs, my inbox was missing the email I was expecting.

I could only assume that he was still in bed with his hot actress, and I tried to put all thoughts of them rolling around together out of my head.

Nothing about Kian and his harem of women does anything positive for my confidence.

My inbox has been quiet since. Not that I've checked it— and my spam—every thirty minutes or so.

Maybe he just doesn't care.

Stretching my legs out on the couch, I forget the movie I was watching and dive into chatting with a man who does seem to want my time and attention.

> Lori: Hey, hunk. How's it hanging?

> Ryde my dick: Little to the left, more than a little hard.

> Ryde my dick: How about you? Any details from your wild weekend that you need to share with me?

> Lori: Nothing wild happening here.

> Ryde my dick: Damn, you really do need me, huh?

> Lori: I guess that depends on what you have to offer…

The photo that follows only goes to prove that he is more than a little hard and more than a little ready to play.

It's the prefect distraction from real life and the fact that Monday morning is going to roll around all too soon.

I stand in front of the elevator in the Callahan Enterprises building with butterflies erupting in my stomach.

I don't want to get inside there. But also, I don't want to climb the stairs to the top of this high-rise building. To be honest, I don't want to be here at all, let alone in the management offices where a certain CFO resides.

But as much as I want to turn around and run as fast as I can, I can't.

I would be stupid to do something to ruin this opportunity. The paycheck is enough to change not only my life, but also my brothers'. And they're more important to me than anything else in the world. Being able to help them live out their dreams will mean everything to me.

Sucking in a deep breath, I watch the small screen as the floors count down to ground level.

You can do this, Lorelei.

It's just an elevator.

You're safe here. Even if the worst happens, no one will hurt you.

The elevator dings a beat before the doors slide open.

Two people I don't recognize spill out—neither of them pays me any mind, their attention focused on leaving the building. Seems a bit premature, seeing as the day has barely started, but whatever.

I take a hesitant step forward, still trying to convince

myself that everything is going to be okay, when suddenly, a large, warm hand presses against the small of my back, guiding me forward.

I want to snap at him, to tell him to get off me, but as I step into the enclosed space, all the words dry up as the doors close us in.

Kian's hand never leaves my back, nor does his overpowering presence behind me.

His breath tickles over my ear and down my neck.

I fight like hell to stop my body from reacting, but it's pointless. All I can think about is him pressing me up against the bar and kissing me senseless on Saturday.

Closing my eyes, I focus on my breathing. But I quickly realize my mistake when I discover each breath is laced with his scent.

"Breathe, Lorelei," he rasps behind me. "I won't let anything happen to you."

Tipping my head to the ceiling, I begin counting seconds. I've no idea if it's to make the time in this enclosed space feel like it goes faster, or my time around him. Honestly, it could be either.

He ditched you for a model-worthy actress on Saturday night.

He isn't worthy of your time or your thoughts.

He never replied to my email either, and I find it really hard to believe that it's because he hasn't read it.

My heart continues to pound as we climb higher and higher.

He doesn't say another word. Or at least, not until we get to the very top, a beat before the doors open and I'm granted freedom.

His hand slips from my back and around my hip, allowing him to pull me back, pinning me against his hard body.

"Ten minutes, my office. I think we need to have a little chat, don't we, Lorelei?"

No sooner have the doors parted than Kian strides out of the elevator as if he didn't just knock my world off kilter.

"Good morning, Melissa," he sings as if everything is perfect. But then, if he spent all Saturday night and yesterday banging Tia Halliwell, I guess he does have something to be spritely about.

Rolling my shoulders back, I hold my head high and walk out of the elevator just as Kian is disappearing into his office.

"Morning, Lori. Did you have a good weekend?" Melissa asks politely.

"Hmm, yeah."

"You looked gorgeous Friday night. It must have been an experience for Kian to have a date with some level of intelligence."

I snort a laugh; I can't help myself.

"And to end the night unsatisfied." She covers her mouth in a useless attempt to hide her laughter.

"Would you like a coffee?" I ask as I abandon my things under my desk and make a beeline for our kitchen.

"No, thank you. I'm sure Kian wouldn't say no, though."

Well, he's going to be disappointed.

With my fresh mug of coffee and another new notebook in my hand, I nervously make my way to his office.

My heart is in my throat as I knock, and it doesn't get any better when he calls out to invite me in.

I take a second to compose myself before throwing the door open and marching in as if I own the place.

Fake it until you make it, Lorelei.

Placing both my coffee and my notebook on his desk, I take my seat. Not once do I look up, but it's impossible to miss the fact I have his whole attention.

Well, that and my notebook which reads "List of people I want to punch in the face...my boss."

Once I'm settled, I finally look up.

My eyes instantly connect with his dark, angry ones and my heart does a little flip.

"You wanted to see me, sir," I say sweetly, aware that it's going to do fuck all to help this situation.

He leans forward and rests his exposed forearms on his desk.

"That email you sent..." My pulse races and my temperature spikes. "I suggest you forget you ever typed it, because it's not accepted."

"W-what?" I stutter.

He shakes his head as if he's disappointed in me. "Never go back on your word, Lorelei. It makes you look weak and indecisive."

"I-I—"

"We need to discuss my schedule. Some unforeseen things have arisen that need my attention."

My teeth clench. "I see."

"It's going to involve some last-minute travel plans."

"Just tell me what you need and I'll get onto it," I force out as my world continues to spin out of control.

40

LORELEI

No sooner had Kian given me the dates and location for his upcoming business trip than I was dismissed from his office. Nothing more was said about my refusal to accept his proposal, nor did he discuss the reason why he canceled our date.

It's fine. I understand well enough that he found a better option. There was a twisted part of me that wanted to see if he was going to be brazen enough to sit on the other side of his desk and lie to my face.

He has to know that there are pictures of him and Tia online. Surely, he doesn't think I'm stupid enough not to have looked...or maybe he does.

That thought possibly hurts more than the fact he chose a hot actress over me in the first place.

Only minutes after I returned to my desk, Kian emerged from his office and announced that he was going to be out for the rest of the day and not to bother him unless it was urgent.

That wasn't exactly a big ask, since he was the last person on the planet that I wanted to talk to.

Mellissa also left soon after to accompany King in some meetings. I had no idea if they were the same meetings that were keeping Kian busy, and I didn't care to ask. Instead, I made the most of the peace and focused on all the things I needed to do.

The day sped by faster than I was expecting, and all too soon I left the building with a little more excitement than I entered with this morning.

I still second-guessed my trip in the elevator, but while I might have had an extra skip in my step after spending hours without being hounded by my boss, I wasn't embarking on the epic trek that would have been taking the stairs.

The sun was shining and the warmth of the fall air instantly wrapped around me like a blanket. And that was just the start of my day turning around.

"Lori," a familiar voice calls, and when I turn around, I find Cory running toward me with a wide smile on his face. "Surprise," he says, animatedly handing me a gorgeous bunch of flowers.

"Aw," I say, dropping my nose into the pretty blooms and sucking in a deep breath of sweetness. "What are these for?"

Cory shrugs. "A little birdy told me that you might need a pick-me-up."

"Tatum," I growl darkly, making him laugh.

"She was meant to come, but she's stuck in a meeting, so lucky you, you get me all to yourself."

A genuine smile spreads across my face.

"Sounds perfect to me. What's the plan then?"

He rolls his eyes dramatically. "Cocktails, obviously."

"It's a Monday night, Cor."

"So? Haven't you heard Mondays are the new Fridays?"

"I thought Thursdays were the new Fridays," I tease.

"Ugh, you are so last year." He laughs, threading his arm through mine and spinning me around in the direction of our favorite Mexican restaurant.

"Miss Lori?" a deep voice calls. "Do you need a ride?"

"No, thank you, Jamie. Why don't you go home and enjoy your evening?" The temptation to invite him out for a drink burns through me. I'm sure Kian would have something to say about that. But I manage to refrain. He's a good egg. I don't want to get him in more trouble than I'm sure I already have.

"I'm not off the clock for a few hours yet."

"I'm sure the boss can cope getting a cab," I point out.

"Oh man, I'd love to see a Callahan hailing a cab on the sidewalk," Cory says loud enough for Jamie to hear.

He laughs, although he covers it quickly in his attempt to be professional.

"It's okay," I assure him. "I won't tell anyone. Thank you, for Friday night, by the way. I really appreciate everything you did."

Cory looks between us with a confused frown on his face.

"Anytime, Miss Lori."

"Aww, my hero." I swear he flushes from head to toe the second those words roll off my tongue.

"Sounds interesting," Cory muses, discreetly tugging me away from Kian's driver.

"Have a good evening, Jamie. Don't do anything I wouldn't do."

He chuckles as we walk away, and I'm pretty sure I hear him say, "I wouldn't dare."

"So, what did Jamie, the hot driver, do?" Cory asks the second we're out of earshot.

I let out a heavy sigh as I prepare to tell the story again. It's not the story itself that bothers me, but the fact that I have to talk about Kian.

"I got stuck in the lift in my building. Jamie and Kian had to rescue me."

"Oh. My. God. Tell me that was only the start of your night."

"Christ," I mutter. "Yes, Cory, it was only the beginning. After rescuing me, both my boss and his driver took me into my apartment and fucked me six ways to Sunday all freaking night."

"Could you say that again but with less sarcasm so that I can at least pretend to believe it?"

"You're a nightmare."

"Sounds like a dream, if you ask me."

"Please don't dream about my boss," I complain.

"Oh, come on. Your boss is one of the hottest men on earth. I don't believe for a second that you haven't had some kind of filthy dream about him."

I don't look over when his curious stare burns the side of my face.

"Oh my god, you have. Tell me everything."

"I need at least three margs for this conversation."

"Lucky for you, that's exactly what is about to happen."

I stumble through my front door—after Cory insists on riding the elevator up to my floor with me so I don't have to navigate the stairs—way later than I should and after one too many cocktails for a Monday night. But fuck it.

My boss is an asshole who casts me aside for hot actresses. Who cares if I turn up a little late in the morning with a sore head?

Certainly not me. Kian Callahan can kiss my ass.

With my front door securely locked, I kick my heels off and crash into my bedroom, mentally listing all the things I need to do. Take makeup off. Put hair up. Shower. Pass out.

I manage to successfully get through my to-do list until the point of passing out, because I make the mistake of pulling my cell from my purse and checking my messages.

I have two. One that infuriates me on sight and another that stirs some excitement.

I go for Ryder's first.

> Ryde my dick: If I were to call you an Uber, would you come and ride me, baby?

Heat pools between my thighs.

Fuck. His offer is so freaking tempting right about now.

Leaving him on read for a bit as I come up with my response, I open Kian's message.

> Boss: Has everything been booked?

"Rude asshole. What's wrong with 'Hi, Lori, have you had a good day? Sorry I haven't been in touch; meetings have been crazy. Or even, sorry I've been MIA, Tia's pussy is just that good.' Argh," I cry as I jump into bed and shove my legs under the sheets.

No matter how good Ryder's offer is, I am not going out.

I am not.

I am not.

As I sit there fuming at the audacity of my boss, I type out message after message that I'm not brave enough to send. Even while I'm on the wrong side of tipsy, I second-guess each of them.

In the end, I return to Ryder and let him down gently.

He isn't happy about it, but unless he's going to get his own ass in an Uber and turn up here, he's going to have to suck it up.

> Ryde my dick: If you're not going to get your sweet ass over here, at least give me something good to jerk off to.

> Lori: Pig.

> Ryde my dick: You love it. Don't even try to tell me that you're not wet, knowing that I'm here stroking my hard cock thinking of you.

> Lori: I can neither confirm nor deny.

I chuckle, picturing him rolling his eyes at my attempt to avoid answering the question.

> Ryde my dick: I know you are. I bet you're touching yourself right now, too. No need to be shy, baby.

He follows that up with a photo that proves just how unshy he is.

"Good lord," I mutter, staring a little too intently at the way he holds his dick.

My pussy throbs, I can't lie. It's been way too long since I saw some action that wasn't of the sexting variety with Ryder.

I could message and demand he come over. But unlike all the times in the past, it feels wrong.

He's good, and I know I'll get what I need. But having him here, in my bed, touching my body, just feels wrong.

I hate to admit it, but he's not the one I want.

He won't kiss me the way I was kissed on Saturday. His touch won't burn the way it did then.

> Ryde my dick: Come on, baby. Let me see those beautiful tits.

Honestly, he's probably already got hundreds of photographs of them saved in his camera roll from over the years. He should probably go back and look at some of the earlier ones, they'll be a little perkier than they are now.

Throwing the covers off, I push myself to my feet, swaying a little as I do.

My watch buzzes on my wrist, but I ignore it, knowing it'll be Ryder trying to convince me to get down and dirty with him.

Grabbing my phone, I open the message before immediately tapping the camera icon.

Pushing my tits together just so, I snap the perfect picture before hitting send.

Deciding that it's best to end it there, I put my cell on airplane mode and plug it into the charger on my nightstand.

After righting my top, I slip back into bed, but as much as I might want to drift off, my body is burning and my heart is racing.

Thoughts of Ryder staring at that photo and jerking off morph in my head to someone else doing the same.

Unable to stop myself, my hand slides down my stomach and slips inside my sleep shorts and panties.

Ryder is right, I am wet. But it's not for him.

It's for a man who shouldn't feature in my thoughts, let alone my filthy fantasies.

In my head, we're back in the gym, but when I press my hands against his chest, it's not to push him away. Instead, I slide them up, curl them around his shoulders, and pull him closer. And we don't stop.

I come with his name on my lips like a plea, my cheeks heating with both arousal and embarrassment.

After cleaning myself up, I crawl back into bed with shame still burning through me. I can't lie though, I do feel more relaxed after the release. Although, it still could have been better...

41

LORELEI

"Oh, shit, shit, shit, shit," I chant as I jump out of bed.

I should already be at work.

With my heart racing and my hand trembling with panic, I rush around my bedroom, dragging clothes on and throwing my wild curls into a messy bun. There is no time to do anything more.

My head lightly pounds, but it's nowhere near as bad as I deserve.

Kian is going to kill me.

By some miracle, I'm out the door and racing down the stairs in twenty minutes. There is no chance I'm risking the elevator this morning. There's no time to deal with that kind of drama should something go wrong.

I burst out of the building in a rush with my Uber app searching for a car.

I should have ordered one the second I woke up, but I was too frantic to think straight.

It's still telling me that it's trying to find one when a voice hits my ears.

"Good morning, Miss Lori. Can I offer you a lift?"

"Fuck," I hiss. If Jamie is here, then Kian knows that I'm late.

Blowing out a slow breath, I walk over.

It's too late to try and cover this up now.

"Morning, Jamie. Yes, that would be fantastic, thank you."

"No problem, Miss Lori. Did you have a good night with your friend?" he asks as he opens the door for me to climb inside.

"Yes. A little too good, actually." He chuckles as I get comfortable before closing the door on me.

I sit back and wait as he pulls away from my building in the direction of Callahan Enterprises. As we get closer, the dread I felt the moment I looked at the clock only gets worse.

Sitting forward, I speak to Jamie. "Is Kian mad?"

He takes a moment as he navigates an intersection, making my nerves quadruple.

"No. Mr. Callahan might be firm, but he's also fair. Plus, he likes you, Miss Lori. He'll go easy on you."

"Does he?" I mutter under my breath.

"You've got nothing to worry about."

I sit back, wishing I felt a little more confident about what I'm going to walk into in a few minutes.

"**W**ould you like me to ride up in the elevator with you, Miss Lori?" Jamie asks as I stand on the sidewalk, my eyes focused on the entrance to the building I should be inside.

"N-no," I stutter, hating that I don't sound more confident.

"It would be my pleasure to escort you."

Turning to Jamie, I smile up at him sweetly.

"I really appreciate the offer, but I'm okay."

What I really need is a very strong coffee, but that's going to have to wait.

"Okay. Have a good day."

"You too," I say before taking off in the direction of the elevator.

My skin tingles as if I'm being watched, but despite what I hope is a discreet look over both my shoulders, I don't find Kian watching me. It soon becomes clear that he's also not waiting to help me into the elevator like he was yesterday.

I hate that I'm disappointed, but there's very little I can do about it.

As I ride up through the building, I focus on what I'm going to say when I get to the top and Kian demands to know why I'm so late.

I come up with a few good lies that revolve around a sudden, unexpected illness, but I figure that he'll know it's a lie the second the words leave my lips.

The only thing I can do is tell the truth.

"Ah, there you are. Kian said you were going to be delayed this morning. I hope everything is okay."

"Y-yeah, everything is great."

"Good. He asked for you to go through to his office once you arrived."

My stomach turns over, but I force a smile on my face. I don't want anyone to know that I'm apprehensive about what's to come.

"I need coffee first," I mutter, more to myself than Melissa, before I dump my stuff under my desk and rush toward the kitchen.

Unlike yesterday, I grab two mugs from the cupboard, and I pay extra special attention to ensure Kian's coffee is exactly as he likes it.

A peace offering, if you will.

"Come in," his deep voice booms the second my knuckles rap against the door.

With both mugs in one hand, I suck in a deep breath and push the door open.

His scent hits me first, and then the second I step inside, our eyes collide and I feel it like a physical blow.

"Good morning, Lorelei," he says, his voice cold and hard. "How wonderful of you to show your face."

"I'm sorry I'm late. I—"

"Went out and got drunk on a school night," he finishes for me. "Thank you," he adds when I place his coffee before him. "Interesting that you chose to make me one this morning."

"I'm sorry, okay? I wasn't even that drunk, but I overslept and..." I trail off, hating that I'm reasoning with this jerk.

I fucked up. I know that. I don't need him making me feeling worse than I already do.

"I'm sorry. It won't happen again."

Assuming he wants me for more than to make me feel about a foot tall for my poor decision-making, I lower my ass to the chair.

He watches me silently as I sit bolt upright, waiting for him to say whatever it is he's holding back.

The air between us crackles, and it only takes me a few more seconds to recognize that there's something different about him.

He's not had a haircut or anything like that. It's nothing physical. But there's something in his eyes that I'm not sure I've seen before.

It's dangerous. Hot. And damn if it doesn't make my thighs clench.

Memories of my moment of weakness last night come back to me and my temperature soars.

Shut it down, Lorelei.

He isn't even that hot.

Fuck. He really is.

"Okay, shall we get to it?" he finally says, snapping out of whatever was keeping him silent.

His eyes drop to the desk. "What? No notebook today?" he asks, quirking a brow.

"Not this morning. What did you want to discuss, sir?" I ask, pushing everything else aside and focusing on work. It's much safer that way.

He talks me through another spreadsheet he's created.

330

Pride oozes from him as it works seamlessly, calculating profit and loss over the various decisions of the company.

It's impressive. Not that I'm going to tell him that. His ego is already big enough.

After explaining it all, he describes exactly what he would like me to do with all the data—in great detail—before finally dismissing me from his office.

"Lorelei," he growls before I'm able to slip away.

"Yes, Sir?"

"I expect this on my desk by the end of the day. No excuses."

My lips part to bark back a reply about my previous performance with hitting deadlines, but I manage to bite it back before it floats free.

I've already been late. I think that's probably enough for the day.

In a rush, and determined to knock him on his ass with the report I'm going to pull together, I finally take a seat behind my desk and set to work.

It's long after lunchtime when I come up for air.

In desperate need for something to eat, I save my document and slide my iPad into my purse with the intention of reading through what I've done so far.

I'm waiting for the elevator to hit the top floor when his footsteps echo down the hallway.

My teeth grind as he steps up behind me.

He doesn't say a word. He doesn't need to. His presence alone is oppressive enough.

When the doors open and I step inside, he follows.

The second we're trapped, the tension amps up.

I thought I was on edge in his office earlier, but it was nothing compared to this.

Not a word is spoken, and he doesn't make a move to touch me, but it doesn't matter. My body is on full alert. My skin is tingling, and my blood is burning.

Something has shifted with him. But I've no idea what it is.

The moment I can escape, I dash from the elevator and toward the doors that will grant me some freedom.

"Good afternoon," Kian says behind me as I assume he greets the doormen I grinned at as I ran past them.

I take off in the direction of the closest coffee shop in the hope that he will let me go.

Wishful thinking.

"Where are we going?" Kian rasps beside me.

"I've no idea where you're going, but I'm going for a sandwich and some peace."

"Sounds perfect."

"It wasn't an invitation," I hiss quietly.

"I don't need an invitation, Lorelei."

"Oh yeah, how could I forget? You do what you want."

I don't need to look over to know he's smirking.

With a sigh, I keep walking with my head held high.

He wants to follow me. Fine. But I will not give him the satisfaction of unnerving me.

He does not hold that kind of power over me.

My stomach growls loudly the second I see the coffee shop up ahead.

I join the line to order and he falls into place behind me.

Thankfully, the line moves fast, and in only a few minutes, I'm sitting at a small table at the back.

With my food and drink on one side and my iPad propped up on the other, I set about the task at hand.

I read a paragraph and swallow one mouthful before a shadow looms over me.

My stomach knots and my heart rate increases, but I don't look up.

His glare burns into the top of my head as I keep my eyes locked on the screen.

"Lorelei," he warns.

I let out a frustrated sigh before finally glancing up,

making sure my face shows just how irritated I am by his mere presence.

"Can I help you, sir?"

"Can I sit?"

I look at the other chair around the small round table and then back up at him.

"I don't think there's enough space. That table over there is free," I say, jerking my chin in the direction of a recently vacated table currently covered in trash.

His jaw pops in irritation, but to my surprise, he spins around and marches in that direction.

Internally, I do a little celebratory dance. Who knew it would be so easy to get rid of him?

My eyes widen when he shoves the trash from the table, places his lunch on top of it and then picks the entire thing up and carries it back over.

"What the hell are you doing?" I shriek as he lowers his newly accosted table next to mine.

Shrugging off his jacket, he drapes it on the back of the chair and lowers his ass to the seat.

"Close your mouth, Lorelei. You don't make a good guppy."

Anger surges through me.

"I'm trying to have a quiet lunch. Alone," I warn, aware that we've caught the attention of a few fellow diners.

"And I'm having lunch with my girlfriend," he states as if he truly believes the words.

My chin drops again at his audacity. But while my anger only increases, he smirks at me like he's won something.

"That's not...we're not..." If possible, the amusement only grows. "You're infuriating."

"So you've mentioned before," he says before biting into his sandwich.

I drag my eyes away from him and back to my screen, but I can no longer focus, and I end up reading the same sentence four times over.

Kian is focused on his cell and thankfully ignores my ridiculous attempt to continue working.

Giving up, I reach into my purse and pull my own cell out.

I've got a handful of email notifications, a stream of notifications from my group chat with my brothers, which reveals the usual—them trying to get the other in trouble—and a message from Tate.

I giggle at the meme she's sent, causing Kian to look up. His attention makes my face heat, but I don't let him know that I'm aware of him.

It's the first time I've looked at my messages all day. It occurs to me that I never received a reply from Ryder after I sent the photo last night.

Tapping out of Tate's message, I scan down my inbox, wondering why.

My eyes drop, and then so does my heart when I find that my thread with Kian is above Ryder's.

No. That can't be right. My heart races and my temperature soars to dangerous levels as reality dawns.

Oh my god.

Oh my god.

Tell me I didn't. Please, for the love of God, tell me that I didn't...

Fuck. My. Life.

My stomach rolls, and I press my hand to it.

I'm going to be sick.

With my cell gripped tightly in my hand, I jump up from my seat and race to the bathroom.

He calls my name in concern, but I don't dare look back.

I can't.

How the hell am I ever going to look him in the eyes again?

I sent my boss a picture of my boobs.

I sent my boss a picture of my fucking boobs.

42

KIAN

"Lorelei?" I shout after inviting myself into the ladies' bathroom in the coffee shop.

She's been gone for almost fifteen minutes.

"You shouldn't be in here," she calls back weakly.

"I'm worried. Are you—"

"Fine. I'm fine. I'll just meet you back at the office."

I frown.

"What's wrong? Are you sick?"

"No, I'm fine," she repeats.

"You're hiding in a bathroom stall. You are not fine."

She huffs in irritation a beat before a toilet flushes.

The lock disengages and suddenly the door is ripped open.

"I am not hiding," she states firmly, marching toward the basins with her head held high.

"Then why are you—"

"I already told you, I wanted to have some peace, Kian," she spits. "Is it so hard to believe that I might need five minutes away from you?"

Her words are vicious, and the look she pins me with in the mirror isn't much better.

"Lorelei, I—" My words are cut off as the bathroom door opens and a woman walks inside.

Her eyes widen at the sight of me standing in the middle of the space, and she gives the sign on the door she's still holding a double check.

"I'm sorry. I'm just leaving," I say before moving toward the door. "I'll meet you back at the office."

Without waiting for a response, I walk out of the bathroom and then soon after, the coffee shop.

"Come in," I call the second a knock sounds on my office door.

Lorelei stalks inside like always. There is no sign of the woman who ran and hid in the bathroom earlier.

"I have the report, sir," she says before placing a folder on my desk.

I study it, reading the first few lines before looking back up at her.

"Thank you."

"I'm going to finish up a few other things, then I'll be heading home," she informs me.

"I trust that you're going to have a more sensible night," I muse.

"Not that it's any of your business, but yes."

She backs away from my desk in favor of the door.

"Good. I need you ready tomorrow."

"Have a good evening, sir."

"Don't worry, I intend to."

She looks over her shoulder just in time to see the smirk that pulls at my lips. She frowns but doesn't respond and a second later she's gone.

I expected her to say something this morning.

To apologize, maybe. To at least ask me to forget I'd ever seen anything.

What I wasn't expecting was for her to say nothing.

My office door closes behind her, leaving the room feeling cold and lonely.

I stare at it, battling with myself about whether I should go after her or not.

I asked Melissa to check on her after she returned from her lunch, and she assured me that Lorelei was fine.

Dragging my attention back to my monitor, I continue with what I was doing, but just like before, my focus is elsewhere.

The buzz of my cell is a welcome distraction; so is the person I find in my messages.

> Makenzie: I'm bored

> > Kian: Do some homework. It's never too late to learn something.

I smirk. Teasing them will never get old.

> Makenzie: I'm already smarter than you, old man. What are you doing?

> > Kian: Trying to work.

> Makenzie: Boooooring.

> Makenzie: You should do something fun.

> > Kian: I am. You should see this spreadsheet I'm working on.

> Makenzie: Yawn.

> Makenzie: Ditch work and come get me? I'm going crazy stuck at home.

> > Kian: It's been three days.

> Makenzie: Three loooooooong days. Don't tell her, but I even miss Tilly.

> > Kian: I'm so telling her.

> Makenzie: Traitor. Come and rescue me and I'll let you off.

> Kian: Blackmail, really?

> Makenzie: Come on, old man. You know you don't have a better offer.

She adds a load of praying emojis, and before I'm aware that I've made a decision, I've saved what I'm doing and turned my monitor off.

> Kian: You have thirty minutes.

> Makenzie: Yessssss!

After changing out of my suit in my private bathroom, I head out toward the elevator.

The reception area is empty and silent, and I can't help but be drawn to Lorelei's desk.

Everything is perfectly tidy. It has been ever since I pointed out her mistake on day one.

The only thing that sits on the top is a notebook.

Fucking notebooks.

I've no idea how many she has, but this is another that I've never seen before.

It reads, "Too busy for your bullshit."

Shaking my head, I refrain from putting it away.

She'll know it was me, and she'll know that she's getting to me.

It does spark an idea, though.

As I descend through the building, I make two calls. One to secure something to put an end to Kenzie's boredom for an hour, and another to my graphic designer.

You want to play, Lorelei?

You chose the wrong opponent.

"Oh my god," Kenzie screams as I take the corner too wide and the car's back end spins out. I knew it was coming, but it still made my heart lurch in my chest. "This is awesome," she squeals as I right the car and floor it down the straight.

I've been coming out here to burn off steam for years. Usually alone, though.

Kenzie has been begging me to bring her out with me. She's an adrenaline junkie—something we have in common.

She's already asked me if we can do a parachute jump for her eighteenth birthday.

I haven't broached the subject with our mom—not that her opinion will matter much to Kenzie. When she sets her sights on something, it usually happens.

Apparently, it's a family trait that hasn't just come down from our father.

Pushing the gas as hard as I can, I watch the speedometer climb higher and higher until I have to brake for the next corner.

I'll have Mom on the phone later, ripping me a new one for bringing her here. But I'm pretty sure Kenzie needs this release just as much as I do.

Nothing but the car and the asphalt matter when you're on the track. The rest of the world and all the issues that come with it fall away in favor of heart-racing adrenaline.

"Why are you stopping?" Kenzie complains when I finally drop the speed and head into the pits.

"Time's up," I say, feeling as disappointed as she sounds.

"You'll bring me back, though, right?"

"Assuming Mom doesn't kill me in the meantime."

"She'll be fine," Kenzie assures me. I'm not sure I agree.

She's always refused to allow me to bring her here, and that was without a broken ankle.

"You hungry?" I ask, not ready to end my evening and head home alone quite yet.

Kenzie laughs. "Obviously. Burgers?"

"You read my mind."

Once we're back in my own car, we head across town at less hair-raising speeds to our favorite burger place.

"Tilly is gonna be pissed."

"Ken," I warn.

"Dude, I'm fifteen. I can say pissed."

I raise a brow.

"Jeez, you're as bad as Dad. I bet you were saying and doing much worse when you were my age."

"Definitely not. I was an angel."

"Bullshit," she coughs, earning herself a hard glare. "Sorry. Sorry. I know I shouldn't listen to Kieran's stories."

"They're all lies," I state firmly.

"Suuuuure."

"So, how's school?" I ask, attempting to change the subject.

"Dull as ever. I'm ready for college."

"You've got a while yet. And anyway, you might not get in."

She throws a fry at me. "I'm going to Harvard, and you know it."

"Tills will. You...I'm not so sure."

"Evil, Bro. Freaking evil."

I'm still buzzing from the drive around the track when I let myself into my apartment later that evening.

Mom wasn't home when I dropped Kenzie off, so I managed to avoid the ass-ripping that I'm sure is to come when she discovers where I took her baby tonight.

After replying to a handful of urgent emails that landed while I was hanging out with my sister, I head for my bathroom, stripping out of my clothes as I go.

The moment I step into my walk-in shower, everything

I've forced myself not to think about today comes rushing back full force.

"Fuck," I groan, my cock hardening and the desire she sparked in me last night surging through me with the force of a tsunami.

Reaching out, I wrap my hand around my aching length.

I jerked off twice to her photo, and then again this morning, but it's barely taken the edge off.

The second she walked into my office, it all came flooding back, and I'm sure I was a heartbeat away from splitting my pants. Thank fuck I didn't have to stand up.

Every single thing about the image was perfect.

The only thing is that I'm pretty sure she never meant to send it to me.

And that's a big fucking problem.

Because it means she's intentionally sending them to someone else.

I swear to God, if it's her asshole of an ex...I'll fucking end him.

He doesn't deserve her after what he did, and if he's still got his claws into her...

Anger collides with my desire, causing something dangerous to explode within me.

I jerk my cock hard and fast, already knowing that it's going to lead to a surface-level, unfulfilling release.

I need more.

I need her.

I had every intention of saying something about the photo earlier, but then she walked into my office and knocked me on my ass. Or at least, she would have if I weren't already sitting on it.

"Fucking Temptress," I grunt as my release surges forward. "Lorelei, fuck. Fuck."

I come into the torrent of water raining down on me, but just like I suspected, it barely takes the edge off.

Resting my palm against the tiles, I hang my head, shame washing over me.

I should have deleted that picture the second it landed on my cell.

But then I guess the things we should do and the reality are often very, very different.

My muscles are once again pulled tight when I crawl into bed an hour or so later.

Propping myself up, I flip my laptop open. I force myself to finish what I started before Kenzie messaged, but it's hard work.

I've never had such a hard time focusing.

It's all her fault.

Lorelei and her perfect tits.

Her lips.

The kiss.

Fuck.

I've got a real fucking problem here.

And I'm pretty sure that my plans for the rest of the week are only going to make the issue worse.

I smirk as I think about what the next two days might hold.

I've warned her time and time again that once I set my sights on something, I do whatever it takes to secure it.

She keeps underestimating me.

Well...more fool you, Lorelei Tempest.

I've decided what I want, and I'm going to use every dirty trick in the book to ensure it happens.

And I'm going to enjoy every fucking second of it.

The second I've finished, I slam the lid of my laptop down and grab my cell.

I've got messages in the group chat with my brothers, but I happily ignore them in favor of my chat with Lorelei.

The second I open it and the photo emerges on my screen, it's like last night all over again.

I might know it's there now, but I'm no less surprised or turned on by it.

She knows I've seen it. The little blue ticks beneath it are all the evidence she needs.

Does she know just how much I've made use of it, though?

My cock jerks, craving more than my own hand can offer.

With a smirk, I tap out a message that is sure to cause a reaction.

It took all my self-control not to reply last night. But it's over. My restraint has run out.

She might think she can outrun me, but she's going to learn that I'll always be one step ahead.

43

LORELEI

Boss: Where's my goodnight photo?

My stomach knots up as disbelief rushes through me.

He hasn't said a word all day. If I didn't realize my mistake at lunch, I'd have no reason to believe he even knew.

Of course, I know that he knows because of those two taunting blue ticks beneath the photo.

How many times has he looked at it?

As much as I tried to convince myself that he was disgusted and deleted it the second he opened it, I knew deep down that he wasn't.

And now I know...

Not only that, he's demanding more.

What the actual fuck am I meant to reply to that message?

I can hardly do as he's requesting and send my boss another dirty picture.

Can I?

No. I absolutely cannot.

But what if he sends one in return...

Fucking hell, Lorelei.

Closing the message, I climb out of bed and pad through

to the kitchen in the hope that in the time it takes to grab a bottle of water, inspiration will hit.

But predictably, when I crawl back into bed with a drink I neither want nor need, I'm still as clueless about how to navigate this situation as I was before.

I could ignore him. But does that make me look weak?

> Lori: I apologize for my previous message. My mistake. Please delete and never think or talk about it again.

I read my words over and over again, my thumb hovering over the send button.

Does it still make me look weak.

Should I be apologizing?

Sure, it was an accident. But something tells me that he's not annoyed about my drunken mistake.

Deciding against it, I delete it all and change tact.

> Lori: Unfortunately, that's the only one you're going to get from me. Enjoy.

I immediately feel better about my response and hit send without second-guessing this time.

He reads it instantly. An image emerges in my head of him sitting in bed just like me, staring down at his cell...at my photo.

Heat unfurls in my lower belly.

Don't think about it, Lorelei.

Do not think about it...

> Boss: Trust me, I have enjoyed it.

> Boss: Many times.

I gasp, my hand covering my mouth as I stare at his confession.

I look around the room, shocked to my very core that he'd admit that.

What do I do now?

Sure, I'm no stranger to a little sexting. But with my boss? That's certainly a first.

I think of Clive, the boss that needs to never take up any brain space ever again, and I shudder.

Maybe things could have been worse than him accusing me of stealing. Imagine his dick pic. I shudder again. I might need to throw some ice-cold water on this situation, but that shit isn't necessary.

Kian drags me from my disgusting musings when his dots begin bouncing.

> Boss: Could really use some new inspiration…

"Fucking hell." I laugh. Brazen much?

> Lori: Goodnight, Boss.

I lower my cell to the bed, proud of myself for not being dragged in. It would be easy, too freaking easy, to fall under Kian Callahan's spell...again.

It helps knowing that I'm not going to see him for a couple of days.

He's got a stupidly early flight tomorrow. I should know. I booked it.

A wicked smirk spreads across my lips as I remember the moment I selected the worst possible flight time just to piss him off. Fucker deserves it for being an ass.

> Boss: Lorelei…

My skin prickles as I hear his deep warning voice as if it's growled in my ear.

> Lori: I'm sure you have plenty of girls willing to send you naughty pics. Message one of them. I'm not interested. You have an early start tomorrow. I suggest you get some sleep.

> Boss: I'm not the one who has an issue with their punctuality.

> Lori: Goodnight, Kian. Sleep well.

I should turn my cell off, but the temptation of knowing if he's replied again is too much to ignore.

But he doesn't, and I drift off feeling disappointed instead of celebrating that I got the final word in.

———

Bang. Bang. Bang.

"What the fuck?" I gasp, sitting upright in bed, my eyes wide and my heart pounding.

A cold sweat covers my skin as I wait for something else.

But there's nothing. Not for a few seconds, anyway.

Bang. Bang. Bang.

Recognizing the sound this time, I throw the sheets off and get to my feet, confident that someone isn't robbing the place.

Ripping my bedroom door open, I march through the hallway toward the irritating noise.

I stretch up on my toes and peer through the peephole to discover which asshole thinks it'll be funny to wake me before dawn.

"Of fucking course," I mutter when I find an impatient man glaring back at me.

"Open the fucking door, Lorelei," he demands, fully aware that I'm on the other side. Fuck knows how.

"Motherfucker."

Pulling my sleep bonnet from my head, I let my curls fall around my shoulders before I unlock the door and pull it open.

"What?" I snap with my hands on my hips and my best resting bitch face in place.

He doesn't dignify my question with an answer. Instead, he barges past me and storms into my apartment like he owns it.

"What the hell, Callahan?" I demand as he continues toward my bedroom.

I rush behind him, continuing to glare as he looks around as if he's expecting to find something.

"What?" I snap again.

"There's no suitcase. You're not packed," he states, spinning around to pin me with a weighted look of his own.

"Why would I need to pack?"

"You're not..." He scrubs his hand down his face in disbelief. As he does so, his dark eyes drop from mine and he finally acknowledges what I'm wearing—or not, as the case may be.

My skin burns despite the thin layer of cotton stopping him from seeing me in all my glory. Not that it matters, he's already seen everything already. My nipples harden as he makes his way back up. There's no way he doesn't notice, but he keeps his expression neutral.

It's not until his eyes meet mine that I see any kind of reaction.

They're molten.

Desire hits me like a freight train.

But like him, I refuse to let my true feelings be known, and I cross my arms under my breasts, effectively pushing them up and stealing his attention again.

"We-we're going on a trip, remember?"

I smirk, loving that I've made this always-in-control man trip over his words.

"No. *You're* going on a trip."

He narrows his eyes.

"No. *We* are. I asked you to book a business trip."

"And I did. Your flight leaves in..." I glance at the clock. "Whoa, an hour and a half. You really should go."

"You're my assistant, Lorelei. You come on business trips with me."

I shrug. "Not this time, hot shot."

"Fuck's sake," he mutters before spinning around and pulling my closet open.

"What are you—"

"Where is your suitcase?"

"Kian, I'm not—"

"This trip requires both of us, so I suggest you wake the fuck up and get packing. Our flight is leaving in an hour and a half," he says, mocking me.

"Your flight. I only booked one seat."

"Then I suggest you get on the phone, because I'm not flying alone."

I watch in horror as he selects a handful of outfits from my closet and throws them onto the bed.

He isn't joking, is he?

"Suitcase, Lorelei. Then call the airline. Where is your—"

"Kian," I shriek when he successfully locates my underwear drawer without my help. "There is something fucking wrong with you," I mutter as I attempt to push him away.

He's bigger and heavier than me, and he doesn't so much as sway when I shove at his shoulder.

Reaching into the drawer, he pulls out a red lace G-string and holds it up.

He studies it for a beat before turning to me and letting his eyes trail down my body.

"Do you have the matching bra?"

"My suitcase is in the closet in the hallway," I tell him, submitting to the fact I'm going on a trip with this infuriating man.

He looks down at my open drawer again with a pout in his lips before he backs away, leaving me to deal with my underwear choices.

"I'm trusting you to select the right ones," he warns.

"My underwear, my choice," I snap as he goes in search of my suitcase.

By the time he returns, I have everything laid out on my bed. All I need are my toiletries.

"Thank you," I mutter insincerely as he places it on the bed. "I need to get ready. Wait for me in the living room?"

For a moment, I don't think he's going to agree and instead insist on staying to watch. But after a few seconds, he finally walks out again.

"Why did I agree to this job exactly?" I ask myself.

"I heard that," he calls, amusement laced through his tone.

Despite Kian's insistence that he should get priority due to the amount of money his family and the company spend on flying every year, I fail to get through to the airline on our journey to the airport.

As we walk toward the check-in desk, we're at risk of missing the flight I had originally booked for him.

"Good morning," Kian says curtly to the man standing at the entrance to the first class and business line. "Kian Callahan. We're flying to Charleston."

"Callahan?" he asks, tapping his screen.

"Yes," Kian sighs in exasperation.

I get it. It's too early for this shit.

"I'm sorry, we don't have you flying first or business with us today."

Kian instantly turns to look at me.

"Oh, whoops," I say innocently. "I think I booked you an economy seat."

His face morphs into one of pure frustration, and I find it hard not to smirk in response.

Don't mess with me, asshole.

I raise a brow.

He never demanded that I book him a first-class seat, just like he didn't tell me to book two. What's a girl to do?

Kian turns his glare back to the airline assistant, who, unlike me, withers under his intense stare. "I am an Executive Platinum member. There's been a mistake. I need to book two first-class seats on the flight to Charleston this morning."

The man practically trips over himself before suggesting that we follow him to the desk.

Much to Kian's irritation, we can't get on our original flight unless we accept economy seats. Obviously, I didn't have an issue with that. I've only ever flown economy and probably always will. But that isn't good enough for Kian Callahan, so we have no choice but to hang around the airport for a few hours to catch the next flight.

"Let's go," he barks once we've got our boarding passes.

His hand grabs mine and I'm all but dragged toward security, which we fly through because of his fancy members' card.

"Sit," he demands once we've been welcomed into the first-class lounge at Chicago O'Hare.

"Could you please be more demanding? I just love it so much," I deadpan, trying not to look awed by my surroundings.

He stills and glares down at me.

A shiver rips down my spine, but it's not fear. It's something very, very different.

His dark, angry eyes bore into mine, and my temperature soars.

I've always known that I'm a little fucked up when it comes to men. It's why I keep falling for the wrong ones and getting my heart broken. But this really takes the cake.

I should be scared, but I'm not in the slightest.

His nostrils flare, and his eyes widen. "You booked me in economy."

I smile up at him, refusing to be intimidated.

"Just wait until you see your hotel room."

Refusing to be blindsided again, the moment Lorelei excused herself to use the bathroom, I called the hotel and fixed our room situation.

Just like she'd taunted, she'd booked me into a basic twin room.

I'll never admit it to her face, but her audacity amuses the hell out of me. I'm not sure there's anyone else on the planet who would dare test me like that. Okay, yeah, my siblings would. They'd get a massive fucking kick out of it, too.

Conversation between us remains focused on work, despite my desire to return to our little texting session last night.

We're away for three days. Something tells me that it'll come up.

I didn't need to bring Lorelei to an airport to know that she was not a seasoned traveler. But seeing her wide-eyed expression as we walked into the lounge...I guess it's easy for this life to become normal.

Hell, it is normal for me. I don't ever remember traveling any differently.

Maybe she's right. Maybe I am nothing but a wealthy, entitled asshole.

I smile. Yeah, I'm definitely that. But there's more if you care to look a little deeper under the surface.

"Are you going to share the reason we're going to Charleston, or is it something I have to guess?" Lorelei asks when she returns to her seat.

"We're going to meet with the management team at The Regency. They've had issues with staff retention recently and their accounts are looking...interesting."

She studies me, and I wait with bated breath for her response.

"And that's a job that requires the CFO's involvement?"

I hold my head high, both annoyed and impressed that she's seen straight through me.

"Normally, no. But I haven't traveled this year like I usually would, and it's time to make my presence known, especially at some of our locations that are struggling. I believe it's important to remind the management teams that despite being miles away, we are watching."

"I see."

"If you have something to say, Lorelei. Please, just say it."

She silently fumes, her head spinning with whatever it is that's bothering her.

It would be easy to think it's the photo that's still burning up my cellphone.

Sending me a picture of her tits by accident probably is a big deal, but she's strong enough to deal with that.

"How's Tia?" she suddenly blurts.

I frown.

"Ti—oh. Tia Halliwell. She's...fine, I believe. Do you know her?"

"Nope. But it seems you know her well."

I haven't been on social media for days, but I'm not stupid. I'm more than aware that there's probably a photograph of us together on Saturday night. Tia loves the spotlight. She'll make the most of any opportunity to turn the attention on her.

It seems that little bit of attention may just have passed by Lorelei's radar.

The corner of my mouth twitches with the beginning of a smirk.

She's seen it, and she's jealous.

Holy shit.

"A few years ago, I knew her well. But we've barely spoken since she moved to Hollywood," I explain, aware that it isn't what she really wants to hear.

"You must have had a lot to catch each other up on, then."

With her eyes focused on her coffee, I'm able to take a few seconds to really study her.

She didn't have time to put much makeup on this morning —not that she needs it. Nor did she have a chance to do anything with her hair. Her curls look beautiful hanging around her shoulders, and the freckles across her nose and cheeks are endearing as hell.

Her shoulders are pulled tight with tension, and she's picking at her nail anxiously.

It's not a look I'm used to seeing on her, and I can't say I like it all that much. I prefer strong and sassy Lorelei.

"Not really. Our lives have moved in different directions. I'm pleased for her, but there isn't anything between us anymore."

Her eyes jump to mine.

"But you canceled on me for her."

Unable to stop it, a laugh tumbles free.

"Is that really what you think?" I ask calmly.

"It's what I know."

I raise my brows and sit back in my chair, crossing my arms over my chest.

"You really shouldn't believe everything you see online, Lorelei."

She glares at me. She wants to believe me, but then I guess when you've been let down by men all your life, expecting the worst begins to come naturally.

"Okay. So why did you cancel Saturday night after making such a song and dance about getting me out on a date in the first place?"

"I had a family emergency."

"Bit convenient. Tate didn't say anything about an emergency."

I'm hardly surprised. King probably doesn't even know that Kenzie had surgery on her ankle.

"Well, maybe Tate doesn't know everything."

Lorelei glares daggers at me as a staff member clears our empty plates.

"So..." she starts the second we're alone again.

"One of my little sisters broke her ankle cheerleading. My stepdad was out of town on a golf trip, so my mom called me to sit with my other sister while she was looked at. Turned out that she needed surgery."

The more I talk, the more blood drains from Lorelei's face.

"Shit. Is she okay?"

Pulling my cell from my pocket, I open my camera roll and find a selfie she forced me to take in the track car last night.

Spinning it around, I let Lorelei see Kenzie's wild eyes and excited smile.

"Yeah, she's as crazy as ever."

"So if you spent the night at the hospital, how come there are photos of you and Tia Halliwell on Instagram?"

"You know, you don't have to say her whole name every time."

"Shut up," she hisses.

"I went for a drink after I left the hospital, and she happened to be there. It was nothing more than a coincidence."

"How lucky after such a long and stressful night. What?" she snaps when I laugh at her comment.

"Nothing. You're jealous because you think I fucked her."

Lorelei sits up so fast, it's a miracle she doesn't break something.

"I am not jealous. I don't care who you spend time with," she argues.

"Is that right?" I mutter under my breath.

"It's just rude to be canceled on for a celebrity."

"Well, I can assure you that that didn't happen. I canceled because of my little sister."

She slumps back in her seat with her arms crossed under her breasts. With her blouse unbuttoned the way it is, I get a great shot of her cleavage. And with the image that's saved secretly on my cell, I can conjure up a very pretty picture of what she might look like if her blouse and bra were to magically disappear.

"You could have just said that."

She's right, I could. "I'm not used to considering other people's feelings in the way I live my life. I should have been more considerate to my...girlfriend."

"I'm not your girlfriend."

Reaching for my coffee, I take a sip, keeping my eyes on her the whole time.

"I've got to tell you, I'm concerned," I say cryptically.

"That I have the audacity to turn you down?"

"Well, yes, obviously. But I'm more concerned that my girlfriend is sending other men photographs of her boobs."

"Fuck off, Kian."

I smirk at her, loving the way she glares at me.

"They've just put our gate up. We should make a move."

Draining what's left of my coffee, I push to my feet.

Lorelei stares up at me with a small frown between her brows.

"What's wrong?"

"I should run in the opposite direction and never look back, shouldn't I?"

My heart slams against my ribs at the thought of her doing just that.

"Probably," I force out. *I'm not going to fucking let you, though.*

The air between us continues to crackle, ensuring my body temperature simmers just beneath boiling.

Holding my hand out, I wait for her to make a decision.

It takes a couple of seconds. While I'm confident that she's not going to run, I'm not sure if she's going to jump into this with as much excitement as I'd like her to.

Eventually, though, she makes the right choice and slips her small, warm hand into mine.

It might be the most innocent of touches, but fuck if my dick doesn't jerk like she reached for that instead.

The second she's on her feet, I tug her closer.

She squeaks quietly in surprise, but she doesn't immediately pull away.

Ducking my head, I let my lips brush her ear. "I can't believe you thought I was taking this trip without you. I thought you were smarter than that, Temptress."

"I was—I mean, I am—mad at you." She tries to sound stern, but she fails miserably.

"No, you're not. You're too busy wishing that I replied with a photograph of my own."

All the air rushes from her lungs, but I don't hang around long enough for her to reply. Instead, I reach for my bag with my free hand and throw it over my shoulder before leading her out of the lounge.

"Wow," Lorelei breathes once we're settled in our first-class seats.

It's a quick flight. We're not surrounded by the kind of luxury I'd expect from a long-haul flight, but it's still a hell of a lot better than the fucking economy seat she booked for me.

"You don't ever need to worry about me treating you right, Temptress."

"Your money doesn't impress me, Callahan."

"You sounded pretty impressed just then."

"Doesn't mean that I wouldn't be equally as happy back there."

I smirk, watching the flight attendant walking up the aisle with mimosas.

"You were saying?" I ask once she's offered Lorelei a glass. A glass that she eagerly accepts.

"It's the least I deserve for having to put up with you for the next three days."

The flight attendant flinches at Lorelei's harsh words.

"I'm sure you felt the same on your honeymoon," I deadpan, making her balk.

"He's joking. There isn't enough money in the world to make me stoop that low."

Unsure of what to make of us, the attendant hurries down the aisle, serving other passengers.

"You're wrong," I state confidently.

"I highly doubt that."

"One day, you'll beg me to put a ring on it."

"Have you heard yourself? Firstly, don't forget that I refused your proposal. Secondly, never going to happen."

"What makes you say that?" I ask, genuinely interested in her reasoning.

She's an intelligent, beautiful woman who somehow manages to challenge me like no other. I'm struggling to see why she's so adamant it won't happen.

She shakes her head before lifting her half-empty glass to gesture to our surroundings. "All this. Your life. It's not who I am. I'm your assistant, Kian. I know my place in this world, and while I might have considered faking it with you for a few moronic moments, I am happy with my life and where I'm at."

"Your place is beside me," I say simply before turning my attention to the screen in front of me that's showing our flight time.

Her eyes burn into the side of my face, and I sense that she has a million and one things to say, but none of them make it past her lips.

45

LORELEI

I watch as Kian marches through the reception of The Regency. I want to say he moves with the authority of a man who owns the place, but let's be honest, he literally does.

Everyone around me senses it too, because I swear, every set of eyes—both male and female—turns to watch him.

The man sitting behind the reception desk he's set his sights on legit looks like he's about thirty seconds from shitting his pants. It's funny as hell, but also...I get it.

Kian Callahan can be one intimidating motherfucker when he wants to be.

I knew I was in for a whole world of pain when I booked the cheap airline seat and then reserved him a budget hotel room. Not that any room in a Callahan Hotel could ever really be considered as such. I'm not sure any of the men in charge of this empire know the meaning of the word.

I was hardly surprised when he admitted on the drive here that he'd called ahead and "fixed" my little mishap.

I smirk, just thinking about the great Kian Callahan squeezing his big body into a small, twin-sized bed.

It's almost a shame that he's figured me out, because as much as I'd hate to share that twin room with him, it would be funny as fuck.

I watch him at a distance as he talks to the young guy with the pale face. Even from here, I swear I can see his hands trembling.

I've no idea if he prewarned the staff here that he was coming, but something tells me that every single person on the payroll will know thirty seconds after he walks away from that desk.

I wonder if they'll have time to give his room a once-over before he unlocks it and walks inside.

After a few short words, Kian spins around with room keycards in his hand and a scowl on his face.

My stomach knots.

Did that guy just lose his job?

"What's wrong?" I ask the second he approaches me.

"Nothing. Come on," he demands, snagging his bag from beside me, throwing it over his shoulder, and grabbing both of our cases before he marches toward the elevators.

Not wanting to be left behind, I take off after him.

The second we're inside the car, he hits the button for the top floor—of course—and we begin to rise through the building.

"Why are you scared of elevators?" he asks simply, distracting me from the classical music that fills the space.

"I'm not scared of elevators, per se. I'm claustrophobic. Or I used to be."

"Used to be?" he echoes.

"I thought I'd worked through it. Apparently, I'm not quite there."

"Why are you scared of enclosed spaces?"

Thankfully, the elevator comes to a stop and the doors open, allowing me to escape the question. There is no way I'm discussing my childhood with him.

Despite not knowing where I'm going, I take a chance and turn left.

I hear him following me, and I take that as a good sign that I made the right decision.

"Lorelei," he demands just before I turn a corner.

Pausing, I turn to the closest door, assuming that it's mine.

After passing me a keycard, he stands beside me and waits for me to let myself in.

I step inside, finding that the carpet is as thick and bouncy as it was out in the hallway. The need to kick my heels off becomes too much and I sigh in relief as I wiggle my cramped toes.

Releasing the door behind me, I expect it to slam, finally cutting me off from my annoyingly hot travel buddy. But the bang never comes.

I barely get a look at the luxury suite before I sense him step up behind me.

Spinning around, I find his eyes and give him my very best glare.

"Why are you in my room?"

One side of his mouth kicks up in a smirk.

"Your room?"

"Yes. My room."

"Ah," he says, ripping his eyes from mine and walking deeper into the room.

He doesn't stop until he's standing at the large windows and gazing out at the view.

I've no idea what he's looking at, and I don't care. My only focus is getting him to leave so I can have a few minutes alone to process all this.

When he asked me to book this trip for him, I never even considered that he'd want me to travel with him. The whole thing has blown my mind.

"There was an issue," he confesses before spinning around and turning those mesmerizing green eyes on me. "They only had one suite left."

I throw my hands up in frustration. "I don't need a suite, Kian. I need space."

He looks around. "There is plenty of space here."

I shake my head. That is not what I meant.

"What happened to the twin room I booked? I'll take that. I'm not as fussy as you." Hell, I'd sleep in the freaking cleaning closet if it meant I got a breather from him.

"Taken. There are multiple events happening in the area this weekend. Everything is fully booked."

"You're lying," I accuse, refusing to believe a word that comes out of his mouth.

"Call down to reception and ask, if you like," he offers, pointing toward the tablet that will connect me to the front desk.

As much as I want to call his bluff, I don't have the energy.

Instead, I stalk toward him, but before I get too close, I turn to the right and march through double doors that lead to the most incredible bedroom I've ever seen.

A huge oak four-poster bed sits pride of place in the center of the room. The bed itself is high, the comforter thick, and there are more cushions than I've ever seen on a bed. All I want to do is run and jump right into the middle of it.

But seeing as I've got company, I refrain from acting like a child.

I walk through to the bathroom, and my eyebrows rise at the two-person whirlpool bath that sits beneath a floor-to-ceiling window.

Rushing over, I find nothing but ocean on the other side.

My muscles ache as I think about relaxing back in that tub and watching the waves crash in the distance.

Heaven.

I take in the his and hers basins. Those really should give me the answer to my next question.

"Is the other room this impressive as well?"

Kian watches me closely as I walk out of the bathroom, slip my jacket off, and hang it over the back of the chair at the vanity.

"There isn't another room, Lorelei. This is a one-bedroom suite. The finest in the hotel."

His words slam into me, and I take a step back.

"No," I breathe. "That's not...we're not..."

"Freshen up," he orders before collecting my case and placing it into the bedroom. "We've got a meeting with the management team in an hour."

And then he walks away as if he hasn't just turned my world upside down.

"Kian? We can't stay in this room together," I argue before he disappears.

"Why not? Worried you won't be able to resist me?"

I sit beside Kian in the hotel's meeting room, waiting for the others who are meant to be joining us.

In true Kian Callahan fashion, we're beyond early.

I get it. I hate being late and unorganized, but there is such a thing as too early.

"So, is this a new manager we're meeting?" I ask, circling back to our previous conversation about why we're here.

"Yes, she started just under a month ago. She seems competent, and she's managed to flag some issues that have arisen with the previous manager."

"With the accounts?"

"Yes."

"You think he was stealing?"

"That's what I would like to find out. If he wasn't, then there is a serious issue here somewhere."

"A serious issue that is your job to resolve?" I raise a brow, desperate for the truth about why we're really here.

"Like I said, it's been a while since I traveled."

His eyes hold mine, and they hide a million words that he's not willing to speak aloud.

Am I crazy to think he only planned this trip because of me?

I shudder, hating even thinking it.

I'm turning into one of those women.

The ones he's trying to get away from who read into every single one of his actions in the hope of finding something more than he's willing to give.

He is not the one, Lorelei.

Not even close.

"Have you visited many of our hotels and resorts?" Kian asks, changing the topic of conversation.

"The Broadway, obviously. Tate and I went to your resort in Hawaii a couple of years ago. But that's it."

His eyes light up. "I guess that means that I get to show you the world."

"Christ, that's cheesy."

He smirks. "Unlike all the men who've come before, I mean it literally. And physically, of course."

I roll my eyes. "As big-headed as ever," I mutter under my breath as voices approach from the other side of the door.

"Ah, here we go," Kian says, reaching into his briefcase and pulling out a notebook.

I frown. That's my job. What is he—

My thoughts are eradicated when he places it face-up on the desk.

Notes my assistant should be taking.

My chin drops, shock rendering me speechless as a woman and two men enter the room.

Kian introduces us both before everyone takes a seat to get started.

Eagerly, Kian flips the notebook open and pulls a pen from his pocket.

It takes a long time for him to place it down on the desk, allowing me to read what is written up the barrel.

If you want a job done right, do it yourself.

Asshole.

As discreetly as I can, I kick him under the table.

It's childish, I know. But I can't help myself.

His speech or attention on the three people opposite us

never wavers. They probably don't recognize the change in him. But I do. I see the way his lips twitch at the sides, making his dimples pop, and just how brightly his eyes shine.

Credit where credit's due, he's taken my challenge and given as good as he's gotten.

It doesn't mean he's going to win, though.

B y the time we walk out of the meeting room, the sun is setting, and I'm beginning to feel the effects of my early wake-up call.

"I've booked a table for tonight," Kian tells me as we ride the elevator back to our room.

"I hope you enjoy it. I'm going to be ordering room service," I deadpan.

"You're funny."

"You're not," I counter.

"You're coming to dinner with me. It's our raincheck date."

"We're not dating, Kian."

When the elevator doors open, I rush out. It's not going to get me anywhere, but any bit of space between us is a positive.

He doesn't say a word, but I feel him behind me, like an unwavering presence determined to drive me to the brink of insanity.

Unlocking the hotel room door, I march inside, but no sooner have I crossed the threshold than a large hand wraps around my arm, pulling me back.

My back hits the wall at the same time the door clicks closed, cutting us off from the rest of the world.

I don't look up, but I don't need to.

Kian is right there, crowding me with his huge body, making mine burn with his proximity.

I want to push him away, slip from between him and the wall, but I can't. My body is frozen.

His touch is light. Light enough that I could slip free if I wanted to.

I want to. I just...

"Lorelei?" he rasps. It tingles all the way down to my toes. "Look up into my eyes and tell me you don't feel it."

I suck in a sharp breath, more than prepared to lie to his face to save my own sanity.

But the second I do as he commands, all the words are gone.

46

LORELEI

"Wear the red dress." His words ring in my ear just as loudly as the moment he whispered them. My reaction isn't any less visceral, either.

A shiver runs down my spine, and my heart begins to race. It doesn't matter that he's not in the room—I can still feel his presence.

I look around the luxury bathroom I've locked myself inside to get ready for our meal.

I should have stood my ground and said no. This "date" is a disaster waiting to happen.

Hell, this whole trip is, and yet...here I am nonetheless.

I'm standing in a black strapless bra and matching panties. My hair has been freshly washed, and my makeup has been reapplied to the best of my ability, but I doubt it's even close to as good as the women he usually spends time with.

All I need now is the dress.

When he was pulling clothes out of my closet this morning, I had no idea that he was being selective in any way, but it seems that I should have given him a little more credit. I've known it all along—Kian Callahan knows exactly what he wants, and he always gets it. I just keep getting blinded by everything else he tries to keep hidden from the rest of the world and forgetting.

Happy with everything, I turn to the dress hanging on the back of the door.

Butterflies flutter wildly in my stomach as I stare at it.

Whatever happens from here on out is the dress's fault.

The second I step into it, I can no longer be held responsible for my actions.

Blowing out a long, slow breath between my lips, I reach for the dress.

Here goes nothing.

"Shit," I hiss when I fail to zip it all the way up.

I wiggle this way and that, but no matter what I do, I can't get it over the waistband.

Quickly, I weigh my options.

Defy him and wear something else.

Or...

Go out there and ask for his help.

Both are way more tempting than they should be.

Abandoning my dress, I slip my feet into my shoes and then give myself one final spritz of perfume before holding my head high and walking out of the bathroom.

The bedroom is empty, but voices coming from the main living area let me know where he is.

The sound of the TV seems to diminish as I get closer. The only thing I can hear is my heart slamming against my ribs.

You're going to regret this, Lorelei, a little voice warns in my head. But it's nowhere near loud enough to stop me.

I'm about to clear my throat to announce my presence, but I quickly discover that it's not necessary, because he turns around.

The second his eyes land on me, I swear, time stops.

Something crackles so heavily between us, I have to take a step back to steady myself.

"Lorelei," he rasps as he shifts to the edge of the couch and then pushes to his feet. "You look--" He swallows, cutting off his words before his eyes drop all the way to my toes and then back up again. His arm lifts and his fingers comb through his hair, dragging it back and ruining any styling he'd done before I commandeered the bathroom. "Fuck, Lorelei."

His words, or more so the desire within them, hit me right between the thighs.

He's dressed since the last time I saw him. He'd walked out of the bathroom with nothing but a towel wrapped around his waist.

I knew what he was doing, and I refused to fall for it.

My eyes refused to fall for it...at least they did until I was closing the door. Then, I looked. And I can confirm his naked back is almost as good as his front. He has those dimples just above his ass. Dimples that I want to—*No, lock it down, Lorelei.*

"I need a little help," I confess, putting the very vivid image of his towel-clad body to the back of my mind.

His brows lift with intrigue a beat before a smirk spreads across his lips.

"Oh yeah?" he muses, moving closer with something wicked glittering in his eyes.

His white shirt fits his body like a second skin, and the sleeves are rolled up, revealing his ripped forearms. And his pants...shit, I'm pretty sure they'll look better from behind than the towel.

"Y-yeah, I need..." I spin around, letting him see.

The second his eyes land on my exposed skin, a shockwave rocks through my body. But it's got nothing on the moment he steps up behind me, his breath brushing over my neck and down my chest.

Suddenly, my bra feels too small. Hell, my skin feels too small.

His fingers brush my shoulder as he pushes my curls out of the way before his knuckles graze lower, making me flinch, the point of contact burning red hot.

No words are said as he drags the zipper up, securing my dress into place.

When he hits the top, I finally release the breath I was holding, expecting him to take a step back.

But he doesn't. If anything, he only moves closer.

"Oh," I breathe when his obvious erection presses against my ass.

"You lied to me earlier," he whispers, his lips brushing my ear as he speaks.

I shake my head, although the movement is so slight, I doubt he'll see it.

"N-no," I breathe. "I didn't."

He laughs, puffing air over me, making me shudder.

He feels it, too.

His hand lands on my hip, dragging me back against him. My core aches. "It's okay, Lorelei. Deny it all you like. I have every intention of proving you wrong."

His nose grazes my neck, and a needy whimper slips free.

Fuck.

Maybe I shouldn't have lied to him, although honestly, I'm not sure it made much difference.

I knew he could see through every single word I said after we walked back into the hotel room not so long ago.

As he demanded, I held his eyes and told him that I didn't feel it.

But I did. I felt it alright. All the way down to the very tips of my toes.

I couldn't tell him that, though.

He's my boss. My wealthy, arrogant, egotistical asshole of a boss.

And...and I want him, damn it.

The little taste I had hasn't been anywhere near enough. I need more, and I'm as excited as I am terrified to take it.

"Ready for dinner?" he asks, sounding completely unaffected by what just happened.

I release a breath in a rush, amused by Mr. Calm and Collected. But while he might act in control, we both know the truth. I just felt it pressed against my ass, and I've no doubt he's feeling it in his balls right now as well.

Kian Callahan wants me...

It's a heady fucking feeling, I'll admit that.

This man could literally have any woman on the planet. Hell, he kinda already has, and yet, he's here and getting hard for me.

Me.

With a shake of my head, I spin around to face him again.

He looks just as composed and in control as ever. I feel like a hot mess, and I can only pray that I don't look like one as well.

"You okay?" he asks.

"Great. Hungry."

I don't think about what I say until I catch his smirk.

"Me too," he agrees as I return to the bedroom to swipe my purse from the end of the bed.

If I were being sensible, I'd lock myself in the bedroom and refuse to go with him. But where is the fun in that?

We're in a different state. The reality of life has been left behind. We're in one of his fancy hotels, which I'm sure has fancier restaurants.

My stomach grumbles as I move toward the door.

He remains in place, watching me intently.

"Are you coming, or do I need to find another man to entertain me while I eat?"

That gets him moving, and before I cross the threshold into the hallway, he's right behind me.

"Let's get this straight," he growls from behind me. His hand is resting on the small of my back, ensuring my blood continues to simmer at boiling point. "The only man getting anywhere near you for the foreseeable future is me."

I smirk, loving the jealous side that keeps appearing.

"I think that's for me to decide, not you."

"We'll see."

A s I expected, Kian leads me to a five-star restaurant on the building's rooftop. I had no idea it was even up here. Something tells me that I'm not the only one. It seems to be something of a secret.

The second he walks up to the desk, he's welcomed by name, and after some pleasantries, we're guided to our table that's located inside its own pod.

I stare upward in complete awe. I've never dined anywhere like it.

We have an unobstructed view of the clear night sky above us. It's hands-down the most romantic location I've ever experienced.

And I'm with my boss.

"You like it?" Kian asks, his attention fully on me instead of the incredible view above us.

"It's incredible."

"Not always a bad thing being a flashy motherfucker, is it?"

"You said it," I mutter.

Ripping my eyes from the stars, find his dark green ones staring down at me.

Desire continues to burn red hot within them, turning the green I'm used to almost black.

"Thank you," I whisper, needing him to know that despite all the shit I give him, I do really appreciate all these experiences he's giving me.

He shrugs like all of this is no big deal. I guess it isn't to him.

"I was hardly going to take you to a McDonalds for our first date, was I?"

I frown, trying to fight my amusement. "Wait, you know what McDonalds is?"

"I'm not that out of touch."

"Are you sure?" I ask as a server approaches to fill our water glasses and take our drinks order.

"Would you like wine?"

The sensible thing to do would be to say no and stick to water. I might stand a chance of not losing my head—or my body—to this man if I remain sober.

But sadly, my lips aren't in agreement with my brain. They seem to have sided with my body, because the words that spill free are, "Sure. Your choice."

I could choose the wine, but without even opening the menu, I already know that I'm not going to recognize a single bottle on the list. I also know that the prices are going to utterly terrify me.

Ignorance is bliss in this situation.

Kian orders us a bottle of red, which I've no doubt will probably be the best bottle of red wine I've ever tasted. There are certainly some perks to fake dating this man.

Not that we're dating in any way...

As if he can read my thoughts, he sits back in his seat and sips his water with a smirk on his face.

"Penny for your thoughts."

"They're nothing you haven't already heard before."

He quirks a brow in interest.

Unwilling to dive into dangerous territory, I finally reach for the menu sitting before me.

"So, what's good here?"

He chuckles. "Everything."

"Of course," I mutter, my eyes scanning the list of food before me and discovering that it's a seafood restaurant. I guess that makes sense, seeing as we're by the ocean.

Casting a look to my left, I focus on the darkness surrounding us. I can just about make out the reflection of the moon in the calm ocean in the distance.

The desire to walk across the sand and feel the cool water lap at my feet burns through me.

It's been so long since I've had the chance.

"You're a million miles away tonight," Kian muses.

"Sorry. All of this is just a little..."

"Overwhelming?" he guesses when I trail off.

"Yeah. My life isn't like this, Kian. I don't stay in fancy hotels or eat at five-star seafood restaurants. I don't even know what half of this is, let alone what I'm meant to choose." As the words continue to flow, my unease grows until I no longer feel like I belong.

Hell, I don't fucking belong.

This isn't me.

I glance around, taking in the polished gold finishes, the expensive bottles of liquor behind the bar, the other diners.

Lifting my hand, I press my palm over my racing heart as my world begins to spin out of control.

Everything around me starts to blur as my panic fully takes over.

You don't belong here.

You're a fraud.

And one day soon, Kian is going to learn everything and kick you to the curb...exactly where you belong.

"**L**orelei," I say a little firmer than usual.

She's freaking out, and I have absolutely no fucking idea how to deal with it.

Rescuing her from that elevator was one thing, but this, in the middle of a restaurant?

Fuck.

I knew there was a good reason why I only date women who want to use my name to help their own careers or social standing.

I've never cared about any of them. Plus, it helps that any tears they shed are nothing more than crocodile tears. I'm sure they work perfectly on their fathers, allowing them to get their own way, but they won't work on me.

This isn't fake, though.

"Temptress?"

The second her body tenses, I know I've got her.

It takes a few more moments, but her eyes lift to mine.

"I'm sorry," she whispers.

"Would you prefer if we went and found a McDonalds?" I offer.

No sooner have the words left my mouth than her lips curl into the most incredible smile.

"No, it's okay. I just..." She blows out a slow, calming breath.

"Did you know," I say, keeping my voice low, "you're the most beautiful woman in this restaurant tonight?"

She shakes her head, refusing to believe my words.

"Kian, you can't—"

"It's true. You've no idea just how beautiful you are, do you?"

"I'm your assistant, Kian. You can't—"

"I'm the boss. I can do whatever the fuck I want," I state arrogantly.

She rolls her eyes, looking much more like herself again.

Our server approaches with the bottle of red I ordered, and after showing me the bottle, he pours a little into my glass for me to taste.

While I do so, Lorelei pulls her cell out of her purse and checks something.

"That's great, thank you," I tell the server, instructing him to fill our glasses and leave us alone.

I'm not feeling very generous tonight. I don't want to share Lorelei with anyone, even the man supplying us with wine.

"Everything okay?" I ask, hating the small frown that appeared when she started reading what's on her cell.

"Yeah, just my brother being...well, my brother."

"Is training going well?"

She shrugs. "If he's training as hard as he's partying, then we should be good."

Reaching out, she takes a sip of her wine.

"Oh my god," she moans the second it hits her tastebuds. "That's so good."

I smirk, sipping from my own glass. "I have good taste."

"That's good, because I have no idea what to order."

"Allow me?"

"Sure. Go for it. We know how much you like to get your own way." My lips part to respond, but I don't get a chance to say anything, even if it is to agree. "Excuse me," she says, abandoning her cell on the table and pushing her chair back.

I watch her leave, my eyes locked on her ass in her tight red dress with my cock aching beneath the table.

The server looks over, asking if he should wait, and I gesture for him to come and take our order.

Once he's scribbled down all my favorite dishes, he disappears and leaves me alone to wait for Lorelei.

She takes longer than she should, and the need to go and find her burns through me.

I wouldn't put it past her to run and hide in our room. A shot of excitement hits me right in the dick.

No, she wouldn't. That would be too easy.

She would make it a challenge.

I'm busy musing over all the places she could hide when her cell lights up on the table.

I lean over to look at the screen; I don't even really have any desire to see who it is. I've no reason to doubt that she was talking to her little brother. But the second my eyes land on the notification and I see a really long name, my curiosity is piqued.

Reaching out, I spin her cell around.

Ryde my dick.

What the actual fuck?

Before I know what I'm doing, I've unlocked her cell—she really needs a better passcode than her birthday—and I've opened the message thread with this asshole.

> Ryde my dick: Feeling lonely tonight, baby. Wanna keep me company?

"Motherfucker," I hiss under my breath.

This is the asshole who was meant to get her titty pic.

Despite how much I want to scroll up and discover what else she's been sending him, I don't. I've already seen too much.

Instead, I close her messages and open her contacts.

I might have second-guessed looking at her conversation,

but I don't have the same reservations about blocking him. And while I'm there, I take out her ex, too.

Lorelei doesn't need either of them in her life. Not anymore.

In a rush, I place her cell back, hopefully in exactly the same position as before.

Not two seconds later, she emerges from the door that leads to the bathroom.

My breath catches in my throat at the sight of her. Her makeup is light and perfect, her red lips making my cock swell all over again. Her thick curls are free around her shoulders, and I can't help but imagine how soft they're going to feel wrapped around my fist. Then there is the dress...I might not have seen all that much of it when I dragged it from her closet, but I saw enough to know that it was going to knock me on my ass. And fuck was I right. It's sinful.

I shift in my chair, desperately trying to ease the pressure on my dick as she retakes her seat.

"Thought you were embarking on a game of cat and mouse, Temptress."

"Just having a moment."

"Am I that much to take?" I ask, cocking my head to the side.

She scoffs. "You've no idea."

"Aw, come on, admit it. You wouldn't want to be anywhere else in the world than sitting here with me right now."

"Awfully presumptuous of you," she mutters before reaching for her wine. "I really need some food to go with this."

"It should be here soon. So tell me, what would you be doing if you were at home right now?" I ask, leaning forward and resting on my forearms. I swear to God if she says sexting her friend with the moronic name, I'll probably tip the thing over.

"Washing my hair," she says simply.

"Sounds riveting."

"If you had curls, you'd understand."

"I'm sure I'll learn to understand."

"Kian," she breathes.

"Stop," I interrupt. "Stop trying to fight what you know is inevitable."

"You know, you're not God's gift to all women. There are some exceptions out there."

"Oh, I have no doubt. But thankfully, you're not one of them."

Her eyes narrow, and her lips purse. She can argue all she likes. I know as well as she does how her body melts into mine when we're close.

"You're blurring the lines all over the place here, you know that, right?"

"Lines? What lines?" I smirk as our starters arrive.

Lorelei's eyes widen when she discovers what I ordered, but she doesn't say a word until we're alone again with a huge platter sitting between us.

"Oysters, really?" she states.

"What?" I ask innocently. "They're my favorite, and you can't get better ones than here."

"Right," she mutters, eyeing the shellfish suspiciously.

"Have you had them before?"

"Oh yeah, used to be on the menu weekly when I was a kid," she deadpans.

"I'll take that as a no, shall I?"

"Asshole," she hisses.

Ignoring her, I pick up the small fork we're going to need and then select my first oyster.

"Pick one," I demand. "And then you need to loosen it." I show her what I mean before waiting for her to do the same. "And then you tip it into your mouth."

I keep my eyes firmly on her as I lift the shell to my lips and tip, letting the oyster slide into my mouth. The incredible taste of the ocean coats my tongue.

While I swallow mine down eagerly, Lorelei is a little more hesitant. And when she finally takes the plunge, her face screws up in disgust.

"Ew, that's gross," she complains, making me laugh.

"It's an acquired taste," I confess. "Not quite McDonalds."

She glares at me.

"Try another. They're really good for you." I wiggle my brows at her.

"You mean, you hope they're good for you," she accuses.

"Not sure I need any help."

"Trust me, your arrogance is the perfect antidote to anything that might be even remotely tempting about you."

"Have another oyster, Lorelei," I demand, aware of how much she hates it, despite the fact she always follows orders.

The second one must go down a little better because she's not so reluctant to reach for the third.

"See, they're good," I say as I wipe my mouth with my napkin.

"Third time's a charm, right?"

We remain quiet as our server takes the empty platter away, and Lorelei speaks once we're alone again.

"So, what would you usually be doing if we were at home right now?"

I check my watch. "I'd probably be at home, waiting to see if I'm going to receive a hot photo tonight or not."

She rolls her eyes. "I can confidently say that you wouldn't."

"How would you know? You're not the only one who's trying to steal my attention, Temptress."

Her eyes widen and her cheeks redden. Jealousy is a really good look on her.

"You're obviously sharing these images with other men. Why shouldn't I be getting them from other women?"

"You can. You can get as many pictures from as many women who are willing. None of my business."

"You're lying to me again."

"Kian," she snaps.

"Life would be easier if you could be honest."

"Oh, that's rich, Mr. Let's Fake Date and Lie to Everyone."

"Doesn't mean I'm hiding what I want, though, does it?"

Her lips purse before she takes another sip of her wine.

"What we show the rest of the world and what we are behind closed doors can be very different things."

"Both are going to see that I'm your assistant."

"You argue too much."

"And you demand too much."

"Only because I know it'll be worth it. For both of us."

Our main dishes arrive, leaving Lorelei with my previous statement.

She knows it's true.

Just as much as we both know that it's a line we probably shouldn't cross. But I stopped playing by the rules a long time ago.

I want her. I'm making no secret of that.

And so what? What's a little sex between the boss and his assistant? We wouldn't be the first colleagues to embark on something similar. It's not like either of us is going to do anything stupid and fall in love.

It's just sex.

Hot. Steamy. Unforgettable. Sex.

My grip on my cutlery tightens as desire sweeps through me again.

"Eat your dinner, Kian," Lorelei warns as I focus on her instead of the plate in front of me.

"But what if there's something else I want to eat more?"

48

LORELEI

"Your dessert will be served outside," our server says, making me frown.

"Outside?" I ask the second he's walked away.

"Grab your wine, Temptress," Kian instructs before pushing his chair back and picking up his own glass. "You're going to love this."

Intrigued, I push to my feet and tuck my purse under my hand. In seconds, he's beside me, his hand at home resting against the small of my back.

Cool evening air rushes over my exposed skin, and I shiver the second we emerge from our private pod.

Feeling it, Kian moves his hand and wraps his arm around me. It's nice. Comforting. Way too comforting.

He leads me through the other diners' pods where they're enjoying their meals and to the very opposite end of the rooftop.

I'm still confused as he opens a wooden gate and the reality of where we're eating dessert is revealed.

"Wow," I breathe as we step into the private outside eating area.

There is a table for two, but it's clear that that isn't where we're sitting. Instead, there is a cozy swing seat with our names on it.

"Come on," Kian says, leading me through the soft fairy lights toward our destination.

After placing our glasses on the side tables, we take a seat.

"This is incredible," I confess, staring up at the stars again. I swear they're even clearer without the pod between us.

"We could have eaten out here, but I was worried you'd get cold."

I smile up at him, completely speechless.

"What?" he asks, his eyes bouncing between mine.

"You're really quite romantic for a man who's never seriously dated."

"I don't do things by halves, Lorelei."

"No," I muse. "That is something I've learned about you."

"See, not everything about me is bad."

"I never said that it was," I confess. "And I must admit, there is more to you than I first thought."

He raises a brow.

"What? It's the wine. It makes me more honest." I swat his shoulder playfully and reach for my glass for another sip.

"I like your honesty. It's refreshing."

"Aw, does having women tell you that you're amazing in every single way get boring, hotshot?"

"I'm not perfect, and I don't appreciate anyone who tries to tell me that I am. I have just as many flaws as everyone else on this planet. Some—you—may even say that I have more."

I consider his point. "Jury's still out."

"Good to know." He laughs. "Anyway, I like that you see me differently to others. You don't care about this," he says, gesturing to himself and then our surroundings. "You see me for who I am, not what I've been made into."

"I dunno," I muse. "I'm pretty sure I see both."

"Do you have a preference?"

"Maybe," I say, watching as our server begins wheeling something toward us.

I shouldn't be hungry after the first two courses we've had, but the second I see the strawberries, marshmallows and chocolate, my mouth begins watering.

"How is this for you, sir?" the server asks.

I didn't look at the dessert menu. Hell, I barely looked at any menu, but I already know that this isn't on it.

"Perfect, thank you."

The trolley he's pushing tucks perfectly up against the swing seat, allowing us to both eat from it without having to move. It's perfect.

"Can I get you anything else?"

"No, thank you. Just privacy from here on out, please."

My stomach twists at Kian's request.

We may have been secluded in our pod, but there were others right outside and able to see everything.

Here, we're totally alone. No one can see what we do...

My stomach twists with a potent mixture of excitement and fear.

We're so close to crossing the line. At this point, I'm pretty sure it's inevitable. But what's going to happen after?

I can't lose my job. We need the money too much.

I would never forgive myself if I fucked this up and in turn ruined Wilder and Hendrix's chance at college.

"Lorelei?" Kian asks, dragging me from my second freak-out of the night.

What is it about this man that turns me into this mess? I'm usually so strong and sure of everything. Yet when I'm with him...I question everything.

He holds a strawberry up that he's dipped into the chocolate sauce and edges it toward my mouth.

Wow, he really isn't messing around.

My mouth moves on instinct and my lips part, more than ready for what he's offering.

His eyes dilate as I bite down on the fruit, and they darken even further when I moan in delight as the sweetness coats my tongue.

"You're playing a very dangerous game here, Kian Callahan."

"Can't help it," he says before throwing the other half of the strawberry I just had into his mouth. "I'm an adrenaline junkie. I love that feeling of not knowing what's about to happen."

"I'm pretty sure you have a solid idea of what you want to happen," I point out as I reach for a marshmallow and dip it into some chocolate before licking it off.

Kian clears his throat. "Doesn't mean it will. It takes two to tango."

"So it does." Loading up a second marshmallow, I hold it out for him.

He takes the whole thing into his mouth, nipping my fingers in the process.

"You bit me," I complain.

"I can do so much worse, Temptress. All you have to do is ask." His words are dark and coated with pure lust. My thighs clench in the hope of putting a little pressure on my clit. I'm pretty sure if this continues too much longer, then I'm going to combust.

"Big promises, hot shot."

"You've Googled me. You know I can deliver."

"As if I believe any of those hussies who've sold their stories. For all I know, you paid them to blow smoke up your ass. You might be a shit lay with a tiny cock, Kian," I shriek when he grabs my wrist and places my hand right on his dick.

He's hard. So fucking hard. And he twitches under my touch.

My mouth waters, and my core aches.

Okay, so he doesn't have a tiny cock.

"How does that feel to you?" he asks, releasing his grip.

I could pull my hand away, but I don't. Instead, I move on instinct and gently stroke him.

A groan rumbles deep in his throat, and I'm hit with a rush of power.

386

I can undo this man with nothing more than a mere touch.

Suddenly, the table between us is pushed away, and when I look down, he's shoving it with his foot, removing the single obstacle between us.

"Kian?" I whisper, barely able to talk.

"You're driving me crazy, Temptress." He reaches out and cups my face, his thumb brushing across my bottom lip. "I can't stop thinking about that kiss." His eyes jump to my mouth before returning to my eyes. "All I can think about is what would have happened if we didn't stop."

His cock jerks beneath my hand again, reminding me that I'm still touching him.

I pull my hand back, but not all the way. Instead, it rests on his muscular thigh as I wait to see what's going to happen next.

"You think about it too, don't you?"

"Kian."

"I know you do. I know you feel this, too. Try to lie as much as you want—I don't believe it. This," he says, his thumb brushing my lips again, "is too potent for you not to feel it."

He's barely finished talking when he throws caution to the wind and leans in, replacing his thumb with his own lips.

"Oh my god," I whimper as he kisses me softly, waiting for my permission before diving in further.

Fuck, his consideration alone is enough for me to jump off the cliff with both feet.

My hand moves again, firmly grasping him through his pants.

"Temptress," he groans before his tongue plunges into my mouth, searching for mine to join.

His fingers twitch against my throat, his grip tightening, possessive even before his other hand slides up my leg until it comes to a stop at my waist.

Shifting closer, he presses as much of our bodies together as possible as the kiss gets deeper.

His tongue licks into my mouth with such determination,

it's like he wants to learn every single inch of me in one kiss alone.

With one of my hands still on his dick, the other sinks into his hair, my fingers gripping his locks tight and holding him in place—not that I really think he's going anywhere.

Our kiss goes on and on as he makes my entire world spin out of control with nothing more than his mouth and his touch.

More. I need more.

I've no idea how much time has passed when he finally pulls back. His erratic breaths rush over my face as I stare into his lust-blown eyes.

"We need to go," he rasps, his voice deeper than I've ever heard it.

I stroke him again, loving the way his jaw ticks and his Adam's apple bobs.

"Lorelei, if you don't stop—" He swallows again, cutting off his words.

"Then what, Boss?"

I gasp when his hand suddenly lands on mine, stopping my movement.

"I'm not going to come in my pants like a teenager."

An accomplished smile pulls at my lips.

"There's no need to look so smug about it," he mutters before nudging my nose with his and stealing another kiss. "I've got other ways I'd prefer this to end."

"Oh yeah?"

"Yeah, and none of them involve either of us being clothed."

"You're bad," I whisper.

"You've no idea," he says before ripping himself away from me and jumping to his feet. "Finish your drink," he demands as he attempts to rearrange himself.

The sight of him trying to bust out of his pants makes my mouth water. I bet he looks fucking incredible without his designer clothes...

"I don't need any more," I confess, getting to my feet.

"Good. It would only waste time." No sooner has he finished talking than he reaches for my hand and practically drags me back through the restaurant.

I'm too impatient to get him alone again to notice if anyone is watching us leave. If they were watching, it's pretty obvious what's about to go down.

Him...I'm hoping he's about to go down.

The second the elevator doors open, I'm shoved inside backward, and I don't stop moving until I hit the wall. I just manage to suck in a hungry breath before his lips descend on mine again.

As the doors close, his hand slides down my thigh, hitching my leg up around his waist. Thank God for the split in my dress.

"Oh God," I whimper when his cock hits me just so.

"That's nothing," he counters. "Just wait."

"I can't," I breathe, sounding more like a desperate whore than I think I have in my entire life.

But I don't care.

I need him. I need him so fucking badly.

All the flirting and foreplay has brought us here. It's built me up until I'm just about ready to explode.

I need it. I need him to drag me over the edge and freefall with me.

I cry out when the elevator dings to announce that we're on our floor, and I complain even louder when he steps back and once again attempts to cover up his boner.

It's going to take more than a little shift to the side, though. His pants are hiding nothing.

With my hand gripped tightly in his, I'm once again dragged down the hallway until we're on the wrong side of our hotel room door.

Nothing moves fast enough. The door unlocks too slowly, and despite his rushing, he doesn't open it quickly enough either.

But then, all the waiting is over and my back collides with the wall beside the door just like it did earlier, only this time, when he presses the length of his body against mine, there is no hesitation, no questions, no nothing but our unfiltered need for each other.

His hands are everywhere and his kiss is wet and dirty, and I am here for all of it.

Grabbing the backs of my thighs, he lifts me from the floor, pinning me against the wall with his hips as he pushes my dress up in search of my ass.

"Oh God." He was right. He knows exactly what he's doing.

49

LORELEI

"Kian," I gasp as he grabs my ass in a firm grip, his lips dropping to my neck. "Oh God."

He smirks, I can feel it against my sensitive skin, but he doesn't say a word as he continues kissing me. His hips roll, ensuring his dick grinds against me in the most dizzying way.

Suddenly, I understand why he stopped me from stroking him up on the roof. I don't want to finish like this either. Too many clothes.

"Bedroom," I force out. "We need—" He sucks on the patch of skin beneath my ear. "Shit. B-bed...room."

"Thought you'd never ask," Kian says smugly, pulling me from the wall and carrying me across the suite as if I weigh nothing more than a feather.

His stride is calm yet strong, purposeful, confident.

With my fingers twisted in his hair, I drop my lips to his neck and bite.

"Fuck, Temptress," he groans.

"You're not the only one with a little bite, Boss."

I shriek when he drops me, but I quickly recover as my feet hit the ground.

He studies me, his knuckles running down my cheek, over my jaw and then down to my chest.

I moan when he brushes my nipple. I might be wearing a padded bra, but I'm pretty sure there isn't enough padding in the world to hide what his touch is doing.

"Lorelei," he rasps as he moves to the other side.

He steps closer, our bodies pressing together as our breaths mingle.

"This dress..." he muses, running his finger over the spaghetti strap resting on my shoulder. "It needs to go. You've teased me with what's hiding beneath, and I need more."

"You want me to get naked, Boss?"

"No," he says so firmly it startles me. "I'm going to get you naked."

Before I can respond, he spins me around. His fingers find the zipper resting between my shoulder blades and he pulls it down slowly.

My breath catches as the sound of our increased breathing fills the air.

"Kian," I whisper as his knuckles bump down my spine, all the way down to the top of my ass.

I swallow, desperately trying to keep it together as he pushes the straps from my shoulders and lets the fabric drop to my feet.

"Christ," he mutters, my skin burning as he lets his eyes drop to my thong-clad ass. "Turn around," he demands, making all the hairs on my body stand on end.

Defying him might be my favorite hobby, but it's not something I so much as consider as my body complies and I spin on the balls of my feet until I'm facing him.

"Fuck," he grunts before unbuttoning his shirt in record time. My fingers itch to help, but there's no way I'll be that speedy, and I need him naked. Fast.

His pants go next, leaving him in nothing but his tight black boxer briefs. And they leave almost nothing to the imagination.

I stand frozen, staring at him.

I've seen some fine male bodies in my time, but Kian...fuck.

He's...I swallow, not wanting to admit what's about to come next...perfect.

I mean, of course he is. I shouldn't have expected anything else from the god that is Kian Callahan.

I'm still lost in the definition of his six-pack and the deep V lines that disappear beneath his waistband to notice him close the space between us. But it all comes crashing back in vivid color when he wraps his hands around my waist, lifts me off my feet, and throws me back onto the bed.

I bounce once, and then he's there right on top of me, his dark eyes staring down into mine.

"Kian," I breathe, my chest heaving, my desperation reaching fever pitch.

"Fuck," he grunts before ducking down, his lips claiming mine again.

Wrapping my legs around his waist, I drag him down on top of me, loving the hardness and weight pressing me into the mattress.

My hands roam his muscular back until I find his ass, gripping him tight and forcing him to grind against me.

"Oh God," I moan when he kisses across my jaw and down to my neck again.

"So beautiful," he muses as his kisses continue to descend.

I arch my back, offering myself up to him, and he makes the most of it by sliding his hand beneath me and pinching my bra open.

I moan the second my swollen breasts are released.

He whips my bra away, exposing me to him.

My skin flushes bright red as his eyes widen in delight.

"So much better in person," he confesses before dipping his head and sucking one of my puckered nipples into his mouth.

"Fuck, Kian," I scream. He rewards me by grazing my sensitive skin with his teeth. He uses the perfect amount of pressure, sending a powerful bolt of lust straight to my clit.

My panties are ruined—I'm amazed he can't feel how wet I am through his boxers.

I need him more than I think I've needed anyone in my life.

Switching sides, he gives my other nipple the same attention before he sinks even lower, kissing and nipping his way down my stomach.

My fingers twist in his hair, pushing him lower to where I really need him.

He chuckles when he feels me trying to speed him up, and his eyes lift to mine.

"Feeling desperate, Temptress?"

"Please, Kian. I need—"

"Something here?" he says, pressing two fingers against my clit through the lace of my panties.

"Yes, yes, please."

"Aw, you beg so beautifully," he praises.

Shifting between my legs, he makes a show of checking out my bare chest before his eyes lock on the only part of me that's still covered.

My lips part to chastise him for taking too long, but I swallow my words when his fingers tuck into the waistband of my panties.

He pulls them down my thighs, and I help him out by bending my legs to free myself as soon as possible.

The second they're free from my body, he balls them up and lifts them to his nose, inhaling my scent.

"Jesus," I mutter, surprisingly turned on by the move.

No sooner has he breathed me in than he throws my panties aside and drops to his stomach, ready for the real thing.

The sight of him between my thighs and ready to strike is something else.

It's also something I'm never going to regret.

This powerful, all-consuming man is on his knees—figuratively—and ready to worship me.

Fuck. I don't think I've ever felt this important in all my life.

He could have any woman he wants, and right now, it's my taste he wants filling his mouth.

"Kiaaaaaan," I cry out when he leans forward and licks up the length of my pussy. Then, he ups the ante and sucks on my clit.

How the fuck he found it so fast, God only knows, but I'm not in a position to question it.

My fingers twist in his hair again, holding him in place as he really goes to town.

The intensity of what he's doing to my body causes my thighs to close as I fight to embrace it, but he's not having any of it. His palms press against my thighs before spreading them back against the bed. He fully opens me to him, and he doesn't waste the opportunity.

He eats me like a man who hasn't seen a meal in a month. He works me perfectly. As if he's been doing so all his life.

I chant his name over and over as my release approaches. But he never lets me fall.

"If you're trying to remind me who's the boss, then I have to tell you, it's not necessary," I snap, desperate.

He chuckles and takes his fucking mouth away.

"What are you doing?" I gasp, my eyes dropping to his glistening mouth.

Oh my god, my boss just ate my pussy.

Standing at the end of the bed, he wipes his mouth with the back of his hand, his accomplished smirk never slipping before he tucks his thumbs into his boxers.

My mouth runs dry when I finally get to see him in all his glory.

I knew he was big. I figured that out the very first time he pressed it up against me. But shit. I wasn't expecting that.

He gives me a second to take it all in before leaning down, grabbing his pants and pulling something from the pocket.

With the small silver packet in his hand, he crawls back onto the bed and settles between my thighs.

"You look nervous," he says softly.

"Well, yeah. Have you seen..." I trail off before gesturing to his dick. "Don't give me that smirk, Mr. Callahan," I chastise when it appears across his mouth.

The sight of it makes my thighs clench around him, and damn if he doesn't feel it.

"Hard not to when you're looking at me like that, Temptress."

He rips open the condom packet with his teeth before letting me watch as he rolls it down his shaft.

Shifting forward, he drags the head of his cock through my folds.

"Oh God."

"Not God, babe," he says, nudging against my entrance. "Just Kian Callahan."

"Oh my god, you did not just—" My words vanish as he pushes inside me.

The only thing I can focus on is the point where we're joined, the way he's stretching me open.

"Relax," he urges as he pushes deeper.

I do as he says, letting my body go limp beneath him, allowing him to push forward, filling me up until I can't take any more.

"Kian," I whimper.

"I know," he says smugly. "I'm a lot to take."

"Fucking hell," I mutter.

I don't get to say another word before he ducks down and steals my lips, kissing me senseless as he begins to move inside me.

At first, he's slow and gentle, allowing me to get used to his size. But the moment he registers that I'm okay, he begins to up the pace.

"Fuck, you feel incredible," he confesses the second our lips part. "So fucking good."

Sliding his palm down my thigh, he lifts my leg, allowing him to hit me deeper and at an entirely different angle.

"Oh shit," I gasp, making him smile.

"Yeah?"

"Stop digging for compliments, you know it's good."

He shrugs one shoulder. "My ego still likes to hear it," he says, slowly dragging his dick out of me.

It makes all my nerve endings tingle in the best possible way.

Throwing my head back, I put everything into my next performance. "Oh, Kian. Yes. Yes. You're such a god, Kian. Fuck me harder."

He growls in frustration, although I'm pretty sure there's a little amusement in there too before muttering, "As you wish."

He lifts both of my legs and throws them over his shoulders before rutting into me with enough force that I shoot up the bed.

"Hold on, Temptress. Let me show you what I can really do."

With his hands locked around my hips, he fucks me like I've never been fucked before. Every strike of his dick is like pure magic, and the way he looks as he does it...

Fuck me.

Hands down the best porn I've ever watched in my life.

His hair is a mess, hanging over his forehead. His pupils are blown wide—he's high. High on sex. High on me. It's a heady feeling. And the way his muscles pull and flex every time he moves is something else.

It isn't even over yet, and I'm pretty sure I already want to do it all over again.

"That's it, Temptress. You squeeze my dick so good."

Shit.

"Look at you," he muses, letting his eyes roam my naked body. The strength of his thrusts means that things jiggle, and not just the good bits, but with the way he watches me, I find it hard to care. The fire in his eyes helps to banish those niggles of insecurity. He likes what he sees, so why the hell should I be freaking out about it? "You look so fucking good on my dick."

"Kian," I gasp, my release beginning to build.

"You're going to come all over my dick, aren't you, Lorelei?"

"Yes, yes."

"Is this what you've been fantasizing about? Getting fucked by your boss?"

"Oh God."

"It was, wasn't it? While you were sending dirty pictures to him, you were pretending it was me on the other end. You wanted me hard and aching for you."

Releasing one of my hips, he presses his thumb to my clit, making me cry out.

"Wanna know something, Temptress?"

My head thrashes from side to side as he controls my orgasm just like he controls everything else in his life.

"I was. I was so fucking hard for you."

50

KIAN

I am exactly where I'm meant to be.

Right here. Right now. This is fucking it.

I haven't had sex in weeks, and this is why.

The universe—or whatever—knew something epic was coming my way, and it made me wait.

I'm so fucking glad I did.

No one else could have come anywhere close to this.

Hell, I don't think anyone I've ever been with has come close to this.

"I want to feel it, Lorelei," I demand, my voice raspy and deep with need.

I'm already riding a knife's edge, but I'm determined to hold it back.

I have a reputation to uphold, after all, and coming before Lorelei is not an option here.

Putting a little more pressure on her clit, I circle my hips, ensuring I hit her in all the right places.

"Kian," she gasps, hungrily sucking in air as I build her body higher and higher.

"That's it, babe. You're squeezing me so fucking tight. I love it."

"Oh God, yes, yes."

"Come for me, Lorelei. Show me how good my dick feels inside you."

I grind against her in a way I'm quickly learning she loves, and with one more graze of her clit, she falls.

And. It. Is. Fucking. Beautiful.

"Good girl," I praise through gritted teeth. It takes everything I have not to come. Every-fucking-thing.

I let her ride out every ounce of pleasure, and then I switch things up. I might love having control, but there is one thing I can't get out of my head...

My back hits the mattress, and Lorelei's weight lands over my waist.

Her cheeks are flushed bright red, and so is her heaving chest as she settles on top of me.

"Fuck me, Temptress. I want to watch you bouncing on my dick."

"Jesus, Kian," she mutters, although she doesn't waste any time in grabbing my length and positioning herself right above it.

Any hesitation about my size is gone as she lowers herself onto me.

"Fuck," I groan, and she sinks lower and lower, my dick disappearing inside her. "Fuck. Your pussy is insane," I confess as I reach for her hips.

I'm not going to drag her down, forcing her to sit on me, but I really fucking want to.

She smiles—but it's nothing like any smile I've seen from her before. It's pure filth. And if it's possible, the sight of it makes my dick even harder.

She gasps when she's finally full of me.

"Did it get bigger?" she asks, wiggling her hips as she tries to get a feel for it.

I smirk. "One can only hope."

"Fucking mor—"

I grind her hips, and her words turn into a moan.

"I want you to come again, Temptress. Then I'm going to fill that perfect pussy of yours."

"Your mouth is obscene, Kian Callahan."

"Tell me that you don't like it," I challenge.

Her eyes drop from mine in favor of checking out my body again.

"I can't. Your dirty mouth might just be the one thing I do like about you."

I thrust up.

"Just one thing?"

"That's okay, too. But you know, there really has been a vast improvement with dildos recently so—"

"Fucking pain in my ass," I mutter before thrusting harder. "There is nothing on the market that compares to this. I can promise you that."

She quirks a brow at me and I thrust again. Her lips part to cry out, but she swallows it down, refusing to give me the satisfaction of knowing I'm right.

Not necessary, I already know. I can feel it in the way she's rippling around me.

"Fight it all you like; you know I'm telling the truth."

Finding her hands, I lace our fingers together and tug her forward. She falls over me, and her lips immediately land against mine.

Our kiss is wild, just like the frantic movements of our hips. There is nothing calculated or precise about the way we move together. It's desperate and erratic, and everything I didn't know I needed.

"Kian," she gasps into our kiss.

"Come," I demand, and not just because it'll give me a free pass to do the same once she has fallen again. I need it. I need to see her fall; I need to know I'm the one who caused it. I need to feel her tightening down on me as badly as I need my next breath.

She shatters, her pussy sucking me even deeper inside her, and I can't hold on any longer.

"Lorelei," I groan as my cock jerks inside her, pleasure saturating my body. It goes on and on, and by the time it ends,

I'm fucking spent. And I didn't even get to watch her ride me. I guess we'll just have to do it again. What a shame.

Rolling onto my side, I drag her with me and then pull her into my arms.

It isn't a conscious thought, but I am vaguely aware that we're cuddling, and I never cuddle after sex. Ever.

But right now, I don't care. I'm still inside her, my dick barely softening, and she's tucked tightly against me, fighting to catch her breath as her body also comes down from the high.

No words are said for the longest time. The only sound that can be heard in our suite is that of our heavy breathing.

Usually after sex, I have the burning need to kick the woman out as fast as possible and jump in the shower to wash her scent off me, but both of those things are far from my mind right now.

"How is that even possible?" Lorelei whispers a few minutes later.

I know what she's talking about. I can feel it just as much as she can.

I shrug the shoulder I'm not lying on. "It's been a while."

"Nice," she seethes before trying to roll away and disconnect us.

It needs to happen, I need to lose the condom, but I don't fucking want to.

Holding her tighter, I move my mouth to her ear. "It was just that good, Temptress. I want to do it all over again."

Her entire body shudders as my breath rushes over her and my words hit their mark.

Pulling back, I reluctantly slip from her body and reach down to pull the rubber off.

"I think we've already made enough mistakes for one night, don't you?"

Her words should sober me up, but they don't. I'm still too high on her.

"There's a long time until morning, Temptress. We can

worry about all the things we shouldn't have done when the sun rises."

"Kian," she warns as I roll her onto her back and settle between her thighs again.

Her pussy is swollen and red. Fucking perfect.

"Are you sore?"

She shakes her head. "I don't think so."

"Shame. I could have kissed it better if you were."

Her hips roll and her fingers fist the sheets. I'm not sure if she's aware she reacts so viscerally to my words, but she does.

"What are you doing?" she gasps when I drop to my stomach again.

She's kissed away her taste, and I need more.

"Kissing it better anyway."

"You're a devi—ANT," she screams as I gently suck her.

"You've seen nothing yet. Good luck walking in the morning."

I wake up in a way I've never experienced before, wrapped around another body like a koala.

At first, I panic.

But then, memories of the night before come flooding back, and if anything, I hold her tighter.

She's going to back away today. She's going to tell me that last night was a mistake and a one-off that's never going to happen again.

That's fine.

But it's not going to stop it from happening again. And again. And again.

She can argue all she likes. But last night was fucking epic.

We'd be doing a disservice to the universe—to sex—if we didn't do it again.

Silently, I laugh at myself.

I'm pretty sure I'm just delusional after the number of times I came last night.

I've blown through the stash of condoms I brought in the hope of getting some action. We only stopped because I ran out. And when I say stopped...we didn't actually stop. We just used other means of enjoying ourselves.

There have been some wild nights in my past, but nothing stands up to last night.

Everything about it was perfect.

Lorelei suddenly tenses in my arms, letting me know that she's awake and already freaking out.

"Morning, Temptress." It's a whisper, barely audible, yet Lorelei reacts as if I just bellowed in her ear.

She moves faster than I thought possible and launches out of bed, taking the sheet with her.

Wrapping herself up, she glares down at me.

"What the hell was that, Kian?"

I can't help it. My lips pull into a smirk.

"What? The cuddling?"

It seems to hit her all of a sudden that I'm lying here completely naked, and her eyes drop. Her expression instantly changes when she catches sight of my morning wood that was previously very happy nestled against her firm ass.

Momentarily, frustration in her eyes gives way to desire, but she's fast to lock it down so that by the time she looks me in the eyes again, there is nothing but exasperation.

"Yes, the cuddling. That..." she says, throwing her arm out toward where I'm lying on the bed. "This..." she says, pointing between the two of us. "Never should have happened."

"Oh," I say, finally sitting up. "I firmly disagree."

She looks up to the ceiling as if praying for strength. "Of course you do," she mutters.

"Lorelei, last night—"

"Was a mistake that's never happening again."

She storms away, wrapped up in the white sheet like some

kind of Greek goddess, but not before she takes one more look at my dick.

Oh yeah, she wants another shot on that.

The bathroom door slamming behind her rocks through me and I flop back on the bed, more than happy to push her reaction this morning to the back of my mind as I relive our night together.

Fuck, it was hot. Wild. Exhilarating. Life-changing.

My cock rests high up on my stomach as I lie there with my hands behind my head, happily remembering what was, hands down, the hottest night of my life.

Who knew my little temptress would be such a wild cat?

Fuck. Who the hell am I kidding? I knew that the moment I met her. And if I needed my opinion solidified then she surely did the night of King and Tate's wedding.

No woman has ever turned me down like she did that night.

If I weren't so shocked, then I'd have been impressed.

I give her long enough to do her business, and then I swing my legs off the bed and press my feet into the luxurious carpet.

With my aching cock bobbing, I saunter toward the bathroom door.

Twisting the handle, I discover that my suspicions are correct.

She didn't lock it.

I can take that one of two ways...

She was too angry to think about it. Or—and this is by far my favorite—she wants me to follow.

The sound of the shower running hits my ears, and then the vision that is Lorelei Tempest emerges before me.

She has her back to me, her head tipped, allowing the water to rain down on her face.

Water runs down her body, highlighting her insane curves. The sight has my dick weeping.

I take the quickest piss of my life, thankfully still

unnoticed, and I freshen my morning breath with some mouthwash before stepping into the huge walk-in shower behind her.

She screams bloody murder, spins around, and punches me in the stomach.

"Oh fuck," I grunt, shocked by both her force and speed. "It's just me."

"The fuck, Kian?"

Recovering from her fist to the gut, I stand tall and edge closer.

She moves back, but she quickly discovers that she's got nowhere to go.

A loud gasp fills the room as she collides with the cold tiles behind her.

"Shall we start the day over?" I ask, my eyes bouncing between hers.

"I think we need to start the week over, if I'm being honest."

"Bullshit. Admit it, last night was the best sex you've ever had."

51

LORELEI

Lie to him.

Lie through your fucking teeth.

Do not let him know just how good last night was.

Don't tell him how you woke up wishing he'd already taken the liberty to embark on the next round instead of cuddling you, waiting for you to rouse.

Swallowing down the truth, I hold his eyes firm and say, "It was okay."

Bald-faced fucking lie right to his face.

Shame burns me from the inside out.

The truth is, it was the best night and the hottest sex of my life. But what good can come of me admitting that?

This thing—if there is even a thing—between us is fake at best.

There is no future where Kian and I could become anything more than boss and assistant.

He might think last night was fun, but it was a one-off. A vacation fling, if you will.

He moves closer still, and his erection brushes my stomach.

Every single muscle in my body clenches.

The memory of just how good he felt inside me last night slams into me full force.

His dick is like none other I've ridden. And not just because of the size. I swear the thing was made for me. The way it hit all of my magical points without even having to try was something else.

Kian was right; even the best dildo in the world can't do that.

Damn it.

How do I move on from a dick like that? I already know that no one else will ever be able to compete.

Every man in my past—Matt, and sadly Ryder included—pales in comparison.

Fuck. I'm royally fucked.

He chuckles, although there is little amusement in it. His eyes are dark, full of desire and determination, and his body is set for a fight.

"You really need to stop lying to me, babe," he warns, looming even closer.

My mouth runs dry, and the second my tongue sneaks out to wet my lips, his eyes drop.

"I-I'm not lying," I argue, sounding anything but convinced by my own words.

"Right, then I think I'd better prove just how wrong you are."

One second he's staring down at me, and the next I'm being hiked up the wall, my legs around his waist, as his lips claim mine.

I hold firm, refusing to kiss him back or join in.

But my resolve to do the right thing is only so strong.

He shifts me, ensuring his length brushes against my sensitive clit, and I gasp in shock, giving him the perfect opportunity to deepen the kiss.

The second his tongue brushes mine, all my fight seeps from my body, and I throw my arms around his shoulders and dive headfirst into this thing.

He kisses me until I'm breathless and grinding against him in search of the ecstasy only he can deliver.

"We're out of condoms, Temptress," he groans, sounding like he's in physical pain confessing those words.

"I've got an IUD," I blurt.

Wrong thing to say, Lorelei.

You should be using the lack of protection to put the brakes on this thing...

"Lorelei, I never fuck bare," he whispers, resting his forehead against mine.

"Nor do I. Ever."

We stand there in a stalemate, our breaths mingling and our bodies burning red hot.

His eyes hold mine, and I'm able to read every single one of his thoughts.

He wants this. He wants this so fucking badly. But he knows that we're about to cross a line we shouldn't be anywhere near.

I appreciate the fuck out of his internal debate.

It gives me confidence that he really does take this seriously.

"Kian, I need—"

"Fuck," he barks before lifting me higher and lining himself up.

He thrusts up at the same time he drops me lower, and as I scream out in delight, he groans deep in his throat.

"Fuck, Lorelei. You've just ruined me for any other woman." I've no idea if he's aware that he says the words out loud, but that doesn't stop me from preening at his praise.

His hips move with precision and accuracy, hitting my G-spot with every thrust.

I slide up and down the tiles, my hands gripping onto his shoulders, my nails piercing his skin as he works us both hard and fast.

Last night was insane. But this right now with nothing between us?

Fuck. It's even better.

How is that possible?

"I can't hold off," he confesses, his muscles pulled tight as he tries to stave off the inevitable. "Clit, babe."

My hand sinks between us in record time, and I cry out as my fingers collide with my swollen, sensitive skin.

"Shit. So fucking tight," he mutters, his eyes holding mine, silently begging me to let go.

He pulls my ass away from the wall a little more, and it's the last straw as he hits me even deeper.

"Kian," I scream as my release floods through my body, making every single nerve tingle in delight.

"Yes. Yes. Yes," he groans before he also locks up, his cock pumping me full of cum.

Oh my god.

I just let my boss come inside me.

Dropping my head onto his shoulder, I suck in a handful of deep, calming breaths.

They do very little to pacify the hurricane of chaos in my head.

As our breathing returns to normal, Kian lowers my feet back to the floor, but he doesn't immediately leave me to continue my shower. Instead, he reaches for the shower gel and sets about washing up.

"Are you for real right now?" I balk.

"What? We can fuck like rabbits, but we can't shower together? Since when was that a rule?"

My mouth opens and closes to respond, but I quickly discover I have no argument.

Eventually, I go with, "I didn't invite you to join me."

"And you think that'll stop me?" He laughs.

"Clearly fucking not," I mutter.

"Are you done?" he asks when I just stand there staring at him rubbing white fluffy bubbles all over his ridiculously perfect body.

"I've barely started," I sulk.

"Then what are you waiting for?"

"You to leave."

"Trust me, babe, watching you shower isn't going to stop me wanting you. You're naked right now. Naked, wet, and—" He reaches out and drags his fingers up my thighs. "You've got my cum running down your thighs." He holds his fingers up to prove his point before moving them to my mouth. "Taste me," he demands.

I should bite my lips together and refuse in an attempt to shut this insanity down. But of course, being the needy whore that I am, my mouth opens, and I happily lick his fingers clean.

His eyes dilate, and out of the corner of my eye, I see his dick jerk in excitement.

The recovery time of this man is incredible.

Swallowing my need for round...I don't know, twenty-five, maybe, I hold my head high.

"I need some space, Kian," I state, my voice hard and unwavering.

I'm not sure if it's my tone, or the fact he really does know that he's pushing his luck, but he agrees and finishes up. He doesn't step out of the shower without giving me a knee-weakening kiss, though.

"That was your last," I say. "Once you step out of this shower, all of that is being put behind us. We came here to work, and that's what we're going to do."

He nods in agreement, but the smirk playing on his lips tells a very different story.

God damn you, Kian Callahan.

Much to my surprise, everything did return to almost normal after my shower.

Okay, so I did find my outfit for the day laid out on the bed, which I didn't have the energy to argue with. My muscles pulled and ached as I dressed, a constant reminder of the night before. And when I emerged with a light covering of makeup on my face, and my hair twisted up into a bun, seeing as I had no choice but to wash it with normal shampoo this morning, causing my curls to turn into the world's worst frizz, the glance he gave me barely held any heat from the night before.

A weird mix of relief and disappointment warred in my stomach, and it hasn't left since.

We ate breakfast in the hotel restaurant like two platonic colleagues. And then we attended meeting after meeting, where we were nothing but professional. Well, as long as you ignore our notebooks, of course.

Clearly, Kian had yet to build as big a collection as me, because he had the same as yesterday. I, however, had another new one.

Behind every average boss is a kick-ass assistant.

And my pen of choice today.

Ringleader of the circus.

Kian really needs to up his game if he wants to play with the big girls.

It's almost four o'clock in the afternoon when Kian scribbles a note and slides it over for me to read. We're watching a presentation on the future plans for The Regency and how the new manager envisions taking it to the next level, given its recent poor performance.

Her ideas are good, but her delivery is dull as hell, and I've found myself drifting off a number of times.

Make an excuse to leave.

Something is waiting for you in our room.

Go relax and then be ready to leave at six.

I glance up at him, hoping that I'll be able to read the answers to my questions in his eyes. But there is nothing.

I study him closer, but he gives nothing away.

"Go, I've got this."

I narrow my eyes. Do you, though?

His returning smirk tells me that he can hear my silent question loud and clear.

I wait for a natural pause in the presentation before I explain that I'm not feeling well and duck out.

My stomach is a riot of nerves as I ride the elevator alone, and it doesn't get any better when I step out and head toward our suite.

Kian could have literally done anything.

My mind runs wild with ideas, most of them kinky as hell, because after the night—and morning—we shared...well...

But as I enter our suite, everything looks normal and smells fresh. The scent of our night is no longer filling the air.

The second I walk into the bedroom, I find a box on the end of the bed, but I quickly discover that isn't it.

Soft, flickering light from the bathroom steals my attention, and my breath catches when I step inside and discover what he's done.

The entire room is filled with scented candles, and the huge tub in the middle of the room is overflowing with bubbles.

My chest tightens, knowing that he did this for me, but it also makes everything even more confusing.

This is boyfriend/relationship territory, and that is not where we're at, or where we're going.

That being said, there is no way that I'm going to let it go to waste. But not before I check the contents of that box. There's no way I'll be able to relax until I know everything.

52

KIAN

If my brothers could see me now…

They'd probably think that I'd had a lobotomy on the flight down here.

But I can't help it. I just want to make her smile and, of course, stop her from trying to convince both of us that last night was a one-time thing.

I like to think that this morning in the shower was a good clue that I'm not happy leaving things at last night, but this is Lorelei we're talking about. Who the hell knows what goes through her head most of the time?

I sit on the couch in our suite, wearing a pair of tan pants and a dark gray polo shirt, waiting for her to emerge for her six P.M. deadline. But just like always, she makes me wait until the very last second.

When I came up with the idea for what we could do tonight, I figured that none of the outfits I packed for her would work. Okay, that's a lie. I just wanted her to wear something that I hand-selected.

I knew the moment I saw it appear on my screen that it was made for her, and now my knee is bouncing with impatience to see just how right I was.

There's movement on the other side of the room, but that

isn't anything new. It's been the same since I returned to our suite to change thirty minutes ago.

I sit up, my eyes shooting to the bedroom door when the noise gets closer.

It takes her a couple more seconds. She's blatantly looking at a clock and waiting for it to tick around to six on the dot before she pulls the door open.

"Oh wow," I breathe the moment she emerges, wearing the denim dress I chose.

It's fitted with a zip up the front that stops in the perfect place to showcase her tits, and rests halfway between her knees and hips. It's also every bit as good as I hoped it would be.

"You've got good taste," she says as she moves farther into the room, letting me see the red pumps and purse I chose to go with it.

She's right. I do have really good taste.

"Not bad for a man who's never bought a woman clothes before, huh?"

Her eyes narrow. "You've never—"

"Nope," I say, cutting her off as I jump to my feet, ready to leave. "Never cared enough before to buy a woman anything more than a taxi ride home."

"You really are a catch, you know that, right?"

"Too fucking right, I am. I got you that, too," I say, pointing at a wrap thing that's resting over the arm of the couch. "In case you get cold."

She studies me for a beat before picking up the wrap and feeling the soft, luxurious fabric beneath her fingers.

"You really have thought of everything, huh?"

"I'll ask you again at the end of the night. Shall we?"

I desperately want to reach for her hand, but I know she won't have it. Not while we're in Callahan territory, at least.

Side by side, we walk out of the hotel, and instead of stepping into one of the taxis that are loitering, I take a left and continue walking.

"Interesting," Lorelei muses beside me.

"I like surprising you," I confess.

"Trust me, you're full of surprises."

We walk in silence for a few minutes, both of us taking in the beauty of the city at dusk. It's not until I'm confident that we've left the world of Callahan Enterprises behind that I make my move.

Spotting an alcove ahead, I finally entwine my fingers with Lorelei's and tug her into the shadowed hideaway.

"Kian," she gasps. "What are you—"

Her words vanish as I press her back against the wall and duck down so our lips are almost brushing.

"You've no idea how badly I've needed to kiss you all day."

"Kian," she warns, pressing her hand against my chest as if that'll be enough to push me away.

"I know you want it too," I state, studying her closely.

"We've returned to real life today, Boss. This needs to stop." She tries to look away from me, but I catch her jaw with my fingers and turn her face back to me.

"I know you don't really mean that," I say softly. "You want this as much as I do."

"What is this, though, Kian?" Her frustration with the situation is clear in her tone.

"It's whatever you want it to be," I say honestly. "Right now, I'm enjoying spending time with you, even when you are trying your hardest to piss me off. Does it need to be anything more than that?"

She shakes her head, sadness seeping into her eyes.

"I don't want to be anyone's secret fuck buddy, Kian. Not even yours."

"When did I say anything about secret? I asked you to date me, babe."

She balks, and I instantly regret the words.

"Fake date. You asked me to fake it with you to have a break from your fan club. That is not asking to date me, you moron."

"So then, date me," I say simply.

A laugh punches from her chest. "No, Kian. I am not dating you."

She pushes harder against my chest and slips from between me and the wall.

I let her go for a few seconds, giving her a little thinking space before I rush to catch up with her.

"I'm not ashamed of being with you, Lorelei."

"I never said you were," she says tersely.

"You did when you called yourself a secret fuck buddy. You deserve more than to be anyone's secret."

"But I'm not good enough to be anything but a fake girlfriend."

Grabbing her wrist, I spin her around to face me.

"I just asked you to date me. Fuck the fake shit. If we have to be officially dating to continue with whatever this is, then so be it."

Her eyes widen in disbelief. "So be it? So fucking be it? Unbelievable."

"What?"

"For a smart man, you can be really fucking stupid, Kian Callahan."

I fall silent.

"It wasn't meant to come out quite like that," I confess when I hear the words I just said.

"It doesn't matter. None of this is happening anyway. Where are we going exactly?" she asks when we come to the end of the street.

Ahead of us is the ocean, and she stares out at it longingly.

The loose tendrils of hair around her face dance in the light ocean breeze, and I lose myself in her beauty.

"Kian?" she snaps as she looks back to find me doing nothing but staring.

"Straight ahead."

"B-but that's the beach."

"And?"

"I doubt there are any five-star restaurants down there."

I laugh. "You underestimate me, Temptress."

We cross over and then take the ramp that leads us to the beach.

"W-what have you done?"

"Oh, me?" I ask, pointing at myself. "Thought I'd bring the five-star luxury to us."

"You're unbelievable," she breathes as we approach our nighttime beach picnic.

We have a gazebo that twinkles with fairy lights, a thick blanket on the sand, and a huge basket with our dinner and a bottle of champagne on ice waiting for us.

"You said you wanted to spend time at the beach, and you also mentioned McDonalds, so..."

"You didn't." She laughs.

"Go and find out."

With a new burst of energy, Lorelei kicks her pumps off and then all but floats toward the blanket.

I stand to the side, watching as she flips open the basket and breathes in the scent of freshly cooked burgers and fries.

"Kian," she cries. "You are crazy."

I kick my shoes off with a wide smile playing on my lips. "I've been called worse, babe. Hungry?"

"Like you wouldn't believe."

Together, we pull everything out of the basket and set it up between us.

But while she eagerly dives into her burger, I hang back, content to watch her.

"Wait," she says, studying her burger as closely as I am her. "This isn't a McDonalds burger."

"Guilty," I confess. "I sweet-talked the chef at The Regency to create something special."

She shakes her head in disbelief, but she can't wipe the smile off her face as she pulls the fries from the basket.

"You're something else."

"Do you like it?"

She looks around, taking in our surroundings before looking back at the food, and finally at me.

"It's perfect. Thank you."

"Anything, Temptress. You only have to ask."

Before I can think too much about what I just offered, I reach for my burger and unwrap the familiar paper covering it. Chef really did understand the assignment here.

"Oh my god," I moan after taking my first bite. "So good."

Lorelei agrees with a moan of her own that makes my dick twitch before devouring her food like she hasn't eaten in a week.

"Pretty good third date, huh?" I ask a while later after all the food has been demolished and we're lying back on the blanket. I desperately want to reach and pull her into my body, but I refrain. For now, at least.

"It's not a date," she argues. "Let alone a third one."

"If you say so."

Rolling onto her side to face me, she blows out a slow breath.

"Kian," she starts, but I reach out and press my fingers to her lips, stopping her from continuing.

"We've got one more night here, and then we go home and return to normal. Can we just have this? We have all the time in the world to argue about what happens once we get back to Chicago. Don't you think last night was too good not to repeat while we can?"

"It's not that simple," she argues.

"Why? Are you worried that you will fall in love with me?" I ask with a laugh. Honestly, the idea of anyone falling in love with the real me is nothing but amusing. Everyone just wants the man they think I am.

She swallows thickly, and panic hits me like a tsunami.

No. Surely not.

"Lorelei?" I whisper, terrified that I've totally ruined everything for good.

"No, Kian," she states coldly. "You don't need to worry about that. I just mean that things will get messy if we—"

"They won't if we don't let them. We both agreed that us dating was a good idea, for both of us. Why not explore it properly?"

Her eyes bounce between mine. She looks utterly terrified.

Well, she's not the only one.

She doesn't say anything for the longest time; she just stares at me, deep in thought.

Eventually, though, she can't deny the chemistry that's crackling between us, and she leans forward.

My heart slams against my chest, and my head spins with all the unknowns I'm opening up here, but the second our lips collide, everything goes silent. The only thing that matters is the woman beside me.

Reaching out, I tug her closer, pinning our bodies together as we tell each other with actions what we're too scared to with words.

"We're going to get arrested if we don't stop," Lorelei says after long, blissful minutes. But she's right. My dick is trying to rip through my pants, and my hands have definitely roamed a little too far for a public beach.

"It would be worth it."

"Let's go cool off," Lorelei says, jumping to her feet and taking off toward where the waves crash against the sand.

"I'm not swimming. It'll be freezing," I call, attempting to adjust my dick so I can get to my feet.

"Pussy," she calls back as she wades into the water. It's easy for her—she's wearing a dress.

She spins around with the water lapping at her calves and a wide smile on her face.

I may not know her all that well, but something tells me that she doesn't smile like that all that often.

Before I can stop myself, I pull my cell from my pocket and snap a photo of her.

She looks so light and carefree.

If nothing else comes from this trip, then at least I was able to give her this moment.

"Pants off, Callahan. The water is lovely."

"Fuck's sake," I mutter as I undo my pants and kick them and my socks off before taking off toward her.

Our laughter rings out into the silent evening around us as we frolic in the ocean like a couple of kids.

I can't remember the last time I felt this free, this relaxed.

It might be the setting, but I know that's bullshit. It's the company.

Lorelei allows me to step out of the skin I'm forced to wear as the CFO of Callahan Enterprises and get a taste of what life could be like without the pressure of my job and my family.

It's something I think I'll forever be grateful for.

53

LORELEI

Kian has been quiet all day. I know why, and I get it.

In just over ten minutes, we're going to land back in Chicago, and everything that's happened in Charleston is going to be behind us.

We agreed we'd enjoy each other on the trip, and then once we're back, it's life as usual with him as my boss, and me as his assistant.

I stand by the decision. It's the right thing to do. That doesn't mean that it doesn't hurt, though.

These past two days have been...enlightening, to say the least.

But it can't continue. I also can't risk agreeing to this fake dating thing.

He's going to reel me in—more than he already has—and then ultimately, he's going to drop me the second someone else —someone more suitable—comes along.

My stomach knots and my heart aches just thinking about it.

The pilot announces our final descent into O'Hare International, and my anxiety about what life looks like outside of this plane only gets worse.

At least it's Friday.

We've got the weekend to cool off. Maybe things will be easier on Monday.

It's wishful thinking, I know that. But it's all I've got right now.

Barely a word is said between us as we make our way through arrivals and then out to where Jamie is waiting for us.

I've never felt on edge when I've been in Kian's company before. I don't like it.

In fact, I hate it.

We're only a few hours into this "new" us and I already miss his heated glances, his burning touches. His kisses, his dirty words.

Fuck. This is going to be harder than I thought.

"Good evening," Jamie greets with a wide smile. "I trust you had a pleasant trip."

"Yes, thank you," Kian says curtly. His tone does nothing to ease the tight knot inside me.

Jamie takes our suitcases after opening the backdoor for me.

"Thank you," I mutter absently before climbing in.

Kian follows, but again, without a word or even a glance in my direction.

Instead, he pulls his cell from his pocket and begins tapping at the screen.

Both of mine, however, sit ignored in my purse.

I know it's a workday and that I have emails sitting in my inbox that I need to deal with. I also know that I have messages from Tate and Cory that need to be responded to.

I've spoken to Tate, told her where I was and who I was with, but other than that, I've been pretty vague. She has questions—lots of freaking questions. Questions I really don't want to deal with.

I let out a heavy sigh and rest my head against the window.

I'm exhausted, both physically and mentally. All I want to do is put some comfy clothes on and curl up in my bed.

My muscles ache for it, and my eyes immediately get

heavy at the prospect of shutting the world out and getting some decent sleep.

I sense Kian glance over at me. My skin burns with his attention, but I don't look back. I can't. I'm afraid that if look him in the eye, something I really don't want or need to say is going to come spilling out of my mouth.

So instead, I focus on the outside and the passing city until my surroundings become more familiar and I spot my building in the distance.

I thought I'd feel excited to finally get some real space from him, but as Jamie brings the car to a stop beside my entrance, all I feel is the dread and confusion multiplying.

I shift to the edge of my seat, ready to climb out the second Jamie allows it. I'd let myself out if I didn't know it would put that sad, puppy dog look on his face. My heart can't handle that right now.

With my eyes locked on the door, I shoot a quick, "Thank you for the trip," over my shoulder.

I move farther forward, desperate to exit before he can respond, but Jamie isn't fast enough.

"Come home with me," Kian says, his voice deep, maybe even a little sad.

"I can't, Kian. We agreed."

The door opens and I finally make my escape.

"Message me when you're inside," he says.

"Okay," I agree quietly, so quietly I'm not sure if he actually hears me.

Jamie carries my suitcase to the elevator, but I refuse to let him escort me all the way to my apartment.

I'm a grown-ass woman; I don't need any man to stand in an elevator with me.

That night was a freak accident. It won't happen again.

I recite those exact words to myself long after I've said goodbye to Jamie, and I don't stop until I spill out into my hallway. It's also the first time in long minutes that I suck in a real breath.

"Get a fucking grip, Lorelei," I mutter to myself as I tug my small suitcase toward my apartment.

But just when I think everything is about to get easier, my eyes land on the busted lock of my front door.

My heart drops into my feet as dread seeps like poison through my veins.

"What the—"

Hesitantly, I push the door open.

I breathe a sigh of relief when everything looks as it should. I mean, honestly, I have nothing worth stealing. Now that Tate has moved out with her designer handbags and shoes, there is nothing worthy of the effort of breaking in.

Abandoning my suitcase, I forge on. The living room is fine, untouched, and I begin to wonder if whoever broke in got spooked and ran before they could do anything.

But then I get to my bedroom.

I freeze in the doorway and stare at the devastation before me.

Everything is trashed. Furniture has been upended. My clothes and accessories are everywhere. My sheets have been torn from the bed and ripped to shreds.

But none of that is what makes acid swim in the pit of my stomach.

It's the massive, spray-painted word above my headboard that makes my entire body tremble with anger.

Whore.

Disbelief and fury rush through me as I stand there staring.

Only one person pops into my head as the culprit. But... surely not.

Surely, he wouldn't stoop so low?

"Lorelei?" I barely register the deep rasp as I continue staring at the destruction of my bedroom.

But the second he steps up behind me and the heat of his body burns down the length of mine, I jump forward.

Only, I don't get anywhere, because his arm bands around my waist, holding me tightly to him.

I might still be shaking, but as he holds me, it's impossible to miss the way his own body trembles violently.

"You need to come with me," he states, his voice at odds with his body's visceral reaction.

He moves us both backward, and for a few seconds, I allow it. But then reality hits and I anchor my feet to the ground.

"No," I argue, ripping free from his grasp.

A bitter, dangerous-sounding laugh spills from his lips.

"This isn't up for discussion, Lorelei," he states. "You're not staying here."

"Then I'll go to Tate's. I'm not going with you."

His brows furrow, before he firmly refuses to accept my suggestion.

"Is there anything else you need before we leave?"

I watch as he picks up my suitcase. My lips part to refuse again, but it would be pointless, and I quickly give up.

Glancing back at my bedroom, a lump of emotion that was absent the first time I saw it crawls up my throat.

The anger has subsided a little and the cold, harsh reality that someone has been inside my personal space, been through all my things and done this is starting to hit home.

Without a word, I hop between the piles of clothes and my other possessions that litter my bedroom floor until I get to the bathroom.

My eyes widen in shock.

I stupidly expected it to be as untouched as the living room.

"Noooo," I cry, assessing the mess.

All of my hair products have been squirted all around the room. Hundreds and hundreds of dollars' worth of purchases in my quest for curl perfection are seconds away from literally going down the drain.

"What's wrong?" Kian asks, rushing in behind me.

When I glance back, his expression isn't as devastated as it should be.

He doesn't get it.

Not that I expected him to.

"My hair products," I explain absently, desperately trying to keep my sobs in.

But despite not making a sound, he knows.

Reaching out, he pulls me into him.

Pressing my face against his chest, I squeeze my eyes closed and breathe in his manly scent.

"We'll buy more, Lorelei," he promises, his lips pressed against the top of my head.

Unable to do anything but agree, I nod.

"Come on. Let's get out of here."

With all my fight gone, I allow him to lead me out of my apartment.

After fiddling with the busted lock, he assures me that he'll call someone to get it fixed.

"What's wrong?" Jamie asks the second we emerge from the building. I'm still tucked safely under Kian's arm. I can only imagine how I look.

"Someone broke into Lorelei's place."

"What?" he gasps.

"Can you call Thomas? Get him out here to secure it."

"Yes. Both of you get in. I'll get it sorted."

Kian pulls the door open as Jamie gets straight on the phone.

"Who is Thomas?" I whisper once we're safely inside.

"King's security guard."

I nod, accepting his answer.

"What happens now?"

"Now, we get you somewhere safe. You don't need to worry about anything else. Thomas can deal with it all."

"The police?"

"He'll sort everything."

Confident he's telling the truth, I allow myself to curl up

against him. I shut my eyes, but the only thing I can see is the word "whore" spray-painted across my wall.

Kian pulls his cell out and begins tapping, but I don't bother looking. He's probably just canceling his Friday night plans.

By the time we pull up outside his building, I'm too numb and exhausted to really see it.

Sure, it's fancy and luxurious, but it mostly passes me by. As does the ride to the very top floor of the building.

He lives in the penthouse. Of course he does.

But as numb as I might be, the second we step into his space, everything changes.

I'm instantly hyper-aware of everything. Of his presence, his touch, his space.

I don't belong here, and I kick myself for not fighting harder for him to take me to Tate's.

She would have looked after me. Ordered my favorite takeout, made me margaritas, and ensured I had all new hair products by first thing tomorrow. That's just the kind of friend she is.

"What do you need?" Kian asks once we're standing in the middle of the colossal space he calls a living room.

I look around. Everything is white, black, and chrome. There's barely any color. It doesn't look like a home. It looks... fake.

"Shower? Nap? Movie?" he prompts.

I look down at myself. I'm still wearing the dress I put on for our morning meetings.

"I— I want to change and—"

He takes my hand and begins leading me through the apartment until we emerge into his bedroom.

His bed is massive, and my eyes lock on it for a little too long.

"You want to curl up in the middle of it?" he asks.

I shake my head, although I think I might be lying.

Pulling that soft-looking comforter over my head and shutting the world out seems like a really good option right now.

"Wait there," he says before disappearing through a door to my right.

He rummages around and returns a few seconds later with a pile of clothes in his hand.

"They'll be too big, but it's all I can offer right now."

I look down as he throws a pair of man's sweats and a hoodie onto the end of the bed and my eyes sting with tears.

"Thank you," I whisper brokenly.

"Do you need help or..."

"I'll be fine," I say. It's true, I will be okay alone. It's not what I want, but it's what I need. "I'll come back out in a bit," I mutter before shrugging my jacket off and turning my back on him.

"Would you like a drink?"

"Yes, please. Whatever you're having," I add before he has a chance to ask.

He hesitates behind me for a few seconds, but he eventually convinces himself to leave, and the second the door closes, I deflate.

54

KIAN

"What's wrong?" Tate asks the second she answers the phone.

"Why does something have to be wrong?" I ask, even though she's right.

"You never call me unless it's an emergency."

"Right," I mutter as I walk through the kitchen and reach for a bottle of scotch. "Lorelei's apartment was broken into while we were away."

"What?" she screeches down the line.

"It's fine. I've brought her home with me. Thomas is securing the apartment and sorting everything out."

"Who would—"

"You don't have any suspicions?" I interrupt.

"I mean, yeah, but surely he wouldn't?"

"Men do really stupid things, Tate. Look what he did in the first place."

"Yeah," she agrees reluctantly. "Those photos of the two of you at the beach sure looked cozy."

"Photos?" I bark.

"Yeah, on Instagram. I didn't know you had it in you, Kian. That was pretty romantic."

"Shit," I hiss.

"Oh, come off it. You're not that naive."

430

"If we were in Chicago, I'd expect it. But we were in a different state."

"People still know who you are. You're always going to be a target, which makes her a target. You know this."

"Yes, all right," I mutter, already feeling like a big enough asshole over this without her chipping in. "I'm going to fix it."

"Then I guess you need to find the asshole and give him another black eye."

"Tate," I gasp.

"What? I'm hangry. Your brother was meant to be home with takeout almost an hour ago. Never make a pregnant woman wait for food, Kian. Never."

"I'll try to remember that," I mutter.

"What do you need me to do? If you have food, I can come over. Oh, I could pick some up on the way and—"

"What hair products does Lorelei use?"

"What?"

"What hair products does Lorelei use?" I repeat.

"Wha—why?"

"Because the asshole destroyed them all."

"He what?" she shrieks, sounding almost as horrified as Lorelei looked when she made the discovery. "You know, that's a little like asking me the secret to world peace."

"It's just shampoo," I argue.

"Do yourself a favor, Kian. Never, and I mean never, say that to Lorelei."

I shake my head. I'm really fucking missing something here. "Do you have the names or not?"

"It's not that simple. I'll order some things for you, but I can't promise they'll all be right. I haven't lived with her for a few months. She could have moved on from what I remember."

Moved on? From shampoo?

Fucking hell, I don't understand women at all.

"Please can you get it here like—"

"Soon? Leave it to me. In the meantime...can we talk more about that romantic beach date?"

"No, we cannot. I need to go and check on your best friend. Talk soon, Ta—"

"Wait," Tatum cries before I get a chance to hang up. "Is she okay?"

"Of course. She's with me," I say smugly.

"That's why I'm concerned."

"I won't let anything happen to her, and I'll take care of her."

She falls silent for a moment. I should hang up. But I don't. And I regret it the second the next words slip from her lips. "There's nothing fake about this, is there?"

"I've no idea what you're talking about. Enjoy your takeout."

I cut the call before she has a chance to give me any more shit over this whole situation.

Is there anything fake about it?

No, there fucking well isn't, but I'm not about to confess that to Tate, or even Lorelei right now. I can barely admit it to myself, if I'm being honest.

Finally, I pour myself a glass of scotch and throw it back.

"Fuck," I breathe as I slam the glass back down on the counter. Closing my eyes, I find the image of Lorelei's trashed bedroom burned into my eyelids.

What would she have done if I didn't go back up?

I nearly didn't. I almost took her lack of message as her usual brand of defiance.

It was on the tip of my tongue to tell Jamie to just leave. Thank fuck I didn't.

She wouldn't have called me for help. Hell, I doubt that she'd have even called Tate. I might still have a lot to learn about my assistant, but one thing I know for sure is that she's independent to a fault. She'd have probably spent the rest of the night scrubbing that spray paint from her wall so she could brush the whole thing under the carpet in the hope it's a one-off.

It may well be. It could have been a chancer. But...I'm finding it hard to believe.

No random robber would have broken in just to trash Lorelei's bed and bathroom. That was a targeted attack.

If I didn't know it the second I saw that word graffitied on her wall, then I did the moment I witnessed her reaction to her treasured haircare products.

Time passes slowly as I wait for her to emerge from my bedroom.

I could have taken her to one of the guest rooms instead, but even considering it felt wrong.

We might have agreed that everything would go back to how it was before once we touched down on home soil, but it was the last thing I wanted.

The past two days have been incredible. Why the hell would I want something that good to end?

She's scared. I get it.

Hell, I am as well. I've never had a connection with a woman like I've experienced with Lorelei the last two days. I'm not going to let that go easily.

I just need to figure out a way to prove to her that it's worth the risk. That I'm worth the risk.

The problem is, I've no idea how to make that happen. And I fucking hate that I don't have the answer.

It's why I like numbers. It might take a while, but there is always an answer.

People and relationships are a very different beast.

When almost thirty minutes have passed, I give up waiting and go in search of her.

"Lorelei," I call after knocking on my own bedroom door. It feels bizarre, but I don't want to make today any worse for her.

There's no noise from the other side, and I begin to wonder if she's crawled into my bed and passed out. I'm weirdly excited about the idea that she's found comfort in my space.

Twisting the handle, I push the door open and look inside.

"Hey," I say when I spot her emerging from my bathroom.

My sweats look massive on her. I can't see her waist because of my equally large hoodie, but something tells me they are beyond cinched and tied tight to keep them up. She looks incredible, but it's not her clothing that catches my attention, it's her red puffy eyes and tear-stained cheeks that make my heart bleed.

"Babe," I start, but she holds her hand up, stopping me.

"Can we not?" she asks, walking across the room and attempting to slip behind me in her quest to escape.

My hand darts out, my fingers wrapping around her wrist, stopping her.

"It's okay to be upset, Lorelei," I say.

"I'm exhausted, Kian," she confesses without looking at me. "The past few days have been a lot. Hell, the last few weeks have."

"Go and sit down on the couch. I'll get you a drink and order food. What would you like?" I ask, half-expecting her to say McDonalds.

"Italian. I need pasta."

"You've got it. I've got the perfect wine for it."

"Sounds good," Lorelei says, although her tone doesn't match her words.

"Temptress," I growl when she attempts to slip from my grip.

Finally, she looks up at me.

Her eyes are glassy and swollen from crying.

All I want to do is fix it, but I've no idea how.

"Everything is going to be okay," I assure her.

"I know," she says quietly before pulling her arm from my fingers and walking away from me.

I watch her go, kicking myself for not doing better.

This is all new to me. I've never cared about how a woman is feeling before. Never wanted to make everything better.

When I get back down to the living area, I find her curled up in the corner of my sectional with her arms wrapped around her legs.

She looks so small, so...un-Lorelei-like.

I hate it.

After pulling up my food delivery app, I find my favorite Italian restaurant and order what I hope is going to be the comfort food she craves before pulling out a bottle of white wine from the refrigerator and pouring us both a glass.

"Here you go," I say, passing it over.

"Thank you," she says absently, her eyes locked on the view of the city before us.

When I first moved here, I would notice it every single day. But at some point, it became normal. But as I lower myself next to Lorelei, I force myself to really look again.

"I've ordered dinner," I assure her. "It shouldn't be too long."

She nods, but she doesn't say a word. She just continues staring.

"Would you like to watch TV?" I offer, unsure what else to do.

She shrugs.

I hesitate, not wanting to do something she doesn't want.

I never second-guess myself. It's weird.

In the end, I choose to put some soft music on instead of the TV.

"Thomas has secured your apartment. He's going to drop new keys off here for you."

She swallows thickly but still doesn't say anything. Instead, she sips her wine.

"He's waiting for the authorities to come and look at the damage. We'll get whoever it was, babe. I promise you that."

Finally, her lips part and her voice fills my apartment. "You don't have to do that. You've already done more than enough."

"Lorelei, I've done nowhere near enough."

"I'll go to Tate's tomorrow. I don't want to cramp your style."

My heart squeezes at the thought of her leaving.

"We'll deal with everything tomorrow. Tonight, just relax."

We fall silent again, losing ourselves in our own thoughts until the buzzer goes off, announcing the arrival of our dinner.

Despite requesting it, Lorelei barely eats anything.

I offer to order something different in fear she doesn't like it, but she refuses.

She's shut down both physically and emotionally.

After she's pushed her tagliatelle around the plate for the fourth time, I finally take it away, suggesting that maybe she should go to bed.

She gets up and shuffles down to my bedroom without question.

I follow only a few minutes later and find her curled up in the middle of my bed.

Looking back over my shoulder, I debate going to crash in one of my guest rooms, but that's about as chivalrous as I get, because I push those thoughts aside quickly and step into my bedroom, closing the door behind me and shutting the rest of the world out.

After cleaning up, I strip down to my boxers and slide into bed with Lorelei.

She moans as I join her, and the second I wrap my arm around her waist, she wiggles back until she's tucked tightly against my body.

She's sleeping and isn't aware of what she's doing. But it doesn't matter. Nothing does while I've got her in my arms.

"Goodnight, Lorelei. Sweet dreams."

I drop a kiss on her shoulder before snuggling down behind her and willing myself to drift off and put today behind me.

55

LORELEI

I wake to a very large, very cold and empty bed.
I don't need to stretch my arm out to confirm what I already know. Kian isn't here.

He was. I remember him wrapping his arm around me. I remember snuggling back into his warmth, where I felt safe.

Everything has felt wrong since I walked into my bedroom and then my bathroom.

Someone invaded my personal space. Someone trashed my bedroom, called me a whore...

There is only one person I can think of who would do that. But why?

I'm not the one who fucked everything up. I wasn't the one lying through my back teeth every single day of our relationship.

But is he capable of something like this?

Yesterday, before walking into my apartment, I'd have said no. Lying is one thing; criminal damage is entirely another. But then, I guess he does have a score to settle after Kian overpowered him. And it's not like I ever really knew who he was. I figured out that much the day I discovered he had a fiancée.

I kick my legs out in frustration. I was hoping that things would feel easier, make more sense in the cold light of day. But right now, I feel just as numb and disconnected as I did last night.

"Argh," I scream, thrashing about in the bed in the hope of banishing what I'm feeling. I stop dead when I feel something weighing down the sheets. My cheeks burn as I consider that I was wrong and that he is here and watching me lose my shit.

Risking it, I crack one eye open, expecting to find Kian staring down at me with an amused expression on his face. But he's not there, and I quickly banish the wave of disappointment I feel.

But while Kian might be absent, I do find a box waiting for me.

It's the same as the box that was waiting for me at The Regency.

I sit up, opening my sore eyes fully, staring at it as if it's nothing more than a figment of my imagination and it's going to disappear any moment.

But it doesn't, and I shuffle closer with my brows drawn together.

Surely, he hasn't chosen a new outfit for me today? The one he bought me in Charleston was nice and all, but he has to know by now that buying me designer clothes isn't the way to my heart. Not that he wants my heart, of course. Just full access to my pussy.

Shaking the thoughts from my head, I knock the top of the box off and reach for the tissue paper covering the contents.

The second what's inside is revealed, I gasp, my hand coming up to cover my mouth.

Staring back at me is a whole box of all my favorite hair products.

A sob rips from my throat.

How did he know?

My fingers graze over all the bottles. Some I haven't used for a while; others have been my go-to recently.

Honestly, my curly hair is a fucking nightmare. But at the same time, I love the challenge. And when it goes right and a product just works for me...well, there isn't much else in this world that feels that good.

Unable to stay in here, hidden away from him, I throw the covers off and swing my legs out of bed. After freshening up in his luxurious en suite, I go in search of my boss.

The living area and kitchen are quiet, but the scent of freshly brewed coffee lingers in the air, letting me know that he isn't too far away.

I search every room I find, learning more about the man who's welcomed me into his home.

I discover old family photos, along with memories from his time at school, and a handful from more recently. Seeing him grow up, seeing some of the things he experienced in his former years, weirdly makes me feel that little bit closer to him.

It's not helpful seeing as I should be pulling away, but I can't help the squeeze of my heart every time I see his smiling face.

A few of the photos are unbelievable. The things he's experienced are so vastly different from what I have. There are photos of him clay pigeon shooting, playing polo, vacationing on lavish yachts and luxury islands.

There were times in my childhood when just escaping the house felt like a vacation. I can't even begin to imagine what it would have been like to live this life.

When I get to the final door at the end of the hallway, I find it ajar.

My heart rate picks up as I press my hand against the dark wood and push.

I don't need to see him sitting behind his huge desk with the Chicago skyline behind him to know he's there. I feel his presence.

Although, it seems that he doesn't feel the same about my arrival because he doesn't so much as flinch or look up from his computer screen. It allows me a few seconds to take him in. He's shirtless, and his hair is a mess. It really is a sight to behold. I'm so used to the put-together, suited version of him that this relaxed side makes me do a second take.

I'm halfway across the room before he looks up.

The smile he gives as his eyes find mine, though...that sure makes up for it.

"Hey, sleepyhead," he says, his own voice still a little raspy from sleep.

"Thank you," I whisper, trying to fight the emotion that wants to break free all over again.

"You're welcome. Is it all okay?"

I shake my head, and his confidence wanes.

"Y-yeah, it's perfect. How did you know?"

He taps the side of his nose. "A little birdy told me."

"Tate," I breathe.

"Yeah. Even I can admit when I need help, Temptress."

My brows rise at his confession.

"Come here," he says, pushing his chair back to allow me space to sit on his lap.

"Umm..." I hesitate.

"I need your opinion on this email," he adds as a way of convincing me.

"Kian, we—"

"Just work, Lorelei. Then you can go and do whatever you do with all those bottles that make your hair so pretty."

"You think my hair is pretty?" I ask, my brain yet to function properly by catching the words before they spill free.

"Lorelei," he sighs. "There isn't an inch of you that isn't pretty. Now get over here and read this," he demands, his "boss" voice flowing back and making tingles run down my spine.

My feet move of their own accord, and I find myself closing the space between us. But I don't lower myself onto his lap. I draw the line there.

Instead, I lean over the desk and scan the email before me.

It's bullshit. Nothing that he needs my opinion on at all.

Just Martin keeping him in the loop with something I'm not even aware of.

I'm about to stand back up and tell him that he's wasting my time when he acts.

His hands wrap around my hips, and I'm dragged into the position he wanted me in.

"Kian," I cry, wriggling in his grasp, but his hold is too tight.

"Stop fighting me, Temptress. It'll only get me harder."

I still, swallowing thickly as his words hit their mark.

"How are you feeling?"

I don't respond straight away. Instead, I let his question bounce around my head for a few seconds.

"Confused."

I startle when he laughs, a warm puff of air racing over my shoulder.

A shudder rips through me, and my nipples harden, pressing against the fabric of his sweatshirt.

"You're telling me," he confesses quietly.

"Why's that? It seems like you just got exactly what you wanted."

"Yeah," he agrees. "Doesn't mean I understand it all, though."

There's a beat of silence before he continues.

"You're driving me crazy, Lorelei. This body," he rasps, sliding his hands up my waist. "These tits," he says, cupping them and squeezing just so.

I suck in a sharp breath as desire pools between my thighs.

"Having you here in my home...it's fucking with my already fucked-up head."

"I can leave," I breathe, offering something I'm not sure I'm capable of doing. This apartment should be everything I hate with its expensive, luxurious everything, but I feel weirdly relaxed here. Or maybe it's just him. Maybe it no longer matters what I'm surrounded by, as long as he's there with me.

Fuck.

"No," he says in a rush. There's more he wants to say; I can practically hear the words dancing on the tip of his tongue, but for whatever reason, he swallows them. Finally, he whispers, "Stay. Stay until you're ready to return to your apartment."

My spine straightens. "I'm not scared of some stupid little boy who thinks he can run me out of my own home, Kian,"

"Never said you were. But you're not going back until it's been cleaned."

I want to argue, but his hand skims down my stomach and tucks under the waistband of my sweats.

"Kian." It's meant to be a warning, but it comes out as nothing but a moan.

"Tell me that you don't want me," he taunts as his fingers slip lower.

"I-I—" I swallow any lie that was about to spill from my lips as he connects with my clit. "Oh God."

"I know you do," he rasps. "You want it just as badly as I do. Can you feel how hard I am for you? Been like this all goddamn night. I've barely slept. All I could think about was you. Fuck," he groans, feeling the result of his words against his fingers.

"You need to let your body lead your decisions, babe. It leads you to much more pleasurable outcomes. This..." He rubs me harder, making me moan. "This is what we're meant to be doing. Fuck fighting it. Enjoy it."

He pushes lower, sinking two fingers inside me, and my body gives in, relaxing back against him.

My head settles on his shoulder and my thighs fall open, giving him all the access he needs.

"That's it, good girl."

Leaning forward, I kiss his neck.

He moans as his pulse thunders against my lips.

"Your pussy is so fucking good, Temptress. My dick is desperate for it."

"Kian," I whimper, unable to deny anything at this point.

"Are you going to come over my fingers like a good girl?"

Another needy whimper fills the air.

"Come for me. Then, I'm going to fuck you over this desk so the only thing you're able to think about is me."

That sounds like heaven and hell all rolled into one.

I'm falling under his spell faster than I can control. He knows it, too.

"Do you want that, Temptress? Do you want to feel me stretching you open and fucking you right here for the city to see?"

My stomach and pussy tighten at his words.

"Yes," I whisper, my release looming closer.

"Yes, what?" he demands.

"Yes, Boss. I want you to fuck me over your desk."

"Good girl. But not until I hear you crying my name as you fall apart."

He finger-fucks me faster, his thumb circling my clit with perfect precision, working me higher and higher and hi—

"KIAN," I scream as pleasure slams into me. My body convulses on top of his as ecstasy seeps through my twitching muscles.

I fall limp against him as he continues working me through it, and the second it's over, his free hand grabs my hair, turning me to him so his lips can claim mine.

His kiss is wild and untamed. We're all tongues and teeth as we devour each other like we haven't been together in years, not merely hours.

"Need you," he breathes against my lips. "Need to be inside you."

Not a second later, I'm on my feet, and just like he promised, Kian is bending me over his desk.

He rips my sweats and panties down. They pool at my ankles before he demands that I kick them off.

I do, eagerly, allowing him to spread my legs wider to give him space.

"Look at you," he muses.

My chest heaves against the unforgiving wooden top of his desk, but my skin burns where his eyes meet.

"Your pussy is calling to me."

"Please," I beg, wiggling my ass in the hope of tempting him back.

"What do you want, Temptress?"

"Your dick."

"Right fucking answer."

He stands, sending the chair he's sitting on shooting out behind him before it crashes into the floor-to-ceiling window. He shifts behind me, and when I glance back, I get to watch the moment he shoves his sweats over his ass, freeing his dick.

My mouth waters as I watch him wrap his fingers around himself and pump a couple of times.

"This what you want?"

I nod, unable to find my voice.

"I need your words, Lorelei."

"Y-yes," I stutter. "I want your dick."

My entire body sings with relief when he finally steps forward and rubs the head of his cock through my folds, coating himself in my juices.

My core clenches around nothing, desperate to feel him stretching me open.

You're not meant to be doing this, a little voice says, but I quickly ignore it. It's easy to do so when I'm on the cusp of pure ecstasy.

"Yes," I cry when he pushes inside me.

"Jesus, Lorelei. This pussy. I'll never get enough of this pussy."

As he praises me, he slowly works himself deeper and deeper, stretching me open for him so he'll be able to fuck me the way he really wants to.

"Kian," I scream the first time he pulls out and quickly thrusts back inside, making my feet lift off the floor.

"Fucking missed this."

"It's barely been a day," I point out breathlessly.

"Too long," he grunts as he thrusts back inside me again.

His grip on my hips is borderline painful, but I don't complain. How can I when he feels so fucking good?

I slide up and down on his desk as he takes me hard and fast.

My heart pounds, my temperature soars, and pleasure saturates my limbs.

My orgasm races forward, leaving my entire body trembling with my need for another release.

"That's it, babe. Come all over my cock. Let me feel you milking me. I'm gonna fill this pussy with—"

I've no idea what else he says because my release explodes within me and I scream out as I ride out wave after wave of pleasure.

He keeps talking, his deep voice continuing to vibrate through me, keeping my release alive for longer than I thought possible.

I fall limp against the desk as he thrusts twice more before finally reaching his climax.

His dick jerking inside me sends little aftershocks from my lingering release shooting around my body.

I could go again. Shit. I've never been this insatiable before.

He pulls out and takes a step back.

"Damn, Temptress. That is one fucking sight."

I jump when his fingers tickle up my thigh.

"You're wasting it," he muses before plunging his fingers inside me, pushing his cum back inside.

"We're not meant to be fucking, Kian," I point out while his fingers are inside me.

"How's that working out for you?"

445

56

KIAN

Despite Lorelei's insistence that she's not staying, she doesn't make much of an attempt to leave my apartment.

After our little session on my desk, she disappears to make the most of my bathroom and all her new hair products.

When she emerges over an hour later, she's dressed and looking more like the Lorelei I've come to know. I'm sure she's about to announce that she's heading home, or more so to Tate's. But as soon as she sees that I'm preparing lunch, she hops up onto one of the stools at my kitchen counter and watches me work.

"Hungry, Temptress?" I ask, taking in her freshly curled hair.

I've no idea what she's done with all those products, but it looks really fucking good.

"Like you wouldn't believe," she says, her eyes dropping to my still-naked chest.

Sure, I could have put a shirt on at any point in the last few hours, but why should I when I know she isn't going to be able to resist checking me out?

"Oh, I would. Did you like my office?"

Her cheeks blaze red. "Wonderful. I'm sure you...come to very good conclusions in there."

I smirk. "None better than today."

She shakes her head.

"Coffee?" I offer. I'd already made her one and left it on the nightstand while she was showering, but I already know she's going to want more.

"I can make it," she says, hopping down and making her way to my machine.

And just like that, the dynamic between us changes again as we work together in my kitchen like...like a real couple.

"What?" she asks when she catches me watching her instead of tending to our lunch.

"Nothing. You just...look right at home here."

"Don't get used to it. Getting you a coffee regularly at work is one thing; I'm not extending those privileges to your personal life."

"What about if I pay you in orgasms?"

Her chin drops at my suggestion.

"I can see you considering it."

"I am not. I—"

"Tell me that someone else has made you come harder than me?" I ask confidently. Although I must admit, I brace myself, ready for her attack.

She knows how violently I react to the thought of her with other men. She often uses it when she wants to make a point. This would be the perfect time to poke that particular button of mine.

But to my surprise, she goes with the truth. "I can't."

The widest smile spreads across my lips, and I puff my chest out like an asshole.

"Knew it."

She shakes her head before returning to her seat with both of our coffees, seeing as I'm nearly done with our sandwiches.

"Here you go," I say, sliding a plate in front of her.

"Money, good looks, a passable personality, can cook. You really have it all, huh?"

"You forgot smart and fucks like a god."

"Silly me," she mutters as she lifts her sandwich to her mouth and takes a bite. "Mmm, that's good," she mumbles. "So, what do you usually do on a Saturday?"

"Usually, I hit the gym first thing. Then I might do some work or spend the afternoon with family."

"Friends?" she asks.

"I've got a few, yeah. Nothing like what you have with Tate, though." I rub the back of my neck, nervous about my next confession. "My brothers are my ride and die. Always have been."

"Aw, that's cute."

"I'm not cute, Lorelei."

"You can be, every now and then. Not very often, though."

"I never really connected with anyone else. Not on that kind of level, anyway."

"I get it. What Tate and I have is special. Sisters from different misters."

"Is your father as bad as hers?"

Lorelei freezes. It's not a surprise; she gets hella awkward every time family or her former years are brought up.

I want to know, though. I want to learn more about her and why she is the way she is, and I think that her past holds the key to a lot of that.

"I don't know who my father is," she confesses after a few silent seconds.

"Oh, okay. So there's a good chance he could be worse, then. Probably for the best you don't know him."

"Yeah," she muses, deep in thought, letting me know that this is a subject she's thought about a lot over the years.

"What about your mom?"

"Do we have to do this?" she asks, abandoning her sandwich on her plate as if she's just totally lost her appetite.

"No, we don't have to. I was just curious about your life before becoming an employee at Callahan Enterprises."

She hangs her head and lets out a long sigh.

"My life was shit until the day I started at college and met

Tate. Nothing before that day—aside from my brothers being born—is worthy of being discussed. I try not to think about it, let alone talk about it."

"Okay," I state before biting my sandwich.

She looks over and narrows her eyes in suspicion.

"Okay? That's it?"

"Yeah. Why? Is that the wrong answer?"

"N-no. I just...I wasn't expecting you to drop it that easily."

"You'll tell me when you're ready," I reply confidently.

"Okay, so afternoon with family, and then the evening on a date with a celebrity or socialite?"

"I might attend an event—"

"With said date," Lorelei adds bitterly.

Joy lights me up inside that she gets just as jealous as I do.

"I don't date every weekend. And sometimes I go to events alone."

"Bullshit," she coughs, making me chuckle.

"No, really. Sometimes I can't deal with the bullshit of having someone else to worry about."

"Lovely," she mutters.

"I don't need to tell you that most of them are hard work and demanding."

"Demanding?" she asks, raising her brows. "I've no idea how you cope, dealing with someone demanding."

"Okay, yeah. Laugh it up."

"Just saying," she mutters, pulling a piece of cheese from inside her sandwich.

"I'm tired of the bullshit. I want...honestly, I don't know what I want. A change, I guess. Something less...superficial."

"Are you trying to tell me that you're ready for a grown-up relationship?"

"Maybe. No. Yes. I don't know."

She studies me for a beat before continuing to dissect her sandwich and eat the contents.

"I know everyone looks at the lives we live and thinks we

have it all. And on the face of it, sure, we do. But the money, the careers, the...fame...it's not always worth it."

"I get that." I glance at her. "Okay, I'm learning that now by getting to know you."

"I know what you used to think of me. You made it more than clear."

"It was a naive stereotype I wish I could take back."

"Is that why you're scared to talk about your past? Because you think I'll put you in a box?"

She shrugs, not as quick to respond now that I've turned this back around on her.

"Maybe."

"I don't care about your past, or what happened before we met, Lorelei. I just want to know how it made you...well, you."

"My past...it...it made me the independent, fierce woman that I am today. It taught me my worth and what I should and shouldn't put up with from other people. Men, specifically."

"Good. That's good. You shouldn't settle for any less than you deserve."

"Like fake dating a millionaire."

"I quirk a brow. Millionaire?"

She drops her eyes to the counter. "I don't care about your money, Kian."

"I know you don't, and I love that about you. You're not interested in me for any of the same reasons any of the others ever have been."

"Who says I'm interested at all?"

"The wet patch on my desk and your scent on my fingers sure say a lot."

"You're a nightmare."

"So, what did you want to do with your Saturday?" I ask, hoping like hell she doesn't ask me to take her somewhere and not bring her back.

"Not really feeling like doing anything."

"Netflix and chill?" I ask.

"Have you ever asked anyone to do that before?"

"Nope."

"And you know what it means?"

"Of course I do. Why the hell do you think I'm asking."

"What did you want to watch?"

"Don't give a shit. I don't watch TV. I just want the chill part."

"You don't watch TV?"

"Not really, no."

Horrified, she lists a whole host of shows, most of which I've heard of but never seen.

"You can keep going, if you like, but the answer will stay the same. I'll watch football if I can't go to Kieran's game, and the highlights, maybe. But that's about it."

"And yet," she looks over her shoulder, "you have a bazillion-inch TV."

"It's not a bazillion inches," I argue.

"Whatever. It's stupidly big considering it's never on."

"Football is killer on it."

"Well, that's okay then."

"Speaking of TV. Did your brother play last night?"

"No. Thankfully, they're on a bye week. Kieran is at home again tomorrow, right?"

"Yep. We're going."

She rears back.

"We are?"

"You enjoyed it last week, didn't you?"

"Y-yeah, but—"

"Tate's going," I add as a way of convincing her.

"Shit, Tate," she says, hopping up from her stool and sprinting toward my bedroom.

"Is that a yes to the game?" I call after her with a laugh.

B y the time Lorelei returns after her long-ass call with her best friend, I'm on the couch with Netflix on, waiting for her to join me.

"Tell me you have been scrolling for something to watch the whole time I was gone," she says before flopping down on the couch beside me.

"Nope," I say, holding up my cell. "Been working and waiting. Your choice."

"Only because you have no idea what anything is?"

"I'm aware...of some of it. I just didn't want to watch something you've seen before."

"Sure."

Snatching the remote from beside me, she scrolls through the recently released list and selects some docuseries.

"Why this one?"

"Haven't seen it. Tate said it's good. Plus, something tells me that we're not going to be fully focused, and I don't want to ruin something I do want to watch."

"Not going to be focused? I thought you were still in denial about this," I say, gesturing between us.

"What's a few more days of enjoying ourselves? Monday will be here before we know it."

A wide smile spreads across my face.

"We get to fuck more?" I ask simply.

"Depends on how much you annoy me."

"As if you'd say no."

"I might," she argues. "Now shush, I want to watch this."

"You pretty much just told me that you didn't."

"Yeah, well, I want to at least try before you distract me with your filthy ways."

"You love my filthy ways."

"Maybe, maybe not."

Throwing my cell to the other end of the couch, I reach for Lorelei instead, tugging her beside me so we can snuggle up together as the opening credits come to an end.

"I'm experiencing a lot of firsts with you, Temptress."

I can't see her, but something tells me that she's smiling. I know that I am.

With my arm locked around her waist and her body tucked up against mine, we embark on my first Netflix series.

Despite her not believing we'd actually watch, it's really interesting and I find myself sucked in after only fifteen minutes. I'm not sure Lorelei can say the same though, because sometime before the first episode is done, her breathing evens out and her body relaxes even more.

Lifting my head, I press a kiss on her shoulder and whisper, "I like having you here a little too much, Temptress."

57

LORELEI

"You're taking me home after the game," I state as I emerge into Kian's living room, tugging the small suitcase I took to Charleston behind me. Thanks to the extra bits I've accumulated in my short stay here, the thing is bursting at the seams, even with the fully loaded tote bag hanging over my shoulder.

"Lorelei—"

"Don't start," I breathe. I don't have the energy for an argument over this.

After my impressively long nap during the Netflix series I said I wanted to watch yesterday, there wasn't much more relaxing.

I had no idea at the time, but our little session over Kian's desk was only the starter.

He ate me out on his couch before fucking me over the back of it. We also christened his kitchen before we finally made our way to his bed and went a few rounds in there as well.

I've no idea what time we finally passed out, but it was late. Or maybe even early.

We woke up late this morning, and Kian surprised me with some new workout clothes before dragging me out of his fancy apartment to run five miles.

I needed it. I needed to clear my head, but my body was not prepared for it. My muscles were already sore and aching from our sexercise.

I struggled more than I usually do, but there was something very inspiring about the man who was challenging me to push harder. I've never liked working out as much as I do when I'm with him.

It's a problem that I'm really going to have to work on. One of many, I fear, after everything that's happened between us in the past few days.

I convinced myself that it was going to be a South Carolina thing. I was adamant that when we got back, things could go back to normal, and I'd just have to put up with him bossing me around in the office.

I was naive. I know that now. I'm pretty sure I knew it back then, too, but it was easy to lie to myself, to pretend that turning my back on this—on him—would be easy.

I let out a heavy sigh.

I should know better.

"I'm just saying that you don't have to. You're welcome to stay here for as long as you need. The paint is barely dry and—"

"I'm not staying here, Kian. We're not leaving for work together and then coming home like a happily married couple a few hours later."

He frowns, confusion passing through his eyes for a beat before he quickly recovers. "Who said I wanted to travel to work together? I'd have left before you."

I tilt my head to the side. "Is that right?"

He smirks. "Come on, we're picking King and Tate up on the way."

Excitement tingles in my stomach at the prospect of spending the afternoon with my bestie.

Without stopping to argue any more about my plans, Kian walks over and collects my things.

"We can't be late, we'll never hear the end of it," he mutters as I trail him to the front door.

I shake my head, thinking of all the demands Tatum has already made to know the truth about what's going on here between us.

I haven't told her anything. At least, not yet. I've been able to—I think—successfully keep her off the scent of what's been going on, on the phone and over messages. But the second she looks me in the eye, I know the pretense is all going to come crashing down.

I can't lie to my best friend. She knows me too well. Knows my tells.

The second we're in the elevator, Kian backs me up into the corner and looms over me.

"I hate the idea of you going home alone," he confesses quietly.

"Kian," I sigh, lifting my hand to rest on his chest. Beneath my palm, his heart beats sure and steady.

He moves closer. "Lorelei."

The tension in the small enclosed space ramps up, and despite the number of times we've been intimate in the past few hours, my clit begins to throb.

It's ridiculous.

I shouldn't want this man. He is everything I've always despised in men—in society. But my body reacts to him like no other. It's like he holds a remote control to my libido and can turn it on at any moment.

He lowers his head, resting his forehead against mine, and stares deep into my eyes.

"You're going to demand that things go back to normal the second we step outside this building, aren't you?"

Anxiety knots my stomach.

Of course I am. It's the right thing to do. I'm not the kind of woman this billionaire needs on his arm. But...

Fuck. I want to be.

My heart thunders harder as I make that admission to myself.

"Yes," I force out.

The elevator comes to a stop, and the doors open behind us.

He wants to argue; I can see the storm of it building in those deep green depths, but he locks it down.

"Okay," he finally concedes.

"Okay?" I echo, confused as to why he's being so cool about this.

"Yeah. Okay. I'm happy to be or do what you want, Lorelei. Will it kill me, not backing you up against the window of our box so the world can see us? Yeah, it fucking will. But I also understand."

Without giving me a second to think about his words, he spins away, collects my belongings, and walks out of the elevator like nothing just happened.

I take a moment, watching his strong, wide gait as he moves. His Chicago Chiefs jersey shows off his wide, square shoulders and slim waist. And his ass in those jeans...fuck me sideways.

He looks back over his shoulder when he realizes that I'm not following and catches me staring right at his behind.

"Like what you see, Temptress? Let me up to your place later, and you can look as much as you like. Bite it, even."

"You're a menace," I hiss, marching out of the small space, pretending not to consider his suggestion.

"Just the way you like me."

After placing my bags in the truck, Kian opens the door for me like a gentleman before taking off to collect our passengers.

"I'll get in the back," I offer when we pull up into the underground parking lot of King and Tate's apartment building. "Let King sit here."

Reaching out, I wrap my fingers around the handle, ready to climb out, but just before I push, something hot and unforgiving lands on my thigh.

"No," he growls darkly, forcing me to turn back to look at him.

"But—"

"No buts. You do not have to give up your seat for King."

"I don't mind. You two can talk then."

"We can talk later," he counters.

There's a fierce expression on his face that I've never seen before.

"That is your seat. It is where I want you."

My eyes bounce between his as confusion wars within me.

Is he just saying that because it's the right thing to say to get me to agree, or does he really mean it?

"I mean it, Lorelei," he warns as if he can hear my thoughts. "I don't care who King is. In my car, in my home, hell, even my office, you do not cower to him."

"I don't cower to men, Kian," I hiss.

"Okay, wrong word. What I'm trying to say is that..." He trails off, and I can't help wondering if he's regretting saying anything in the first place. "For once in his life, he's going to have to get used to not being the most important person in the room."

My chin drops, and all the words I wanted to say vanish in a heartbeat.

"There they are," he says, almost sounding relieved that I don't have a chance to respond.

Tate immediately makes a beeline for the back, whereas King approaches the passenger side, obviously expecting it to be empty.

He pulls the door open, and I cringe.

"Oh, Lorelei. Hey, how's it going?"

"Great, thanks," I say, forcing a smile onto my lips.

"You're in the back with your girl, Bro," Kian informs him. "No funny business, yeah?"

King rolls his eyes and slams my door closed.

Tatum is either oblivious to the tension around her or

chooses to ignore it, because the second she's inside, she pokes her head through the seats and looks between us.

"You two had sex," she announces.

The need to curl up in a ball and hide from her is all-consuming.

"Do you know what? This was a really bad idea." I reach for the door handle again. "I'll get an Uber home. Enjoy the game."

I push the door open and almost get a foot on the ground when Kian's deep voice vibrates through the air.

"Get the fuck back in, Lorelei. You're not going anywhere."

I freeze, my body reacting to his demands without permission from my brain.

His eyes burn into the name branded across my shoulder blades.

Callahan.

Just like the moment I pulled it on, his possessiveness wraps around me.

I might be in a jersey supporting his little brother, but it's still his surname, and that's enough for him.

No one says another word as they wait to see how I'm going to react. There is a huge part of me that wants to be a stubborn bitch, to get out and walk off with my head held high. But, there is a bigger part that really wants to hang out with Tate and go to the game. And eventually, that part wins.

"Fine," I huff, falling back into my seat with as much sass as I can muster.

"Behave, Brat," King mutters under his breath before Tate must reach out and slap him because he complains a few seconds later.

Thankfully, talk quickly turns to the game and everything is forgotten. Or at least, it is for the guys. I already know that there is no chance of Tate forgetting. And I'm only proven right, the second we get into the stadium and I'm dragged into the ladies' bathroom.

Thankfully, it's empty.

Reaching for my hand, Tate stops me from escaping her and hiding in a stall. Instead, she spins me around and locks her eyes on mine.

"Tell. Me. Everything," she demands.

Excitement lights up her face; all the while, I want the ground to swallow me whole.

Is there anything more cliché than admitting to your best friend that you've been fucking your boss? Your hot boss that every other woman on the planet wants to fuck? Your billionaire, stupidly hot and charismatic boss? The man you so adamantly hated when you accepted the job?

"Fucking hell, Tate," I mutter, covering my burning cheeks with my hands.

"Okay, let's start with the best bits," she suggests. "Is he good?"

I don't look at her, but I know that her eyebrows are wiggling in the way they do when she wants the juicy gossip.

"BestI'veeverhad," I admit so fast it comes out as one word.

She hears it, I know she does; I don't need to look at her and see the smug grin playing on her lips to have it confirmed.

"What was that?" she asks.

"You heard," I snap, giving up on hiding in a stall and instead marching toward the sink to look at my own reflection.

There may be dark circles under my eyes from my lack of sleep the night before, but there is also an unmissable twinkle in them, too. Even without the chemistry between me and Kian crackling away in the car, there was no way Tate was going to miss it.

"Best you've ever had," she says thoughtfully as if she needs to let the confession settle into her mind before believing it. "That's saying something because you've had some hot nights."

"Dude, are you calling me a whore?" I snap, jokingly.

"Moi?" she asks, resting her hand over her heart. "Never. We both know I'm the biggest whore out of the two of us. Or used to be, at least," she says before dropping her hand to her growing belly.

"Good. And don't forget it," I tease.

"So...details, girl," she prompts.

"He's your brother-in-law."

"Exactly. In-law. It's not like you're fucking Miles." She gasps. "You haven't fucked him too, have you?"

"Shut up." I laugh, rolling my eyes at her dramatics. "I wouldn't touch him with a barge pole."

"He has no idea what he's missing out on," she mutters. "But enough about him. Tell me everything that Kian isn't missing out on."

So I do. Right there in the middle of a bathroom in the Chicago Chiefs stadium, I spill all the dirty details to my best friend. And fuck, do I feel better for it once I word vomit all over her.

"That fucking grin, man," King says, slapping me on the shoulder as we step into the box reserved for us.

Lorelei practically fled to the bathroom the second she saw the sign approaching, and Tate quickly followed. I can only imagine what they're talking about right now.

"Fuck off," I mutter, picking up speed to get away from his smug ass.

"What? It looks good on you."

"Whatever," I say under my breath as I grab us both a chilled beer and walk toward the windows that allow us an unobstructed view of the field. The cheerleaders are out doing their thing, helping to rile the crowd up, ready for the game to start.

Just like always, a weird mixture of excitement and nerves flutters in my stomach as I think about our little brother being down in the locker room getting ready. He'll be solidly in the middle of his weird pregame ritual.

I smile. King and I used to roast him for it when we were younger, but it never stopped him from doing it, and even adding more over the years. It works for him, so I guess it doesn't matter how much we tease him.

"So, are you officially dating your assistant after what...two weeks?" King asks, reminding me that I'm trying to avoid his questioning.

I knew it was going to come. He knows me too well, and he's too damn nosey to keep his suspicions to himself.

But I could really do without the one-man firing squad right now.

Lorelei wants to go home after this game. That's enough for me to obsess over right now.

"No, we are not officially dating. We're—"

"Fucking?" he asks, coming to stand next to me.

Rubbing the back of my neck, I tip my face toward the ceiling and close my eyes, praying for strength.

"Yes. No. I don't know."

"Well, I'm glad you cleared that up," King mocks.

"You're an asshole. Do you know that?"

"That's what big brothers are for, right?"

"I'll ask Kieran."

"You know you're going to lose the best assistant you've ever had, don't you?"

"Not necessarily," I mutter.

"Bro, come on. You can't be fucking around with your assistant and expect it to work out. You'll be a dick to her, and she'll get pissed and leave. Or...she'll meet someone else and move on because you can't offer her what she wants."

Jealousy bubbles up inside me like a volcano about to blow at just the mention of her being with someone else.

"How do you know what she wants?" I snap, unable to keep a lid on my emotions.

"Interesting," King muses, continuing to study me closely.

My fists curl with the need to punch that smug fucking look off his face. He always thinks he knows better. I know he's older and has a couple more years' worth of life experience, but that doesn't mean he knows everything.

"I don't want to be stereotypical here, but she's a woman,

K. She might say she's only looking for a bit of fun, but I guarantee that she has one eye on the future."

I think about some of the things she's confessed to me, and my stomach knots.

He's right, I know he is, and I fucking hate it.

"We're just...enjoying working together," I muse, hoping it's enough to get him off my back. Unlikely, but it won't stop me from trying.

Thankfully, King lets the subject drop when I switch lanes and begin talking about work while we wait for the girls to return.

I want to say I'm fully focused as he discusses the British hotel chain he's still pining after, but honestly, I've got one eye on the door, waiting for Lorelei.

How the fuck can I miss her when she's been with me almost twenty-four-seven for the past few days? It's weird. I have never, ever craved another person's presence like I do hers.

The second the door opens, I turn away from Kingston, confirming—if he wasn't already aware—that I'm not listening.

"Hey," Lorelei says the second she finds me watching her.

"Everything okay?" I ask, studying her closely.

She smiles, but it's tight. "Of course. What have we missed?"

"Oh, nothing much," King says, wrapping his arm around Tate the second she's in reaching distance.

Seeing them together, getting to experience my big brother going all sappy for a woman, is pretty awesome, but this time as I watch his lips press against her temple gently, I feel different.

My chest does this weird lurch and I get the sudden urge to pull Lorelei into my arms and do exactly the same thing.

Only, I can't.

She's not actually mine.

It kills me to keep my hands at my sides and not reach for her. But I do it.

For her.

As if he senses that something is wrong, King glances at me, his brow furrowed.

"It's okay, you two can—"

"The Chiefs are coming out," Lorelei says, cutting my brother off and stepping closer to the window.

I want to say that it's a good thing that the game starts, distracting everyone from the internal war I'm battling. I've never really given much thought to a woman's concerns before. Never needed to. But suddenly I'm holding back on everything I want to do because I know it's what she'd want.

What is this bizarre alternate universe I've found myself in?

The Chiefs' win was easier than last week. I can't say that I was surprised. The Saints are in top form this year and probably their biggest competition for the Lombardi Trophy. But no matter how good the game was or how many touchdowns Kieran managed to score, I couldn't fully focus with Lorelei standing right beside me.

Is it always going to be like this now? Am I always going to be so aware of her presence, of every little move she makes?

Things haven't gotten any better since the four of us left the stadium and headed toward a restaurant of King's choice for dinner.

The food has been great—not that there's ever a concern about that if King is involved in the decision-making—but it's not the epic wings that Lorelei had last week. It's much... healthier.

I glance over at her as she tucks her cell into her purse as we get ready to leave.

She's been messaging on and off throughout the meal. It's her brother. She told him earlier today that she was heading to the game, and he's been messaging ever since.

Before, I'd have been worried that she was messaging her ex, or the douchebag she was sending titty pictures to. But I'm confident that she's lost both of them now thanks to that little block button.

Unease twists up my stomach.

She might have lost her ex's texts, but it's more than obvious he's still present in her life.

King and Tate take the lead, and I gesture for Lorelei to go ahead of me, although I'm not very far behind.

"Are you sure about this?" I ask quietly.

"It's my home, Kian. No one is scaring me off. I'm not a weak woman that—"

I laugh. "I know that. Trust me, I do."

"I need to go home," she states, making my heart sink.

But what if I don't want you to?

I shake my head as I take the door from King and hold it open for her, remembering that I should be putting her first.

But would demanding she comes back to mine be so bad?

She'll be angry, sure. But Lorelei is hot as hell when she's mad. It would ensure some epic angry sex...I've never really experienced that before.

The car ride to King and Tate's apartment is much quieter than this afternoon. Tate is curled up against King's side, half asleep, and King's concern is on his wife. As it should be.

I shouldn't be complaining—at least he isn't focused on me and trying to figure all this shit out.

No sooner have I pulled up in the underground parking lot than King and Tate are out of the car.

"Have a good night, guys," Tate says, suddenly perking up.

"Take her to bed, King," Lorelei instructs, not taking any of her friend's teasing.

"I have every intention of doing just that," he happily confirms.

"For sleep. She's exhausted."

"Sure." He winks before nodding at me and taking off toward the elevator with his girl still tucked into his side.

"They're cute, aren't they?" I muse once we're on the road again.

"Ridiculously so. Tate deserves it."

"So does King," I agree before falling silent.

There are a million and one questions spinning around in my head, but I don't really want to voice any of them for fear of what the answer will be.

We drive for another five minutes before I summon the courage to ask the question King sparked in me earlier.

"Is that what you want?"

"Is what, what I want?"

"What King and Tate have?"

"A relationship?" she asks, sounding confused.

"Yeah, I guess. A relationship, a marriage, kids. The whole happily-ever-after thing."

"Of course," she says without having to think about it. "But sometimes I wonder if it isn't in the cards for me." Her voice turns sad, dejected even, and it pulls at my chest.

"What makes you say that?" I ask, pulling up to a stop light and glancing over at her.

"My choice in men. Every single guy I've been with has been a liar, a player, or just completely emotionally unavailable. It's like a curse. Karma, maybe."

"Why would it be karma?" I ask, confused.

Lorelei shrugs.

"My life...it hasn't been anything like the American dream everyone wants. It would be naive of me to think that it could change."

"Living our lives the way everyone expects isn't all that's possible. There is no rule that says you must get married and have two-point-four kids."

"No, I know that. I just..." She lets out a heavy sigh, and I feel it all the way down to my toes. "I want it. I want a normal, happy family life. I want to know how it feels."

"Lorelei," I breathe, feeling weirdly choked up by her confession.

"No," she snaps. "Don't do that. Don't pity me because—"

"I'm not," I argue. "I would never pity you. I do understand, though."

She gives me a double take at that confession. "How?" she breathes.

I get it. I'm sure that on the face of it, from the outside, the Callahan family looks like one of those all-American families that Lorelei is dreaming of.

"I know our lives have been very different. But just because things may look good on the surface, it doesn't mean that everything is rosy beneath it."

"I guess not."

"I get that you don't want to talk about your past, your childhood, but please don't let that be because you don't think I'll understand. I promise you, I will."

My grip on the wheel tightens as my other hand sneaks across the center console and rests on her thigh.

She tenses the second I connect with her, but to my surprise, she doesn't push me off.

"What about you?"

"What about me, Temptress?"

"You want the happily ever after?"

My lips part, but before I can shoot out my standard response of "hell no," I second-guess myself.

"Honestly?"

"No, Kian. I want you to lie to me," she mutters. I don't look over, but I know she rolled her eyes at me.

"I don't know what I want. I've always worked too much to ever really consider anything else. And I've certainly never met a woman who's made me think that it might be worth trying for."

I pull the car to a stop outside her apartment and gaze up at the building.

Please don't go in there.

"It must be hard when you're such a workaholic."

"King's figured it out," I counter before turning to look at her. "I guess that's what happens when you fall in love."

My eyes bounce between hers, my heart steadily thumping against my ribs.

"Yeah," she agrees sadly. "Must feel pretty awesome, huh?"

When I don't respond straight away, she reaches for the door handle.

"Wait," I demand.

She instantly pauses, but she doesn't look back at me.

"I need to go home, Kian. Thank you for...for everything. I really appreciate it."

"But—"

"It's time to go back to reality. I'll see you at work in the morning, Boss."

Before I get a chance to respond, she's out of the car and rushing around to the trunk to grab her bag.

I reach for the button to open it for her, hating myself for not getting out and being a gentleman.

But if I do, I'm not sure what I'll say, what I'll do. And call me a pussy or whatever, but I'm not ready for that, and I know for a fact that she's not.

I hit the button and the trunk releases, but I'm unable to stay inside.

"Fuck," I breathe before pushing the door open. I climb to my feet and wait for her to walk toward the entrance of her building.

"Please," she begs. "Don't follow me."

I swallow thickly. "You know I can't do that."

"Kian," she breathes as I step up behind her.

"I can't leave until I know everything is okay. Humor me."

She twists around to look back at me, but something down the street catches her eye and she sucks in a sharp breath.

I follow her stare but find nothing.

"What is it?"

"Cat," she explains before taking a step forward, leaving me to trail behind her, telling myself that I'm going to do the right thing.

59

LORELEI

My hand trembles as I push my new key into my new lock and let myself into my apartment for the first time since I found it vandalized on Friday night. The second the door is open, the scent of fresh paint hits my nose.

It takes everything I have to keep my unease and fear hidden.

Kian is watching me closely. He's made it more than clear that he doesn't want me staying here, but what's the other option? Move in with him until we get answers? And so far, there doesn't seem to be anything in the way of those.

When I asked about progress, Kian told me his guys are taking care of it, and I had no choice but to believe him. It's either that or demand to know why I haven't been interviewed by the police and have it confirmed that they're not necessarily going about this the way I would.

"Everything's fine. See?" I say, hoping my voice sounds stronger than I feel as I gesture to my peaceful apartment.

There's a small part of me that's happy to be home, but that's being easily engulfed by the bigger part that wants to run into Kian's arms and demand he takes me with him.

You are a strong, independent woman, Lorelei. You do not need a man to protect you.

471

But right now, I really want one.

Unwilling to take my word for it, Kian surges forward and sets about searching every inch of my apartment.

"Okay?" I ask when he finally returns.

"Do I have a choice?" he mutters.

Standing a little taller, I hold his eyes firm and say, "No, you don't. Now, if you'll excuse me, I've things I need to do tonight."

I smile at him. It's forced at best, but if he can see it, he doesn't say anything.

I spin around, directing him toward the door, and he hesitantly complies.

"Lorelei," he breathes. The rasp in his voice sends a shiver skating down my spine.

Fuck. Please, don't do that.

I stare up at him, hoping that he can read the plea in my eyes.

Remember what he said in the car about never meeting a woman to make him consider a future with one.

Remember who he is.

Forget about how good it is to be in his arms, to feel his kiss...

"Kian," I say firmly. "The last few days have been fun. Really fun," I add when his lips part to speak. "But what I said in the car was true. I want more than to be someone's fake relationship or fuck buddy. I want something real, and this..." I say, pointing between us. "Nothing about this is real."

He swallows thickly, and I frown in confusion.

Surely he isn't seeing this as more than it is, is he?

He's my boss. He's Kian freaking Callahan. There is nowhere for this...this fling between us to go.

My heart aches as the harsh reality of the situation becomes known again.

"Thank you for everything. I'll see you in the morning."

Before I can talk myself out of it, I close the door.

"Shit," I hiss, collapsing against it.

My eyes burn, and a messy lump of emotion crawls up my throat.

Before I know what's happening, a single tear slips free, and I hang my head in shame.

You did the right thing.

Kian isn't your King.

He's your boss.

And a super-hot lay, but that's by the by.

I rest there way longer than I should, trying to decide if he just walked away like everything between us meant nothing, or if he's even a little bit affected by it all.

When I eventually stand up straight, the peephole taunts me.

Just look. See if he's still there...

But despite the little nagging voice in my head, I turn my back on the peephole. I already feel empty enough right now; I don't need evidence of the obvious to make it worse.

Kian doesn't care. Okay sure, he cares. He wants me to be safe in my own home. He cares that I enjoy myself when we're together. But he doesn't care care. Not in the way I crave a man to care for me.

Ignoring the living room, I walk into my bedroom and immediately stop in the doorway.

"Wow," I breathe.

Not only has any evidence of the damage been eradicated, but the entire room has had a facelift.

The wall behind my bed is now a deep, gorgeous emerald green that...

"Fuck," I bark.

It's the same color as his eyes.

Unable to look at it without falling apart again, I focus on my suitcase that he abandoned in the middle of the bed and set about unpacking.

Anything to keep my mind off my reality.

I didn't stop all night. After finding homes for all my new hair products, I pulled on a pair of sweats and a tank and set about cleaning every inch of the apartment. Anything to stop my mind from wandering. And not just to Kian and our hot few days, but also to what happened here not so long ago.

If I so much as think about someone invading my privacy and doing what they did, I get a little closer to running out of the door and never looking back.

Once everything was sparkling, I found my cell and called both of my brothers. Wilder kept his conversation short. He was heading out to hang with friends, but Hendrix was happy to keep me entertained for a while. We switched to a video call, and he allowed me to help him with an assignment, which is something he only ever does when he knows I need a connection to home.

He never asked what was wrong, and I never offered up any information. But I was more than grateful for the distraction.

By the time the sun set, I was emotionally and physically exhausted. But neither was enough to put me into a deep, restful sleep.

Instead, when my alarm went off this morning, I barely felt like I'd gotten an hour.

"Good morning," Melissa greets me with her usual cheer as I walk into the office ten minutes before I'm meant to start with two coffees in hand.

Things will probably be weird as hell between the two of us today, so I figured I should at least come armed.

"Morning," I say, attempting and failing to sound as enthusiastic.

She eyes me suspiciously. "Weekend that good, huh?"

"You've no idea," I mutter before taking a sip of my cappuccino with a double shot of hope.

"He's not in," Melissa says, changing the subject suddenly.

"Huh?"

Her eyes drop to the second coffee in my hand. "Kian. He's not here."

"Oh. Is he due in or..."

"I've no idea. He didn't say anything to you?"

I shake my head, not liking the feeling that bubbles up inside me.

He usually keeps me fully informed about his whereabouts.

"Could be a nice quiet morning then." I want to say that I'm relieved, but mostly I'm confused. Kian doesn't just not turn up to work.

The second I place his coffee on my desk, I pull my cell from my purse, expecting to find a message or an email from him.

But there's nothing. It's been the same since I closed the door on him last night.

I almost message him asking where he is. My thumb hovers over my screen, but just before I begin typing, I remember that he's an adult and has absolutely no reason to check in with me. I'm just his assistant.

Once my computer loads, I open his diary and find the entire week has been cleared out, all meetings gone.

What is he playing at?

Forcing my feelings down, I open my laptop and get to work.

Him not being here is a blessing in disguise. Thanks to our trip last week, I've got a mountain of emails to get through and jobs to complete.

I should be grateful.

I also shouldn't be looking up every time I hear a noise that could be Kian arriving at the office.

It didn't matter how many times I looked up—it was never him.

King and Michael both came and went. Neither of them asked about Kian's whereabouts. A couple of others I didn't know arrived for meetings before leaving again without so much as glancing my way.

I didn't leave for lunch. Instead, I asked Melissa to grab me something when she popped out in favor of continuing with work. Or at least, I told myself it was so I could make the most of catching up. Deep down, I was lingering in case Kian showed his face.

It had been radio silence all day. Not a single message, email or phone call. No demands—not one. It was weird. Too weird.

I stay late, again because I want to work...and by the time I leave the Callahan Enterprises building, the sun is already setting behind the tall buildings.

I stop on the way home to grab myself some dinner, and after showering and pulling on some comfortable clothes, I once again open my laptop and continue working. I don't have anything else to do.

It never used to be like this. No matter what, I was always able to come home to my best friend. No matter how bad my day had been, she was always there to distract me and make me smile.

I thought I appreciated it while she was here, but now she's gone, I realize that I didn't.

I miss her. I miss her so fucking much.

Emotion bubbles up again, and I fight to batter it back down.

Reaching for my cell, I wake it up to find nothing.

Even Matt is avoiding me now.

Ryder has gone, probably found a girl who was actually willing to meet and give him some action that wasn't through a screen.

And Tate...she's just busy moving on with her life. She's

married with a baby on the way. I'm no longer the most important person in her life. I get it. I really fucking do, and I'm ecstatic for her. But it still hurts.

In a moment of weakness, I open my messaging app and find my conversation with Kian.

The "message has been deleted" comment from where I removed the picture of my tits taunts me, reminding me that all of this is my fault.

If I never sent him that message, then maybe we wouldn't have ended up here. Did I lead him on with that photo? Did I let him believe I was just like all the other women around him?

No.

I refuse to believe that.

I'm not them. I don't want to walk around with my arm threaded through his in the hope of the photo of us together ending up on social media.

I'd rather remain hidden. It's why his suggestion of us fake dating was so ridiculous. I understood the concept, but I'm not the woman for that. And not only because I think it would be entirely too easy to begin to fall for him.

I've always fallen easily. That's no secret to me. It's why I always end up hurt so badly. I have this uncanny ability to ignore all those wild red flags and I fall head over heels. Swept away by a guy's charm, lies, and wicked touch.

Just look at Matt. He was one giant walking red flag, and yet I fell hard and fast. Almost as if I hadn't been hurt before.

I always end up with a broken heart. It's something I can guarantee from the get-go.

Closing my messaging app, I lower my cell to the couch and let out a pained sigh.

Nothing good can come of sending him anything. He's made it very clear today that he doesn't need or want to talk to me. I'm not going to be that woman who's scratching around trying to get any crumbs of attention he's willing to offer. I have more self-respect than that.

Focusing back on work, I do my best to force thoughts of him aside.

It's easier said than done.

And as the next few days pass, and his lack of presence in my life only gets more oppressive, it becomes harder and harder to forget everything he brought to my life in those few days we had together.

60

KIAN

I slouch back on the couch, my eyes focused on the London skyline on the other side of the windows. But I don't see it like I should. I certainly don't appreciate it.

All I can think about is what—whom—I left behind in Chicago.

I knew I couldn't stay the second I walked back into my apartment without her on Sunday night. Her scent still lingered in my home, and everywhere I looked, she was all I could see.

I wanted to say that inviting her into my life, into my home was a mistake. But it wasn't, and it isn't anything I'll ever be able to regret.

She opened my eyes to something new. A life I could have. The kind of life I'm watching my big brother build with Tate.

Maybe. Just maybe it could be out there for me as well.

Lorelei too.

A pained sigh passes my lips as I let my head fall back against the cushion and close my eyes.

I wasn't meant to be here. The meeting I had set up with the financial team of the hotel chain King wants to buy, was virtual. But no sooner had I returned home on Sunday night than the idea popped into my head.

Traveling without Lorelei sucked. Not getting to witness

her awe in the first-class lounge or at the service on the airplane...just not having her with me was worse than I could have expected.

Landing in London, seeing the city, the sights, the history. Fuck. She'd have loved it, and I instantly felt guilty for not allowing her to experience all of this with me.

But that wasn't the point of this trip. It was to get away, to put some distance between us in the hope of figuring out why it hurt so much the second she cast me out of her life and closed the door in my face.

It was selfish of me to leave, especially after what happened in her apartment last week. But I haven't left her unprotected. She may or may not have figured it out yet, but I have people watching her, keeping me informed of anything untoward happening around her.

So far so good.

Maybe we were wrong, and it was someone random who broke in and—

No. It was a targeted attack. It was too personal.

"Fuuuuck," I groan, pushing to my feet. I pace back and forth in front of the floor-to-ceiling windows in the hope of burning off some of the anxious energy pulsing through me.

It's been four days since I spoke to her. There are four thousand miles between us right now, but still, I can barely think of anything else.

As much as I hate to admit it, the meetings I've had here have been great. For the first time since King brought this acquisition to the table, I can understand why he latched onto it.

Sure, I'll stand by my opinion that, financially, it's a fucking mess. But having met the senior management team, I now have a better understanding of what's gone wrong. And since visiting some of their more successful properties across the country, I get why King fell in love with it.

I don't stand a chance of arguing against this now. I'm pretty sure that was why King didn't argue when I told him where I was. Instead, his voice turned smug with understanding. He's been trying to get me out here to see for myself for months; he knew the second I discovered more that I'd no longer be able to fight him.

Maybe he's right. Maybe life isn't always about having the figures add up. Maybe sometimes you do have to just follow your heart, even if none of it makes any sense.

It's almost dawn. The first light of a new day is beginning to warm the dark sky. I should be sleeping. But just like every night I've spent here, sleep eludes me and my cell calls to me.

I lasted until Tuesday afternoon before I caved and sent her an email.

It was all business, no niceties. No discussion of how much I enjoyed spending time with her last week, no mention of how much I liked having her in my home. But even still, I felt better just for seeing her name on my screen.

Fucking pussy.

We've exchanged a few emails since, but all of them have been work-focused.

I've lost count of the number of times I've picked up my cell and almost typed out a message to her. I've had to talk myself out of hitting dial on her number more than I'm willing to confess.

But tonight...it's harder than ever.

I'll be back in Chicago tomorrow. I'll have to face her again. But how can I when there has been so much left unsaid between us?

Before I can talk myself out of it, I hit her contact.

My hand trembles as I lift my cell to my ear, and my heart rate kicks up the second the dial tone rings through the air.

She'll decline it, a little voice says. But despite hearing it loud and clear, I don't hang up.

I've started this now; I can't be seen to run away.

It rings and rings. It's late evening in Chicago. She's probably sleeping, but even still, I can't hang up.

Convinced it is going to either ring out or go to voicemail, my adrenaline begins to wane, and I prepare to return to the silence of my suite. But then...my heart jumps into my throat as the line crackles and then the most amazing sound comes down the line.

"K-Kian?" she stutters, her voice raspy with sleep. "Is everything okay?"

I collapse on the couch once more and drop my head into my hand.

Is everything okay? Now, that's a loaded question if I've ever heard one.

Silence passes between us as I battle to come up with a reasonable answer.

"Kian?" she eventually asks again. "Are you there?"

"Yeah, I'm here. I—" I swallow thickly. "I'm sorry, I shouldn't have called."

I've no idea what she hears in my voice, but the rustling of fabric down the line lets me know that she's sitting up, prepared to give me her full attention.

I glance at the clock and cringe.

I really shouldn't have called her at this time.

"It's okay. What's going on?"

"Nothing. I'm in London and—"

"I know, Kian. What is it you need me to do?"

I shake my head as fear wraps around me.

She doesn't get it. Which means...fuck.

Which means she doesn't feel the same.

"I don't need you to do anything. I just...I can't stop thinking about you, Temptress."

Silence.

"I know you don't want to hear it. But it's true. Fuck, Lorelei," I say, dragging my hand down my face. "You've done things to me. Things no one else ever has."

I've no idea what I'm saying, what it is I want from the confession. All I know is that I need to get the words out in the hope it helps.

I can't settle. I'm restless and anxious, and I fucking hate it. My focus right now isn't on work, and that isn't how I roll. I don't get distracted by anything or anyone. Ever.

Until now.

"I came here to figure things out. Leaving you at your apartment on Sunday night fucking killed me." Her gasp on the other end of the phone is the only sign that she's still there and listening, and it spurs me on. "No other woman has ever spent the night, let alone the weekend, at my apartment, but having you there made the place feel more like a home than it ever has before.

"When I returned and you weren't there...I hated it. Do you have any idea how hard it was for me not to come back for you?"

She still doesn't say anything.

"I've been here four days, Lorelei, and I still don't have a fucking clue what I'm doing. You've messed me up, babe. But I think it's in a really good way."

Say something. Please say something.

"Kian," she breathes, her voice rough and broken, and I fear it's not just from sleep. "You need to figure your shit out because we can't be more than we've already been."

"Why?" I blurt without even thinking.

Am I even asking for more? I've no idea. I just know that I can't keep running halfway around the world to try and escape...this.

"Because you're you, and I'm me. It won't work, and you know it. We're from different worlds."

"I don't give a fuck about where you're from," I state, a little firmer than I intended.

"It's not that simple, Kian. How can't you see that? I'm your assistant. You literally pay me to spend time with you. I'm—"

"I swear to God, Lorelei, if you call yourself a whore because we—"

"I wasn't," she interrupts. "But thanks for bringing that up. We made a mistake last week, Kian. It was fun, but it was a

483

momentary lapse in judgment on both our parts. It's done. And if you can't accept that, then I guess I need to start looking for a new jo—"

"No," I bark, panic flooding through me. "No, you're not going anywhere."

"Then you need to figure this out," she says firmly. The emotion that had drained from her voice earlier is long gone, replaced by strength and determination. "I need to go. It's the middle of the night. Some of us have work in the morning."

Before I get to argue the fact that I've been working all week, the line goes dead, severing my connection to her once again.

"FUCK," I roar, throwing my cell onto the couch cushion beside me and watching it bounce and then crash to the floor. "Fuuuuuuuuck."

E very minute since she hung up on me drags on forever.

My flight back to the States seems to take a fucking age, and by the time I step back onto American soil, I'm exhausted, angry, and even more fucking confused than I was before.

I spent the entire nine-hour flight trying to read between the lines of what she said on the phone, but no matter how I spin it, I still come up with the same conclusion.

She doesn't feel the way I do.

Last week meant nothing to her.

I mean nothing to her.

A bitter laugh spills out of me as I carry my small suitcase toward where the taxis are waiting, where I hope Jamie is waiting for me.

It's late. My flight was delayed thanks to the shitty weather in London. The working week here is over. Everyone is heading home and putting the past five days behind them; whereas I feel like I'm stuck in last week.

The second I step out of the building into a cold and miserable Chicago evening, I find Jamie standing beside my car with a wide smile on his face.

At least someone missed me.

"Did you have a good trip, sir?" he asks, taking my case from my hand. "It's wonderful to have you back."

"It was great, thank you," I lie as he opens the back door for me.

He quickly places my luggage into the trunk before dropping into the driver's seat.

"Would you like to go home?"

My kneejerk reaction is to say yes, but I think better of it before the word spills free.

I'm not ready to face my apartment yet.

"No, could we please go to the office?"

"Of course," Jamie says, his eyes meeting mine in the mirror. I might not be able to see the lower half of his face, but I know he's smiling.

He's always happy.

How does he do that?

I'm still wondering what his life might be like outside of driving me around at all hours of the day when he pulls away and heads toward Callahan Enterprises.

By the time we get through the city traffic, it's late enough to ensure that the building should be almost empty.

"Do you know how long you're going to be?" Jamie asks as he lets me out.

I shake my head. "Go home, Jamie."

"Are you sure? I don't mind wait—"

"Enjoy your evening," I insist before marching into the building and then the elevator that will take me to the top floor.

As the elevator doors open, familiarity wraps around me

like a warm blanket, and the scent of my second home wafts through my nose.

Confident about my decision to come here instead of going home, I walk around the corner, expecting it to be deserted. But it quickly becomes clear that I'm very, very wrong.

"What are you still doing here?"

61

LORELEI

This week has been hell.

It shouldn't have been. It should have been blissful.

A whole week without my demanding, overbearing asshole of a boss.

But it was anything but.

Instead of loving the peace, I found myself craving his presence more and more every day.

We only exchanged a few emails, each one caused butterflies to erupt the second his name appeared on my screen.

It also felt safe. He was on the other side of the pond. I could let that excitement flutter, all the while hoping that it would lessen and that by the end of the week, I'd have forgotten what it was like to be with him twenty-four-seven. All memories of his touch, his kisses, his everything really would have faded into nothing, allowing me to focus on doing my job and moving on with my life.

I want to say that it was going well, but I'd be lying.

I put every second of my waking hours into work this week so I didn't have to think about the issue with my apartment and the man who was ultimately responsible. But working meant dealing with things for Kian, which meant I never managed more than a few minutes without thinking about him, no matter how hard I tried.

Even when Tate dragged me out for dinner on Tuesday night, he was the main topic of our conversation. She wanted all the ins and outs—literally—that I refused to give her in the bathroom at the Chiefs stadium on Sunday afternoon.

Talking about it hurt more than I expected it to. It brought everything I was trying to squash back up to the surface, and I missed him all over again.

I almost thought I had a handle on it by the time I left on Thursday night. Thoughts about finding new employment disappeared as my confidence in myself to move forward from last week began to grow.

I just fucked my boss...over and over...it'll be fine. Right?

So what, if it was the hottest sex of my life? It was just a... what? Four-night stand?

It's cool. He'll come back next week and it'll be business as usual.

But then my phone rang in the middle of the night, and everything came crashing down around my feet with just a few little heartfelt words.

I may have been the one to end the call, but it was only out of pure desperation and self-preservation.

I couldn't listen to it anymore. Everything he was saying was exactly what I wanted to hear. It was the thing of fairy tales.

But just like fairy tales, it wasn't real.

Kian was blinded by hot sex and a carefree business trip where reality ceased to exist.

Of course he was thinking of me; it was hot. But I'm pretty sure sex with the next woman he finds will be, too.

I'm just the most recent.

My stomach knots painfully and my chest aches as I think about him being with someone else.

The second I hung up the phone, I burst into tears. Tears

of sadness, of loss—even if it was of something I never really had. Tears of confusion and loneliness.

I should be living my best life right now. I've got a job I love that pays enough to look after my brothers. I have incredible friends and a lovely home. Everything I've ever wanted.

Well, almost everything.

I didn't manage to get to work on time this morning. When I finally rolled out of bed, my eyes were sore, red, and swollen, and my heart wasn't in much of a better state.

I lied and messaged Melissa to say that I'd forgotten that I had a doctor's appointment this morning and gave myself a few hours to put myself back together.

After doing both a hair conditioning treatment and a face mask, I had the world's longest shower, where I shaved and scrubbed my body until I was sure I'd washed the heartache from it. I spent longer than ever before on my hair and makeup and pulling on a dress I wouldn't usually choose to wear to the office, I took myself out for brunch.

It didn't come anywhere close to fixing anything, but at least I felt good on the outside, even if the inside was a broken, battered, and confused mess.

I arrived just as Melissa was leaving for lunch, and I settled in to work.

One more day in the office without my boss.

Or at least, that's what I was expecting.

I intended to leave by seven to be home in time to watch Wilder's game.

I only had an hour to go, and I'd be free for the weekend— as free as I could get when it was my own thoughts that were tormenting me.

But at just past six o'clock, the elevator door opens, and a heavy yet confident set of footsteps moves toward my desk. Not a second later, Kian appears around the corner, looking as gorgeous as ever in a black fitted suit with an emerald green tie that makes his eyes twinkle.

My heart jumps into my throat, and my lungs cease to work.

Our eyes connect, and I swear he may as well just take a baseball bat to my chest.

But while I freeze in shock, he gets angry.

His expression hardens, and his eyes narrow.

My stomach knots, and damn it if my thighs don't clench beneath my desk.

Damn it, Lorelei. This is why you have such bad luck with men.

Your taste is toxic.

His lips part and I brace myself for what's going to spill from them.

I already know it isn't going to be good.

"What are you still doing here?"

My own frustration builds and I push to my feet, sending my chair shooting out behind me with enough force that it crashes back against the wall.

"I'm working; what the hell does it look like? We don't all get to disappear to London at the drop of a hat because we feel like it."

For a second, disbelief overrides the anger in his expression.

"Because we feel like it? You thought I went because—" He cuts himself off with a huff of disbelief.

He stands in front of my desk with his chest heaving before both his hands lift, his fingers combing through his hair and pulling until it has to hurt.

Briefly, he glances up at the ceiling as if he's praying for strength.

If it's possible, the air around us grows thicker and thicker until I can barely suck in a breath.

But then he looks back at me and everything takes another turn.

His eyes are blazing with a potent mixture of anger and

desire. It's impossible not to react to the sight as he looms even closer.

"You've no idea, have you?" he rasps, his voice low and terrifying.

I don't respond. I can't. I'm locked in his dark stare and completely at his mercy.

"It's you, Lorelei. *You* have done this."

"I-I haven't...I haven't done anything."

My chin drops when he throws his head back and barks out a manic laugh. It's like nothing I've ever heard from him before.

It's as terrifying as it is thrilling.

I cause this reaction in him. Me.

I have never felt more powerful in my life. But I'm not entirely sure I like it.

He's hurting, that much is obvious. I heard the pain in the middle of the phone call. That was hard enough to deal with. But this...hearing it *and* seeing it...

It's too much.

Way too much.

"No," he agrees, forcing me to remember what I said only a few seconds ago. "You haven't done anything. You're just here," he says, tapping his temple with more force than necessary. "Always in fucking here. Driving me fucking insane."

"I-I can't help that," I cry, at a total loss for what to do here.

"I don't want you to help, Lorelei. I want you to..." His words fade to nothing and I frown, needing the end of that sentence almost as much as I need my next breath.

"You want me to what?" I beg, needing to know what I can do to make this better.

But he never responds. Instead, he spins on his heel and marches down the hallway to his office.

Now would be a really good time to run, a little voice screams in my head.

But I don't run. Not from men. Not even Kian Callahan.

So instead, I stomp after him.

"You can't just march off halfway through...through... that," I shout, throwing my hand back toward where we were as I storm into his office.

I don't see him right away, but I sure hear him as he growls, "Yes, I can. I can do whatever the hell I want."

I jump forward when the door suddenly slams, and when I spin around, I find Kian right behind me.

He's lost his jacket, and his tie is hanging loosely around his neck, his collar undone.

My heart rate races to dangerous levels, and it only gets worse when he steps closer.

His eyes bounce between mine and then down to my lips.

Oh my god. Why did you follow him?

You're fucked. Totally fucked.

"I need you to admit that you feel this too. I need to know that I'm not the only one losing my goddamn mind."

I shake my head, still refusing to accept that there is anything here. It's too terrifying to consider that what we had last week was anything more than a naughty hookup.

"Kian—"

"No," he bellows, his voice echoing off the walls around us as he surges forward. "You don't get to lie to my fucking face. Not again."

His warm, minty breath rushes over my face as the heat from his body calls to mine.

"Give me something. Anything to assure me that I'm not alone here," he begs, his eyes still alternating between mine and my lips.

Oh my god, just kiss me already.

He moves closer still, and I step back, attempting to keep a safe space between us. It works for about five seconds, then I bump into his desk, and not a moment later, his hands land on either side of my hips, trapping me.

492

"Temptress," he whispers, ducking low and dragging his nose up the line of my jaw.

My fingers curl around the desk, and I squeeze my eyes closed in a lame attempt to ignore the powerful charge of electricity that shoots through me at our limited connection.

I don't breathe. I don't move. I don't do anything.

His lips find my ear, and his breath sends a shiver racing down my spine.

"Give me something," he whispers. "Please."

It doesn't escape my attention that this man standing before me has probably never begged for anything in his life.

But right here, right now, he's begging me to tell him I feel something.

Me.

My body burns red hot. My skin tingles everywhere we're even close to touching. And my heart...that is completely out of control in a way I've never experienced before.

"Kian, I'm not the kind of woman you want—"

"Fuck that, Lorelei," he snaps, pulling back to stare me dead in the eyes. "Fuck the pretences and the expectations. This..." he says, pointing between the two of us. "It's more than any of that bullshit. It's real. It's real, and raw, and fucking painful. Tell me that you're with me. Please, for the love of God, tell me that you feel it too."

My heart slams against my ribs as he silently begs me to finally confess the truth.

My body acts without instruction from my brain and I find myself nodding. "Yeah," I whisper. "I feel it."

The confession has barely passed her lips before I'm on her. My mouth collides with hers as one of my hands wraps around the back of her neck and the other slides down her thigh, hitching her leg up around my waist.

Fuck, I need this.

I need it like I've never needed it in my entire life.

And it's not just the release. It's her. I need her so fucking badly.

"Lorelei," I groan into her mouth as her hands slide up my arms before wrapping around my neck.

She moans in response, and it only makes me burn hotter for her.

Closing the final bit of space between us, I shove her dress up around her hips and spread her legs, allowing me to press against her.

"Oh God," she cries, throwing her head back and breaking our kiss.

"Fuck. Look at you," I groan before leaning over her and kissing and licking down her neck.

"Yes, yes," she cries, reaching for my loose tie and pulling it free. The second it's gone, she starts on my buttons.

My hands move of their own accord, squeezing her breasts and making her moan louder.

Seeing her as desperate for me as I am her...it's everything. Every-fucking-thing.

She abandons my buttons when she gets halfway down and is unable to reach any more and instead slides her hands up my chest and over my shoulder, pushing the fabric away.

My teeth grind at the first touch of her hands. My skin burns, and I feel it all the way down to my dick.

Despite craving it, I haven't seen any action—even my own hand—since we were last together on Sunday morning.

I figured that if I didn't have her, then it wasn't worth getting off. Something that's both a blessing and a curse right now. I love that I waited because I know it'll be totally worth it. But I'm still dressed, she's barely touched me, and I'm riding a knife's edge already.

"Missed you, Temptress," I confess as I set to work on the tie that's holding her wrap dress together.

It's like she knew...

It takes a couple of seconds to wrangle the clasp, but I eventually manage it and throw the fabric aside.

"Fuuuuck," I groan at the sight of her black lace lingerie.

"Please," she moans, arching her back from the desk, ensuring she continues to grind against me.

"You don't need to ask me twice," I mutter, dragging my half-open shirt over my head and discarding it on the floor, and then sink to my knees.

As desperate as I am to get inside her, I also need a reminder of just how good she tastes.

"Kian," she gasps when I tuck my fingers under the sides of her panties and drag them down her legs.

My mouth waters at the sight of her swollen and glistening for me.

Her whimpers fill my office as I blow a stream of air across her heated skin.

She reaches for me, her fingers making little grabby actions, but she can't reach me.

"Please, Kian," she begs.

I smirk. Oh, how the tables have changed.

Pressing my hands to her inner thighs, I lean forward and drag my nose through her folds, breathing in her scent and committing it to memory.

Her legs tremble and my smile grows.

I'm not the only one feeling like this. She might not want to admit it, but she gets it.

The knowledge finally allows me to relax, and I feel like I breathe properly for the first time in days.

With her fingers finding purchase in my hair, I allow her to drag me closer, and the second my lips lock onto her clit, I suck. Hard.

She screams, her entire body trembling with her need for release.

But she's not going to get it that easily. I haven't waited this long and tortured myself all week for this to be over too quickly.

I work her to the edge, over and over, with both my tongue and my fingers. She curses me out every time I pull back. My smile grows and my heart swells each time.

I don't understand it, and I'm starting to figure out that I'm okay with that, but I'm so fucking addicted to everything about this woman.

I don't know when or how it happened, but nothing makes sense if it doesn't involve her.

This week has been fucking pointless. Everything I've done, everything I've seen, all I wanted to do was experience it with her, or at least be able to share it with her. It was fucking weird.

Everything is fucking weird. But it's exciting too.

"Are you trying to kill me?" she squeals as I slow my pace again, letting her come down from her almost orgasm.

"Definitely not. I like you too much to do that."

"Then prove it. Please," she begs.

I make a noise to let her know that I'm considering her demand, letting her feel the vibrations.

Her grip on my hair tightens until I'm sure she's going to pull both handfuls out, but I don't give a fuck. I'll shave the lot off as long as I get to keep doing this.

"Oh God, yes," she cries when I work her clit and G-spot at the same time. "Yes. Yes. Kian. Kian."

Fuck, hearing her chant my name does strange fucking things to me.

She continues and this time, I can't stop. I need to hear my name spilling from her lips as I push her over the edge too badly.

"Kian. Kian. KIIIIIIIIAN."

Her body convulses on my desk, the wet patch under her ass only growing.

I'm never going to look at this desk the same way ever again.

In record time, I push to my feet and shove my pants and boxers over my ass, letting my dick spring free.

Lorelei lies back on my desk, her chest heaving and her skin flushed red as she comes down from her high.

She's never looked more beautiful.

"More," she begs the second I drag the head of my cock through her folds. Her pussy clenches the moment I'm at her entrance, trying to suck me inside.

"Jesus, Lorelei," I groan, pushing the tip inside. "I can't get enough of this. Of you."

Lifting her legs around me, she digs her heels into my ass, trying to push me deeper.

"You need my dick, babe?"

"Yes, yes," she eagerly agrees.

"Thought you'd never ask."

I push forward. It's not as fast as either of us might want, but after four days of not being together, I need to treat her a little gently. I have every intention of this being just round one; I can't break her yet.

My teeth grind and my grip on her hips tightens as her heat surrounds me.

"Fuck, you're so tight," I hiss, grinding my hips until I'm fully seated inside her.

"More, Kian. More," she begs.

"You're perfect," I confess as I begin to move. "So fucking perfect."

Sliding my hands up her sides, I slip one behind her and unhook her bra, letting her tits spill free.

"Oh my god," she cries when I squeeze them both.

"That good, Temptress?"

"So good. So good," she chants as the sound of slapping skin and heaving breaths fills the room.

My thrusts pick up speed and soon, I'm forced to hold her hips again to stop her shooting up the desk and away from me.

Not happening.

Mine. You're mine now, Lorelei.

"Fuck. You're going to come on my dick, aren't you?" I groan when I feel her beginning to squeeze down on me.

She nods erratically as her body builds higher and higher. It's incredible to see.

"I want to feel it, Lorelei. Come for me," I demand. "Come for me, all over my dick where the rest of the city can see who owns you."

Her head jerks to the side, and her eyes widen as she discovers where we are.

The office is dark enough that we can see everything outside the windows. It doesn't matter that it's one-way glass. She doesn't need to know that right now because her pussy just gushed and she's a heartbeat away from coming.

"Hot, right? Everyone can see that you're mine."

"Oh God. Oh God," she whimpers before her orgasm drags her under.

Her heels dig into my ass harder, to the point I'm sure she's drawing blood, her back arches from my desk, and she screams out as her body milks my own release out of me.

"Fuck," I gasp, refusing to close my eyes as pleasure consumes me.

My grip on her tightens to the point she's going to have bruises tomorrow, but I can't stop. I can't.

The second I'm done, I collapse over her, both of us breathing heavily as we come down from our highs.

"Kian," she whispers after long, blissful seconds, forcing me to look up.

"Yeah, babe?" I ask with a satisfied smirk playing on my lips.

The second our eyes collide, it's like her words just dry up. Whatever she wanted to say vanishes, and in its place, there's nothing but fear.

"What's wrong?"

She glances at the window.

"Don't worry, no one can actually see you. It's—"

"It's not that," she says, wiggling beneath me as if she wants to escape.

"Then what is it?" I ask, pushing myself from her and shuffling back, giving her the space I sense she needs.

She pushes herself up so she's sitting and stares at the floor for a beat.

"Lorelei?"

Sliding from my desk, she puts her bra back into place and then wraps her dress back around herself, covering up her beautiful body.

"That was a mistake. We shouldn't have—"

"You have got to be fucking kidding me?" I bark in disbelief.

How is it possible to go from a high like that to total rejection in a heartbeat?

"Kian," she breathes.

"No, don't do that. Don't go back to pretending like this is nothing."

I reach out and grab her arm as she makes a beeline for the door.

"This is something, Lorelei. You just said so yourself."

Desperation bubbles up inside me.

When she said she felt it, I thought we were starting something. I thought that was it.

"You're my boss, Kian. I need this job."

My brow wrinkles as I try to figure out what she's saying.

I shake my head. "I never said anything about you losing your job."

"No, but that is what this will come to. It might be next week, next month, or next year. I'm the disposable one here. Not you. I'm the one who's going to have my life turned upside down when you decide that being with me is too boring, when there are a million others out there vying for your attention."

"W-what?" I stutter.

Hasn't she heard a word I've said to her?

"There isn't anyone else. I'm not interested in anyone else. Don't you get that?"

"Right now, you're not, no. But what about in the future?"

My mouth opens to respond, but the words die on my tongue.

I don't know what I'm doing tomorrow yet—although I had hoped it would be Lorelei—let alone next month and next year.

"I want you, Lorelei. Not any of the other women out there," I say, throwing my hand out toward the window.

She pauses for a moment and just stares at me. My heart pounds against my ribs as I wait for her to make a decision, fear oozing through my blood like poison.

"I don't know if it's enough," she says simply before spinning around and marching through the door.

I will myself to give chase, to do or say anything that will prove my words to her. But my body doesn't move. I stay frozen to the spot as she walks away from me. Again.

63

LORELEI

I run out of the Callahan Enterprises building like the place is on fire.

My heart pounds and I can barely suck in the air fast enough as I try to outrun what just happened.

My body trembles so badly, I've no idea how I keep moving instead of crumbling to the ground. With my eyes focused on the end of the street, I continue moving faster than I should be able to while wearing my highest pair of heels.

But I don't have a choice.

If I stop, I'll have to think about what I just did.

And I can't. Not while I'm in public.

Hell, I don't really want to deal with it when I'm shut away safely in my apartment, but I'm going to have to.

I'm so lost in my head, I don't register anyone I pass as I keep moving.

The easiest thing to do would be to flag a cab or call an Uber. But that means stopping. And stopping means thinking and...a sob erupts and I run faster.

I can't.

I just can't.

I'm almost clear of the busy street, and I have my eyes set on the corner that will allow me to slip onto the quieter back streets that will lead me home. My chest hurts from both the exertion and what I've left behind in that office, and the balls of my feet burn.

Home.

Just get home.

I take the corner too wide, my legs moving faster than the rest of my body. A shriek rips from my lips as I stumble.

This is going to really hurt...

I plummet toward the sidewalk, my muscles tightening as I brace myself for impact.

But it never comes.

Instead, a large pair of hands grab my upper arms, stopping me from impending physical agony to go right along with the emotional pain I'm already in.

"L-Lorelei? Are you...are you okay?"

The male voice is familiar, but in my panicked haze, I can't place it.

I blink, clearing my vision as he puts me back on my feet and everything becomes clear.

"Ryder?"

"What's wrong?" he asks with a deep frown marring his brow as he rips his eyes from me to stare over my shoulder. "Is someone chasing you?"

I look back, my head spinning at a million miles a second.

"No. No one is chasing me."

His attention returns to me, his eyes darting over my face.

I've no idea what he can see, and to be honest, I'd rather not know.

"You look like you're running away."

Yeah...from my mistakes.

I shrug, wishing I could come up with some credible reason for the state of me. "Friday night."

His brows lift.

"Wilder's game is about to start, and I don't want to miss it."

Mentally, I give myself a high five for even remembering the game right now.

Ryder stretches out his arm and looks at his watch.

"You've got time," he says. "But to make sure you don't miss anything…" He immediately flags down a taxi, which comes to a stop right beside us.

I shake my head. It's a move that only men like Ryder and Kian could ever pull off.

My chest constricts the second I even think his name.

"Come on," Ryder says, holding the door open for me.

I hesitate, remembering why I didn't call a car for myself, but the longer he stands there staring at me, waiting for me to do something, the less fight I have to argue.

"Your place?" Ryder asks after sliding in beside me.

"Y-yes, but you don't have to come with me."

His eyes bounce between mine, and I cringe.

Can he tell I've just been fucked on my boss's desk?

"Let me just see you get home safely," he says as if this is a normal thing for us to do.

Sure, we've hung out plenty of times over the years, and not just to hook up. But this…this is different.

There is concern in his eyes and he's knitting his brows. It's not a look I like being aimed in my direction. Ever.

I nod, unable to speak, before turning to look out of the window as Ryder gives the driver my address.

We take off, and it only takes me a second to realize that we need to drive straight past the Callahan Enterprises building in order to make a U-turn at the next intersection.

My teeth grind as the building appears before me, and I force myself to look down at my lap.

I don't know how I'll react if he just so happens to be walking through the doors right now.

I bet he'd look perfect. No one would ever know that he'd just fucked his assistant over his desk.

A heavy sigh spills from my lips, forcing Ryder's attention to turn my way.

"I'm all ears if you want to talk," he offers.

I attempt to swallow down the emotion that's clogging my throat before muttering, "Nothing to talk about."

"Have you met someone?" he asks.

"No," I say too quickly, giving away the truth.

Although, is it the truth? Have I met someone, or am I just fucking up my life all over again with my ridiculous choice of men?

"I assumed that maybe you had when you stopped replying to my messages last week," he says. There's no accusation in his words, more curiosity.

This is why it's always been so easy with us and also why our relationship is never going to be anything more than a friends-with-benefits situation.

I remain quiet for a few seconds as guilt bubbles up inside me. I know he doesn't care, but I'm usually a better friend than to ignore messages.

"Work has been really busy and—"

"It's okay, I get it. Are you sure you're okay, though? You look...stressed."

A humorless laugh erupts from somewhere inside me.

"Oh yeah, I'm great. Everything is just fucking fantastic."

"Well, when you say it like that," he deadpans.

The taxi pulls to a stop outside my building, and I let another heavy sigh spill free.

"Did you want me to come up?" Ryder offers softly.

For the first time since we got into the car, I turn to look at him.

His eyes are kind yet curious.

"No, I'm okay."

"Lorelei," he breathes.

"I promise. It's just been...it's been a crazy couple of weeks."

"Okay," he agrees, albeit reluctantly. "If you need anything, just call me, yeah?"

I agree, although we both know that I won't be calling him anytime soon.

"Thank you," I say sincerely. If it weren't for him catching me, well...who knows what kind of mess I would be in right now.

"You're welcome. Message me, yeah? Let me know you're okay."

I nod before climbing out of the taxi.

The second I'm inside my building, I pull my heels off and hit the stairs. I'm too fragile right now to deal with the elevator.

Every inch of my body hurts by the time I pull my keys from my purse and let myself into my apartment, but there isn't a single part of me that hurts more than my heart.

"It's real. It's fucking real, and raw, and fucking painful. Tell me that you're with me. Please, for the love of God, tell me that you feel it too."

His words slam into me with the force of a freight train. All the air rushes from my lungs as I stumble into my apartment and slam the door behind me.

A loud, ugly sob erupts, and I crash into the wall before sliding down and landing hard on my ass.

Pulling my legs up to my chest, I wrap my arms around them and lower my head to my knees.

Tears spill down my cheeks faster than I can control as the pain of walking away from him after everything he said drips through my veins.

Everything he said was so perfect. Everything I'd convinced myself I didn't want to hear from him. Everything that would hurt like hell if I allowed myself to be swept away by it all, only to be forgotten about down the line.

I've no idea how long I sit there, purging everything through my tears, but when I eventually look up and catch sight of the large clock on the living room wall, I panic.

Wilder's game has already started.

I scramble to my feet and race toward the TV, turning it on and finding the channel through blurry, tear-filled eyes.

Walking backward, I fall onto the couch the second my

calves hit it and force myself to forget everything that happened tonight and focus on my brother.

They're ten minutes into the game, and they're down by three. Wilder is going to be pissed. They killed this team last year. When I spoke to him yesterday, he was confident that they had this one in the bag.

Looks like it's going to be harder than he expected.

I sit on the edge of my seat, watching as his team tries to pull it back. But every time they get ahead, the other team comes out fighting.

It's a good game. Or it would be if I weren't nervous as hell for Wilder.

There are only fifteen minutes left on the clock, and they're tied again as Wilder's offensive line gets into position, ready to secure the win.

My nerves are shot, but I'm grateful for the distraction.

My cell has been ringing incessantly out in the hallway, but I've refused to answer it.

Tate knows that I'll be watching the game. But I also suspect that she's had a call or at least a message from Ryder asking her to check in with me.

I should appreciate the support. I mean, I do appreciate the support, but right now, I don't want to talk. I just want to be left alone.

"Come on, Wild Child," I whisper, my eyes glued to the ball as it flies toward Wilder.

He's ready for it. I can see the determination in his eyes and the set of his shoulders.

"Yesss," I hiss when he makes the perfect catch and takes off toward the end zone. "Come on, come on," I will, perched on the edge of my seat, waiting to celebrate right along with him.

He's almost there, so fucking close he must be able to taste it, when one of the other team's defensemen appears out of nowhere.

"Oh my god," I gasp when he takes my little brother down on a dirty-looking tackle.

Wilder hits the grass hard and I jump to my feet, moving closer to the screen as if it's going to help.

The defenseman gets up and shakes himself off, but Wilder doesn't move.

"Get up," I whisper, getting even closer to the screen. "Wilder." My voice cracks with emotion.

But no matter how much I beg for him to get up, he continues lying there, lifeless.

My tears return, and I swear my heart shatters into a million pieces.

"Wilder, please. Please," I beg brokenly.

When my cell rings this time, I go running to the hallway and pull it from my purse.

I don't bother looking at the caller ID. I already know who it is.

"Everything is going to be okay," I lie.

Honestly, I have no fucking idea if anything is going to be okay again. But Hendrix doesn't need to hear that.

"He's still not moving," Hendrix whispers. He sounds like he's in complete agony.

"I'm coming, okay? I'm getting on the first plane out of here."

Putting my cell on speaker, I grab my suitcase from my closet and run into my bedroom.

"What's happening?" I demand as I absently throw things inside.

"Nothing. He's still lying there."

"Where is the medical team?" I bark, frustrated that I can't do anything.

It's not the first time Wilder has been injured. But it's the first time he hasn't immediately gotten up. It's also the first time I've felt that soul-deep fear when he went down.

"They're there. Shit."

"What?"

"I don't know. I can't see anything."

"Get your ass down there, Rix. He needs you with him."

"Excuse me. Sorry," a soft female voice says down the line.

Noelle.

At least she's with him.

"Excuse us. We need to get down there," she says again, taking charge while Hendrix freaks out.

"What if they don't let me?" he asks nervously.

"I don't give a fuck. Make them. Do whatever you have to do to be with him."

"Okay," he whispers.

"We'll get you to him," Noelle promises from a distance.

"I'm packing, okay? I'm coming for you both."

I run in and out of my bathroom, grabbing bottles. Fuck knows if they're the ones I need or not, but they're bottles nonetheless.

In less than ten minutes, I'm racing back down the stairs to meet the Uber I've called to the airport.

I don't have a flight. I have no idea when the next one is. But I'm not sitting around here waiting when Wilder and Hendrix need me.

Fuck the rest of the world. They are the two most important people in mine, and they need me.

64

LORELEI

"You've what?" Tatum barks down the line as I run through LAX with my suitcase bouncing around behind me.

I've been on a flight for just over four hours, and other than the messages I received when I put my cell on when we landed to let me know that Wilder is in the ER but stable, I have no idea what the hell is happening.

"I've just landed in LA."

"The hell, Lor?"

"Wilder had a bad tackle at the game. He just...he was just lying there, Tate. I thought he was dead," I cry as I dodge an older couple in my quest to get out of the fucking airport.

Noelle is waiting for me on the other side with my car. Hendrix is in the hospital with a concussed Wilder.

He's okay. He's okay. He's okay, I repeat over and over.

But it doesn't matter how many times I say it, I won't believe it until I see it with my own eyes.

"Shit. Is he okay?"

"Concussion, apparently. I'm going straight to the hospital now."

"Do you need anything?"

I shake my head, forgetting that she can't see me.

"Lori?"

"No, I'm okay. Everything is okay." I hope.

"Good. That's good."

"What?" I snap, knowing her well enough to know that she's holding back.

"It's just...Kian is freaking out."

Shit.

My stomach knots.

I'd be lying if I said I haven't thought about him.

I was stuck on an airplane for four hours. While Wilder's condition might have been something of a distraction, Kian was never far from my thoughts.

No matter how hard I try, he's always freaking there.

"Why?" I ask, trying to sound unconcerned.

"Lorelei," Tate warns as I finally emerge through the doors to the arrivals and find Noelle waiting for me.

It's the middle of the night, and she looks exhausted. But she looks just as concerned as I feel.

She is by far the best thing that's ever happened to my little brother.

I just wish the two of them could realize how perfect they are for each other.

"Hi," I mouth as I step up to her before releasing my suitcase and pulling her in for a hug.

She holds me tighter than I was expecting.

"Lorelei?" Tate repeats after a few seconds.

"Sorry, I just got to Noelle. I should go."

"You're smarter than to avoid him," she warns ominously down the line.

"Things are complicated, Tate," I attempt to explain as Noelle leads the way toward the exit.

"When aren't they? You just walked out on him."

"So he told you then," I mutter, unsure if I'm relieved that I don't have to do the talking or pissed off he's spilled our secrets to my best friend. It's not that I wouldn't tell her, of course I would. I just...I want to decide where and when that conversation happens.

"Well, not really. He went to your place and couldn't get an answer. He then turned up here to get me to contact you."

"Fuck. How long ago was this?"

"Hour or so. I sent him home to think about what he's done and to give you some space."

"Fuck," I breathe as I drop into the passenger seat of my own car to allow Noelle to drive us to the hospital.

"What's really going on here, Lori?"

"Not now," I say, feeling exhausted now that I'm here and the adrenaline is ebbing away. "Just...please don't tell him where I am," I beg.

"You want me to lie for you?" she asks.

"Yes. I can't deal with him as well as this. Just...please."

"Babe, you know I'll do it without question. I'm just making sure that that's what you really want."

"It is. I'll deal with him when I get back."

"And what should I say in the meantime? I've never seen him anything but calm and collected. But earlier...well. Whatever happened, you fucking rocked him, Lor."

I close my eyes for a beat, and immediately, his face as he stared down at me only a few hours ago and told me all the things I could only dream of, comes back to me.

My stomach knots and my chest aches all over again.

"Tell him you don't know. Tell him that you won't tell him. I don't care, Tate. Just...don't tell him the truth. If he comes here..." I trail off as panic sets in. "He *can't* come here."

"Okay, okay," she soothes. "He won't."

"Thank you."

"Just...call me tomorrow, yeah? I need to know more about what's going on here."

"Yeah," I agree, sinking lower in the seat as Noelle pulls out of the airport and hits the highway.

It's about a thirty-minute drive to the hospital they've taken Wilder to, and then another thirty to the town I'd happily never visit again.

"I'll call you tomorrow."

"Love you, Lor. I've got your back. Always."

"Me too."

I cut the call and lower my cell to my lap as the weight of the world presses down on my shoulders.

"Rix called while I was waiting for you. Wilder is awake and responsive."

A huge puff of air rushes past my lips as relief floods through my body.

"Fuck," I breathe.

Noelle reaches over and takes my hand. Tears immediately burn my eyes at her thoughtfulness.

"He's going to be okay, Lori."

"Thank you," I force out. "For being there for them."

She glances over and smiles.

She'll never know how grateful I am for her presence in their lives. I know she's the same age as them, but she's such a good influence on them.

Sure, she's Hendrix's friend really, but she cares for Wilder too, in her own way.

"Anytime," she whispers.

"So, how's school?" I ask, knowing that it's the easiest subject to talk to her about.

Just like us, Noelle's home life is...hard.

She chats away, telling me about classes and what it's like to finally be a senior.

Just like Wilder and Hendrix, Noelle really wants to leave this place and go to college.

She's hoping to get a scholarship, but she's also realistic.

Not many kids from towns like ours are lucky and get out.

I wish there was more I could do. I'd give the three of them the world if I had it.

But as it is, I struggle to look after the three of us. Sure, my new job helps massively, but with two boys in college, my extra funds aren't going to last long.

It'll be worth it, though. Anything that gives them the chance of a better life is worth it.

Before I know it, she's pulling into the hospital parking lot. I jump out the second she comes to a stop and take off toward the main entrance with her hot on my tail.

"Third floor," she says as I slow to a stop in front of the elevators.

The second a set of doors parts, I race inside. There's no time for hesitation when my brothers need me.

She directs me to the ward they've moved Wilder to, and after being welcomed by a nurse at the desk, I rush into his room.

"Lori," Hendrix cries, jumping to his feet and wrapping me in his arms.

Emotion crawls up my throat and my eyes sting once more.

He's grown again, and his embrace is stronger than ever.

I miss these boys every single day, but I don't realize just how much until we're together again.

His hug is only brief before he guides me to Wilder's bedside.

He looks rough. His skin is gray, his eyes dark, and he's got a nasty bruise on his jaw.

"Hey, Wild Child," I say, forcing a smile onto my face as I reach for his hand and squeeze.

I hate that he can see how worried I am. I wish I could hide it, but it's impossible.

"How are you feeling?"

"Like I got flattened by a three-hundred-pound linebacker," he deadpans.

"Bro, he was not three hundred pounds," Hendrix argues.

"How the fuck would you know? He wasn't on top of you."

"Too right he wasn't. That's not how I roll."

"Jesus," I mutter, glancing back at Noelle, who's standing just inside the room as if she's not sure if she's welcome or not. "Glad to see everything is normal here. What has the doctor said?" I ask.

"Nothing," Hendrix confesses. "They want to speak to you. Apparently, I'm not grown up enough to be Wild's guardian."

I look between the two of them with a question dancing on the tip of my tongue.

"We haven't even called her," Hendrix confesses, able to read my mind. "We told the doctor you were coming and that you'd deal with everything."

I nod. "I've got you," I say, squeezing Hendrix's shoulder.

"We know," he states proudly.

"You didn't need to drop everything and come, though," Wilder argues.

"It's okay, I think she was glad of the excuse," Noelle says helpfully.

"Oh yeah?" Hendrix asks.

"It's nothing," I argue.

"Didn't sound like nothing," Noelle teases. "Sounded interesting."

"Have you met someone?" Wilder asks with hope in his eyes.

I don't make a habit of sharing details of my love life with my little brothers.

Sure, they're old enough now, but I still don't see the point of telling them anything until I've found someone I'm willing to introduce them to.

"No," I sigh, shooting Noelle a glare. Not that she cares.

"I'm missing a killer party for this," Wilder complains after a few minutes of me holding my tongue.

I didn't want to talk to Tate about it, so I'm certainly not telling my seventeen-year-old brothers that my boss screwed my brains out on his desk not so long ago.

"I'm sure you can cope," Hendrix deadpans.

"The cheerleader I had lined up won't," Wilder mutters.

"Oh, how my heart bleeds."

If looks could kill, Hendrix would be six feet under right now.

Thankfully, a doctor interrupts their argument before it can really get started.

He gives me a rundown of Wilder's concussion and gets me to sign some paperwork before letting us know that as long as his vital signs are okay over the next hour or so, we'll be able to take him home.

Home...

Quite honestly, I think I'd rather spend the night here.

"You okay?" I ask as Hendrix and I help Wilder into the trailer.

I didn't think it was possible, but the place looks worse than the last time I was here.

How it's still standing is a miracle in itself.

"Yes," he groans. "I am still capable of walking, you know."

"The doctor said you could get dizzy spells. We're just—"

"Being overprotective."

"Don't blame us. There was a moment we thought you were dead, man," Hendrix snaps, his concern for his twin brother coming through so strong that Wilder doesn't say another word until we lower him to his bed.

"Thank you," he says quietly. "I really do appreciate it."

He looks at Hendrix first, then at me.

"We'd do anything for you, and you know it."

He smiles before looking between us at Noelle, who's once again loitering in this family moment.

"I'd do the same for you."

"But thankfully, we're not stupid enough to risk our lives every Friday night," Hendrix muses.

"It's not my fault that you're not as cool as me."

"Matter of opinion," Hendrix says before turning toward me. "Are we really not allowed to let him sleep?"

"Nope. Not for a few hours yet."

"I'm hungry," Wilder complains.

"He must be feeling better," I point out with a smirk. "What do you all want? I'll order takeout. What?" I ask when they all just stare at me.

"No one will deliver at this time," Noelle explains, reminding me that I'm no longer in Chicago.

"Shit. Do you have anything in?" I ask, but I already know the answer.

Fuck's sake.

I hate this. I really fucking hate this.

Only a few more months and they can all get out of this shithole and start over somewhere better.

"I can go to the store," Noelle offers.

Before Hendrix or I get a chance to respond, Wilder begins rattling off a shopping list.

He really must be feeling better.

After forcing Noelle to take my credit card to pay for it all, I get settled on Hendrix's bed so that we can keep Wilder awake.

I suck in a breath and look at the two of them.

"I love you both," I say honestly, "and I'm so fucking proud of you."

"Kian," Tate complains. "I'm not telling you where she is."

My teeth grind in irritation. I haven't seen or heard a peep from Lorelei since the moment she fled from my office like her ass was on fire on Friday night.

It's now Sunday, and I'm losing my fucking mind.

She told me that she felt it. She agreed that there was something between us, and then she just fucking ran.

I comb my fingers through my hair and drag it back until it hurts.

I have never, ever lost my mind like this over a woman. I'm usually glad when they leave...

After spending longer than I'm willing to confess knocking on her front door and calling for her loudly enough that her neighbor came out to see what the fuck was going on, I finally gave up and called Thomas.

It took some convincing, but eventually, he gave me the master key to her apartment.

I was terrified when I let myself in. I knew it was unlikely, but the thought of finding her dead was a constant concern that I couldn't banish.

Thankfully, that wasn't what I found inside her quiet

apartment. Unfortunately, I also didn't find the woman who had escaped my clutches.

The only thing I knew for sure was that she was trying to outrun what we'd found.

She's scared. I fucking get that.

I'm scared, too.

But I'm not so scared that I'm going to run away from this. Run away from her.

For the first time in my life, I want to embrace it. I want to jump in with both feet and see where it takes me.

Of all the women I've met over the years who were so desperate to start up something serious with me, the one I decide I want to see where things go with is the one who'd rather leave town—assuming she has—than face me when shit gets real.

"Tatum, this isn't fucking funny. She's been gone all weekend," I sneer, my fists curling.

"I know, Kian. I fucking know that she's been gone all weekend. But she specifically asked me not to tell you where she is. I'm not breaking her trust in me. Not now, not ever."

"So you have spoken to her?"

I assumed she had. I know how close they are. But up until her last comment, she was keeping her cards very close to her chest.

"Kian," she breathes. "She wants time and space. Give it to her."

"I did," I argue. "I gave it to her last week when I fucked off to London. Look what good that did," I shout, a little too loudly.

"No wonder she ran," Tate mutters down the line.

"Okay, fine. Maybe I came on a bit strong. But...fuck, Tate. She's stronger than this. She should be here facing me and telling me that she doesn't want me if that's the case."

My brows pinch when Tate's reaction to my comment is to laugh.

"The fuck, Tatum?"

"Of course she wants you, you idiot. That's exactly why she isn't here. If she wasn't interested, trust me, she would be telling you to your face. You should be pleased she ran."

"Pleased?" I balk. "How could I be pleased that I sent her running after we—"

"Screwed on your desk?" she finishes for me. "Hot, by the way. I love it when King bends me—"

"Tatum," I bark, not wanting or needing to hear this.

"She cares, Kian. You're scaring the ever-loving shit out of her, and she doesn't know how to deal."

"So tell me where she is and let me go and attempt to fix it."

"I can't," she repeats, sounding exasperated.

"Let me talk to King. Maybe I can get it out of—"

"No. Just wait. She'll be back."

"When?" I demand.

"When she is ready."

"She has work tomorrow. She can't bail on her job."

Silence greets my comments.

"I swear to God, Tate, if you're about to tell me that she's handed her notice in..." I trail off, not really knowing where I'm going with that threat.

"She hasn't. She's put in a request for emergency leave, though."

"Emergency? What's—"

"I need to stop talking before I say too much."

"That's exactly why you need to keep talking," I counter.

"Lorelei is fine, and she will be back when she's dealt with her— fuck. I'm going. Bye, Kian."

She cuts the line, and silence descends around me.

"Fuuuuck," I groan as I fall back on the couch and drop my cell into my lap.

I stare out of the window, watching as the sun descends for the day, the unease in my stomach only growing.

If I were to push Tate, I know that she'd eventually crack

and tell me everything I need to know. But I don't want to do that.

I want Lorelei to call me. Return one of the many messages I've sent her. Hell, even a work email would be something at this point.

Reaching for the television remote, I turn on the game and attempt to push my concerns about Lorelei aside.

It's pointless. No matter how hard I focus on the game, she never leaves my head.

I had tickets for this game. I also had flights and a hotel for two booked.

Wishful thinking? Maybe.

Probably.

But I couldn't help myself. Watching Kieran play with her by my side has become one of my new favorite things to do.

Hell, who am I kidding? Doing anything with her by my side is my favorite thing to do.

Unable to stop myself, I unlock my cell and open up Instagram.

I might have an account, but I hardly ever post on it.

Our marketing team insisted we all have profiles, but it's not really my thing. The few posts I do have are courtesy of a previous assistant who turned out to love social media more than getting paid to be an assistant. It was about all she was good for before her inevitable departure.

I hit the search bar, ready to type in Lorelei's name, but it soon becomes apparent that it's not necessary.

It's the only option from my previous searches.

I shake my head at my own patheticness and tap on it, opening up her profile.

Honestly, I wasn't expecting much, but I'm still disappointed when I discover that she hasn't posted since a night out with Tatum a few weeks before she started at Callahan Enterprises.

Despite having looked at them all a million times in the past week alone, I scroll through past photos of Lorelei in the hope it's enough to get my fix when I already know it won't be.

I pause when I find a photograph of her with her brothers.

She might have given me a little more detail about them, but I still have very little knowledge about her life before Chicago.

Opening the post, I tap on Wilder's tag and go to his account.

His first post stops me dead in my tracks.

He's in a hospital bed.

"Shit," I hiss, sitting up straight, my eyes dropping to the content of the photo that was posted yesterday. "She's in California. She's gone home."

I'm at my front door with my shoes on before I realize I've made a decision, and only ten minutes later, I'm in my car and heading toward her apartment again.

I need their address.

Sure, Tate will have it, but she's made it more than obvious that she won't be telling me shit about Lorelei's location.

If I want to find her, then I need to do it alone.

I t only takes me five minutes to hack into her iPad to find her contacts, and thankfully, she has Wilder and Hendrix listed with the same address.

And then it takes me another hour to pack a small bag and be at the airport for a flight that leaves in just over thirty minutes.

There is one seat left. An economy seat.

If I hadn't already told her how I felt, then this should confirm it.

I sit with my thighs practically pressed to the people on either side of me on the really fucking hard seats and a scowl on my face.

I have no interest in talking to anyone for the next four hours and twenty minutes, and I'm more than happy to let them know it.

I pay for the downright awful WIFI and attempt to deal with some emails, but my inbox barely loads let alone sends anything.

By the time I get off the flight, I'm more than ready to put this fucking day—this weekend—behind me.

The airport is a fucking nightmare, and it takes me forever to get to the car rental and collect the car I organized from O'Hare.

It's late by the time I hit the road, the GPS telling me that I've got almost an hour's drive to get to the address I found back at Lorelei's apartment.

I've been to LA before. The sights around LAX aren't new to me. But before long, I leave the bright lights of the city behind. The landscape changes quickly and not long later, so does the feel of the place.

The houses get more and more dilapidated as I pull into a town I've never heard of before, and there are more cars abandoned on the side of the road than actually going anywhere.

I'm hyper-aware of everything as I make my way down what I assume is the main street. The odd street light flickers, allowing the few people staggering around a chance to see their hands in front of their faces. But other than that, there's nothing.

The majority of the businesses that line both sides of the street seem to be boarded up. And if they're not, the windows are smashed, and they're covered in graffiti.

The place is depressing as hell. The thought of Lorelei and her brothers calling a place like this home fills me with dread.

They deserve so much more.

And things only get worse as I close in on the destination I tapped into the GPS.

"Oh shit," I gasp, the car bouncing after falling into the world's biggest pothole as I drive into the entrance of a trailer park. "Fucking hell."

My eyes are wide as I take in my surroundings. This place looks like hell. And the darkness is probably hiding the worst of it. I can only imagine what it'll be like come dawn.

I shudder at the thought.

Suddenly, all of Lorelei's first impressions of me make much more sense.

She wasn't lying when she said that we grew up in different worlds.

Only a few minutes later, the GPS happily tells me that I've reached my destination, and I pull to a stop outside a trailer. It's one of a handful with the lights on, and I can only hope that's a good thing.

As I kill the engine, I let out a heavy sigh and look around once more.

It occurs to me that they might have moved, but something tells me that they haven't.

Swallowing down my apprehension, I push the door open and step out straight into a deep, muddy pothole.

Wonderful.

With my head held high, I walk toward what I assume is the front door to the trailer and knock.

My heart jumps into my throat the second I hear movement and voices on the other side of the door.

I don't allow myself to consider the fact that some stranger with a gun—or worse—is about to come to the door.

Lorelei is in there. I know she is. And she will hate me for doing this.

66

LORELEI

The second there's a knock at the door, both Wilder and Hendrix look my way.

"What? It's probably another one of Wilder's fan club coming to check on him and bring him goodies."

I laugh, but actually, the candy and chocolate the girls have been bringing for him have gone down really well.

Plus, it's given Hendrix and me plenty of reasons to tease our favorite patient.

Obviously, I knew that Wilder was popular with the girls at school. I've heard more than enough tales from both of them. But hearing about it on the phone and seeing it in real life are two entirely different things.

Wilder's eyebrows wiggle. "Booty call, you say?"

My eyes narrow. "Absolutely not," I say firmly. "You might rule this place while I'm away, but I am not sharing this shithole trailer with some screaming Wilder Kemp fan."

"Thank fuck for that," Hendrix mutters, returning his attention back to the series he and Noelle are watching.

"I'll go then, shall I?" I ask when Wilder doesn't make a move to get it despite the fact it's more than likely for him.

Wilder gives me one of his megawatt smiles, the one that gets him all the attention from the girls, before I push from the lumpy couch that's older than all of us put together and walk toward the door.

My eyes drop to the baseball bat that lives propped up by the entrance to our trailer.

There was a time when I wouldn't answer the door here without having it in my hand. Honestly, it's probably good practice to do it still. But when I get to the door, I only reach for the handle.

The second I pull it open, a waft of man's aftershave hits, and I can't help but take a small step back.

I know that scent.

I—

Then I see him.

My eyes widen, and my chin drops at the sight of Kian Callahan standing before me in this shitty trailer park in the kind of town I'm sure he probably thinks only exists in TV shows.

My heart begins to race and my hands tremble as I stare blankly at him.

I have to be dreaming. Right?

He doesn't say a word, nor do I—something that Wilder notices a few seconds later.

"Who is it, Lor?"

I blink, the sound of my brother's voice bringing me back to earth.

"It's..." I swallow thickly as he continues standing there on the other side of the door wearing a Ralph Lauren polo and what I'm sure are stupidly expensive designer jeans.

He does not fit in here. Not in the slightest.

"N-no one."

Kian's brow quirks at that.

In a panic, I attempt to swing the door closed.

I've no idea what I'm doing. All I know is that he can't be here. He can't see this.

He does not belong here.

But he's faster than me, and before I get a chance to slam the door in his face, his hand lifts, stopping me from shutting him out.

"Lorelei," he growls quietly, his voice broken and rough. "Don't do this."

He takes a step closer, and his scent gets stronger.

Some of the tightness I haven't been able to shake since I ran from his office two days ago loosens, and my stomach knots with a mixture of anticipation and confusion.

"You can't be here," I blurt, keeping my defenses up despite knowing it's probably too late.

"And yet, here I am," he says, getting impossibly close.

I might be inside the house and at his eye level but I feel tiny under his intense stare.

My heart rate becomes even more erratic, and it only gets worse when I hear footsteps approaching from behind me.

"What's going on? Who's—" Wilder's words are abruptly cut off as he steps up behind me and finds Kian on our doorstep. "Pretty sure you've got the wrong town, mate. No one wears Ralph around here. Well, not unless you want to get mugged in daylight."

"I'm in the right town. I'm at the right house, too," Kian confirms before sticking his hand out for my brother.

"It's good to finally meet you, Wilder. I'm Kian, Lorelei's—"

"Boss," I blurt, stepping aside a little to see what Wilder will do with the proffered hand.

It's not the kind of way people around here greet each other, so color me intrigued.

"Can't say she's mentioned you," Wilder says, his own hands staying firmly at his sides.

"How are you feeling? I saw your tackle. You took quite the hit."

Suddenly, everything makes sense and I turn to glare at my brother.

"You posted about it?"

He shrugs. "Of course I did. My fan club, remember?"

"Jesus," I mutter while Kian snorts in amusement.

"So, are you coming in or what?" Wilder asks after looking between the two of us for a few seconds as if he'll figure everything out.

If only it were that easy.

"N-no, Kian is—"

"I'd love to," Kian says, giving me a wide grin and slipping into our shitty trailer.

Fuck my life.

I stand there in the doorway, watching as he follows Wilder to the couch.

The TV has been forgotten and both Hendrix and Noelle are watching the scene play out before them, curiosity burning bright in their eyes.

I glance around our home and cringe.

The boys—okay, Noelle—do a pretty good job of keeping it tidy, but there's only so much you can do to make this place presentable. Something tells me that Kian has never seen anything like this before in his life.

Wilder drops into the spot he vacated and gets himself comfortable while Kian perches himself on the edge of the couch as if he's scared of breaking it.

"Would you like a drink?" Noelle asks politely before she gets up and walks to the kitchen.

"Yes, please. Whatever you guys are having."

She rushes into the kitchen and pulls the refrigerator open, plunging us back into awkward silence.

"Why are you here, Kian?" I ask bluntly.

His eyes hold mine, his expression softening. "Because you are."

Wilder coughs, and when I glance over, I find that he's trying to hide his smirk. Hendrix doesn't bother trying to hide his curiosity; he looks between the two of us with a soft smile playing on his lips.

My mouth opens and closes, but no words appear.

What the hell do I say to that?

"You shouldn't be here," I eventually repeat.

"We should give you some space to talk," Noelle says after returning with a can of soda for Kian.

It's an unbranded can from our local store, but if Kian notices he doesn't react. A smile twitches on my lips as he thanks her, cracks the top, and immediately takes a drink. He doesn't so much as wince despite the fact that we all know just how awful it tastes. It's just...it's the best we can afford right now. Beggars can't be choosers and all that.

"No," Hendrix says, speaking for the first time. "I think we need to hear why Lorelei's boss has come all this way."

Kian startles. I can only imagine what he must be thinking right now.

"I'm sure they will explain. Come on," Noelle says softly, grabbing the arm of Hendrix's shirt, ready to physically pull him away.

"No, it's okay," I say quickly. "We'll go. You guys stay put."

"Go?" Kian asks, lowering his can and staring up at me with hope and fear filling his eyes.

"I think we need to talk, don't you?" I admit, my chest tight with my own anxiety over this situation. Plus, I really need to get him out of this trailer and away from here.

"Yeah," he agrees, slowly rising to his feet. "Lead the way."

My heart is in my throat as I spin around and march back toward the door.

I'm reaching for the handle when Hendrix speaks again.

"Hurt her, and we'll come for you."

Disbelief and a huge surge of love for my little brother rush through me.

My lips part to speak, but Kian beats me to it.

"I have no intention of hurting her. I'm here to hopefully do the opposite."

"You care about her," Wilder muses.

"More than she's willing to believe."

Oh my god.

Ohmygodohmygodohmygod.

"No offense, but we're not going to take that at face value. We're going to need solid evidence. We don't trust just anyone with our big sister."

The smile that spreads across my face is unstoppable, and it's still firmly in position as I step out of the trailer and descend the rickety old steps that lead me to ground level.

"I like them," Kian states behind me.

"They're both a pain in the ass," I say lightly.

"Anyone who protects you as fiercely as that is good with me."

I pause, the weight of his words pressing down on my shoulders.

He steps up behind me. The warmth of his body burns down my back and his breath rushes over the exposed skin of my neck.

My body sags in relief. The need to lean back into his is almost all-consuming.

But just before I do, I remember where I am and keep walking forward, my eyes widening when I take in the car sitting in our driveway.

"You brought a Mercedes here?"

I look back just in time to see him shrug.

"I just rented a car."

"Well, I hope you took out the extra coverage, because if you stay here much longer, I can guarantee that you won't be taking it back with four wheels attached."

"I guess that all depends on how long I'm welcome for."

"You don't want to stay here," I say dejectedly as he pulls the passenger door open for me.

"Says who?" he asks, lowering down and getting into my space. "I certainly don't want to be in Chicago without you."

My breath catches. The honesty shining in his eyes makes mine burn with emotion.

"Get in, Lorelei, and then tell me where to drive so we can talk."

My legs follow orders and a heartbeat later, my ass hits the soft leather seat and he closes the door on me.

I sit there in a daze as he joins me and then backs out of the space.

I keep my eyes on my lap. I know exactly what we're driving through; I spent the best part of my childhood trying to survive here. The thought of Kian seeing it too makes shame bubble up inside me.

I don't want to be the girl from the trailer park in the deadbeat town everyone's forgotten. Not when he's the high-flying CFO of Callahan Enterprises.

We don't fit, and I fear we never will.

"You're going to need to tell me where to go," Kian says lightly as he pulls to a stop at the exit to the trailer park. "Left or right?"

"Uh...left."

He takes the turn and we fall back into silence.

The only time I speak is to give him directions. But he's not quiet because he doesn't have anything to say—I can practically hear all the thoughts whizzing around his head. But for as much as I want to hear them, I know they're going to floor me.

I'm not ready, but I no longer think I have a choice.

I ran when it got too hard, and he chased me.

If I ever needed proof that he meant everything he said to me Friday night, then I guess it's currently staring me right in the face. Or at least, sitting beside me.

"Pull up over there," I say, pointing to the farthest corner of the parking lot I directed him to.

He brings the car to a stop and kills the engine.

"So—"

"We're not there yet," I say, pushing the door open and jumping out.

Without waiting for him, I walk around the front of the

car and then take the well-trodden track that leads to the beach.

It's been a long time since I came to hide down here. It seems like the perfect spot for the conversation we need to have.

67

KIAN

I follow Lorelei down onto the dark, silent beach.

The moon is sitting high in the sky, and there are stars twinkling down at us.

It's beautiful. Peaceful. Two things that I'm not sure are often used to describe this place I've found myself in.

Finding a spot she likes, Lorelei suddenly drops down, crossing her legs and staring out at the calm ocean before us.

Lowering myself to the patch of sand beside her, I follow her lead, waiting for her to speak first.

It takes long, torturous minutes, but eventually, her soft voice rings through the air.

Her words might be predictable, but they don't sting any less than the first time I heard them.

"You shouldn't have come here."

"Because you're afraid that I'll judge you for where you grew up? Or because you're terrified to face me and the reality of this thing between us?"

"Because you should be in Chicago getting ready for work in the morning."

"So should you," I counter.

"Kian," she sighs.

"No," I snap, a little harsher than intended. "Don't do that. Don't make out like you're not as important as me."

"I'm not. I'm just your—"

"Everything?" I ask, cutting her off.

A bitter laugh spills from her lips.

"You need to stop."

"No, *you* need to stop. I know you're scared, Lorelei. I know I terrified you with everything I said on Friday night. But...don't you think that I'm scared too?" I ask, reaching for her hand.

I expect her to pull away instantly, but she surprises me and allows me to lace our fingers together.

She hangs her head and lets out a huge breath.

"I didn't think anyone with the surname of Callahan was scared of anything."

"Then you don't know me as well as I thought you did."

She doesn't respond, and for a handful of seconds, I fall quiet too.

"I was livid when you ran away without a second glance on Friday night," I eventually explain. Her breath catches, but she doesn't say anything.

"I thought..." I shake my head. "I stupidly thought for a moment there that you were with me.

"I spent all week in England trying to figure my shit out, and just when I thought everything had fallen right into place, you pulled the rug right out from underneath me again. No one has ever had the power to affect me like that before, Lorelei. Never.

"But you..." I let out a breath I didn't realize I was holding as relief floods through my veins.

She might not believe the words, or be brave enough to do anything with them, but I feel better for saying them.

"I came for you, you know. I practically knocked your door down trying to get to you. I think your neighbors hate me, by the way."

I glance over just in time to catch the small smile that appears on her lips.

"I begged Tate to tell me where you were. That woman is stubborn as fuck," I say with a laugh.

"She's good people," Lorelei says, her voice so quiet it barely carries over the sound of the ocean filling the air around us.

"She is, if she's keeping your secret. When you're the one who wants information, she's annoying as hell."

"How did you find me if Tate didn't—"

"After stalking you on Instagram and finding Wilder's post, I convinced Thomas to give me the master key to your apartment. I searched until I found your iPad and then their address. And here I am."

"Here you are," she mutters.

My heart drops when she pulls her hand from mine and gets to her feet again. I sit there for a moment, watching as she moves closer to the ocean.

She stares out at the horizon silently, and it does nothing to soothe the unease I can't shake.

Climbing to my feet, I move closer to her—as close as I can without touching her.

"I want you, Lorelei," I confess. "You drive me crazy, and I know I do the same to you. We're different, I get that. Really fucking different. But I love that. I love that you're not the same as every other woman I've met. You challenge me, surprise me. You fight me. Fuck, do you fight me. But it wouldn't be the same if you didn't.

"Since you started at Callahan, I look forward to coming into work in the mornings in a way I never have before. And not only that, but I'm better for it. I know I'm overbearing and controlling, and generally just an asshole, but I need you to know that I trust you. I always have.

"I don't care where you come from, Lorelei. I don't care that you weren't privately educated or have fancy vacations every year. Do you know what I do care about, though?" I ask, reaching for her arm and spinning her around to face me.

"I care that you do everything you can to give your brothers the best chance at a future. I care that you dropped everything the moment Wilder was hurt so that you could be here to support him.

"I love how fiercely you love them, and how fiercely they love you in return. I love that you've taken hold of every opportunity that's come your way to try and better your life. I love that you call me out on my bullshit and make me look at things in a whole new light."

Reaching out, I cup her jaw, my eyes holding her watery ones so she has little choice but to really hear what I'm saying.

"I love your smile. I love the wicked things that come from these lips," I say, dragging my thumb across her bottom one.

"I love—" A tear splashes against my knuckles, and my words falter.

"Kian," she whispers brokenly as her entire body trembles.

Leaning forward, I press my brow against hers.

"I love...falling in love with you."

All the air rushes from her lungs, tickling over my face as more tears spill free.

"I know all the reasons why you don't think we work. But I think you're forgetting the most important thing..." Her eyes search mine, waiting for what I have to say. "Despite all of that, Temptress, we work. We make sense. And you know it just as much as I do. You just need to be brave enough to take a chance on me. On us."

My fingers wrap around her throat. Her pulse pounds against them, giving away how she's feeling right now.

Silence rings out between us. Only the sound of the crashing waves can be heard as the cool evening ocean breeze blows around us.

She doesn't say anything for the longest time, but she wants to. I can see it in her eyes. What I don't know is if I've said enough. If she's brave enough to take the next step with me.

Sucking her bottom lip into her mouth, she chews on it for

a moment before fucking sucking in a deep breath, ready to speak.

"I'm really mad at you," she finally says.

An unexpected laugh bubbles out of me. "I guess that's something we'll both have to get used to. I'm going to fuck up, Lorelei. I've no idea how to do this."

She closes her eyes for a beat before staring back up at me.

There are so many emotions swimming in her eyes I don't stand a chance of identifying them.

"I'm serious, Kian," she states.

"I know," I assure her, although I'm not entirely sure what I've done. "But I'm okay with that. Be mad. Shout at me. Scream. Hit me if you want. I came here for you, to tell you how I feel, to tell you that this is real, to tell you that I'm yours. If you want me. Fuck everything else."

"You blocked Ryder on my cell," she seethes.

"Ah, yeah. I did do that."

She shakes her head, her anger palpable.

"Why?" she whispers.

I smirk. "Because you're mine, Lorelei. Mine. Not his."

"I've never been Ryder's, Kian."

"Maybe not, but you were sending him photographs of something that belongs to me."

"I'm not yours either," she argues.

"Maybe not, but you're going to be." I search her eyes, needing her to see just how serious I am. "I blocked Matt, too. I don't see you arguing about that one."

"No. I should have done that myself a long time ago. But it probably has a lot to do with the state of my apartment last week. Has your team found him yet?"

My nostrils flare. "You know they haven't," I confess.

"And you think that's okay?"

"No," I bark a little too forcefully. "It is not okay. Nothing is okay while he's out there and could possibly hurt you."

My hand trembles where it's still holding her neck. The thought of him getting anywhere near her makes me feral.

That's the exact reason why I insisted that we weren't calling the authorities. He'd have been let off with a slap on the wrist and be free to continue tormenting her.

I want him gone. And I want him to face the wrath he deserves for hurting her.

"He won't—"

"He might, and that's not fucking happening, Lorelei. I'll do anything in my power to protect you. Anything."

Tears continue to fill her eyes, but she manages to keep them contained for now.

"What do you want, Lorelei? Forget your fears and apprehension. What do you really want?"

She lowers her eyes as she continues to fight between her head and her heart.

All I can hope is that her heart wins this time.

My thumb brushes over her cheek, reminding her that I'm here and praying that she can feel how desperate I am to hear her give us a chance. A real chance.

It feels like an eternity has passed when she lifts her eyes again.

My heart jumps into my throat as I wait for her answer.

"I want..." Her voice is rough and cracked with emotion. "I want...you."

The final word is so quiet, it almost gets carried away in the breeze, but I hear it. I hear it loud and clear, and it makes my entire body come alive in a way I've never felt before.

This isn't some woman telling me that she wants a night with me because of my surname, my money, my connections. This is a woman who is terrified of being hurt but willing to put her heart on the line. For me.

Fuck. She brings me to my fucking knees.

My lips part to respond, but I quickly discover that I don't have any words.

There aren't any worthy of this moment. Only actions are good enough.

I lean forward and let my lips brush against hers.

Our first kiss is hesitant, as if we're testing each other out all over again, confirming that what we've said is correct before diving in too deep.

But then as the seconds tick by, the air around us and the connection crackling between us amps up.

The second my lips part and my tongue sneaks out, so do hers. We collide with an expression of desire as I wrap my arm around her waist, pinning her body against mine as my fingers sink into the hair at the nape of her neck, angling her exactly as I want her.

Her moan mingles with mine as we devour each other right there in the middle of the deserted beach.

Not that it matters it's empty; we could be in the middle of a crowd right now and the only person I'd be aware of is her.

"You can't take it back this time. I won't let you," I rasp as I drag my lips from hers and kiss across her jaw and down her neck. "You're mine, Lorelei Tempest. Mine."

"Kian," she moans as I suck on the patch of sensitive skin under her ear. "Yours. I'm yours."

"Fuck. Say it again," I demand as I drop my hands to her ass and lift her from the sand.

She instantly wraps her legs around my waist and I turn around, walking away from the ocean a little before dropping her onto her back in the sand.

"I'm yours, Kian Callahan. Please..." She gasps as I settle myself between her legs. "Please be gentle with me."

"With your heart, always. In the bedroom...never."

68

LORELEI

His kiss makes everything disappear.

I forget about my anger, my frustration, my confusion.

The only thing I feel is relief, and it's stronger than I ever could have expected.

My body trembles as his hand skims up my side before wrapping around my throat, holding me in place as he licks deep into my mouth.

The weight of his body presses me into the dry sand beneath me. His hips grind between my legs and in only seconds, I'm burning red hot for him.

We make out on the beach for the longest time, sealing our promises from only a few minutes ago with a kiss to rival all kisses.

He's rock-hard. It's impossible not to feel him against me.

My body aches for him. To feel him touch my bare skin, to feel him push inside me.

It would be so easy to throw caution to the wind and take what we both need right here.

But as hot as it would be...if we're going to do this, then I want to do it right. And a tumble in the sand isn't it.

I suck in a deep, greedy breath when he drags his lips from mine, kissing across my jaw and down my throat.

"Shit, Temptress," he groans, pressing his forehead against my shoulder, fighting to catch his own breath.

"I know," I whisper.

Kissing him. Being with him. It's like nothing I've ever experienced before.

It's scary and exhilarating.

It's everything I've ever wanted, just...not the kind of man I ever expected.

"I should get you home before we do something we might regret," he says roughly.

"You'd regret taking me on the beach?" I ask, quirking a brow.

"I'd regret not treating you the way you deserve. And," he says, pushing up so he can look down at me, "have you ever had sand burn? Puts you out of action for days, and..." His eyes drop to my lips and he sucks his bottom one into his mouth. "That can't happen."

Heat rolls through me.

"I want to take my time with you, Lorelei. Worship every single inch of this body," he explains, sliding his hand back down my side, brushing over my breast before hooking my thigh higher around him, grinding into me in a way that makes me gasp.

I want to tell him that we can do that later, that we can have both, but before I can find the words, he lifts me to my feet. Thankfully, he doesn't leave me to stand on unsteady legs. Instead, he wraps his arm around my waist and pins me to his side.

Silently, he leads me back to his rental car and opens the passenger door for me.

Reluctantly, I allow him to deposit me into the seat before he closes the door and takes a step back.

He doesn't immediately join me. Instead, he looks up to the sky, almost as if he's praying.

I'm struck with a bolt of anxiety. Surely, he's not already regretting this.

But then his gaze drops. His eyes find mine before lowering to my lips as his hand moves to his crotch.

My attention follows, and I find him hard and ready against the tight fabric.

My mouth runs dry and desire rushes through my veins.

I need him.

With a wicked smirk playing on his lips, he finally walks around the front of the car and joins me.

"Problem?" I taunt.

"Temptress," he groans. "You have no idea how hard it's been."

I can't help it—I bark out a laugh as he backs out of the space and sets the GPS to our address.

I cringe all over again, remembering that he's now witnessed the part of my life I try to keep as far away as possible from my new one.

Sensing that I'm freaking out, he reaches over and takes my hand.

"I don't care, Lorelei. Stop worrying," he says, lifting my hand to his mouth and kissing my knuckles. "This place, it doesn't change you. If anything, it only proves how strong you really are."

"I hate it," I confess. "My brothers are the only good thing about it."

"And they'll be done soon. All of you can put it behind you, if that's what you want."

"It's what I want," I say without missing a beat. "I've saved every single cent I can to make sure it happens for them. Wilder will hopefully get a scholarship, but Hendrix..."

Kian squeezes my hand. "We'll make it happen."

"No, Kian. They're not your responsibility. You don't—"

"Lorelei, they're your brothers. Of course I'm going to help."

Emotion burns my throat. I'm grateful, of course I am, but his offer goes against everything I've ever known.

"We don't take charity, Kian."

He chuckles. "Good thing I'm not offering anything."

"Kian," I warn.

He lifts my knuckles for another kiss.

"We're doing this, right?" he says, quickly glancing over at me. "Me and you? Us?" His question makes my heart beat faster.

'U-um..."

"Lorelei," he growls.

"Y-yeah, we are," I agree hesitantly. It's not because I don't want it. I do. Everything he's said, everything he said he wants, I want it too.

It's just...a lot to process on top of everything else.

"You don't sound very sure."

"I am. It's just..." I trail off, unable to find the right words.

"I know. I get it," he agrees, giving me an out. "You're mine, Lorelei, and together, we'll give your brothers the future they deserve."

"And Noelle?" I blurt. There's no way I can leave her behind after everything she's done for them. For us.

"Of course," he agrees without question.

My heart swells with something terrifying.

He told me out on the beach that he loves falling in love with me. And...I can't help but agree.

I thought I'd fallen before, but I'm pretty sure they were all just warm-ups for the real thing, because it's never felt this huge before.

The excitement, the exhilaration, the fear.

They're all-consuming, just like the man who's causing them.

All too soon, we're pulling into the trailer park. My heart sinks lower with every pothole we bounce into.

"There are only two motels in town, so you'll probably be better driving over to the next one. But a questionable four-star hotel is all you're going to find," I say quietly as he pulls to a stop outside my childhood home.

He kills the engine and looks over.

I love the expression on his face, a little bit of confusion, some awe, and a lot of understanding.

"Were you planning on coming with me?" he asks.

"N-no, I need to be here for Wilder." It's not true. He's fine now and should be going to school as usual tomorrow. Even if he weren't ready for it, something tells me that he'd be there anyway, just to soak up all the attention.

"Then that's where I'll be too," Kian says firmly before pushing the door open and climbing out.

"Kian," I breathe when he opens my door and tugs me out by my hand. He pulls me into his body and cuts off my argument with his lips.

The second we connect, there's an eruption of noise from the trailer beside us.

"Oh my god," I mutter into his kiss before turning around to look at the window.

Both of my brothers are standing there watching us with wide smiles as they bang against the window.

"It's not too late to change your mind about the motel. They only have a minor case of cockroaches."

Kian's chest vibrates with laughter. "I think I'll take my chances here," he says before pushing me forward.

"So, Lorelei," Wilder teases the second we're inside. "Would you like to reintroduce us to your friend?"

I clear my throat, suddenly nervous about letting them into a part of my life I've always kept separate.

"Wilder, Hendrix, Noelle" I say, formally introducing them all. "This is Kian, my—" I swallow thickly, stumbling over the word.

"Boyfriend," Kian finishes for me.

The way he says it makes my knees go a little weak.

I, Lorelei Tempest, am Kian Callahan's girlfriend.

Not just his girlfriend. His first girlfriend.

Maybe his last, too...

I shut that thought down before it can take flight, because this is already big enough.

"If it's okay with both of you, I'm going to stay the night before taking Lorelei back home," Kian explains.

"You...you want to stay here?" Hendrix asks like it's the most insane thing he's ever heard.

"Of course, it's your home and—"

"It's a shithole," Wilder interrupts. "Your family owns some of the world's most luxurious hotels and you want us to believe that you're happy to stay here?"

My eyebrows shoot north. I didn't give either of them details about my new job.

"What?" Hendrix asks. "You think we don't keep tabs on you, big sister?" He rolls his eyes, and I can't help but laugh.

"I'll stay wherever Lorelei is," Kian confirms. "Nothing else matters."

A ripple of silence goes through the air as my brothers take in Kian's words.

"Okay, but I should warn you," I start, my eyes shifting to the couch. Kian's gaze follows mine. "That's my bedroom."

"It's cool. I've never slept on a pull-out before."

Wilder laughs. "This place really is going to be an education for you, huh?"

Kian shrugs, taking everything in his stride.

I study him closely, trying to figure out if it's an act or if he really is happy to embrace all of this. But I can't find any hint of a lie. I think he's genuinely happy to jump into our lives with two feet. For one night, at least.

"We should warn you, though, this trailer rocks."

Kian frowns.

"And it's not soundproof," Hendrix adds.

"Fucking hell," I mutter. Since when did my brothers get old enough to be warning me about this?

"We know, Wilder. Trust us. We know," I half laugh, half cringe.

"Hey, you don't have to share a room with him."

"You didn't that night. You topped and tailed with me," I

point out, laughing as I think about the night in question last summer.

"He still refuses to tell me if they used my bed."

Kian claps Hendrix on the shoulder. "Take it from someone with two brothers to contend with...he definitely used your bed."

"Motherfucker."

"Hey, now, just because I'm not scared to have fun, doesn't mean that your bed feels the same," Wilder counters.

"I'm not scared," Hendrix starts. "I just—"

"Don't worry," Kian interrupts, saving Hendrix from himself. "I'll respect your home. And your sister."

"What?" I balk, still reeling from putting the brakes on things at the beach.

"Lorelei," Wilder and Hendrix gasp at the same time.

"Oh shush. I'm a fully grown adult with needs."

"Stop talking. Stoptalking. Stoptalking," Wilder teases, pressing his hands to his ears.

"Such an asshole," Hendrix says loudly before taking off toward the kitchen.

"Hey, I heard that," Wilder barks.

"You were meant to," Hendrix counters.

Leaving them to bicker, I slip behind Kian and walk toward what will be our bed for the night.

I throw the cushions off and bend down to pull the bed out. Kian's attention burns my skin as I do so.

"What do you think?" I ask once the thin mattress we're going to have to sleep on has been revealed in all its glory.

"I think that I'm going to have you right beside me, and nothing in the world could be better than that."

To my surprise, no one teases his sappy comment, and when I look back, I find that Wilder and Hendrix have made themselves scarce.

I stare up at Kian with my heart thumping steadily in my chest and butterflies fluttering wildly in my stomach.

"Are we really doing this?"

"Yeah," he whispers, taking a step closer and cupping my face in his hands. "We're really doing this."

His kiss is sweet, gentle, and the perfect tease for what I really want.

"The bathroom is down the hall on the right," I say when we part.

"Trying to get rid of me already?"

"Trust me, you won't want to spend any longer in there than necessary."

"If you're not coming with me then no, I won't be hanging around."

I chuckle. "The fact you think we could both fit just proves how disappointed you're about to be."

"I've nothing to be disappointed about because you'll be out here waiting for me."

"Smooth talker," I tease.

"Just telling the truth, Temptress."

69

LORELEI

Kian was almost right. Being in his arms again was almost enough to put aside just how fucking uncomfortable the pull-out is.

Almost.

Much to my frustration, he remained true to his word and mostly kept his hands to himself.

I respected the hell out of his need to do the right thing and not give my brothers any more reasons to have nightmares.

We kissed until long past midnight. It was incredible, and everything I didn't know I needed. Okay, I knew. I just refused to accept it.

But with him here, with my limbs entwined with his, it's impossible not to accept the truth. Everything makes more sense when I'm in Kian Callahan's arms. Everything seems easier, lighter, more achievable. I feel like a better person just because of his presence. Is that what real love is? Because if it is, I think it's safe to say that I've never experienced it before. I thought I had, but it seems every relationship of my past pales in comparison to this. I already knew that no other man could compete. But the feelings he evokes in me...they're beyond everything I've ever known. I'm almost as obsessed with them as I am him. Almost.

The sun is shining bright, the thin curtains at the windows no match for the ones that keep Kian's apartment in complete darkness until he's ready to greet the day. There is no chance of sleeping in this morning. It's just another of the things I hate about this place.

A groan from behind me lets me know that my bed buddy is rousing.

"I think my back is broken," he complains as he shifts his hips, ensuring his erection pokes me harder in the butt.

"Baby," I laugh, rubbing my ass back against him, making him groan again, only for a very different reason.

"Hmm, I could be convinced to stay lying on this rock for a little while longer."

"I gave you the option of a four-star hotel," I tease.

"I'd have chosen this every time."

He shifts again, rolling me onto my back and settling himself between my thighs.

"What time do your brothers wake up?" he whispers in my ear before nipping my earlobe.

"They're seventeen-year-olds," I remind him. "They're lucky if they're awake this side of midday."

He chuckles, his lips tickling my neck and sending goosebumps skating across my body.

"You're going to need to be quiet," he murmurs.

"What happened to respecting my family home?" I tease.

"I'm a patient man, Lorelei. But even I have my limits."

His palm lands on my breast, and a moan rumbles in my throat as my back arches.

"Kian," I gasp when he pinches my nipple through the thin fabric of my tank.

"Yeah, Temptress. I'm right here."

Dragging my tank down, his lips wrap around my nipple and he sucks hard enough to send desire shooting to my clit.

Suddenly, I regret my decision last night. Maybe I should have insisted he stay in the hotel and I should have gone with him.

"Please," I whimper when he moves to the other side, teasing me in only the way he can.

Sinking beneath the cover, Kian kisses down my stomach before tucking his fingers into the sides of my panties.

He's barely moved them when both of our cells start ringing.

"Keep going," I demand, reaching out and twisting my fingers in his hair to hold him in place.

A deep chuckle rumbles in his throat before he does as he's told.

But no sooner have our cells stopped than they start again.

"Fuck's sake", he mutters, moving so he can reach over the side of the bed. Lifting my arm, I look at my wrist.

"It's Tate."

"It's King," he says at exactly the same time.

We share a look before answering the calls.

This can't be good if they're both ringing.

"What's going on?" I bark the second the line connects.

"You dirty little whore." Tate laughs down the line while Kian climbs from the bed.

"He's done what?" he roars, ensuring that Wilder and Hendrix are also awake with dawn.

"What's going on, Tate?" I ask, my stomach knotting with fear.

"Someone has leaked photos of you and Kian on the beach last night."

"They've what?" I shriek, sitting up so fast it makes my head spin. Kian looks back at me with a mixture of fear and concern warring in his dark green eyes. "Who even knew that we were there?"

"We're trying to find out," Tate assures me.

"Find him," Kian demands. "I don't give a fuck what it takes. Find the motherfucker. No one does this to her."

My chest swells the second I hear the possessive tone in his voice at the same time acid drips through my veins.

"It was him, wasn't it? He's punishing me for turning my

back on him," I say quietly as Kian gets swept up in a conversation with his brother.

"We don't know that."

"We do, though. No one else cares enough about what I'm doing with my life."

"We'll find him. And if it's him, he's going to regret it," Tate says dangerously. "King called Aubrey."

My breath catches. I love Aubrey. She's the kind of badass I aspire to be. But she's also dangerous as hell. You'd never believe it by looking at her, but uncover a few layers and she's freaking lethal.

"She won't let him get away with this."

"What will she do to him?" I whisper, hating how her promise makes me feel.

"Who gives a crap? He's trying to ruin your life. The things he's said. I'll—"

"What?" I ask, confused. She said there were photos, she didn't say anything about words.

"Lorelei, please, just...stay off the internet today, yeah?"

I'm already lowering my cell as her voice rings through the line.

I type Kian's name into my search bar—because why would I type my own? No one knows who I am. But I very quickly discover that assumption is beyond incorrect.

Kian Callahan making the most of his new assistant after hours.

Kian Callahan's assistant isn't afraid to get her hands dirty.

And there are more. So many more.

My hand trembles as Tate's voice continues to fill the air, but I don't hear a word she says. Instead, I stare in horror at the news everyone is waking up to this morning.

"Kian," I whisper, tears filling my eyes.

He looks over and instantly freezes at what he sees.

"Get rid of it all, and then call me when you find him. Nothing else is worthy of a call."

He hangs up, throws his cell onto the bed and rushes over.

"It's going to be okay," he says, crawling onto the bed and taking my face in his hands. "King is going to get it all taken down."

There's movement elsewhere in the trailer before Wilder comes storming in, and he doesn't stop. Or at least not until he's dragged Kian from me and thrown him against the wall.

"What the fuck did you do?" Wilder bellows, getting right in Kian's face.

"Wilder," I cry, scrambling from the bed just as Hendrix comes running in.

"Dude, put him down," he states as I tug at Wilder's shirt, trying to drag him back.

"He didn't do this, Wilder," I cry. "Please."

Thankfully, my words get through to my brother and he releases his grip on Kian.

"It was someone else," I explain as I rush to Kian's side.

"Who?"

"That's what we're trying to find out. But I can promise you, I have nothing to do with it. No one has the right to talk about Lorelei like that," Kian says so fiercely it's actually a little scary.

"We think it's my ex," I explain as Wilder continues to glare at Kian with his chest heaving, ready to fight for me.

I appreciate it. I really do. But Kian isn't the one he needs to be glaring at.

"Where is he?" Wilder demands.

"We don't know," I say softly in the hope of calming him down. "Kian has people looking for him."

"But he's here. Do you have people here, Kian?"

"We will find him, no matter where he is," Kian explains calmly.

"That's not good enough."

"Wilder," I warn.

"Do you all want coffee?" Hendrix asks, sounding much more composed than his hot-headed twin.

"Yes," I all but cry. "Yes, we all need coffee."

Taking Kian's hand, I lead him back to our bed and tug him to sit.

He's tense. His shoulders are practically bunched around his ears.

"I'm sorry," he whispers as Hendrix demands that Wilder help him.

"Hey," I say, cupping his jaw and turning his eyes to me. "None of this is your fault. My relationship with Matt started long before there was anything here."

"I should be protecting you," Kian hisses, clearly irritated with himself.

"You are," I assure him.

"He's also targeting you because of me."

I swallow thickly, because he is partly right there. "He'd have done this no matter who came next in my life. He just lucked out that people know who you are, giving him a larger platform for his bullshit."

Kian's eyes bounce between mine as he absorbs my words.

"I'm sorry he ruined last night."

"Again, not your fault."

Wilder walks over with a mug of coffee for Kian, and he holds it out for him as a peace offering.

"Thanks, man," Kian says, taking the mug and almost instantly taking a sip.

The second the taste hits his tongue, his eyebrows shoot up in shock.

He tries to hide it, but he can't, and he ends up spluttering.

"I'm taking you all for breakfast," he announces, abandoning his mug and pulling his discarded clothes back on.

I want to argue, refuse to take his charity, but this time, I manage to keep my mouth shut.

He just wants to do something nice.

"That sounds great. Go and get ready—we can drop you at school after."

"Really?" Hendrix complains, obviously hoping for a day off.

"Really," I state firmly.

He rolls his eyes and I laugh.

"He just doesn't want to watch my fan club fawn over me."

"Too fucking right," Hendrix complains.

"Go and get ready, and we'll head out," I say before kissing Kian and walking toward the bathroom to clean up.

———

"Can I drive?" Wilder asks the second we emerge from the trailer.

"The kid with the concussion?" Kian deadpans. "Yeah, I don't think so."

"Dude, that's harsh."

"And yet true," Hendrix mocks as he pulls the back door open and climbs in.

Wilder blows out a heavy breath but does the same thing.

Kian is shaking his head, waiting with the passenger door open for me.

"Ignore them." I laugh.

"Never, they remind me far too much of me and my brothers," he confesses as he wraps his arms around my waist.

"I can only imagine," I muse, staring up at him with my heart pounding a little too hard in my chest.

What is it about Kian Callahan that makes all the ugly things surrounding us seem like nothing?

Of course, I feel totally violated that our private moment last night has been plastered all over the internet. Of course, the toxic things that were said about me stung, but they're just words written by a hurt man. A hurt man with a questionable state of mind.

It might be hot news in certain circles now, but give it an

hour, and it'll be old and forgotten. Someone more famous will do something much more gossip-worthy.

"We were trouble," he says with a smirk.

"Some might say you still are."

"Touché."

My stomach growls as he holds me.

"I guess I should feed my girl. Do you know somewhere good to eat?"

"In this town?" I ask, cocking my head to the side.

Disappointment washes through his expression.

"Of course I do. There is only one place to go for breakfast."

I quickly peck him on the lips before dropping into the car, waiting for him to join us.

70

KIAN

"So, are you two a couple?" I ask innocently after Lorelei and Noelle excuse themselves to use the bathroom.

I know the answer, but I can't help myself.

Wilder barks out a laugh while Hendrix's cheeks blaze bright red.

"No, we're just friends."

"Riight," I muse while Wilder continues to laugh.

"He's too much of a pussy to do anything, but he's totally in love with her."

"I'm not," Hendrix snaps. "She's my best friend."

"Who you want sucking your cock," Wilder points out.

The two of them continue bickering and I sit back with a smile playing on my lips. It reminds me of good times with my brothers.

Sure, we're still fairly close. Or at least, King and I are. Since Kieran embarked on his own path, we've lost our tight team, and I'm not too old and independent to admit that I miss him sometimes.

The second Lorelei returns, I wrap my arm around her and press a kiss to her temple.

Hendrix and Noelle watch us closely while Wilder is

distracted with his cell, and I can't help but wonder if they're both wishing they could have something similar.

I guess only time will tell.

"Are you guys ready to head out?" Lorelei asks, keeping an eye on the time and ensuring they're not late for school.

She's going to be a great mom one day.

The thought hits me out of nowhere and my entire body freezes, something that she doesn't miss.

Turning to look at me, she gazes into my eyes, forcing me to breathe again.

"You okay?"

I breathe out, my chest aching in the best kind of way.

"Yeah, I'm good. Are you sure you're okay to return to Chicago?" I ask, changing the subject.

She doesn't want to. I can see it in her eyes. But she also knows that we need to return to reality.

Wilder is fine now; plus, he's got Hendrix and Noelle to look out for him.

I would say he has their mom too, but she seems to be MIA. When I asked about her, I got quickly shut down and the conversation changed around me.

Something tells me that meeting their mom might have pushed Lorelei a little too far. Letting me into their home, their lives, was hard enough. Their mom is an entirely different issue.

She shrugs one shoulder. I get it. Half of her heart lives here. But it won't be that way for much longer. The second these two have got senior year done, they're free to move anywhere they want. Is it weird that after spending only a few hours with them, I want them in Chicago with us?

"Work calls, I guess. And my boss, he's a control freak. I dare not piss him off."

"I've heard he's the worst kind of tyrant."

Lorelei smiles. "That and a few other things."

"Sexy?" I whisper in her ear. "The best fuck of your life?"

Lorelei giggles like a schoolgirl, and Wilder and Hendrix groan as if they're in pain.

"Stop it," Noelle chastises. "It's cute. And Lorelei deserves it. I'm going to take these two knuckleheads to school, leave you guys to it."

"You don't have to do that, we can—"

"Enjoy the rest of your morning," Noelle says, sliding out from the other side of the booth.

"Thank you," Lorelei says, pushing to her feet and pulling the younger woman into her arms. "We'll see you soon, yeah?"

"Yeah. You know where we'll be."

"Not for much longer," Lorelei promises.

"Still feels like a lifetime away."

Lorelei squeezes her hand as they part before turning to her brothers.

As she hugs Hendrix, Wilder holds his hand out for me.

"Thank you," he says, holding my eyes. "We're trusting you to keep looking out for her."

"I won't let anything happen to her. You look after yourself, yeah? We'll be watching."

"Do you know any college scouts?" he asks hopefully.

"I'll do everything I can," I promise him before he nods in acceptance and turns to Lorelei.

Hendrix doesn't give me a warning; he just shakes my hand and thanks me for being there for his sister.

Only a few minutes later, we stand there as the three of them walk out.

Reaching for Lorelei, I pull her into my arms the moment they disappear from view and hold her tight.

She trembles and my heart breaks for her.

I can't imagine being so far away from my brothers. It's weird enough when Kieran is out of town for an away game.

"You'll see them again soon."

"I hate leaving them," she whispers. "I hate knowing that they're here."

"They're so lucky to have you, Temptress."

She blows out a shaky breath and holds me closer.

"Take me home, Kian. I don't belong here anymore."

"I thought you'd never ask."

I throw a load of bills onto the table to cover the check and lead my girl out to the car.

My girl.

Fuck. There are two words I never thought I'd say.

"Your place or mine?" I ask once we've pulled out of the airport parking.

Lorelei hesitates, and I can't help but wonder if it's because she wants to go home alone or if she's scared I'm going to suggest she move in with me.

Honestly, if I didn't think she'd freak out then I would.

I know what I want, and I'm more than happy to dive in with both feet. But something tells me that she's going to need a little more time to get her head around all of this.

She glances over at me.

"I need to get some things from mine, but—"

"Say no more," I say, taking a turn at the last minute that will lead us directly to my place.

"But my apartment is—"

"You don't need to pick anything up, Temptress. Everything you could possibly need is already at my place."

"What have you done?" she asks suspiciously.

I smirk and push my foot harder against the gas, needing to get her home so that I can finally have her to myself.

Last night was nice and all, but I need more.

I need everything.

We're pulling into my underground parking lot in record time, and only a minute later, I have both our luggage in my hand and I'm racing toward the elevator.

"Did you just remember you left the oven on or something?" Lorelei teases from behind me.

I look back over my shoulder and let my eyes roam down the length of her body.

"No, it's more important than that."

The second I'm inside the elevator, I drop the suitcases on the floor with a loud thud in favor of reaching for her.

Her shriek of fright fills the small space as I push her against the back wall.

"Do you have any idea how badly I need you," I ask, my eyes locked on hers.

She swallows thickly. "I-I have a good idea, yeah."

Without warning, I push my hand inside her jeans.

"Oh my god, Kian."

I groan the second my fingers connect with her soaked pussy.

"Yeah, you get it," I muse, pressing my hard cock against her hip, letting her know that I feel her frustration just as potently.

I push lower, letting my fingers dip inside her, teasing her with what she could have before quickly pulling them away again.

"Tease," she breathes, her eyes blown with desire as I lift my fingers to my lips and suck.

"Delicious."

Her chin drops and her eyes darken. But before she gets a chance to act, the elevator dings and the doors open.

"Home sweet home," I muse before picking up our luggage and marching toward my front door, leaving her to rush after me.

There's no doubt she will—she was just about to climb me like a tree.

My chest is heaving and my cock is trying to bust out of my pants as I let myself into the apartment and stalk into the kitchen.

I once again drop the luggage, but I don't do anything else for a couple of seconds. Instead, I take a moment to breathe.

The calm before the storm.

"Kian, what are you—"

The second she's in reaching distance, I pull her in front of me and wrap one arm around her back. The other lifts, my fingers sinking into her hair as I slam our lips together.

Our kiss is frantic. Our hands are everywhere as we tug at clothing in the hope it disappears.

She shoves my t-shirt up around my chest, and I help her out by reaching behind me and pulling it off. The second my skin is exposed, her hands are roaming, making a violent shudder rip down my spine.

"Lorelei," I groan, dragging her shirt off, quickly followed by her bra.

"Yes," she cries when I duck my head and suck on her nipples.

She throws her head back, giving me free rein of her body.

In seconds, I have her jeans open and I'm dropping to my knees before her and dragging them down her legs.

They're so skinny, it's a fight to get them off her feet, but I finally manage it, and her panties quickly follow before being discarded somewhere behind me.

"Jump up on the counter, Temptress," I demand, my voice deep and rough even to my own ears.

She doesn't hesitate, and the second her ass hits my cold granite counter, she hisses in surprise while I push her legs apart.

The sight of her glistening pussy makes my mouth water, and without missing a beat, I shuffle forward and lick up the length of her.

"Holy shit," she cries, sliding forward so that she's right on the edge, giving me all the access I need.

With my hands pressed against her thighs, I eat her like she's my last meal.

Her entire body trembles with her impending orgasm, but I don't let her have it. Not until I'm ready.

Her taste floods my mouth, and I do my best to memorize it. Not that I need to. This is it now. She's mine, and I'm going to be able to do this over and over.

In the past, I've always thought that settling down with one woman would be boring. The thought of only experiencing one pussy, one body for the rest of my life terrified me. But no more.

Thinking about having Lorelei every single day excites me. The thought of being able to learn every single thing about her, all the ways I can make her come...it's a bigger turn-on than fucking a different woman every night ever was.

"Kian, please. I need—"

"What do you need?"

"You, Kian. I need you."

"That's what I like to hear."

I up the ante, sucking her clit harder, curling my fingers deeper inside her, making her scream as her release barrels into her.

The way she clamps down on me makes my head spin and my cock weep.

She's barely come down from her high when I push to my feet, lose my pants and boxers and drag my cock through her folds.

She trembles, her pussy sensitive and swollen.

"So pretty," I muse, watching intently. And my fascination only gets stronger as I push inside her, observing the moment we connect.

It feels like it's been a lifetime when in reality, it's only been days. But no matter how long it's been, it's too long.

There were too many secrets and far too many miles between us this weekend.

"You're mine, Lorelei Tempest. Mine. All. Fucking. Mine," I state before thrusting forward and stretching her wide open.

My teeth grind and my grip on her hips tightens as I embrace just how fucking good she feels wrapped around me.

"Yes, yes. I'm yours, Kian. Yours," she screams as I pull out and thrust back in harder, deeper.

"Good. Don't forget it. Ever."

71

LORELEI

Kian was right. There wasn't anything I needed from my apartment to spend the night with him. He'd already organized everything.

I had clothes, lingerie, toiletries, and of course, more bottles of my beloved hair products. There were even sanitary napkins and tampons in the bathroom cabinet. If I wasn't already falling hard, then looking around his home and finding hints of myself everywhere really would have done it.

But as incredible as spending the night and then waking up with him was, I'm still nervous as hell as we step out of the car outside the Callahan Enterprises building the next morning.

I've no doubt that a huge percentage of the people who reside inside this building on a daily basis would have seen the footage of Kian and me on the beach, and worse, the slander that was attached to it.

Kian was keen to embrace our relationship in the office as well as outside, but I wasn't as eager. I wanted to remain professional at work and just focus on being his assistant. Kian was insistent that he wanted everyone to know that I'm much more important than that.

We walk side by side, our shoulders almost touching, our

hands grazing each other. He wants to grab mine—I can sense it without looking at him. He also wants to whisper assurances in my ear that no one is looking at me.

I keep my eyes on the elevator ahead of us, refusing to look at any of the people loitering at the entrance, but I know they're looking. Looking and judging. I shouldn't care; I know I shouldn't. But suddenly, I'm not just worrying about me. I've got Kian to think about now. I know I'm punching above my weight; I don't need anyone to tell me that, and I'm terrified of showing him up.

I'm just a girl from a bad town in California. I'm not worthy of his life, this job, but for some reason, he's chosen me, and I'm too exhausted to keep fighting it because...I want him too.

I love being with him. I love the way he makes me feel. I love the expression on his face when he looks at me.

I love...him.

The second we step into the elevators alone, he turns to me.

"No one here cares, Lorelei," he assures me, staring down into my eyes.

"They do. They care more than you can understand. They're just also scared of you and King, so they won't do or say anything."

He smirks. "That's good enough for me. If anyone dares say a single thing to you, they'll be unemployed faster than they thought possible."

I shake my head, both loving and hating his words.

"Can we please just do our jobs?" I beg.

With Him gone all last week, and both of us absent yesterday, our to-do lists are piling up fast. We don't have time to get into an argument about him being an overbearing asshole. Not right now, at least.

"Does that mean I can't molest my assistant whenever the need strikes?"

Heat rushes through me and memories of our time on his desk Friday night flash through my mind.

"During working hours, we're boss and assistant," I confirm.

Disappointment covers his face before he lifts his arm and checks his watch.

His smile grows once more, and before I know what's happening, his lips are on mine and he's giving me a knee-weakening kiss.

He releases me quickly, leaving me gasping for breath when he looks at his watch again.

"We had another minute. Had to make the most of it."

The elevator dings, the doors part, and Kian walks out, shouting, "I require a coffee on my desk in no more than ten minutes."

A laugh tumbles out of me as he disappears around the corner. I did ask for business as usual.

I jump out of the elevator as the doors threaten to close on me and emerge into the front office to a smiling Melissa.

"Good morning, Lorelei," she says with a knowing glint in her eye.

Safe to say that she's seen the photographs of us, then.

"Good morning. Would you like a coffee?"

She shakes her head. "I'm fine, thank you."

Needing to dive into action instead of allowing myself to think about what everyone in Callahan Enterprises now knows about me, I abandon my things at my desk and make a beeline for our kitchen.

No sooner have I stepped inside than I set the coffee machine to work and reach for two mugs.

"You don't need to hide."

"Holy shit," I gasp, almost dropping the mug in my hand.

"Crap, I'm sorry," Melissa says softly as she steps farther into the room with me.

"It's okay," I whisper before turning back to the coffee machine.

"No one here will judge you, Lorelei. You know that, right?" she says, going in for the kill.

"Of course they will. I'm not like them," I mumble, refusing to look back at her.

"I know that Kian has had a privileged life, and there are a few others here that have too. But trust me when I say that they're the exception. Most people under this roof are here because they're good at their jobs and they work damn hard at them.

"This office contains people from all walks of life. It's not just the wealthy. There are many more people like you." She takes a step closer. "People like us," she says with a new layer of understanding in her voice.

"This isn't how I grew up, Lorelei. I got my first job when I was twelve to help my mother pay for food for my little brothers and sisters. I didn't even graduate high school," she confesses, raising her brows to drive the point home.

I take a step back, surprised by her words.

"Life isn't about the past, Lorelei. It doesn't matter where you came from. The only thing that's important from here on out is your future. And you get to choose what to do with that."

She grabs a bottle of water from the refrigerator and then spins around and leaves me with those words.

Resting my ass back against the counter, I can't help but believe them.

Why should I be ashamed of where I've come from when Kian isn't? He has never made me feel any less than him, even now he knows. He's happy to embrace that it's a part of me. So why shouldn't I?

And Melissa is right—it's in my past. As soon as Wilder and Hendrix graduate, it'll be in all of our pasts. Mom...hell, we don't even know where she is...she made her choice years ago. She probably won't even notice that they've left. It's a sad but true fact. One that all three of us will have to learn to live with. I just hope that it's made us all stronger.

With two mugs of coffee in hand, I make my way to Kian's office.

Melissa is on the phone as I pass, but she gives me a soft smile and I happily return it, hoping she can read the gratitude in my eyes.

I knock once before letting myself in, and then kick the door behind me.

"Eight minutes. Not bad," Kian teases.

"Yeah, yeah, whatever," I mutter, lowering our mugs to his desk and taking a seat. "So, what have we got this week then, Boss?"

He watches me closely before reaching for his office drawer.

"You forgot your notebook," he points out before passing something to me.

My eyes drop from his and I swear, they almost bug out of my head.

"List of coworkers who don't think you're sleeping with the boss."

"Kian," I gasp as I take it from him.

"Open it and see the list," he encourages.

Without thinking, I follow orders and find nothing but empty pages staring back at me.

A laugh rumbles in Kian's throat and when I look up, I can't help but join in.

"You're an idiot."

"Maybe, but at least I'm a funny one. I got you a pen, too."

"Oh Christ," I mumble as he passes it over.

"Wake up happy. Sleep with your boss."

"Fucking hell."

Kian shrugs. "True though, right?"

"Maybe," I say, popping the top and flipping the notepad open.

I scribble today's date on the page and then sit back to listen to him discuss what's happening and list out my epic to-do list.

Sure, we could have done this at home—I mean, at his

place—but we need to figure out how to keep work and play separate, at least until we figure all this relationship stuff out.

It takes a bit of convincing, but eventually, Kian manages to pull his boss mask back on and set to it. Although, it doesn't stop him trying to add "fuck your boss in his private bathroom" to the list every now and then.

We're just finishing up so he can log in to his first meeting of the day when a knock sounds out on his door.

"Come in," Kian calls, his voice all deep and commanding. I'd be lying if I said it didn't send chills skating down my spine. From the look he gives me, he knows it too.

The door opens, and a familiar face appears before me.

"Aubrey?" I whisper, my previous desire giving way to unease.

She looks between the two of us. "Is now a good time?"

"It is, as long as you're giving us good news," Kian states, gesturing for her to come in and shut the door behind her.

"Some of it is good."

I close my eyes as dread slowly drips through my veins.

Oh my god.

I'm not sure I can cope with another attack.

"Fucking hell," Kian groans, scrubbing his hand down his face. "Start with the bad."

Aubrey smirks and pops a hip. I instantly relax. Maybe this isn't going to be as bad as I first thought.

"Your security team needs better training. It took me less than an hour to find that motherfucker's location."

"Not everyone can be as good as you, Kendrick," Kian teases, making her smirk grow.

"Well," she says, flipping her hair back. "You said it."

"Have you found him?" I ask, ignoring the two of them.

"Yep, and he squealed like a pig. Fucking pussy."

Her words make me sink back into my chair.

Deep down, I knew. But assuming and knowing for a fact are two very different things.

Hurt and disbelief wrap around me as both Kian and Aubrey watch me closely.

I put so much trust and hope in that man, and all he ever did was cast it—me—aside.

It was never about us, about our future. It was all about him. I was just the fool along for the ride.

"He did it all?"

Aubrey nods. "Yes, but not personally. He's too weak to get his hands dirty, but we also have the man he paid. He was just as easy to find."

"What are you going to do with them?"

She tilts her head to the side. "Do you want to know?"

Acid swirls in my stomach. Despite appearances, Aubrey is lethal. She just covers it with a sweet smile and a banging body.

"Do whatever with the man he paid. I don't know him, nor do I care to. But..." I glance at Kian, scared that he's not going to approve of my next request, but when I find his eyes, all I see is understanding.

He nods, encouraging me to continue.

"Hurt Matt as much as you like, just...let him go after."

Aubrey agrees, although she doesn't look overly thrilled by the idea as Kian pushes from his seat and walks toward me.

Taking my hand, he pulls me to my feet and wraps me in his arms.

"You sure?" he asks.

"Very. No matter how bad his past is, everyone deserves some kind of a future."

He drops his lips to my ear, and I shudder the second his breath rushes over my skin.

"You're incredible."

My entire body sags with happiness and relief, and he happily holds me up.

"I should probably go," Aubrey says, slinking toward the door. "Call me if you need me."

Before I can thank her, she's slipped through the door, leaving us alone again.

"It's over?" I whisper, blinking up at Kian.

"No, babe. It's just starting."

72

LORELEI

It's been two weeks of pure heaven.

The kind of heaven that I never thought I'd have.

Sure, there have been times with my previous boyfriends that I thought were good. But I'm quickly discovering that those times weren't all that, because this right now? Bliss.

Is it just the honeymoon period? Maybe. But I'm not worrying about what is going to come next or how our relationship might change. I am fully embracing what we have right now. And it is incredible.

By day, we work seamlessly side by side. Of course, Kian is as demanding and as overbearing as ever, and he still drives me insane most days, but now, he always soothes the annoyance with a little kiss or cuddle where he can.

And then, as soon as we walk out of Callahan Enterprises, we forget about being colleagues and focus on being a couple.

More often than not, we head back to his place and he either cooks or we get takeout.

We have been to my apartment, but it's only been to collect things that I need.

Every time I've gone back there, I've expected to feel like I'd gone home. That I'd want to stay. But I don't. It's tainted now. Tainted by him.

I've tried my best not to think about him and what he did. I have questions. So many freaking questions. But I also have very little confidence that I'd ever get the answers. I'm not even sure he has them.

Aubrey did as I asked, and she assured me that I'll never hear from him again. While I don't feel like I've had any real closure on the situation, I can live with it.

He's nothing but a liar and a cheat who craves love and attention. He's clearly unfussy about how he achieves them, based on his recent actions.

If I felt anything for him other than disdain and regret, then it would be pity. But I don't care that much.

"Wait, aren't you going the wrong way?" I ask, suddenly realizing that Kian has missed the turn that will lead us to the Chiefs stadium for this afternoon's game.

Last weekend, we traveled to Detroit for an away game. It was my first experience of a Chiefs game away from their own turf, and it was incredible.

I may not be a true football fan, but I love watching Kieran almost as much as I love watching Wilder.

We've got plans to attend one of Wilder's games in a few weeks. Not that we've told him yet. We're going to surprise him, and I can't wait. Watching him on TV is one thing, but seeing him live in action is another entirely.

"I know," Kian says smugly. "We've got to make a pitstop first."

"I thought you dragged me out a bit early. Where are we going?"

"Surprise," he teases.

"Ugh. Really?"

He glances over with a wide smile playing on his lips. "Really."

My head spins with ideas, but I soon get a good clue and my stomach flutters wildly with excitement.

By the time Kian pulls into the parking lot that's out front of O'Hare Airport, I'm practically bouncing in my seat.

There are only two people he could surprise me with who might be arriving. Everyone else I love is here in this city with me.

"Kian?" I whisper.

"Come on. We don't want to be late," he says, killing the engine and jumping from the car.

I follow not a second later and meet him at the front.

"Did you really do this?"

"Just for you, Temptress," he says, stealing a quick kiss before I turn and run into arrivals.

There are people pouring through the doors, and my eyes dart between them all, searching for ones that look so much like my own. We might have different dads, but the similarities between us are striking.

"They'll be here in a minute," Kian says with a laugh as I bounce on the balls of my feet.

It's only been a couple of weeks since we saw them. We usually go a lot longer, but it still feels like a lifetime.

There is a break in the stream of people, and there right at the back, I spot Hendrix.

"There," I point before taking off.

I'm pretty sure it's against the rules, but whatever. I charge through the people and fall into their arms.

"You're here," I cry, fighting and failing to contain my tears.

"Had an invite we couldn't refuse," Hendrix says as Kian joins us.

Wilder steps up to Kian and holds his hand out. "Thank you," he says. I think he's trying to be all grown-up and manly. It's as cute as hell, and I love him even more for it. But it gets even better when Kian tugs on his arm and pulls him in for a hug.

I swear, my heart explodes right there on the spot.

The twins still have some contact with their father, but their relationship is nowhere near what they'd like it to be. So to see them bonding with Kian...it means everything to me.

Not just because they're getting along and both sides are making an effort, but because the boys are going to have a positive male role model in their lives. I don't think Kian understands just how important he's going to be to them in the coming years.

"Good to see you, man," Kian says as he slaps Wilder on the back. "Did you have a good flight?" he asks before turning his attention to Hendrix.

"Dude, you flew us first class. It was fucking epic," Wilder announces happily.

I look at Kian. "You...of course you did," I mutter, shaking my head.

"What? Everyone deserves a little luxury every now and then."

"Like our coffee machine. That thing is fucking ace. Thanks, man."

"You're spoiling them," I say once my brother releases my boyfriend back to me.

"They deserve it," he says again. "Come on then. We don't want to be late."

"I am so fucking pumped for this," Wilder says, sounding like a little kid again.

"Oh, really? You should have mentioned it another couple hundred times. I swear to God, there isn't a single person at school who doesn't know. Even the principal wished me a good weekend when I left on Friday," Hendrix says, sounding exasperated.

"What? I'm excited. And he was probably just being polite."

"He followed it up with a 'go Chiefs.' He was not just being polite."

"Coach must have told him."

Kian and Wilder spent the entire ride to the stadium talking stats and plays and all kinds of things that go over my head. But even still, I sit there with a wide smile on my face.

I might have fought against this. But giving in to my

feelings for Kian and letting go of all my fears was definitely the right thing to do. Not only is he good for me—no, incredible for me—he's also good for them. And to think, if he hadn't chased me to California, I might still be holding back from introducing them.

Wilder is like an excitable toddler as we step into the box —the only box I've watched home games from.

"Oh my sweet fucking god. This is insane."

He pulls his cell out and starts recording. I stand back and watch him with a sappy smile on my face. It reminds me of Christmas morning back when he and Hendrix believed. The magic. The excitement. Okay, so Hendrix isn't nearly as excitable, but he still looks around with nothing but awe in his eyes.

"I think they're happy," Kian whispers, his hands clamping down on my hips and pressing the length of his body against my back.

A shiver rips down my spine as his breath tickles down my neck.

"They're definitely happy. And so am I." Spinning in his hold, I stare up at him. I'm sure there's as much awe in my eyes as I look at my man as I just saw in Wilder's. "Thank you for doing this for them."

"Anytime." He leans forward and whispers in my ear, "Do you want me to let you into a secret?"

"Go on then."

"I didn't do it for them. I did it for you."

A smile spreads across my lips.

"Is that right?"

He pulls back and looks me dead in the eyes again.

"Yeah, Temptress. I did. I'd do anything for you."

"Aw, such a big softie," I tease, reaching out to cup his jaw.

Silence stretches out between us as the connection I always feel when we're close crackles away.

"I—I love you, Lorelei."

My breath catches as his confession echoes around me.

Time continues ticking, but I swear right there, my entire world grinds to a halt just for a second.

I've known for a while just how strongly I feel for him. I've wanted to tell him. Hell, there have been times in the past couple of weeks that I could have blurted it out. But I held it back. I've no idea why; maybe I was waiting for this moment. Who knows.

"I love you, too," I reply brokenly. "I love you so much."

Wrapping his hand around the back of my neck, he pulls me in for a sweet kiss. One that steals my breath and the last remaining piece of my heart.

"Ew, guys. Seriously?" Wilder complains when he notices us. "You're going to miss the start."

We part with a laugh and one more heated look before we turn toward the windows to watch Kieran obliterate the opposition.

He scores more touchdowns than I've seen him achieve before. He's on fire. And every time he scores, he looks up to one spot in the crowd.

"Has he got some kind of lucky charm up there or something?" Wilder comments, having noticed the same thing.

"Something like that," Kian says cryptically.

"Who is it? Has he got a girlfriend?" Now I'm intrigued.

I don't know all that much about Kieran, but I do know that him having a girl would be huge fucking news, and I've heard nothing.

"Nah. How's Noelle, Rix?" Kian asks, changing the subject. "Shame she couldn't come too."

"Yeah, Rix. How's Noelle?" Wilder sings, earning himself a slug in the shoulder.

"Is this for fucking real?" Wilder asks in amazement, trailing behind Kian and me as we slide past security, heading toward the family area of the arena. "I'm really going to get to meet some of the team?"

"Yep," Kian agrees. "I've got someone else for you to meet before the players emerge, though."

"Really? Who?" Wilder asks, intrigued, as I glance at Kian.

"Yeah, who?"

"Just wait," Kian laughs.

"Not my forte," I mutter.

"Don't I fucking know it."

Only seconds later, he's holding the door for us and then guiding us through the room toward a man I've never seen before.

"Ah, Kian," he says the second he spots my boyfriend.

"Richie, good to see you. This is Wilder. Wilder, this is Richie Carson. He's a scout for Trinity Royal College. He's heading out your way in a couple of weeks."

I swear to God, I've never seen Wilder's chin drop so low before. I've also never, ever seen him lost for words. But in the seconds that follow his introduction, it's like they suddenly cease to exist.

"Wild," Hendrix hisses, shoving his brother in the back and forcing him to step up to Richie.

"H-Hi," Wilder stutters, nervously holding his hand out to the older man. "It's good to meet you."

"You too. I've heard a lot about you, Son."

The warmth of Kian's hand wraps around mine before he pulls me away.

I watch Wilder interact with the scout for a few more seconds before turning to my boyfriend.

"You did this?" I whisper. I've no idea why; no one else can hear me.

Kian shrugs one shoulder. "I might have spoken to Kieran, who in turn put the feelers out."

"You..." I cut myself off from chastising him for using his connections to boost Wilder's chances of college football. Wilder deserves this, and hell knows I couldn't do it myself. "You are going to make his entire world, you know that right?"

"No, he's going to do that himself. He's a fantastic football player, Lorelei. He'd get a killer scholarship with or without our backing."

"If you say so."

I turn to look at Wilder again, and my eyes fill with tears.

"I love you, Kian Callahan. You are everything we were missing in our lives."

"You are everything in my life." Pulling me closer, he kisses me right there in the middle of the Chiefs' family room. It's only the ruckus of the players finally joining us that tears us apart.

We stand back and watch as Wilder takes it all in. My face hurts, my smile is so wide, and it only grows when Kieran appears and makes a beeline straight for him.

So maybe I was wrong...maybe taking the job at Callahan Enterprises wasn't the biggest mistake of my life...

EPILOGUE

Lorelei

I stand at the edge of the box the Callahans managed to snag for the Chiefs playoff game, staring down at the field with my hands trembling and my stomach in knots.

I'm not sure I've ever been this nervous for someone else.

Even on the flight to San Francisco, I was anxious.

I can only imagine how Kieran must be feeling right now.

Everyone is here to support him. Micheal and Jackie, Kian's stepmom. King and Tate, Wilder, Hendrix, and Noelle.

It's the first time all season that we've all been in attendance. But it feels right. And if the Chiefs manage to secure a win tonight, then we'll do it all over at the Super Bowl in two weeks' time.

I feel sick just thinking about it.

I want it for them. I want it so freaking badly.

I glance over at Wilder. He looks as green as I feel.

Over the past few months, he's struck up a friendship with Kieran. At this point, I'm pretty sure Kieran has a god-like status in Wilder's life. But I can't complain. For a wild child himself, Kieran's been nothing but a good influence on my little brother. I just wish Wilder didn't have access to Kieran's social media to see what he gets up to off the field. I'm pretty sure Kieran's active dating life is one of the reasons Wilder is so keen to go pro. He's worked his way around the jersey chasers at school; he's ready to dip his toe into a bigger pool of willing women. God help them all.

"They're going to do it. I know they are," Tate says confidently, cradling baby Prince against her.

My eyes drop to my godson, and I swear my heart explodes with his cuteness.

Chubby cheeks, stunning green eyes, just like his daddy.

Just another Callahan boy to steal all the ladies' hearts. "Yeah," Kian agrees, eagerly waiting for Kieran to emerge. But as confident as he might sound, I know he's worried.

Kieran has been off his game a little recently. He's missing his good luck charm, and tonight is going to be no different.

"He's got this," I say, twisting my fingers with his and squeezing. "He's probably on the phone to her now."

"Yeah." He laughs, a smile playing on his lips as he thinks about his little brother's pregame ritual.

The next three hours are a blur of screaming and shouting, of excitement, disappointment, and frustration.

It's a good game. A really good game. But it also means that the Chiefs are behind just as much as they're in front. It's the epitome of a nailbiter.

Kieran is struggling. The rest of the fans in the stadium who are screaming for their beloved Chiefs might not notice, but we do.

A piece of his puzzle is missing, and while in the grand scheme of things it shouldn't matter, it does.

As the clock counts down, the teams are tied. The home team are about make a play and the nerves about how this is going to end are ramping up.

"I can't watch," I say, turning around in favor of getting a drink, the pressure too much.

"Get back here," Kian says, pulling me into his side and

pressing a kiss to the patch of skin just above the neck of my jersey.

My skin erupts in goosebumps as a roar sounds out around us.

"Shit," Kingston curses before Prince begins wailing. It's like he knows.

"Come on," I urge, glancing at the clock.

But it's too late. The home team is already celebrating.

The final minute passes slower than any I've ever known before. Each second is more painful than the last.

Kieran's Super Bowl hopes are over.

The final whistle sounds and everyone sags in defeat. The home team fans erupt with excitement as Chiefs fans' hearts shatter across the country.

"They did good," Tate says, but there's nothing but sadness in her voice.

"He should be proud of himself," I say despite the fact my heart hurts for him.

Watching Kieran stare up to the sky with his shoulders slumped in defeat is painful.

"You think you can hack this in the future?" Hendrix asks Wilder.

It takes him a couple of seconds to respond, and I know it's because he's feeling Kieran's pain right alongside him.

"Can't win them all," Wilder mutters sadly.

"We're celebrating tonight," Kingston says loudly as he stands in the middle of the room with Prince in his arms. "Kieran has had a killer season, and he deserves to celebrate that. Next year, he'll be back, and we'll all watch him lift that trophy."

"Hell yeah," Wilder shouts as Kian wraps me up in his arms.

With smiles on our faces, we head out in search of the youngest Callahan brother to remind him just how awesome he is.

"He'll be okay, you know," I say as we make our way into our suite later that night.

It's almost midnight, but I'm still buzzing from the excitement of the day.

Kian is too.

It doesn't matter that we didn't win; the adrenaline is still there.

"Yeah, I know. It's just a bitter pill to swallow. Especially when he feels like it was his fault."

I watch as Kian pulls open the sliding doors. It's cool out, but I don't argue.

There's a swing seat under a small outdoor heater.

Ignoring the seat for a moment, I walk over to the railing and look out over the city.

We've barely had a chance to explore yet, but I'm looking forward to the next few days here.

In just a few short months with Kian, I've traveled more than I ever thought I would. It's been incredible, seeing just a small part of the world with him.

I shiver as the light breeze blows around me, the loose tendrils of hair tickling my face.

I expect Kian to join me, but his warmth never comes.

He isn't far away, though. My skin tingles with awareness, just like it always does when he's watching me.

"Lorelei," he says, his deep voice cutting through the air.

"Yeah?"

"Turn around," he demands.

Just like always, I follow orders, ripping my gaze from the view in favor of finding him.

I spin around, but I don't find what I'm expecting.

Kian isn't standing before me, waiting to cuddle up on the swing seat. Instead, he's...

"Oh my god," I gasp, my hand lifting to cover my gaping mouth.

He's on one knee.

He's on one freaking knee.

My heart begins to race, yet I'm pretty sure I stop breathing as Kian holds out a small black box.

"Lorelei, you rejected me from the get-go and ensured that I would never forget you," he starts, making me laugh. "From the first moment I saw you—which, by the way, was long before my brother's wedding—I knew there was something different about you. Even then, you weren't scared to voice your opinion and tell me what you really thought of me. You enthralled me, confused me, and captivated me.

"The day I saw you inside Callahan Enterprises, I just knew I couldn't let you work for anyone else. You were there for me. You just didn't know it yet.

"Every day, you make me a better person. A better brother, uncle, friend, boyfriend, and hopefully one day, a better husband.

"Lorelei Anne Tempest, will do you me the honor of agreeing to be my wife and spend the rest of your life by my side?"

"Kian," I breathe, unable to believe what I'm seeing and hearing.

Kian flips the ring box open, but I can't take my eyes away from his for a second to look at it.

I'm lost in the emotion and hope that's swimming inside them.

Seconds pass, but I barely notice as I lose myself in the feeling of the moment.

The surprise. The joy.

The love.

"Temptress, I think it's about now that you're meant to say something," he says almost nervously.

Surely he doesn't think I'd even consider saying no?

"Yes, Kian. Yes, of course I'll marry you," I cry.

In a heartbeat, I'm on my knees before him, my arms locked around his neck and my lips on his. Any thoughts of the ring have been long forgotten as I lose myself in my fiancé.

Holy shit, I'm marrying Kian Callahan.

"I'm not sure you should be laughing right now," he says when I break our kiss.

"It's happy, I promise."

He studies me closely before his own smile emerges.

"You just asked me to marry you," I say in disbelief.

"I did. And...you said yes."

I sit back as he holds the jewelry box between us, and I finally look down.

"Oh wow," I breathe, taking in the untraditional ring. There's a large emerald with smaller diamonds on either side. The green is the exact same color as Kian's eyes. I haven't put it on yet and I'm already obsessed.

Kian plucks it from the cushion and holds it out for me. My hand trembles as I lift it, and it only gets worse as he slides the ring into place.

"Oh my god," I whisper, the significance of the moment hitting me full force. But it's soon forgotten when Kian suddenly bellows, "She said yes," scaring the ever-loving shit out of me before a loud cheer erupts from the balconies around us.

"They knew?" I ask, although the answer is obvious.

"Well, I asked Wilder and Hendrix for permission to marry their big sister, and it just kinda got out."

"You did not," I gasp.

Kian shrugs. "I totally did. I needed to make sure the most important men in your life approved of me being their big brother."

A laugh tumbles from my throat.

"I love you."

"I love you too, Mrs. Callahan."

By His Play

Prologue
Effie

"You've got this, K. Get out there and smash them. I'll be watching, I promise."

"I know. I just hate you not being here." I vividly picture the pout that's currently playing on his lips. But unlike usual, it doesn't make me laugh. Sure, he still might be being over dramatic and a drama queen, but I'll give him a free pass today.

He's playing in the conference championship. The final step to the Super Bowl. It's been his dream for as long as I've known him. And it's been a pretty long time at this point.

Memories of sixth grade, when we were put next to each other and forced to be lab partners, flicker through my mind.

All these years on, we're still the most unlikely of friends. It works, though. I like to think my presence in his life helps keep him grounded. Without me...hell knows what kind of situations he'd end up in. I mean...he's still wild. Always has been and always will be.

A bitter laugh threatens to escape. I'll never understand what he sees in me that has kept us connected all these years. Honestly, I've mostly given up thinking about it.

Kieran Callahan is an enigma that even I, as his best friend, can't figure out.

"You don't need me there," I assure him. "And anyway, I'll be screaming so loudly at the TV you'll probably hear me anyway."

"Maybe if we were at home. But out here..." he trails off.

His anxiety over the upcoming game is clear down the line.

He's not going into this game pumped for the win like he usually does. He's stressed and feeling the pressure. I hate that I can't fix it.

"Enough of the negativity, Callahan. You get your head out of your ass and go out there fighting. You're going to be the best goddamn running back on that field. You get out there and make sure every motherfucker watching knows it."

I cringe at my own pep talk. But sometimes, I've just got to swallow my pride and tell my best friend how it is.

He's the best football player I've ever known. Okay, so he may also be the only football player I've ever known, but he doesn't need to know that right now.

"I've got this," he says, a little hesitantly.

"It's just another game," I assure him. "I'm watching, your brothers are watching. And we'll all be there with you for the next one too."

He's silent for a moment. My nerves grow as I wait for what he's going to say next.

"We're gonna do it, Luck. We're gonna fucking do it."

"Hell yeah, you are. Now get out there and show them who's boss."

"You got it. I'll see you on the other side."

"I'm with you all the way," I promise.

We both pause for a beat before we simultaneously chant, "Three. Two. One. Win."

And then just like always, Kieran cuts the call.

I blow out a breath as I lower my cell to my chest and close my eyes, praying that he gets himself into the right headspace.

I give myself ten seconds before I force myself to look down again, and when I do, my eyes immediately lock on the ring on my finger.

My stomach knots, guilt rushing through my veins like poison.

It's okay, I tell myself.

He'll never know.

I'm just doing what I have to do.

Blowing out a long, slow stream of air, I tuck my cell into my pocket and walk toward the room I stepped out of only minutes ago.

The TV shows the build-up to the game and a mix of excitement and nerves flutters in my stomach as I think of Kieran in the locker room going through the rest of his pre-game ritual. I became a part of it junior year of high school. It was the last game of the season and he wanted to make a killer impression on their coach before embarking on his final year. They won that game by a mile, and he put it down to me. He has called me before every single game he's played since that day, without fail. And no matter where I am or what I'm doing —usually, I'm sitting either in the stadium or in front of a TV ready to watch—I take the call.

I'm sure it's a habit that many would say that I should have broken a long time ago. But I can't. It means too much to Kieran, and I love that I'm able to help him and be a part of his success.

I love watching his career go from strength to strength. He deserves it. He's an incredible player, and a wonderful person.

"Everything okay?" Grams asks the second she notices me lowering into the chair beside her.

I look over, relieved to see the usual sparkle in her eyes that I love so much. It's becoming less and less every day now.

Sadness tugs at my chest. Grams has been the one constant in my life. Well, apart from Kieran since the first week of sixth grade. The thought of losing her, of living a life without her terrifies me. But there isn't much I can do about it. Not only is her mind giving up, but her body is too. Every single second that passes is one less I get to spend with her.

It's why I'm not in San Francisco right now, supporting Kieran in person.

I hate that I'm not, but also, I couldn't leave Grams.

I fight the pained sigh that threatens. It's like my heart is being ripped in two with the need to be in both places at once.

But Grams needs me more right now. Kieran will have

more games, and anyway, I'm watching, I'm supporting him, just...from a distance.

"Yeah, everything is great. Kieran is a little nervous."

"Well, that's to be expected. He'll want his fiancée by his side for big days like this," she says so confidently that I'd question her diagnosis if I didn't know better.

My stomach knots and my eyes drop to my ring again.

"Yeah," I muse.

"I just can't believe it...after all these years. I mean, I knew. That boy has loved you from the first day you met. But I never thought I'd see the day when he figured it out. I just want to be there on the big day."

A giant ball of emotion crawls up my throat. My nose itches and my eyes burn.

"You're going to make the most beautiful bride, Effie."

Pain shoots up my arms as I curl my fists, digging my nails into my palms in an attempt to distract myself.

"You'll be there," I choke out. "You're too stubborn not to be."

It's a lie.

She's not going to make it. And not just because of her declining health. But because all of this is fake.

Kieran friend zoned me a long time ago.

But what are you meant to do when your only grandmother's dying wish is for you to get engaged and marry the man of your dreams?

You give her exactly what she wants, knowing that it'll make her happy. Even if it rips your own heart to shreds at the same time...

Want more?
PRE-ORDER BY HIS PLAY NOW!

Want to be the first to know about my books in progress? You

can join my Patreon for sneak peeks, special edition paperbacks, and more!
SUBSCRIBE NOW
https://www.patreon.com/tracylorraine

Have you met Zach?
Turn the page for a sneak peek of Hate You, book #1 in my spicy contemporary romance series, Rebel Ink.

HATE YOU
SNEAK PEEK

Prologue
Tabitha

I stare down at my gran's pale skin. Her cheeks are sunken and her eyes tired. She's been fighting this for too long now, and as much as I hate to even think it, it's time she found some peace.

I take her cool hand in mine and lift her knuckles to my lips.

"It's Tabitha," I whisper. I've no idea if she's awake, but I don't want to startle her.

Her eyes flicker open. After a second they must adjust to the light and she looks right at me. My chest tightens as if someone's wrapping an elastic band around it. I hate seeing my once so full of life gran like this. She was always so happy and full of cheer. She didn't deserve this end. But cancer doesn't care what kind of person you are, it hits whoever it fancies and ruins lives.

Pulling a chair closer, I drop onto it, not taking my eyes from her.

"How are you doing today?" I hate asking the question, because there really is only one answer. She's waiting, waiting for her time to come to put her out of her misery.

"I'm good. Christopher upped my morphine. I'm on top of the world."

She might be living her last days, but it doesn't stop her eyes sparkling a little as she mentions her male nurse. If I've heard the words 'if I were forty years younger' once while she's been here, then I've heard them a million times. She's joking, of course. My gran spent her life with my incredible grandpa until he had a stroke a few years ago. Thankfully, I guess, his end was much quicker and less painful than Gran's. It was awful at the time to have him healthy one moment and then gone in a matter of hours, but this right now is pure torture, and I'm not the one lying on the hospital bed with meds constantly being pumped into my body.

"Turn the frown upside down, Tabby Cat. I'm fine. I want to remember you smiling, not like your world's about to come crashing down."

"I know, I'm sorry. I just—" a sob breaks from my throat. "I don't know how I'm going to live without you." Dramatic? Yeah. But Gran has been my go-to person my whole life. When my parents get on my last nerve, which is often, she's the one who talks me down, makes me see things differently. She's also the only one who's encouraged me to live the life I want, not the one I'm constantly being pushed into.

That's the reason I'm the only one visiting her right now.

When my parents discovered that she was the one encouraging my 'reckless behaviour', as they called it, they cut contact. I can see the pain in her eyes about that every time she looks at me, but she's too stubborn to do anything about it, even now.

"You're going to be fine. You're stronger than you give yourself credit for. How many times have I told you, you just need to follow your heart. Follow your heart and just breathe. Spread your wings and fly, Tabby Cat."

Those were the last words she said to me.

Chapter One
Tabitha

The heavy bass rattles my bones. The incredible music does help to lift my spirits, but I find it increasingly hard to see the positives in my life while I'm hanging out with my friends these days. They've all got something exciting going on— incredible job prospects, marriage, exotic holidays on the horizon—and here I am, drowning in my one-person pity party. It's been two months since Gran left me, and I'm still wondering what the hell I'm meant to be doing with my life.

"Oh my god, they are so fucking awesome," Danni squeals in my ear as one song comes to an end. I didn't really have her down as a rock fan, but she was almost as excited as James when he announced that this was what we were doing for his birthday this year. Although I do wonder if it's the music or the frontman who's really captured her attention. She'd never admit it, but she's got a thing for bad boys.

I glance over at him with his arm wrapped around Shannon's shoulders and a smile twitches my lips. They're so cute. They've got the kind of relationship everyone craves. It seems so easy yet full of love and affection. Ripping my eyes from the couple, I focus back on the stage and try to block out that I'm about as far away from having that kind of connection with anyone as physically possible.

I sing along with the songs I've heard on the radio a million times and jump around with my friends, but I just can't quite totally get on board with tonight. Maybe I just need more alcohol.

"Where to next?" Shannon asks once we've left the arena and the ringing in our ears has begun to fade.

"Your choice," James says, looking down at her with utter devotion shining in his eyes. It wasn't a great surprise when Shannon sent a photo of her giant engagement ring to our group chat a couple of months ago. We all knew it was coming

—Danni especially, seeing as it turned out that she helped choose the ring.

Shannon directs us all to a cocktail bar a few streets over and I make quick work of manoeuvring my way through the crowd to get to the bar, my need for a drink beginning to get the better of me. The others disappear off somewhere in the hope of finding a table

"Can we have two jugs of..." I quickly glance at the menu. "Margaritas please."

"Coming right up, sweetheart." The barman winks at me before his eyes drop to my chest. Hooking up on a night out isn't really my thing, but hell if it doesn't make me feel a little better about myself. He's cute too, and just the kind of guy who would give both my parents a heart attack if I were to bring him home. Both his forearms are covered in tattoos, he's got gauges in both his ears, and a lip ring. A smile tugs at the corner of my mouth as I imagine the looks on their faces.

My gran's words suddenly hit me.

Just breathe.

My hand lifts and my fingers run over the healing skin just below my bra. My smile widens.

I watch the barman prepare our cocktails, my eyes focused on the ink on his arms. I've always been obsessed by art, any kind of art, and that most definitely includes on skin.

I'm lost in my own head, so when he places the jugs in front of me, I startle, feeling ridiculous.

"T-Thank you," I mutter, but when I lift my eyes, I find him staring intently at me.

"You're welcome. I'm Christian, by the way."

"Oh, hi." A sly smile creeps onto my lips. "I'm Biff."

"Biff?" His brows draw together in a way I'm all too used to when I say my name.

"It's short for Tabitha."

"That's pretty. So... uh... how do you feel about—"

"Christian, a little help?" one of the other barmen shouts, pulling Christian's attention from me.

"Sorry, I'll hopefully see you again later?"

I nod at him, not wanting to give him any false hope. Like I said, he's cute, but after my last string of bad dates and even worse short-term boyfriends, I'm happy flying solo right now. I've got a top of the range vibrating friend in my bedside table; I don't need a man.

Picking up the tray in front of me, I turn and go in search of my friends. It takes forever, but eventually I find them tucked around a tiny table in the back corner of the bar.

"What the hell took so long? We thought you'd pulled and abandoned us."

"Yes and no," I say, ensuring every head turns my way.

"Tell us more," Danni, my best friend, demands.

"It was nothing. The barman was about to ask me out, but it got busy."

"Why the hell did you come back? Get over there. We all know you could do with a little... loosening up," James says with a wink.

"I'm good. He wasn't my type."

"Oh, of course. You only date posh boys."

"That is not true."

"Is it not?" Danni asks, chipping in once she's filled all the glasses.

"No..." I think back over the previous few guys they met. "Wayne wasn't posh," I argue when I realise they're kind of right.

"No, he was just a wanker."

Blowing out a long breath, I try to come up with an argument, but quite honestly, it's true. My shoulders slump as I realise that I've been subconsciously dating guys my parents would approve of. It's like my need to follow their orders is so well ingrained by now that I don't even realise I'm doing it. Shame that their ideas about my life, what I should do, and whom I should date don't exactly line up with mine.

Glancing over my shoulder at the bar, I catch a glimpse of

Christian's head. Maybe I should take him up on his almost offer. What's the worst that could happen?

Deciding some liquid courage is in order, I grab my margarita and swallow half down in one go.

I'm so fed up of attempting to live my parents' idea of a perfect life. I promised Gran I'd do things my way. I need to start living up to my promise.

By the time I'm tipsy enough to walk back to the bar and chat up Christian, he's nowhere to be seen. I'm kind of disappointed seeing as the others had convinced me to throw caution to the wind (something that I'm really bad at doing), but I think I'm mostly relieved to be able go home and lock myself inside my flat alone and not have to worry about anyone else.

With my arm linked through Danni's, we make our way out to the street, ready to make our journeys home, and Shannon jumps into an idling Uber while Danni waits for another to go in the opposite direction.

"You sure you don't want to be dropped off? I don't mind."

"No, I'm sure. I could do with the fresh air." It's not a lie— the alcohol from one too many cocktails is making my head a little fuzzy. I hate going to sleep with the room spinning. I'd much rather that feeling fade before lying down.

"Okay. Promise me you'll text me when you're home."

"I promise." I wrap my arms around my best friend and then wave her off in her own Uber.

Turning on my heels, I start the short walk home.

I've been a London girl all my life, and while some might be afraid to walk home after dark, I love it. I love seeing a different side to this city, the quiet side when most people are hiding in their flats, not flooding the streets on their daily commutes.

My mind is flicking back and forth between my promise to

Gran and my missed opportunity tonight when a shop front that I walk past on almost a daily basis makes me stop.

It's a tattoo studio I've been inside of once in my life. I never really pay it much attention, but the new sign in the window catches my eye and I stop to look.

Admin help wanted. Enquire within.

Something stirs in my belly, and it's not just my need to do something to piss my parents off—although getting a job in a place like this is sure to do that. I'm pretty sure it's excitement.

Tattoos fascinate me, or more so, the artists.

I'm surprised to see the open sign still illuminated, so before I can change my mind, I push the door open. A little bell rings above it, and after a few seconds of standing in reception alone, a head pops out from around the door.

"Evening. What can I do you for?" The guy's smile is soft and kind despite his otherwise slightly harsh features and ink.

"Oh um..." I hesitate under his intense dark stare. I glance over my shoulder, the back of the piece of paper catching my eye and reminding me why I walked in here. "I just saw the job ad in the window. Is the position still open?"

His eyes drop from mine and take in what I'm wearing. Seeing as tonight's outing involved a rock concert, I'm dressed much like him in all black and looking a little edgy with my skinny black jeans, ripped AC/DC t-shirt and heavy black makeup. I must admit it's not a look I usually go for, but it was fitting for tonight.

He nods, apparently happy with what he sees.

"Experience?" he asks, making my stomach drop.

"Not really, but I'm studying for a Masters so I'm not an· idiot. I know my way around a computer, Excel, and I'm super organised."

"Right..." he trails off, like he's thinking about the best way to get rid of me.

"I'm a really quick learner. I'm punctual, methodical and really easy to get along with."

"It's okay, you had me sold at organised. I'm Dawson, although everyone around here calls me D."

"Nice to meet you." I stick my hand out for him to shake, and an amused smile plays at his lips. Stretching out an inked arm, he takes my hand and gives it a very firm shake that my dad would be impressed by—if he could look past the tattoos, that is. "I'm Tabitha, but everyone calls me Biff."

"Biff, I like it. When can you start?"

"Don't you want to interview me?"

"You sound like you could be perfect. When can you start?"

"Err... tomorrow?" I ask, totally taken aback. He doesn't know me from Adam.

"Yes!" He practically snaps my hand off. "Can you be here for two o'clock? I can show you around before clients start turning up. I'll apologise now for dropping you in the deep end, we've not had anyone for a few weeks and things are starting to get a little crazy."

"I can cope with crazy."

"Good to know. This place can be nuts." I smile at him, more grateful than he could know to have a distraction and a focus.

My Masters should be enough to keep my mind busy, but since Gran went, I can't seem to lose myself in it like I could previously. Hopefully, sorting this place's admin out might be exactly what I need.

"Two o'clock tomorrow then," I say, turning to leave. "I'll bring ID. Do you need a reference? I've done some voluntary work recently, I'm sure they'll write something for me."

"Just turn up on time and do your job and you're golden."

I walk out with more of a spring in my step than I have in a long time. I'm determined to find something that's going to make me happy, not just my parents. I've lived in their shadow for long enough.

I look myself over before leaving my flat for my first shift at the tattoo studio. I'm dressed a little more like myself today in a pair of dark skinny jeans, a white blouse and a black blazer. It's simple and smart. I'm not sure if there's a dress code—D never specified what I should wear. With my hair straightened and hanging down my back and my makeup light, I feel like I can take on whatever crazy he throws at me.

With a final spritz of perfume, I grab my bag from the unit in the hall and pull open my door. My home is a top floor flat in an old London warehouse. They were converted a few years ago by my father's company, and I managed to get myself first dibs. They might drive me insane on the best of days, but at least I get this place rent-free. It almost makes up for their controlling and stuck-up ways... almost.

Ignoring the lift like I always do, I head for the stairs. My heels click against the polished concrete until I'm at the bottom and out to the busy city. I love London. I love that no matter what the time, there's always something going on or someone who's awake.

The spring afternoon is still a little fresh, making me regret not grabbing my coat, or even a scarf, before I left. I pull my blazer tighter around myself and make the short journey to the shop.

The door's locked when I get there, and the bright neon sign that clearly showed it was open last night is currently saying closed.

Unsure of what to do, I lift my hand to knock. Only a second later, the shop front is illuminated, and the sound of movement inside filters down to me, but when the door opens it's not the guy from last night.

"Oh... uh... hi. Is... uh... D here?"

The guy folds his arms over his chest and looks me up and down. He chuckles, although I've no idea what he finds so amusing.

"D," he shouts over his shoulder, "there's some posh bird here to see you."

My teeth grind that he's stereotyped me quite so quickly, but I refuse to allow him to see that his assumptions about me affect me in any way.

"Ah, good. I was worried you might change your mind."

"Not at all," I say, stepping past the judgemental arsehole and into the studio reception-cum-waiting room.

"That's Spike. Feel free to ignore him. He's not got laid in about a million years, it makes him a little cranky." I fight to contain a laugh, especially when I turn toward Spike to find his lips pursed and his eyes narrowed in frustration. All it does is confirm that D's words are correct.

"Is that fucking necessary? Posh doesn't need to know how inactive my cock is, especially not when she's only just walked through the fucking door. Unless..." He stalks towards me and I automatically back up. I can't deny that he's a good looking guy, but there's no way I'm going there.

"I don't think so."

"You sure? You look like you could do with a bit of rough." He winks, and I want the ground to swallow me up.

"Down, Spike. This is Tabitha, or Biff. She's our new admin, so I suggest you be nice to her if you want to stop organising your own appointments and shit. I don't need a sexual harassment case on my hands before she's even fucking started."

I can't help but laugh at the look on Spike's face. "Don't worry. I'm sure you'll find some desperate old spinster soon."

He looks me up and down again, something in his eyes changed. "Appearances aside, I think you're going to get on well here."

I smile at him. "Mine's a coffee. Milk, no sugar. I'm already sweet enough." His chin drops.

"I thought you were our new assistant. Why am I still making the coffee?"

"Know your place, Spike. Now do as the lady says. You know my order."

"Yeah, it comes with a side of fuck off!" He flips D off

before disappearing through a door that I can only assume goes to a kitchen.

"I probably should have warned you that you've agreed to work around a bunch of arseholes."

"I know how to handle myself around horny men, don't worry."

After finishing my A levels, before I grew any kind of backbone where my parents were concerned, I agreed to work for my dad. I was his little office bitch and spent an horrendous year of my life being bossed around by men who thought that just because they had a cock hanging between their legs it made them better than me. I might have fucking hated that year, but it taught me a few things, not just about business but also how to deal with men who think they're something fucking special just because they're a tiny bit successful and make more money than me. I've no doubt that my time at Anderson Development Group gave me all the skills I'm going to need to handle these artists.

"So I see. So, this is your desk. When you're on shift you'll be the first person people see when they're inside, so it's important that you look good. But from what I've seen, I don't think we'll have an issue. I've sorted you out logins for the computer and the software we use. Most of it is pretty self-explanatory. I'm pretty IT illiterate and I've figured most of it out, put it that way."

D's showing me how they book clients in when someone else joins us. This time it's someone I recognise from my previous visit, although it's immediately obvious that he doesn't remember me like I do him. But then I guess he was the one delivering the pain, not receiving it.

"Biff, this is Titch. Titch, this is Biff, our new admin. Be nice."

"Nice? I'm always nice. Nice to meet you, Biff. You have any issues with this one, you come and see me. He might look tough, but I know all his secrets." Titch winks, a smile curling at his lips that shows he's a little more interested than he's making out, and quickly disappears towards his room.

It's not long until the first clients of the afternoon arrive, and I'm left alone to try to get to grips with everything.

Between clients, D pops his head out of his room to check I'm okay, and every hour I make a round of coffee for everyone. That sure seems to get me in their good books.

"I think I could get used to having you around," Spike says when I deliver probably his fourth coffee of the day. "Only thing that would make it better is if it were whisky."

"Not sure the person at the end of your needle would agree." He chuckles and turns back to the design he was working on when I interrupted.

My first day flies by. D tells me to head home not long after nine o'clock. They've all got hours of tattooing to go yet, seeing as Saturday night is their busiest night of the week, but he insists I get a decent night's sleep.

DOWNLOAD NOW to keep reading.

ABOUT THE AUTHOR

Tracy Lorraine is a *USA Today* and *Wall Street Journal* bestselling new adult and contemporary romance author. Tracy recently turned thirty and lives in a cute Cotswold village in England with her husband, baby girl and lovable but slightly crazy dog. Having always been a bookaholic with her head stuck in her Kindle, Tracy decided to try her hand at a story idea she dreamt up and hasn't looked back since.

Be the first to find out about new releases and offers. Sign up to my newsletter here.

If you want to know what I'm up to and see teasers and snippets of what I'm working on, then you need to be in my Facebook group. Join Tracy's Angels here.

Keep up to date with Tracy's books at
www.tracylorraine.com

ALSO BY TRACY LORRAINE

Inked (A Rebel Ink/Driven Crossover)

Rosewood High Series

Thorn #1

Paine #2

Savage #3

Fierce #4

Hunter #5

Faze (#6 Prequel)

Fury #6

Legend #7

Maddison Kings University Series

TMYM: Prequel

TRYS #1

TDYW #2

TBYS #3

TVYC #4

TDYD #5

TDYR #6

TRYD #7

Knight's Ridge Empire Series

Wicked Summer Knight: Prequel (Stella & Seb)

Wicked Knight #1 (Stella & Seb)

Wicked Princess #2 (Stella & Seb)

Wicked Empire #3 (Stella & Seb)

Deviant Knight #4 (Emmie & Theo)

Deviant Princess #5 (Emmie & Theo)

Deviant Reign #6 (Emmie & Theo)

One Reckless Knight (Jodie & Toby)

Reckless Knight #7 (Jodie & Toby)

Reckless Princess #8 (Jodie & Toby)

Reckless Dynasty #9 (Jodie & Toby)

Dark Halloween Knight (Calli & Batman)

Dark Knight #10 (Calli & Batman)

Dark Princess #11 (Calli & Batman)

Dark Legacy #12 (Calli & Batman)

Corrupt Valentine Knight (Nico & Siren)

Corrupt Knight #13 (Nico & Siren)

Corrupt Princess #14 (Nico & Siren)

Corrupt Union #15 (Nico & Siren)

Sinful Wild Knight (Alex & Vixen)

Sinful Stolen Knight: Prequel (Alex & Vixen)

Sinful Knight #16 (Alex & Vixen)

Sinful Princess #17 (Alex & Vixen)

Sinful Kingdom #18 (Alex & Vixen)

Knight's Ridge Destiny: Epilogue

Harrow Creek Hawks Series

Merciless #1

Relentless #2

Lawless #3

Fearless #4

Callahan Billionaires

By His Vow #1

By His Rule #2

Never Forget Series

Never Forget Him #1

Never Forget Us #2

Everywhere & Nowhere #3

Chasing Series

Chasing Logan

Made in United States
Orlando, FL
28 December 2024

56631440R10367